PRAISE F[...]

"A captivating tale of psychological suspense."

—*Publishers Weekly*

"When Emma Donoghue, the bestselling author of *Room*, describes a book as 'A vivid and sensuous domestic drama . . . ,' you read the book . . . Guys, this book totally lived up to Emma's promise."

—*Hasty Book List*

"Blakemore's skill at bringing the past to life is used to great effect . . . The 250+ page book is a slim volume that packs quite the punch, while adding more diversity than often shown in historical mysteries."

—*BOLO Books*

". . . a slow psychological burn."

—Criminal Element

". . . a very clever and vibrant novel, compelling so that it pulls the reader along at speed . . ."

—*NB Magazine*

"Blakemore's descriptions are rich and vivid . . . Secrets, eavesdropping, sinister happenings, and a forbidden relationship all make for a riveting historical thriller reminiscent of Sarah Waters, *Burial Rites* by Hannah Kent, or *The Confessions of Frannie Langton* by Sara Collins."

—Historical Novel Society

"A vivid and sensuous domestic drama, *The Companion* is also an atmospheric crime story."

—Emma Donoghue, bestselling author of *Room*

"Sarah Waters fans, welcome to your next obsession. *The Companion* is an elegantly written tale of beautiful lies and ugly secrets, a reminder that love's transforming power makes not just angels, but monsters. Telling one from the other will keep you guessing until the end."

—Greer Macallister, bestselling author of
The Magician's Lie and *Woman 99*

"*The Companion* is a brilliant study of all that makes us human—our terrors, regrets, and passions, and the lies that shape our worlds. Kim Taylor Blakemore's novel is both astonishing and captivating, and it will leave readers spellbound."

—Lydia Kang, bestselling author of
A Beautiful Poison and *The Impossible Girl*

"As her date with the gallows approaches, Lucy Blunt is struggling to understand why she is at odds with society. In a literary tradition stretching from *Jane Eyre* to *Alias Grace*, her intoxicating account took me to another time and place. A confession with the illicit excitement of a thriller, *The Companion* offers everything I like about modern historical fiction: a resonant voice that brings women's lives out of the shadows."

—Jo Furniss, bestselling author of
All the Little Children and *The Trailing Spouse*

"A vividly rendered and chilling tale of murder, desire, and obsession."
—Sophia Tobin, bestselling author of *The Vanishing*

"*The Companion* is a totally absorbing read—beautifully written, atmospheric, and intriguing. Kim Taylor Blakemore's characterization is both convincing and compelling as she evokes the gritty reality of nineteenth-century life to great effect. I loved this book."

—Lindsay Jayne Ashford, bestselling
author of *The Woman on the Orient Express*

"The narrator is riveting. The prose, gorgeous."

—Ron Hansen, National Book Award–nominated author of *Atticus*, *The Assassination of Jesse James by the Coward Robert Ford*, and *Mariette in Ecstasy*

"Kim Taylor Blakemore's novel *The Companion* is the absorbing tale of Lucy Blunt, a young woman condemned to death and deeply haunted by her past. Blakemore skillfully immerses the reader in the tactile world of antebellum New Hampshire with her exquisite choice of details and gorgeous writing style. The novel has everything—complexity, mystery, murder, betrayal, forbidden love—even a ghostly presence. Treat yourself to a few evenings with this captivating story as you explore the mind and experience of a tortured young woman from another time. You'll be glad you did."

—Amy Belding Brown, author of *Flight of the Sparrow*

"Moody and atmospheric, *The Companion* is a compulsively readable treat. Blakemore's meticulously researched world captured me from the very first page, and her intriguing, unpredictable characters kept me guessing until the end. An utter delight for lovers of classic gothic literature!"

—Elizabeth Blackwell, bestselling author of *In the Shadow of Lakecrest* and *On a Cold Dark Sea*

PRAISE FOR *AFTER ALICE FELL*

"Kim Taylor Blakemore hits her stride in this well-plotted page turner of a novel. The prose shines with her unique lyrical voice. Cannot recommend highly enough!"

—Terry Lynn Thomas, *USA Today* bestselling author of *The Silent Woman*, *The Family Secret*, and *House of Lies*

"*After Alice Fell* is an enthralling, haunting, and harrowing gothic mystery that sweeps the reader into a post–Civil War New England that consists of broken families and even more broken minds. Easily one of my favorite books of the year, this story stayed with me long after I'd read the last page. I absolutely loved it!"

—Emily Carpenter, bestselling author of
Burying the Honeysuckle Girls and *Reviving the Hawthorn Sisters*

"Blakemore pulls you deep into the mind of a woman haunted by a harrowing past and the fallen ghost of her sister. Family secrets, terrible regrets, and hints of murder lurk around every dark corner of this well-drawn, Civil War–torn world. As the mystery of Alice's death slowly unravels, you simply cannot look away!"

—D. M. Pulley, author of *The Dead Key* and *No One's Home*

"Superbly crafted, Kim Taylor Blakemore's *After Alice Fell* is an enthralling story of absolving guilt and seeking the truth. It's a captivating historical thriller that kept me turning the pages way into the night."

—Alan Hlad, internationally bestselling
author of *The Long Flight Home*

"Taut, tense, and terrifying, *After Alice Fell* is a harrowing novel that will make skin crawl and hearts break. Blakemore's latest is a sophisticated, meticulously woven historical suspense of loyalty, loss, and deception. With a nod to Shirley Jackson's claustrophobic settings and intricately drawn characters, Blakemore has created a haunting thriller that will pierce the security of her readers."

—Amber Cowie, author of *Loss Lake*

THE
DECEPTION

THE
DECEPTION

A
NOVEL

KIM TAYLOR
BLAKEMORE

LAKE UNION
PUBLISHING

Published by Lake Union Publishing, Seattle

www.apub.com

Amazon, the Amazon logo, and Lake Union Publishing are trademarks of Amazon.com, Inc., or its affiliates.

ISBN-13: 9781542037037
ISBN-10: 1542037034

Cover design by Faceout Studio, Jeff Miller

Printed in the United States of America

For the Litwits:
Tonya Mitchell, Robert Gwaltney, and Jacqueline Vick.
Your fierce, funny, and creative friendship got me
through this book.
&
For Dana, always.

Spring, 1877
Harrowboro, New Hampshire

Dear Miss Watkins,
I am in difficulty. My guardian spirit is unruly and serves
distemperately. You have been recommended as a helper
of those in need. If you could observe a sitting and give
your thoughts and advice as to how I might amend my
mediumship, I would be most grateful. I have included
a card with my hours.
Yours in Faith,
Maud Price

Dear Miss Price,
Yes. I will help.
C—

Chapter One

CLEMENTINE

Clementine Watkins hooked her thumb to the parlor curtain, tugging it enough to spy out on the proceedings of the room. It was a late night. A Wednesday. Her head hurt from too much whiskey the night before. Her bum, pressed to the window, had chilled to a state of numbness. The trousers and jacket she wore gave no protection from the seeping damp cold beyond the glass panes and shutters. She wriggled her toes in her socks, curling them under then stretching them out.

A yawn threatened. She swallowed it down and forced herself to ignore the cold behind her and take heed of the goings-on.

Or lack thereof.

Five people sat around a table, hands clasped, eyes shut, faces wobbling and gleaming in the light of a solitary candle. Two men, three ladies. The family Ott and a Mr. Sullivan, to be precise. Clem was close enough to touch the shoulder of Mr. Ott. He would have done better with two chairs. Now he shifted his weight from one buttock to the other and every so often let out a discomfited groan. To his right sat a young girl of longish neck and pinkish nose, her mouth already curved like her mother's—the next participant at the table—in a permanent scowl. The mother wore the finest of mourning: soft velvet ribbons, hard jet buttons, crinoline that glimmered in the low light. The broach at her neck boasted a braid of hair and a dangling ruby. Next to her sat Mr. Sullivan. He had come alone, trailing behind the family and twisting his hat in his hand. He had bobbed his head in a mumbled greeting before the medium requested they sit.

The medium herself—Maud Price—sat still as a statue, elbows locked straight, shoulder blades pushed against the slats of her chair. She wore a simple dress of organdy, pale as her skin and hair. She was of no great beauty, with a high forehead, a pinch of nose and chin. Beauty, of course, had naught to do with psychical gifts, not at all. Still, Clem was of the opinion it did not hurt.

Suddenly, Maud Price lifted her shoulder—an inadvertent jerk of movement, enough to alert the others that *soon* there would be communion, *soon* the dearly departed would join the circle—causing the stiff material of her skirts to rustle.

The girl's eyes snapped open and she watched Maud.

Clem slipped the curtain back, lest her hiding place be spied. She had seen the sharp spark in the girl's eye. Doubt.

Well, after all, they had been sitting now for an impossibly long time. And Maud had made no movement save that twitch of shoulder and a few bobbles of her eyeballs under the translucent skin of her lids.

Mr. Ott cleared his throat. "So sorry."

"It's the weather," the mother said.

"Horrible spring."

"Why are your eyes open, Celia?"

"Why are yours?" the daughter answered.

Then Mr. Sullivan began to burble and broke into a sob. "Would you all be quiet?"

Clem leaned against the window frame and picked at her thumbnail. This would be the time for a good, long disembodied screech.

She was tempted.

But this wasn't her place. Her place was to observe.

I am in difficulty.

The note had come to Clem's boardinghouse, slipped under the tea mug on the breakfast tray and nearly used as a napkin by Russell. But Clem had nicked it in time, and now she was here in the too-hot room with the too-cold window.

"You're squeezing too tight, Mother."

"Pay attention."

"I don't believe in ghosts. I—" The girl gave a shriek.

Clem flicked the curtain.

The candle had been snuffed. The wick glowed orange and umber and then went out.

An odor curled through the room, like cat urine and last week's offal. Clem pinched her nose to it.

Someone gagged at the reek.

Maud moved. The organdy dress hissed.

Maud spoke. "Aaaaaahhhh."

Nothing but a long groan, but still, Clem felt relief that *something* had happened.

"Are you there, Matthias?"

My guardian spirit, she had written, *is unruly and serves distemperately.*

Nothing then but breath drawn and released.

"Matthias is . . ." Maud's voice rose to a keen, then dipped to a whisper. "Here. He is here."

"Is it our Tom?" Mrs. Ott's voice quavered.

Clem turned her head away. How often she heard the plaintiveness, the scraping ache of a mother for a son.

"Is it my Maisie?" Mr. Sullivan asked. A wife, a sister, a mother, a sweetheart. Gone too soon and leaving a grown man in fits of sobs and sighs.

The girl whined, and then stopped herself.

Mr. Ott moaned. "Tom?"

Then came the clapping. Solitary. Winding round the room, ricocheting from corner to corner, then circling closer and closer. *Clap* behind the girl's back, *clap* behind her mother's. Sullivan's shoulders hunched to his ears in readiness. *Clap.* The claps floated to the ceiling and faded into the plasterwork. *Clap clap clap clap . . .*

"Tom misses . . ." Maud's voice was that of a child's. ". . . everything. No, Billy."

"Billy?" the father asked. "Who's Billy?"

"Quietnowquietbe." The deep voice shot down Clem's spine.

"Who's Billy, I ask?"

"Billy's my new friend. Billy play." Maud gasped, her breath rasping in short bursts. "No, no." Her shoulders shook, and she hunched over until her forehead touched the table. "They have left me."

The air sagged, sinking back into itself.

"That is all."

☙

You have been recommended—but here the words bled from a drop of cider. Russell had picked up the enclosed calling card, holding it to the tavern's whorled window.

> Miss M. Price
> MEDIUM
> 328 Hall St H'boro
> Circles at 7p Mon–Sat.
> 25c All Welcome

Russell scratched his stubble. "Here we go, Clem, here we go."

☙

Nothing much happened after. A chair scraped. A match fizzed and flared. Maud leaned over the table to light the candle. She cupped the flame, moved to a sconce by the fireplace, opened the glass and lit that before dropping the match to the grate. Then she crossed her hands before her, one resting upon the other on top of her skirt. How small she was, how unassuming and bland, sloped shoulders and downcast gaze. "Perhaps tomorrow, Mr. Sullivan. Perhaps then."

Clem could see only a sliver of the group now. Mr. Ott's bald pate and circling curlicues of gray. The girl's mouth hanging open. The mother curled into herself.

"Sometimes the veil is too thick." Maud dipped her head. "We can try again tomorrow?"

"Yes. If you think Maisie—"

"Thank you, Mr. Sullivan. For your confidence."

The father twisted from his chair.

"I won't come again. There's Mrs. Martin. We'll go to her."

"Yes, of course, Mr. Ott. If you must." Maud's real voice was no more than a murmur.

"Where is Tom now?" Mrs. Ott had moved to the door. "Where is he, Miss Price?"

"I do not know. I think he needs guidance."

"Which you cannot give."

"Not tonight."

Clem sat on the window ledge and listened to the shuffle of chairs, then the quiet as the room emptied. The rain plonked against the glass. She watched a spider spin a tendril of web in the fold of curtain, then climb the web to spin another length of silk.

"You can come out."

Clementine pushed the curtain aside, then dropped it behind her. Maud sat in a stuffed chair by the cold fireplace, her hands gripping the wooden arms. "Oh." She tilted her head and puzzled over Clem's gray serge trousers and vest.

"It allows me the night." She shoved her hands in her pockets, strode across to the door, and peered out to the hallway. The stairwell was dark, as was the entryway. The only illumination came through the arched window above the front door, a pallid glow from the streetlight. Clem's brown beaver-felt bowler hung from the rack near the door. Her umbrella rested in a tin bucket.

"Hello?" Her voice echoed and was not answered.

She closed the parlor door and looked at Maud. "The smell."

"I'm sorry?"

"How do you do the smell?"

"I don't—"

"It's clever."

Clem ran her gaze along the wall, peering into a curio cabinet that held nothing but aperitif glasses and a single half-empty crystal decanter of liquor. She pulled its stopper and sniffed. Sherry.

The room held very little. Just the chairs, the table covered in a lace cloth. The glass globe sconces. Two portraits: a scowling man with wild brows and high collar facing a woman of great resemblance to Maud. White walls. Heavy curtains, but it was still April, and the days too dismal to change to a lighter set. Rag rug on a dark, scarred wood floor. And Maud herself in the chintz chair with an antimacassar starched and neat on its back.

Clementine followed a ceiling beam across the breadth of the room, then snapped her fingers. "The fireplace. Very good. But easy to spot." She leaned down, hands to knees, twisting to look up the chimney. It smelled of old ash. But easy for the maid or an accomplice to toss some oils and cat piss when the timing was right.

"No. No, that comes when—if—Matthias comes." Maud raised a hand to her forehead and smoothed her hair. "I sent Margaret away. She doesn't approve of these nightlies."

"She let me in, though. Well, she left the kitchen door open."

"She's Catholic."

"They have their spirits."

Maud let out a great sigh. "Never mind the maid. She's only one of slews."

"Who gave you my name?" Clem pulled a chair from the table and sat. The room had cooled, now that there were only her and this Maud to heat it. "A fire would be nice."

"Yes. Oh, I . . . I've sent the maid home."

"You said. May I smoke?"

"I . . ." Maud shook her head. "If you must."

"I must." Clem flipped open her jacket and removed her pipe case. She set it on the lace cloth, opened the leather pouch of tobacco, and stuffed it into the pipe bowl. "What do you think you need from me, Maud Price?"

"I have a reputation."

"It precedes you."

"But you see the room." Maud gestured. "It once held twenty."

"And you enraptured hundreds. I saw you then. When I was a child and you were too. At a fair in Laconia."

Maud's mouth quivered and then rose in a smile. "Yes."

"The Maid of Light. I remember."

"Yes."

"It was on a banner. Tied to the side of the wagon cart. You sat on a white chair."

"You watched."

"Mm." Clem remembered. The sky the bluest of blue. The girl in her poplin, holding white roses and swinging one white-booted foot. Her father in his shiny suit with apple-red cheeks and swaggering walk.

"O Wonder, O Light, hear the dead speak."

But Clem's mother had dragged her past, turning only to spit. "Godless."

The tobacco tasted of apples and cherries, which made Clem's stomach growl. How long since her last full meal? And damn the last of the whiskey. She gave a shake of her head. "How did little Tom die?"

"He . . . he didn't tell me. He's with Billy."

"Who is Billy? Another of your . . . ?"

"I don't know. Another child lost. Perhaps someone come to bring him to the other side. It was so faint."

"You should've known the child's death before sitting with his grieving parents." Clem crossed a leg and swung her foot. "Now they're twice as upset and sure to visit someone else. There's no shortage of you all."

"If I know this beforehand, I leave myself open to accusations of fraud. I am not a fraud, Miss Watkins."

"I am not accusing you. It's just . . . clapping and rapping. I see no planchette. No levitating tables. Do you know a three-hundred-pound man levitated at Mrs. Martin's last week? He still has a bruise on his crown from smacking into the ceiling. You can bet those around that table will return to her."

"The spirits speak through me. They are not circus performers."

Clementine leaned forward, an elbow to each knee. "You need a three-legged monkey."

"A three-legged *what*?"

"You need fish that drop from the ceiling, or floating goblets—and you definitely need to know what poor Tom died of, and darling Maisie, and if you had a bauble or two to return to the grievers? Well, that's the three-legged monkey."

Maud just stared at Clem.

"An act. You need an act."

"That's fraudulent."

"It's a small necessity. For when your Matthias disobeys."

"Harriet said—"

"Ha. Mrs. Martin sent you. I'll have to thank her." Clem shrugged. Harriet was as fake as a medium could be.

"She said you helped."

"I do."

"Not like that. I don't want that. Flying trombones and . . . I feel I fail those who seek me now. I serve, Miss Watkins, that's—"

"You don't have money for the maid because you don't hear the voices. Your guiding spirit takes runners when you need him most. What money you do have comes from paltry twenty-five-cent entry fees, not leaving people to their own generosity. You're serving no one."

"Miss Watkins—" Maud rose from her chair and stood directly in front of Clem. She smelled of lavender and cedar. "There's a spirit right next to you." How keen she was, her breath coming in quick gasps as she ogled something just past Clem's shoulder. "Very weak, but there, nonetheless."

Clem forced herself not to turn. "There's nothing behind me."

Maud studied her. "It's there. Touching your shoulder."

"You should have done that during the séance. When the girl opened her eyes. That would have sold her." Clem emptied the ash into the candleholder, packed the pipe in its case, and stood.

"But it follows you."

"No. Nothing follows me."

"You are not a true believer."

"My convictions are as strong as yours."

"It is beautiful. To believe."

"Yes." Clem glanced at the empty fireplace grate, then back at Maud. She lifted a shoulder and dropped it. "You found me before. Send a note. If you want a full parlor, I can help."

"I was mistaken to have you—"

"Tom Ott fell from a tree. He broke his neck. His sister Celia was the one watching him, or supposed to have been, anyway. She is torn with guilt and she's afraid of her brother's ghost because she blames herself."

"He fell?"

"An oak in the yard. It's been cut down. What mother would want to look on that every day? It's like a murderer leering from the edge of the yard. What comfort she could have if she knew little Tom felt no pain. If just once she could feel a kiss on her cheek. Something, anything. But you know all this."

Clem opened the door and took her hat from the rack. She twisted her hair into a bun and tucked it under the brim. "I don't know about Mr. Sullivan's Maisie, but I can find out for you."

Maud followed her to the foyer. "I do wish to bring solace. That has always been the aim."

"Then we are agreed." She lifted the umbrella and pointed it across the entry at Maud. "It's never about the dead, Miss Price. What counts, in our line of work, is bringing comfort to the living."

～∂

Clem pulled the collar of her coat tight around her neck and jumped the steps to the street, grazing the edge of a puddle. She tipped the umbrella to shield herself from the rain, now coming at a sharper angle than it had been earlier in the day. At the shadow's edge of the second gaslight, she turned to look back at Maud Price's.

The woman was certainly spare with her candles. Clem spied only one at a second-floor window. She wondered if Maud had carried it from the parlor table. Perhaps this was her last candle, the very last, and after it was gone, soon the maid would go, and then the cups and saucers and carpets, and finally the house itself.

Then Maud would be left chasing her unreliable, unruly Matthias straight to the poorhouse, and no one there believed in ghosts. If they did, of course, the road to the asylum was short.

Maud seemed like a nymph those years ago. Now the woman's bland visage gave little away. Her hands, though, were smooth, dimpled on the knuckles and obviously not wont to labor.

Was the woman a true believer? An actual born medium? How many really were? Oh, the *Banner of Light* reported many spirit

12

manifestations, and flying tables, and rooms caked with ice. Mr. F. H. Hawley stated he conjured seven spirits from seven various Abenaki tribes and commanded them light seven separate woodstoves at his Portsmouth manse. And Mrs. J. H. Conant healed a girl with scarlet fever and cleared the gout from a neighbor, all while entranced and channeling the healing wisdom of dead Dr. Fisher. Harriet Martin's room swelled with the cacophony of floating violins and an oboe (here Clem made a bow to herself for her cleverness).

Miss Price did none of these things. She sat in her chair and waited for the spirits to speak. Not the other way around. God alone knew how many nights had been spent like this one, with the dead too stubborn to converse, and the table of mourners crumpling ever further into their grief.

And that figure Maud saw, just behind Clem's shoulder?

It had given Clem a fright, and very, very little did.

The candle in the window was now out. Or had been moved to a rear bedroom. Either way, the glass was black, leaving only the reflections of the streetlights in the windowpanes and on the brass knocker.

Clem sniffed and rubbed her nose. "I could make you a pretty fortune."

A carriage rumbled past. Clem leapt back from the spray of water and continued her walk. She tapped her finger to the tips of a wrought iron fence. Harriet's house was just down the way. Might as well stop in; she, too, held late hours. Clem could check the drawing room setup. Get a few coins for the extra care. Maybe a drink and a meal.

And ask after Maud Price.

A heavy arm wrapped around her shoulders. She stumbled forward, the umbrella falling to the ground.

She smacked her hand to the stomach of the assailant. "Get your fat hands off, you bastard."

"I'm insulted now. There's not an ounce of fat on me."

"You got fat for a brain, Russell." She grabbed her umbrella and swung it up, forcing the man to twist away.

He cocked his head and peered under the canopy at her. "Did you catch your fish, Mrs. Sprague?"

"Don't call me that. I'm not your wife."

"We could make it more so."

"I like my own name."

"Still."

"I like my own life."

Russell ducked under the umbrella and took the handle. "I'll crook my neck regular and permanent if you keep hold of that. Let me."

She shoved her hands under her jacket and underarms, hurrying her pace to keep up with his. "Look what you've done, fat brain. I'm going to die of pleurisy. Then what'll you do?"

He looked back at her with a slow grin. "I'll conjure your ghost, woman. What do you think I'll do? Your spiritual magnetism won't be able to resist my animal magnetism."

"Is that so?"

"'Tis so, my girl."

She jogged up to his side and wrapped her arm around his waist. "I couldn't resist if I tried."

"Well, that's that then. What are you on for this fine drab and damp eve?"

"Harriet Martin's for a drink."

"Ha!" He switched the umbrella and pulled her close. "Harriet's it is."

꩜

Mrs. Harriet Martin was not a missus. She eschewed marriage, having witnessed her sister's personality turn "the color of week-old linens." Clem suspected her name wasn't Martin, either, though she had yet to find out what exactly it was. She had been through every nook and corner and cranny of the three-story house. First it had been to suss out the areas to set up the necessary equipment. Walls were plastered and replastered; none but Clem was aware of the pulleys and strings she'd rigged through the slats and along the joists and between the floor-boards. A high D plunked on the pianoforte set off an echoing call from an invisible violin. An angle of silvered glass instead of brass behind a gaslight gave just the right shimmering image of a searching hand.

Raps and knocks were for amateurs.

Though they had their place, if only to startle.

"I want them to weep in wonderment," Mrs. Martin said.

"Wonderment is expensive," Clem answered. She did not need to mention the price to keep secrets. Mrs. Martin paid it all.

With each successive envelope of cash—no banker's check, upon mutual agreement—Clem grew more and more curious. She came by more frequently to "check the lines" and sneaked her way through clos-ets of feathers and velvets and deep purple wools. She'd rifled the sec-retary for bills—only to find the ledger blank, as well as the stationery.

She was a woman after Clem's heart.

Now, she leaned across the table to pass Clem the clotted cream. When Russell reached for it, Clem ground her heel on the top of his foot.

"No need for that." Russell smiled and gestured for the creamer to continue its way from Harriet's side of the table to Clem's. "She should be a cat," he said.

Harriet raised an eyebrow and settled back in her chair. "A sleek Siamese."

"An alley cat." He humphed and dug his fork into a mound of scrambled eggs. "Meow."

Clem took a scoop of cream and spread it on her toast. Then she took another and let the silk and sweet of it melt on her tongue. "I like breakfast at 1:00 a.m." She sighed, leaning back and angling her head to watch the blue flames in the lamps. There were three of them with simple clear globes. The table itself was set with mismatched silverware and plates with nicks and cracks. The only honest room, Clem thought. The breakfast room was one of the few Harriet left to its own uses. It wasn't a maze of ferns and vases and peacock feathers and stuffed pigeons and marmots. Even the séance room had its share of marble busts and ruby-red crystal chandeliers.

She had witnessed more than one soul faint away at the frowning Caesar on his plinth by the front entrance.

"Maud Price," Clem said.

"Yes? What of her?"

"You gave her my name."

"She is . . ." Harriet slid her eyes to the side. "An earnest woman."

"A once famous woman."

"Yes."

"Yes."

Harriet's green eyes sharpened. "You have a trick up your sleeve."

"No trick. She did not wish my services."

"Her creditors might disagree."

"But she will. I'll provide her a small gift. Then she can decide one way or the other."

"And the gift?"

"I don't give my secrets away. You know that."

"And you don't give free gifts. I know that too." Harriet stirred her coffee, then ran the spoon across her tongue before setting it to the saucer. "I have a man coming Friday night. Herodotus Parker. He is a very rich man with a very dead wife. You can get me something, can't you? Of hers?"

Clem tucked her thumbs to the pockets of her jacket. She flipped the gold chain of her watch against her vest, then slipped out the timepiece and snapped open the lid. "Herodotus Parker's very dead wife is very well buried. As of 10:00 a.m. yesterday."

"They were believers."

"I know that. I have read his musings on the nature of ethereal mists."

"Can I have the cream now?"

Clem slid it to Russell and watched him put a dollop on half a biscuit and then eat the whole in one bite.

"They have been here often. Their two boys . . ." Harriet lowered her gaze. Then she gave a shake of her head and looked out to the hallway.

"Their two boys and all the others killed in the war have made you rich."

"Nevertheless." Harriet pursed her lips and stared at Clem. "She had a bracelet made with the boys' hair twined and set in a glass bead. I want to give that."

Russell bit into the other half of biscuit and chewed. He rubbed a crumb from his lip. "It's on her wrist, isn't it?"

Harriet's cheeks rose as she smiled. "Think of the solace it would give. Were it to drop from the heavens to his lap."

Clem twisted in her seat. What Harriet wanted—it was too damn cold and wet to dig up another grave. Horse Hill was notorious for its muck and mud.

But Harriet was a consistent and discreet client. "I'll have what you want."

"My man will wait for it tomorrow night. At the usual spot."

Chapter Two

Maud

Maud shook her head and turned her gaze from the dining table to the window. It was a disconsolate morning. The rain had not stopped throughout the night, and now it slid in sheets down the glass. She rubbed her hands together, then pushed them under her thighs and into the warm folds of her skirt. Perhaps she should run up and down the stairs—that would get her blood stirring. Maybe her toes would stop feeling as if they might snap off in the cold, and her legs along with them.

She peered out to the entryway, her stomach growling as it awaited the morning coffee and toast and bacon. Which were not going to appear.

Margaret had knocked very early, and she had that tense fighting line to her shoulders when Maud pulled open the door.

"I am a Catholic," Margaret said. She stepped past Maud and didn't seem to notice how her skirts and cape dripped water all over the parquet floor. "I'll wait for a reference."

Maud rubbed her eyes of sleep. "But I need a maid."

Margaret sniffed and stared at the ceiling.

So a letter was drafted—Maud wrote the same content as in the previous six—and Margaret folded it into her purse. "You need God, Miss Price."

But Maud thought at this moment that what she really needed was the coffee and toast and bacon.

And Matthias to mind and obey.

Well, that Watkins woman witnessed it, and instead of offering guidance, some new sort of conjuring or a new method of trance, she had offered a theory involving a three-legged monkey. Well.

Harriet needed a talking to. Maud would pull her aside at next month's psychical meeting.

Which Maud was meant to speak at. She had not written a word. What could she honestly say? *My Fellow Spiritualists, I stand before you a trickster and a liar.*

That odd woman in her suit had caught out the cat piss and ash. It had been one of Margaret's last duties. Maybe that, rather than some loyalty to Catholic piety, had turned her away. And the clapping, well, how hard was that? Or pulling a string on a window and letting in the cold?

Clementine Watkins knew exactly what Maud was up to. And she was not impressed.

Maud glanced at the ceiling, running her gaze across to the parlor. Her father's room sat above it. Maud piled the bills on his secretary still, though he'd been dead and buried six years. The stack was precariously high. It needed attending. Which she did wish to do, sometime, even if it was to sidle in and sneak the top paper and pray it was a notice for last week's meat and egg delivery and not Mrs. Amberstone's for the last hat.

Maud had to stop with the hats.

She winced and shook her head. Tsked at her own shortcomings, much as Father had.

But really, this was all Matthias's fault. Who ever heard of a spirit-guide leaving a medium in the lurch? Well, he had. Matthias Turnbull had tormented her as a child and now his absence tormented her too. If she could say one thing about spirit-guides, it would be to steer clear of them.

But in the past, when she called for him, he came. She asked his acquaintance and was answered. He held open the veil when she requested, and the paradise on the other side blinded her with beauty.

The lines of those waiting to see her! It seemed they went on to the horizon. Some weeping, some still, mothers and grandfathers and sweethearts and wives and little children. All those souls lost on battle-fields, succumbing to bullets and dysentery and infectious blood. All those poor men.

Matthias came directly when called. *Hello, my dear. I am so glad to be here with you. I have a loved one here to speak.*

Father told her it all went down better if she had a tear in her eye and held the mourner's hand.

The days had turned to weeks and weeks had turned to . . . years. She could not deny it. And each successive séance brought less and less, only glimmers, sometimes a sound or two, those who meandered and were lost. If only Maud could grab them all up and hold them.

Now she could barely look a mourner in the eye. All the faith they had in her to find their loved ones, to join the living and the dead in final goodbyes and trading of secrets and whispers of joy, and simple hope for the next world—the weight of her failures nearly crushed her.

She had once been the Maid of Light. She had given comfort. She had been useful. She couldn't bear to have it all go away.

Her stomach growled. She flung herself out of the chair. If she wanted coffee, she would need to get some all on her own, wouldn't she? It wasn't that difficult. She didn't need a maid. Half the rooms were empty anyway, dustcovers draped over piano and cabinet and bed frames alike. She could pick up a mop and dustpan and clean the remaining rooms lickety-split.

Her slipper landed in a puddle. She hopped on the other foot, then reached down to pat the rag rug, following the sodden wool to the baseboard under a side window. She stood to peer behind the china cabinet at the wall itself and cringed at the buckled paint and plaster.

She clenched her jaw and thumped her hand to the cabinet's top. "Hell and damn."

A loud thump answered. A pewter candlestick wobbled and shot off the wood, landing with a *clomp* by her feet.

She froze. Stilled herself. Her fingers grew chill, numb. Her breath blew out in a white mist. Was he here?

"Matthias?"

Nothing. Just damp and cold.

A rap sounded on the door.

She smoothed her hair and looked out a front window. The stoop was empty. No one was on the street. She turned the lock and opened the door. A small leather pouch swung from the knob. She freed it, then leaned out to check the street again, but nothing stirred, save the rain drenching the new spring leaves and cascading over the roof edges on the white clapboard houses across the street. The bells in South Church rang six.

She held the bag by its drawstring, surprised at how light it was, as if it held only air. She sat on the bench in the hall, undid the string, and turned the bag onto her lap.

A miniature soldier with blue coat, red trousers, and drum slid out, landing face up, its black-dot eyes staring at her. The base held two initials, carved neatly into the balsa: *T. O.*

Tom Ott.

A small piece of paper fluttered atop the toy. *Tom Ott fell from an oak tree. Celia blames herself. There is a match of this toy in her room. Give her this. The family is in great grief. Give them solace. Your gifts are needed.*

$\backsim\!\!9$

It took Maud much of the day to determine what to do. It would, she felt, bring much comfort should she meet with the family. Lift the guilt from Celia's heart, for certainly it was there; she'd felt it so clearly at the sitting. Along with Celia's fear of her parents' rejection, should little Tom appear in spirit and blame her for his fall.

She could not leave them like this. The dead child like a limb chopped off, there and then so quickly not there. It was too much to bear. It was her calling to light their path, and if the means were a bit muddled, the result was the same, was it not?

So the decision was made. She found a hack idling at the street corner, as if it were waiting just for her to hail it. She handed the driver the Otts' address, and off they had gone.

And now they were here. A white crepe ribbon hung on the Otts' door, the sign of a child having died, a sign to give a quick prayer to the babe and the family inside. The shutters remained fully shut, as if the Otts had departed for an extended trip. But smoke curled from the brick chimneys; the family was in residence.

She knocked on the glass between herself and the driver. The carriage swayed and lifted as he hopped out to unfold the step and open her door.

"You'll wait for me?" she asked, taking his hand as she exited.

He nodded and returned to the warmth of his seat.

The garden, she thought, would be lovely in a month or two. Now the grounds were bare but for the hedging along the drive and up to the portico. On either side, the land rolled away in greens, grasses flattened and muddy, stone circles and walkways awaiting new pebbled paths and flowers to rise and blossom. She spied it then, the space where the oak had been, the turned earth like raw gums after a freshly pulled tooth.

She strode forward, the toy soldier now wrapped in a piece of blue velvet, secure in the deep pocket of her cloak. A gift to give to the Otts, to stave off their fear that Tom dwelt lost and frightened in the land of Nod.

A twinge of guilt stopped her from knocking. She shouldn't have come. This was . . . this was beyond her small necessities. Clementine Watkins's smug smile floated in front of her.

No. She should not. Her stomach hurt from the lie of it.

The door opened. The daughter peeked from the narrow gap. Delia? Celia.

The girl's mouth knotted and twisted. She stared out at Maud.

Maud fumbled in the purse on her belt and produced her calling card.

Celia glanced at it. The skin around her eyes was puffy and dark gray. "I know who you are."

"It's not your fault." The words tumbled from Maud's mouth. "You cannot blame yourself. He doesn't want that."

Celia plucked the card and shut the door, leaving Maud to wonder if she had been turned away.

But almost as soon as the door shut, it swung wide open. Mr. Ott stared down at her. "You are not welcome here."

Maud lowered her head and stared at the tips of his shoes. "I come only with a gift."

"Your gift was to bring us Tom."

"The spirit-presence does not have a switch." But what was there to explain? Just hand over the toy and give condolences.

She unwrapped the soldier and held it out. "This came to me. I believe it is meant for you."

Mr. Ott's face drained of color, his jowls slackening. He turned the toy around and around, then tipped it and dragged his nail over the initials. "My God. Is he with you now? Nancy! Celia!" He stepped back to bellow for them once more, then reached for Maud's elbow to usher her inside. "Come, come. You must come in. My God."

Now Nancy—Mrs. Ott—came to the door, her lips a sharp line when she recognized Maud.

"Look, Nancy." Ott held the little soldier up to her gaze.

"Where did you get that?" she asked.

"It was brought as a gift, Mrs. Ott," Maud said. "I found it on my doorstep."

Nancy gripped her mourning skirts and stepped back in the hall. "We buried that with him. We buried it with Tom."

◦━◦

It was Celia's expression that kept Maud talking. Celia, who should be in the bloom of youth, but whose face was already lined from guilt and grief.

Maud had not left as she should have.

She sat instead on the edge of the sofa and twisted her napkin, demurring an offer of another piece of plum cake, another cup of tea, and talked and talked.

"Tom says he plays with two other boys now, chutes and ladders. He did like playing that, didn't he?" Miss Watkins's notes had been right, for Mrs. Ott cried harder and Mr. Ott patted her hand.

"You must believe, Celia, that he is well now. You shouldn't blame yourself at all. God called him to the beauteous beyond."

The girl hid her face in her hands.

"Celia." Maud reached to lay her hand on Celia's knee.

The girl's shoulders juddered as she held back a sob. "He promised to stay on the lowest branch. He promised. I only turned my back for a moment because the dog—"

"The toy soldier is for you, Celia. Tom spoke very clearly to me. You are to bring it home to him when it is your time. You gave it to him as a gift once. He has returned it for your safekeeping."

"Me?"

"You."

Maud's mouth felt dry as sawdust. She stared at the watery light and the blank sky out a paned window. A flash of yellow caught her eye. A canary perched in a metal cage. It pecked at a seed block. "Does it sing?"

The Otts looked at the bird.

"No," Mr. Ott said.

"He will." Maud squeezed her eyes tight and prayed it would be so.

Celia threw her arms around Maud, clawing at her back, thumbs pushed into her shoulders, her sobs long and low, breath hot on Maud's neck.

"There, there. Feel peace. Tom is at peace. Tom loves you all."

⁓

The driver had waited as requested. He sat under an umbrella, and when Maud neared, he tipped his hat before climbing down to assist her inside.

"All well and good then, miss?" He smiled, lips pulled higher on one side, and scratched at his bushy beard as if he had something more he wanted to say to her.

"Yes?"

"Just asking after yerself, miss."

She sat without answering, bit the inside of her cheek and hunched over, squeezing her sides. The driver gave a look of concern and hesitated before the passenger window, as if he would ask after her again. She yanked down the black blind to shut him out. Her head ached.

The cab lurched and began its journey.

She pushed her fists to her stomach, willing away the threatening nausea.

It was for the living. This was for the living. She had seen the loosening of guilt on Celia's face, the softening of heartache. Now the family could lay their grieving to rest. Tonight the house would sleep.

She sat up, dragged in a breath, and transferred the twenty dollars from her fist to her reticule.

"If I had more . . ." Mr. Ott had said.

Maud had not declined the money as she had the cake. She had done the right thing. Yes. The kind thing.

Perhaps. The thought curled round her skull. *Perhaps.*

Chapter Three

CLEMENTINE

The path Clem took was narrow, worn to ruts by mourners who'd carried so many a coffin up Horse Hill and returned empty-handed and in silence after the burial. She zigzagged through oaks and birch and then cut through a stand of pines before dropping to the water. The river, swollen from all the rain, grabbed at the long grasses. Her lantern swung and spread little light, the mist thick as pudding. At least the horrid rain had stopped. The fresh grave slopped with mud, and every dig of the shovel let another rivulet of water fill the hole. The ground grew even more slippery, and not once, but twice, her boot slipped and she had to claw her way out. But Harriet needed her "proof" for tomorrow night's circle.

Russell had taken himself off somewhere. He said to the theater, for Ogden Sparks was set to play Hamlet. Russell hated Ogden, as if the traveling actor were directly responsible for Russell's own lack of any meaningful talent. He vowed to throw evil looks and loud boos the actor's way.

Earlier, Russell had clad himself in driver's gear and rented a hack from McClennan's. "I will judge your Miss Price myself. Besides, I know how to drive a set of horses and you do not."

It was one of the more reasonable things he'd said.

So she traveled the old coffin path and waited for the gravekeeper to take to his cottage for evening psalms and a meal.

Almira Parker, devoted wife of Herodotus, was now with the Lord at eighty-seven years old. Clem lifted the lid and squatted to bring her candle close.

"Happy to be dead, Mrs. Parker?" The old woman's mouth was curled into a grin, a rictus of toothless eternal joy. Clem patted the cold cheek. Then she set the candle on the woman's chest and proceeded to snip a lock of her hair, unfasten her lace collar, and roll the beaded velvet bracelet from her wrist.

She folded them in linen, stuffed the bundle into her wallet, then blew out the candle and filled the hole.

The trip back took half the time as the trip up. Midway, she jogged to a stand of oak, unbuckled the rucksack she'd stashed there earlier, and peeled off her wet clothing. All of it was shoved into the sack, along with the iron cat's paw (so much more efficient than a crowbar—she was glad she'd stolen it last year) and pair of pliers. She patted the chest pocket of her coat to confirm the takings remained intact. Dressed now in simple widow's blacks, she meandered the rest of the way down the hill, then out the gate.

The trees lining the street dripped rain on her bonnet. She whistled a bit, then grew tired of it.

Harriet's man should have been waiting at the far corner of the street. But he wasn't. A small brown-and-white dog snuffled around a white wrought iron fence and then gave her a leery glare before loping back to its warm house and treats from its owner.

"Damnation," she muttered. She dug out her watch. Ten forty-six. She was late. It wouldn't do for her to be loitering along such a pristine street, widow's habit or not.

The genteel world stopped at Main Street. The brick buildings here hugged the sidewalks in a long, undulating line. Most doors were locked. Most windows were black. The gas lamps gave a modicum of light, as did the spill of lamplight from a few of the windows she passed. By morning, the street would be a cacophony of horse carts and wagons, as the industrious of Harrowboro sold and manufactured their wares. The meeting hall, pious in its white-clad simplicity and well past its useful life, blared with light. Drivers idled on the side street, smoking their pipes and chumming from man to man, while their horses hung their heads and no doubt prayed for a sunny pasture someday in their miserable lives.

Clem turned into a side alley, then pushed her shoulder against a worn wooden door and tiptoed up the steep back stairs of the boardinghouse. Her hand glossed the rough wall as she ascended.

Russell said nothing when she entered their small room, just kept pushing aside the curtain on the front window and peering out. He was drinking a bottle of cider. His slouch hat was on, tilted back so tufts of blond hair curled around his forehead and over his ears. He touched the brim with the bottle's mouth in greeting and returned his gaze to the window.

She put out the lantern and set it on a square table. "Who's gathered?"

"The ladies' rights auxiliary. It was the men's brass band night—you should have seen the fuss. A tuba was gravely injured by a sharp parasol. Horrible business." He rubbed his nose and looked at her. "You're a fine mess."

"You're observant tonight."

"Good dig?"

Clem nodded. "A happy corpse."

"That's how it goes sometimes."

"Harriet's man wasn't there."

"Again?"

"I was late. I'll drop the goods off in the morning." Clem stuck her fingers into the top of her boot to scratch. Her skin felt damp, puckered, waterlogged. Like the woman's in the box. She untied the boots, glad for the relief, for they pinched at the toes. She pulled them off and set them by the stove. "How was *Hamlet*?"

"Moaning."

"And the elephant?"

"Drugged. He swayed and stumbled into the wings and wasn't seen again."

Clem removed her jacket and hung it from a wooden dowel, then took the leather wallet from the chest pocket and deposited it in a dresser drawer. The drawer squealed and shimmied; Clem shoved it closed with her knee.

"I don't understand what you see in that Maud Price, Clem. She is so very . . . solemn." Russell twisted to lie back on the bed, one arm slung under his head and the bottle held out for her.

"Did you ever see Charlotte Cushman act?" She took the bottle, glad for the sweet bite of cider down her throat. "I saw her play Juliet once. Just a year or two before she died. Had to have been thirty years too old for the part. Here, unbutton my shirt, will you? My hands are fumbly frozen."

Russell sat up and pulled the shirttails from her skirt. "I'm not letting you in the bed without a scrub down."

"You'll have to bring up more wood, then."

"I'll have to lug up water, too, so how about a quick rubdown with the pitcher we've got?"

She stepped between his knees and patted his cheek. "I just dug up a grave; I'm not dragging the crumbs and pieces between the sheets. So, you'll get water and wood. But first listen to me—I'm telling you about Juliet."

A half loaf of black bread and a pot of jam sat on the side table. Clem leaned over and tore a piece off, then dragged it through the jam. She popped it in her mouth and chewed and swallowed. "Could have left the meat."

"Only cold cuts. Mrs. Epp refused to give more."

"Listen. Charlotte Cushman was too old to play Juliet. The actress playing Nurse was twenty years her junior. And yet the theater was packed to the gills. It didn't matter how wrong it was to cast her as a fourteen-year-old girl. Her reputation is what pulled people in."

Russell's hand stopped at her collar. "You've torn it."

"So we suspended disbelief. And for that evening she *was* Juliet. There wasn't a dry eye in the house when she plunged that dagger to her breast." Clem shrugged out of the shirt and unbuttoned her skirt. She let it slide to the floor and stepped out of it, leaving her in a chemise and men's long underwear.

"Maud Price once had that reputation. And that, Russell, will make a thousand clawing, grief-stricken mourners from every forsaken village and grand opera house return. And believe."

"Not a dry eye in the house."

Clem kissed him on the lips. "Not one damn dry eye."

He swung himself up, grappled for his pocket watch, and returned to the window.

Clem wrapped her arms around his waist and pressed her nose to his back. She loved the smell of him, the tang of horsehair and leather, the linger of his sweat. She slid her hands under the rough wool of his vest and ran her fingertips over his chest, smiling at the catch in his breath. "I'm much more interesting than the ladies' auxiliary."

"Yes. You are." He leaned forward then, palms to the window frame as he stared into the street.

His back tensed. "Get your clothes." He turned from the window, grabbing up clothes and tugging the blanket from the bed. He slung her coat at her, followed by her boots.

She tied the laces together and draped them around her like a necklace. The heels banged against her chest. She threw open the wardrobe, shoving costumes aside, reaching toward the back, behind the shoes and boots.

"Come on, Clem." Russell reached out his hand.

"I need my kit." She tugged the leather handle of a heavy satchel and lugged it out.

"Come on, come on." Heavy thumps echoed in the stairwell. "They're at the second floor."

Clem smacked his hand away, ducked under his arm, and ran for the door. Her ears throbbed and clanged. Had someone followed her? Had someone seen? She'd been so careful replacing the soil. Always so careful.

"They're up there." Damned Mrs. Epp and her horrid, snot-filled voice. "I've warned them before. You do not pay, you do not stay."

The steps grew louder. Two sets. The police.

Clem bit her lip, took in a breath, and slipped into the hall, taking the last flight to the roof. Russell followed behind, arms loaded with scarves and cloaks, the blanket trailing. They paused at the roof door, thankfully without a lock, for Russell had been clever enough to remove it once upon a time. He gave a quick nod, and they tumbled through, not slowing until they'd made the rooftop door of the Archer's Dry Goods warehouse and taken the steep flight down.

They froze at the landing to the offices. A single gas light glowed in the hall and reflected on the glazed glass windows of each office door.

"It's all right. We just need to get to Harriet. We get those materials to her and it's all fine as a fat goose." Russell turned to her, running his eyes down her body. "You are nearly naked."

"And you didn't pay the rent."

$\sim\!\!9$

The privy stunk, as privies do. Clem pulled on the brown wool skirt Russell had tossed her before stuffing her in the small space and leaving her to her own devices. She tugged a cotton shirt over her head—his shirt, not hers—and tucked it in as best she could.

This was not how things should turn out. Clem twisted around to wiggle on a boot. She blamed the entire state of affairs on Mrs. King and her damn integrity. Her betrayal, more like.

The fire was not Clem's fault.

But Mrs. King—Clem clenched her teeth and ground them—would hear nothing else.

You sure it's not an angry spirit? Clem had ventured to ask. *You stir enough of them.*

That comment got Clem kicked out of Portsmouth proper. Blacklisted from a nonexistent list.

She tilted her head to the outhouse's vent pipe and pretended the air was fresh. She looked at the sky. It was much like peering through a telescope. A star glimmered, faint and far away. A thin wisp of cloud slid by.

No. Not cloud at all. Tobacco smoke.

The door rattled. "Oy."

Clem unlatched her satchel and double-checked the buckles on the inks, the tightness of the lids, the latch on the toolbox. Then she hefted it under her arm and unhooked the door.

A man swayed and tottered back. His clothes were splotched and stained. He had the shoulders of a wool driver or baler, the jacket puckering under his armpits and too short at the cuff.

"Move aside." She stepped to the ground.

He took a drag from his pipe. "What's in the bag?"

"Nothing to concern you."

"Maybe that's for me to figure. Give it to me."

Her hands shook. "No."

"We could trade, then." His arm snaked out to grab her elbow.

She swung the bag directly at his face. It shuddered in her grip. He staggered back, clutching his nose, and blood poured around his fingers. "Whore!"

"Serves you right, doesn't it?" She grabbed her skirts with her free hand and bolted down the alley, swinging through the light of the street and thrusting herself into the shadows of a storefront. She gasped and leaned against the door.

Across the way, a group of women came down the steps of town hall. The women's auxiliary must have won the fight. How neat and tidy they were in their evening coats and matching umbrellas and gloves and befeathered hats. Carriages and hansom cabs awaited. One by one the women departed, the horses chawing their bits, the drivers flicking the reins, the wheels slicing through puddles.

The street grew quiet.

But not empty.

A woman stood on the bottom step. Her hat was ridiculous. Like an upturned bucket with cascades of feathers and silk roses. She kept her hands tucked to her muff, her umbrella hooked over her arm. Her cloak swung as she descended to the walkway. She looked neither left nor right, but straight forward.

Straight at Clem.

Maud Price.

Clem blew out a breath and lifted her chin. The boy's toy had been impossibly easy to get. It was his small fingers, skin so unbearably soft, that she couldn't shake from her dreams.

She would deny everything.

Maud crossed the street. She stared at Clem, her eyes so pale they were nearly silver. "Find out what happened to Maisie Sullivan."

Chapter Four

MAUD

She had not made a mistake. It was Clementine she had spied across the street, and it was Clementine who now shifted her shoulders back and smiled. Her teeth were very straight; Maud inadvertently raised a hand to cover her own. Then she stopped herself and grabbed the handle to her umbrella.

The woman's lips tightened into a smirk. She cocked an eyebrow. "Thank me first."

"For what?"

"The Otts. The toy."

Maud swallowed. "Yes."

"That is not a sufficient thank-you. I'm disappointed. Truly." With a shrug and a sigh, Clementine reached behind her and picked up a leather valise. She swung it in front of her, both hands curled to the brass and leather handle. "Have a good night."

"Have a good . . ."

"Night, day, life. Have a good Otherworld, if that suits. Oh, wait, they've closed the doors to you. Anyway."

Clementine brushed her aside with a wave and sauntered to the street. She turned once to nod, then kicked out a boot from under her skirts and walked off. Her hair, tied in a long braid, swung like a pendulum against a shirt three sizes too big. The tails flipped and fluttered. A sleeve flopped down. Clementine folded it up.

"You look ridiculous," Maud said.

Clementine contemplated Maud.

She dropped to a curtsy, her arm drifting gracefully up and then across her bosom. And once again she performed the routine, ending with a kiss blown to Maud.

Then she straightened, attention turned to a nearby street. Her eyes stayed glued to it as she circled back to take Maud's arm and jerk her forward. Maud stumbled and jogged to keep up. "Don't pull my arm off."

Clementine didn't answer. She tugged Maud again, this time through a doorway and into a dank hall empty but for a flight of stairs, sagging and black with grime. The wallpaper had once held a pattern, but it now hung in strips.

Maud jerked her arm free of Clementine's. "What are you doing?"

"Getting us and the dead pheasant atop your head out of the rain." Clementine frowned and looked Maud up and down. "Do you have money?"

Maud's heart battered her chest. "Are you robbing me?"

"I might be. And then I might not. I might be saving you."

"How is this—"

A door cracked against a wall upstairs. Clementine put her finger against Maud's lips. Then she leaned close to Maud's left ear. "You are going to give me the money you most certainly made at the Otts' today."

"I don't have it."

"Yes, you do." Clementine shifted back. "You can call it a loan. If that makes you feel better."

"It doesn't."

Clementine shoved and pawed at Maud's coat and skirts with her free hand. The valise swung and bumped Maud's knees.

"Stop it." Maud grabbed the woman's wrist. "It's in the reticule on my belt."

"Thank you."

Maud flinched as it was torn away, the beaded bag tossed to the floor and the money crumpled in Clementine's fist.

"You see, Miss Price? Thank-yous are very simple." She sidled through the door, leaving Maud in the stench of the hallway. Old cabbage and mold. Her reticule lay in a puddle of oily liquid. Something seeped from the landing above.

Then something moved in the corner. Maud froze. She blinked, forcing herself to see in the dimness. "Who's there?"

It moved again, a streak of gray mist and chittering ice, scratching along the pocked wainscoting, then flattening and slipping under the door. A cat. The last she saw of it was the swish of its tail. Then it was gone.

A match flared above her, followed by the acrid smell of a cigar. Two stories up, a man with thick black sideburns and a bald head rested his elbows on the railing and watched her as he smoked. The tip of the cigar glowed red, then went black. Ash drifted in the stairwell. A sharp gust set it to swirl as Clementine swept back in.

Clementine wiped her arm over her eyes and pushed back the hair stuck to her forehead. Her clothes were soaked through. Water beaded and stained the valise. "I will find your Maisie Sullivan's fate for you."

"It's raining." Everything was fuzzy around the edges of Maud's vision. She opened her mouth to speak, but the words seemed to be stuck like syrup in the back of her throat.

"Are you all right?" Clem asked.

"Who follows you?"

A door thudded. The smoker had returned to his room.

"No one. At the moment." Clementine held open the door. Rain sheeted the sidewalk and bounced in great glops on the road, stirring up mud and the low fog. "We'll share your umbrella. I'll tell you my services and prices along the way."

"Where?"

"To your house, of course." A single thin wisp of mist coiled Clementine's skirt. "I'll be glad for a bath. I'll want that first."

⁓

It wasn't like Maud. None of this was. She trailed behind Clementine in her plain brown skirt, her battered satchel bumping against her leg. Clementine stroked the leather as she strode along, as if she were soothing a child. Once, after they had left the main streets and the sodden rain had become a light drizzle, the woman stopped under the arch of a tree, leaned back against a wrought iron fence, and sighed.

It was a heavy sigh, the kind that shudders all down the body. She turned her head and stared at Maud.

"We were supposed to share the umbrella," Maud said. "And discuss prices."

"Thirty percent of all takings, plus expenses."

"Thirty percent. That's outrageous."

"You have no money. Thirty percent of zero is zero. You can afford me." Clementine shifted the satchel from under one arm to under the other, pushed her heel off the brick base of the fence, and started off again. "I'm very good at what I do."

Maud tipped her umbrella to avoid the worst of the weather and jogged forward, though she was not near close to catching up. The farther they walked, the farther Maud lagged.

Her heart raced and her breath grew reedy. She feared that, should she lift the umbrella enough to peer down the road, it would not be Clementine trudging forward, but her father, his hands in fists and swinging industriously forward and back, his stride long and impossible to match, his coattails flapping against his calf.

"Come along, girl. Come along."

But he didn't slow. That was not something he ever did. Just expected her to scamper and lunge along in her white leather boots and pretty frocks and somehow catch up. Then when she didn't—for how could one, at ten years old with stubby legs, or at twenty and still recovering from scarlet fever?—he bellowed and circled around and snapped up her hand in his and shook it once. He leaned down, jowls and ruddy cheeks and stubbly sideburns and scowl the whole of her vision. "Why do you lag so?"

"I can't keep up."

"But you must. You must. It is urgent."

Always such. Everything was so urgent. "Mrs. S— requires a reading. Mr. T— asked especially. Little M's yearning for his mother. Now look at that line of mourners! Look, daughter, how many need your Matthias to speak."

Another yank of the arm. "He will be with you, won't he?"

Maud's umbrella swung to the side. The rain spattered her skin. She blinked and screwed her eyes shut.

She felt Clem tug on the umbrella and tightened her grip.

"Here we are."

And indeed, there they were.

"It's awfully dark." Clementine sprang up the steps to Maud's front door. Her eyes grew wide, and she scanned the street, much as the villain in a melodrama would. Maud half expected a sneer and the rolling of a mustache. "I wonder if anyone is home." She knocked before putting her ear to the wood.

"What are you doing?" Maud swung the umbrella up and was glad for the reprieve from watery spit.

Clementine put a finger to her lips. "Shh."

"Who are you?"

"I said be quiet."

"How dare—"

Clementine snapped her fingers. A flame sputtered and burned from her fingertip. "Ah. Better now." She reached for the doorknob, turned it, and pushed the door open wide.

Maud stared at the vestibule. It was dark, save the thin glow from the flame now balanced on Clementine's palm.

"I locked that."

"If you say." Clementine swept into the hall, lighting one sconce, then the next, before blowing out the flame cupped in her hand. Her boots clacked against the wood as she returned to stare down at Maud. "Are you hungry? I'm starved."

Chapter Five

CLEMENTINE

It was such an easy trick. Snap and there's fire. Easiest trick in the book, but it did always stir a bit of awe. Even Mrs. Bletham hesitated in the swing of her cane, giving the back of little Clem's thighs a much-needed rest. Clem did not respect the orphanage rules, did not like the mealy food, and definitely did not like the punishments, which were both harsh and swift. The fire trick put a pause to them, and when the wonder of that wore off, Clem practiced another skill, and then another (Arthur Asher had been good enough to write them down before dumping her) until she was left well alone. At least, nearly alone. But enough of that.

She took a bite of the molasses bread Maud had managed to find in the kitchen and chewed. She draped her arm on the back of a spindle chair and stretched out, tapping a toe to the leg of the kitchen table. Maud stood across the room, worrying away a towel and biting her bottom lip with much disquiet. Her frown was deep, eyebrows nearly touching as she kept a wary gaze upon Clem.

Water burbled in two large pots on the stove. Maud had lugged a tin tub to the middle of the floor. Clem smiled and swallowed her bread. She lifted a small glass half-full of cider to her lips and tossed it all back. She pushed her foot at a chair across from her. "Sit."

"The water—"

"Is it boiling?"

Maud leaned over to look. "It's rolling."

"Then it's not boiling. You can sit." Clem scratched her thigh. Maud had given her a chemise and drawers in exchange for her sodden and heavy skirts and shirt. Both hung on a drying line that ran from the corner near the larder to a hook by the hallway entrance. Maud had not changed. Her skirt was stained along the hem and she shivered.

"I'm all right here."

"Suit yourself."

"I do." Maud scooped up a wooden spoon and stuck it in the pot and stirred. The windows and wall behind her beaded with steam. Her hair, mousy and limp, grew even limper and hung about her face.

"Double double, toil and trouble . . ."

"That's not funny." Maud removed the spoon and set it with a clack to the counter. She clutched a towel to the pot handles, lugged it up, waddled to the tub, and tipped it. The water sloshed against the sides.

Clem sighed. The tub looked deliciously steamy. She was cold through and through, as if the rain had managed its way to her marrow. But of course it had: she'd started the evening in the pit of a grave and ended it cowering in a corner to evade the police and the wrath of Mrs. Epp. It was a minor miracle Maud had come along when she did. Who knew where Russell was—who knew how many months he'd forgotten the rent but remembered the whores and dogfights. She blew out a breath. *Hamlet*, indeed.

She would need to return to their room in the morning; the twenty dollars she'd dragged from Maud's reticule would hold the police off only so long. No doubt there'd be a few idling around the door, waiting for another bill before giving her access. But she didn't have it, nor the bracelet she'd slipped from the arm of a dead woman. One went with the other: without the bracelet she had nothing to give to Harriet Martin and thus Harriet Martin had nothing to give to her.

Yes. Maud was a minor miracle. Though the conjuring of little Tom's toy had egged it along.

The clatter of a pot brought back her attention.

Maud made a sweeping gesture toward the bathtub.

"Ah." Clem stood, pulling her chemise over her head and dropping it to the table.

Of course Maud's cheeks would pink. Of course she'd turn her gaze to the door. "I'll just . . ."

"Don't go." Clem pulled the string on the long underwear, then shimmied out of them. Damn, the room was cold. She curled her toes up, wanting nothing more than to dart to the hot bath and jump in. Instead, she swaggered over and leaned down to touch her index finger to the water. "It is exactly right."

Maud twisted a thumb and stepped from one foot to the other. She took a half step to the door.

"Don't you want to know how I got the toy?" Clem lowered herself down, her limbs softening and buzzing at once. She leaned back, resting her head on the towel Maud had kindly folded to the rim.

"Are you staying the night?"

Clem opened one eye. "Didn't I mention it? Thirty percent plus expenses *plus* accommodations for the length of the contract. Which we could settle tonight on a handshake and put to ink in the morning."

"Are you in trouble?"

"Of course not."

Maud's eyebrow arched.

"Just a confusion with the landlady," Clem said. "Over the rent."

"And the twenty dollars you stole from me. That didn't help?"

"That won't keep her from throwing everything out the window." She pushed her hair from her forehead; it was already frizzing from the steam. Then she sighed and frowned and bit back her next words. The money hadn't been stolen. It was as much Clem's as it was Maud's. She sighed again.

"I'll make up a room." The woman slipped out the door and pulled the latch tight.

Clem listened for footsteps. There were none, though the hall floor in the back of the house had no rugs. She peered up at the ceiling, then to each wall of the kitchen, her eyes passing over the door to the larder and the dark shelves, the mugs and plates and a few errant pieces of porcelain. A vase with a girl in a white feather hat and ballooning blue skirts. A teacup painted with roses. Just behind the cup, a tiny cross was scratched in the plaster.

She scooted back and sat upright, elbows hooked over her knees. Another cross was scratched just behind the milk jug. Two more above the hall doorframe. One in a corner of the exit to the yard. She peered up at the ceiling. There. Faint—oh, so faint one could think them shadows or dust motes—cross was linked to cross, from corner to corner. Some were straight and neat, others stabbed and slapdash, leaving the plaster pocked where the scissors or knife had dug deep.

The maids, it seemed, did not like the goings-on at 328 Hall Street.

A loud thunk made her jump. The water splashed and sloshed.

Clem's chest tightened and burned. She pushed her fingers hard to her sternum and felt the quick thuds of her heart just under the bone.

A drawer scraped open in the room directly above her. Footsteps passed and the drawer scraped shut again.

She let out a breath and gave a quick shake of her head. It was only Maud. Getting the bed linens out, she supposed, or finding an extra blanket because the house was cold as a witch's tit.

As was the water.

Clem rubbed her face and under her arms, then clambered out and roughed the towel on her skin. She shrugged on the underclothes and lifted the oil lamp from the table. Another loud thunk.

This one from the wall behind her.

She swung the lamp to the noise. The clothes on the drying line cast shadows along the floor. She ducked underneath and shined the light along a bare wall and long empty counter. The chill grew sharp. She spied the square of the coal chute, the door swung open. A chunk of coal dropped to a wooden bucket.

"I need a drink." She pushed the heavy, wet skirts aside, strode across the kitchen, and yanked the hall door open. Maud sat on a bench directly opposite, still as marble. Her hands lay flat on her thighs, her shoulders hunched forward. Her eyes stared straight ahead, fixed and glassy.

Clementine pushed out her lower lip and studied the woman. She set the lamp to the side and squatted in front of her. Then she poked her knee.

Maud blinked and squinted. Her mouth twisted. Then she slapped Clem.

Clem put a hand to her ear and cheek. "What in the hell?" She thudded back to the floor. Her ear rang. "What the hell?" she said again.

"Don't ever touch me." Maud pulled a breath through her nose. Her nostrils widened and then narrowed. She stood, skirts gripped in her fists, and stepped over Clem. "Your room is at the top of the stairs. I left extra blankets."

Clem watched her walk down the hall. She stopped in front of the dining room and stared into its darkness. "You will help me?"

"I promise."

Then Maud stepped into the black.

The blankets did nothing. Clem pulled her knees to her chest and tucked the corners of the outrageously thin quilts (not even a bit of wool between the two) around her feet and thighs and then grabbed the bulk of it tight to her neck. The batting clumped all along the edges, leaving only thin cotton and needles of cold along her skin.

The stove in the corner was useless—empty of coal, gray with a coat of dust. The generously shared stump of candle Maud had provided had hours before given up the ghost. The window just by her head did not shut properly and the pillowcase she had wedged between the frame and ledge only helped to keep out the keen of the wind.

She thought of Russell and bit the inside of her lip.

Tomorrow he'd get a piece of her mind for running off and leaving her to fend for herself in the rain.

A sharp cry came from across the hall. Maud was a troubled sleeper. Between the cries and mewls and mumbling, Clem wondered if the woman suffered from excessive fatigue. It would explain the purply circles under her eyes and the general mealiness to her manner.

Clem plumped up her pillow so her head burrowed as far into the fold as she could get it without suffocating. The feathers smelled of mildew.

The room smelled of mildew.

The borrowed nightshirt smelled of mildew and an inordinate amount of vinegar.

Maud coughed. The woman might as well be hovering over the bed.

Thin walls in the belly of the house, no insulation on the bones of it.

Clem sat upright. The clapping at the séance. It had traveled in an arc, directly above the table, and swirled into an ever-larger circle before fading out.

She slipped from the bed, dragging the blankets tight around her. The floor was no friend to her bare feet. She tiptoed both to stay quiet and to have the least amount of skin touching the wood.

The pattern of the house continued to take shape. This room sat above the kitchen. Maud's bedroom was directly across the hall. The clapping wouldn't emanate from here. Too far away, even with the echoes.

She twisted the door handle and waited. Maud's door was an inch ajar. The moon glazed the room, illuminating her form on the bed. She lay on her back, mouth half-open, arms flat to her side, just a single sheet for comfort.

Clem slinked across the hallway to spy in. There was as little to pay notice to as there was in her room. A narrow dresser. Comb and brush. Water jug and mirror. Empty blue walls, save a circle of dark braided hair behind glass and an elaborate mahogany frame. A book on the bedstand, spread open and spine cracked. She supposed there was a wardrobe on the wall she could not see. It would, no doubt, be filled with a week's worth of plain white dresses and that horrible hat.

She turned, for the room held little else of interest, and ran her finger along the stair banister as she crept to the front of the house and the room above the parlor.

Depending on the layout, the room could explain the clapping and cat urine and even the gust of wind. Maud's small necessities, as she so rationalized it. But everyone had their slippery morals, so she couldn't fault her for it. Not in a house so bare of luxury—and one that should have been stuffed to the gills with comfort. There was a time one couldn't open a newspaper or turn a corner without seeing her luminous face. Her younger face. The child seer.

The Dead Speak!
The Spirits Live!
Come Say Hello!
Maud Evangeline Price
World Traveling Child Clairvoyant, Trance and Prophetic Medium
Bring Your SORROWS to the Maid of LIGHT

Clem trailed the railing and then ran her forefinger along a glass-fronted cabinet, a smooth plaster wall, and a door to its knob.

It was locked.

She pulled a pin from her hair, checked once down the hall, then jiggered the pin in the rim lock until she heard the familiar click.

She slipped in and ran shin-first into something hard and sharp. She squeezed her mouth tight and held her breath, one hand to her now throbbing shin and the other flailing out to find the culprit. A carved leg held the glass of a mirror.

She clambered around it, but her hip caught the corner of another piece of furniture. It shimmied and slid and squealed. She reached down, fingers recognizing the drawers of a dresser and its caster wheels. The source of the offending squeak.

And just past it were the curtains. Wool and silk. She had a mind to take them back to bed with her.

She parted them just enough to allow in the yellow glow of a streetlight.

A man's room, by the look of it. A canopy bed with newel posts and heavy damask. The mattress bare, unadorned pillows neatly propped at the head. A rolltop desk stacked with papers. One stack held down by a square ashtray. An oil lamp with beaded rose glass atop another. A wardrobe too tall for the room. A rag rug in front of it. The fireplace mantel without decoration.

Clem stepped to it and sniffed. It smelled of old ash and nothing else. Above it hung a portrait of a woman, stern and proper. The black, sullen eyes stared back at Clem and did not waver. A small rip marred one cheek.

"Miss Watkins?"

Clem jumped. She twisted to peer at the doorway, though it was empty, and the voice came from the opposite corner of the room, just between the desk and the wardrobe.

"Miss Watkins."

Now it came from the windowsill, which was empty, as much as the wall by the desk was bare.

"What are you doing in here?"

Maud now stood in front of her. Close enough Clem had to step back, her shoulder blades against the mantel. Then Clem bent to the fireplace, stuck both hands under the lintel, and clapped. The noise ricocheted, sharp like an arrow.

"You hold your circles in the room below."

Maud's gaze brushed the floor. "Of course."

Clem tipped her head. "Remarkable."

"I'm sorry?" Maud's brows touched one to the other.

47

"No one's asked to investigate? To see which maid or newsboy you paid to clap and stomp up here?"

"I have a sterling reputation."

"Even so." Clem shuffled around Maud, patting her shoulder as she passed. "These things are required when the spirit is weak, eh? Nothing to be ashamed of."

"This was my father's room."

Clem ran into the hall and stopped dead center on the landing. "Say that again."

"I won't. I just want you to leave it."

"Ha!" She bounded down the stairs, skidded into the séance room, and made a wide circle around the table. "Clap," she whispered. "Then proceed to your room."

"I won't."

It was as if Maud floated just to the left of her.

All of Clem's skin tingled. The sound in the house traveled oddly. But there was a pattern; she was certain of it. Everything had a pattern. And everything thus understood could be capitalized on.

At Harriet's, the thick walls precluded such bending of sound. Each room seemed its own separate island. It took five lines of catgut and two spirit trumpets to even come close to this. And Harriet always forgot where to sit. Mrs. King refused such endeavors. "We've all moved on from the raps and taps and voices," she'd said. Though she wasn't averse to syncing her prude little mouth to Russell's guttural broken words. The Wise Maharaj did bring in the crowds. But this—

Clem tapped the table and smiled. Disembodied taps caused ever so much shivering and belief in séance devotees. But disembodied voices?

"We have much work to do, Miss Price." She rapped the wood and stared up at the ceiling. "I know you hear me."

"I do."

"Much work."

Chapter Six

Maud

Maud heard Clem as clear as if she sat cross-legged on William Marcus's bed. She wanted to reach right out and slap her. Instead, she curled her fingers into tight fists to keep from swinging at air. She knew the house had . . . idiosyncratic acoustics. It was old. The kitchen had been in service since the first Elias Price cut down the trees and hewed rocks and boulders for the foundation. In 1769, a fire had engulfed it, taking everyone in its flames save a wee toddler who'd crawled out to the goldfish pond to dig sticks in the mud. The smoke stains still seeped through the thick kitchen walls, no matter how many coats of paint they swallowed.

Travis Jedediah Price. Survived the fire, but not yellow fever.

How many cups of tea she'd had with him as a child, his fat fingers clumsy with the dainty cup she offered, the tea sloshing down his spirit throat and all over the rag rug.

How often Mother had yanked her up by the elbow and given her a thwack to the bottom and an hour in the closet under the stairs. "You mustn't."

Travis shared the dark with her. Knee to knee and whispers to ears.

That's Sylvie with the wash. That's Father helping her down the stairs. That's Mother muttering in the parlor and Pie the bad dog sick on the rug.

Travis liked to braid her hair, three braids instead of two. Travis liked to tell her the future.

Not the far future; not what she'd get for Christmas or when her grandmama would finally leave in summers. Just what happened a breath away. *The milkman will trip and break a bottle. Sylvie will yell and step on the orange cat's tail.*

Mother's headaches were like an extra child in the house—underfoot and uncontrollable. Laudanum and locked doors helped but did not tame. The dark hung about her like a cloak of black gum and tarred rope. Sometimes the coils of it tripped Maud as she passed her in the hall. Sometimes Mother's eyes glittered so bright Maud thought them glass beads that threatened to pop out of their sockets, roll along the carpet, and bounce down the stairs.

Once, Maud closed herself in the understairs closet and Travis crossed his chubby legs and slapped his bright-skinned knees.

Your father's going to knock the glass over. Sylvie will cut her thumb on the glass. Pie is choking on a chicken bone and won't—there, he's coughed it up. Your mother's got a sick headache and isn't ever getting up.

Maud scrambled from the closet. She found her father in the dining room. He ministered to Sylvie's poor cut finger. Shards of glass sat on the sideboard.

Pie crossed the doorway and gave a great raspy cough.

"Mother's dead," Maud said.

Sylvie blinked, her black eyes big as saucers. She tugged her hand from Maud's father's, tore from the room and up the stairs. "Mrs. Price. What have you done?"

Maud stared at her father. "William Marcus"—for everyone called him such, including little Maud—"what will you do?"

His mouth curved into a deep frown, spreading his mustache hairs so Maud saw each follicle and the pale skin between. Like the chicken

Sylvie had plucked that morning. His gaze swung to the dining room door and then back to Maud.

"Travis said—"

"Your mother is not dead."

"She wants to be." It came to Maud in solid certainty that this was the case. "Yes, William Marcus, she wants to be."

William Marcus covered her mouth and twisted her up tight to his chest so her ribs hurt. Her legs flopped around and her heels kicked at his waist as he climbed the stairs. "Come see your mother, little one." His voice bounced loud off the ceiling. "Carolina, my love, are you unwell?"

His hand loosened on her mouth. Maud pulled in a shallow breath. His skin smelled of soap and tobacco. Then the smell changed—it became sour and musty damp.

Mother lay on the narrow bed in the back room, nearly lost amidst the comforters and feather pillows. She picked a scab on her cheek and glanced at Maud from heavy-lidded eyes. "I saw the most beautiful world, Maud."

"You see," William Marcus said. "Not dead."

He set her to her feet. "You need to control your spirits, daughter. Lest they control you."

Maud looked around the room for Sylvie, but she was not there. Just Maud and William Marcus and Mother and that rotten sour smell. Sylvie must have gone down the servants' stairs, Maud thought, mayhap to get Mother some broth.

"Kiss her good night."

Maud didn't want to. The scab on her mother's cheek dripped blood, which made the stink dizzily sweet.

William Marcus took a handkerchief from his vest pocket and wiped his wife's cheek until the skin pinked and only a small stain remained. "You'll be all better in the morning, Carolina." He pushed Maud's shoulder. "Kiss your mother good night."

She shuffled forward, swallowing saliva and holding her breath. How she hated this. Hated Mother and the nights and days she spent like this. Only up to berate poor Sylvie or the greengrocer when he forgot a cabbage or leek in the delivery. Only to wander the halls and square of yard with the grass that never greened.

Maud thinned her lips and leaned over to peck her mother's cheek. Her mother's hand wrapped around her head, holding her down.

Voices babbled like water on stone. White light burst behind Maud's lids. It wavered and patterned into diamonds, dissolved, and reconfigured into feet and legs and faces that shimmered and transfigured man to woman. Then there was only blue. The most beautiful blue imaginable.

"You see it." Her mother stroked her hair, her fingers lazing on the back of Maud's neck. "Don't let him take it."

"Good nights said." William Marcus set his hand to Maud's shoulder.

No more blue.

Stench of old vomit.

Mother's eyes glazed, smile fixed. One hand waving in the air as if pushing aside the curtains to take in the sun.

Travis took Maud's hand as they left the room. *Isn't it beautiful?*

The men came in the morning, early so as not to wake the neighbors. Mother did not fight. She stayed quiet and didn't look up at Maud. Just pulled the long white cloak she'd been given tighter and tighter to her throat. Climbed in the wagon without assistance. Eyes to the floor as the door swung closed.

Sylvie washed the sheets and scrubbed the floor.

Sylvie wept and William Marcus comforted.

Travis no longer took tea.

She saw him only once more, when her mother well and truly died. He sat on the coffin as the men lowered it into the ground. His squeals and screams descended with her, blunted by the first clod of dirt to the box.

"Two circles a week." Clem's voice jerked Maud from that world to this. "We'll have all the chairs full and a semicircle near the back for the audience."

Maud rubbed her hand to her chest and waited for the room to stop shimmering. "Two circles?"

"Scarcity, Miss Price. It drives desire. Which drives up your unspoken fee. You will see." Clementine clapped once more and laughed. "Come. Get a lamp and show me every room."

Maud began the tour on the top floor, where Sylvie once slept before she joined William Marcus in his grief and his bed. Here the floors warped and the hallway creeped in tight to the shoulders. Four doors, two facing two. Whitewashed walls and a simple cross hung where the hall came to an end. She wondered who had hung it.

"Most of the maids liked to sleep in the room off the kitchen." Her breath flicked the candle flame so it lengthened and spit.

Clem rattled one knob, then another. "Why are they locked?"

"Why wouldn't they be?"

"Hm." Clem ran her fingernail along the whitewashed wall as she wandered toward the cross. She made a clicking sound and stomped her foot every few steps, then leaned an ear to the floor and nodded.

"Mm-hmm," she said. Then she clicked and swung around in the small hall to shake the knobs again. She snapped her fingers and held out her hand. "Key, please."

"I don't have it."

Clem's left eyebrow lifted and then settled. She raised her hands to her head and pulled two hairpins from the mess of curls. "Let me, then."

She watched Clem fiddle with the pins. "Do you do that for a living?"

"Never ask what you don't want the answer to."

The lock clicked. Clem pushed the door and stepped into the room. She moved to the single set of drawers. Opened it and peered inside. Hooked her finger over each of the wooden dowels that once held aprons and skirts and caps. Knocked along the plaster walls. Shoved the cot to the wall, the wheels shrieking loud enough Maud hoped the Parkers would not awaken next door. Never mind their maid. That girl could be found leaning from any window to see the goings-on.

Clem jimmied the window open and shut with a thud. She picked at the floorboards.

Soon all four rooms were explored and catalogued.

Maud wondered if she should get Clementine a pencil and ledger.

"No, I don't need that." Clementine sidled around her and into the hall. "Attic?"

"There's nothing in there."

"But there's always things in the attic." Clem's eyes grew wide, and her smile leered in the candlelight. "Monsters. Generally, by the name of Mr. and Mrs. Rat."

"Just furniture. Mostly furniture."

"Well, lead on." Clem gestured, waving a hand in quick flicks. "Or is that locked too?"

∽

Of course, there was more than furniture. Her mother's trunks, the clothes dusted with lavender and neatly packed by Sylvie. Her old rocking horse, the tail hairs chewed by some generation of Mr. and Mrs. Rat and the stuffing pulled from the rump to make way for a nest. The scowl of her grandfather, eyes stark black and full of scorn. Her mother had hauled it up here.

"I won't have the man in my home," she'd said.

At least she hadn't burned it, which was the fate of the matching grandmama.

William Marcus had put his foot down at the portrait of his sister Margot, though he hung it in his study to keep the peace.

Clementine shifted aside a stack of wicker chairs, each with something missing—a back, a leg, an arm—and flipped up a corner of cotton sheeting from the object leaning behind.

Maud lunged forward but caught her foot in all the wicker. This was ludicrous. How dare this woman?

"Well." Clementine tugged the sheet. It slipped to the floor in a billow of dust. She sneezed, shook her head. "Well."

Maud didn't need to look. She knew what was there. A billboard glued to wood. Little Maud in her white chair, in her pristine dress with her hands dainty and crossed on her chest. A planchette on her lap, awaiting the words of the dead. Eyes closed—unless one looked just so—from the side or quick and then away—eyes open. A repeat of those curious eyes painted like tattoos on the backs of her dimpled hands. The chair lifted two inches from the base of the painting, as if levitating and about to spin against a background blue and cold. Glittering gold (now flaked—attic heat and damp ruin everything) words in the corner: *Seek the dead and ye shall find.*

"It was meant to be my mother," Maud said. "She wasn't of the right—"

"Not in her right mind?"

"Personality. Not the right personality. She hated to travel. In this world."

Clem frowned but said nothing.

"She traveled the Otherworld often. But she refused to share it." She shook off the darkness that settled on her shoulders and focused on the gaudy painting. "We were on tour—"

"I remember. I had one of your dolls when I was little. It looked just like you."

"It's rather . . . vulgar. That."

Clementine lifted and dropped her shoulder. "I loved it. Do you still have the planchette?"

Maud nodded. "We used it as a prop."

"Let's really use it." Clementine rubbed her nose and paced in front of the old billboard. "I'll modify it, show you a neat trick. The mournful can't get enough of letters from the Otherworld."

"Matthias doesn't—"

Clementine stepped around the wicker and flicked at the crystal drop beads on a lamp with a broken shade. "You'll teach him."

Maud shook her head and wanted to answer that no, Matthias did not take to teaching. But there was Clementine, her hand clapped on Maud's shoulder. "I like dolls. Yours had lids that blinked open and closed. Wonderful." Then she nodded, cupped a hand to the candle flame, and strode to the hall. "Come. The rest of the house, please."

"All I want, Miss Watkins, is to know about Mr. Sullivan's wife."

"And what will you do after giving him the news of her demise? Mr. Sullivan is the type of man who, once that veil is open, will return again and again. Every night he will sit across from you, hoping and wishing and yearning for a glimpse of his wife. The soft whisper of her voice. A letter, perhaps. I hope your Matthias knows where to find her. Or"—she rapped her knuckles to the doorframe—"we make sure he does. Or we don't. If you wish to tatter your reputation that much further—"

"I don't. And I do see the dead." She swallowed, but it did nothing for the dryness in her throat. "I do not wish to disappoint those who suffer."

"Then let us not disappoint them."

❧

Clementine Watkins had not disturbed Maud's sleep; Maud had been awake. Perhaps not wide-awake, but in that drifting shimmery space that left openings for Matthias and any other wandering spirit to slip into the room. Some mornings in the far past she'd awake surrounded by the dead, translucent spirits draped on the dressing table, curled around the bedposts, or sitting at her side, asking her to find this person or that. Singing happened in so many keys Maud stuffed cotton in her ears. *Hellohellohello,* they'd shout.

I see you, she'd say. *I hear you,* she'd also say. This satisfied the majority, and the rest faded and disappeared with the morning sun and the maid's tray.

Lately, the room had been so empty, the quiet so brittle, that Maud wondered if she should take to laudanum to pass the silent hours.

But this morning, she watched Clementine across the hall. Watched her wake and rise. Followed her figure as she stretched her arms and swung out of bed. As she lit a candle and set it atop the dressing table, then poured water from the pitcher and splashed it on her face. Clementine shook out the sheets and blanket, folded the quilt. Stopped to stare out the window, and then across to Maud's half-open door. She tipped her head one way and the other, as if considering something.

Then she crossed the hall, quiet as a cat, slipping through Maud's doorway, pausing to peer down at her. She crept to the wardrobe, pulling it open just enough to reach in but not set the hinges to whining.

"You only need to ask," Maud said.

Clementine froze. Her hand remained in the cupboard.

Maud grabbed up a match from the box on her bedstead, struck it, and lit the oil lamp.

"Hello," Clementine said. Her gaze did not waver from Maud's. She did not even blink.

"Do you need something?"

"A blouse." Her lip twitched and then she smiled. "I didn't want to wake you. But now you are awake."

Maud sat up. "You aren't as quiet as you think."

"I'm not?"

"No."

"Well. That will need to be worked on. May I borrow a blouse? We're near the same size."

Maud lifted and dropped a shoulder. The woman would take the blouse no matter what Maud answered. "I doubt your skirts are dry."

"I doubt they are. It was a dismal night. May I borrow that too?" She peeked into the wardrobe. "Do you have anything but white?"

"To the left."

She chose a plaid skirt, russets and greens. "Bustle?"

Maud pointed to the dresser. Clementine dressed. Used Maud's brush. Primped her cheeks in the mirror.

"I need the attic. If we're to assist—"

"We?"

"Mm. I need space for materials and tools. There's a good, solid table up there. And my choice of servants' rooms. You won't be bothered by me at all. Though I do think we'll need use of the library too. It's a sad little place now, isn't it? But it backs your parlor, and that makes it of utmost usefulness. I think new wallpaper . . . I'll help you pick. We'll go to town, not today—another day—but it will be great grand fun."

"Are you moving in permanently?"

"Oh no. Only until you're on your spiritualist feet." She twisted a lock of hair around her finger and let go. It sprung like a coil, as untamed as the rest of her hair. She turned from the mirror to face Maud. "Why are you looking like that?"

"I'm not looking like anything."

"Good. When I return, we shall meet your Matthias."

"You don't believe he'll come back."

"You will make him."

"I can't—"

"I've looked through your bills. You're two steps from the poorhouse, Miss Price. You might be more forceful in your pleas to him."

That was it. No other words. Just a smug nod of the head and off the woman went to do God knew what.

Chapter Seven

CLEMENTINE

Clementine was grateful to Maud for the lending of the clothes. Truly she was. It was a far superior outfit to the one she'd worn the night before, even if it was quite precious in its old-fashioned cut and trimmings of lace and slope shoulders and staid high collar. She twisted the top button until the thread snapped, then stretched her neck in relief. At least the woman had not offered a hat. God knew what the rest looked like.

The day had broken bright, the sun sharp enough that everyone she passed blinked desperately or kept their eyes to their feet. Two dazzling puddles ran the length of the carriage ruts, the sun glinting as if diamonds had been tossed to them. Clem put a hand to her forehead to shadow her gaze and stared at the sky. Not a single cloud.

If Clem believed in omens, which she assuredly did not, this morning boded well.

She smiled, laughed out loud, and followed it with a clap. "That house!"

Clem's skin itched in anticipation. Harriet's wonderments would be nothing compared to this. Clem could relaunch Maud Price's career.

Not could. Would. She'd take this moldering, odd little woman who no one remembered and make her what she was and more.

The grand reentry, Maud's return to the upper echelons, would come later. Parlor to meeting house. Private homes and invitations turned down. The opera house here, in Keene, in Concord, in Boston. The world. Oh, by then!

But Clem stopped herself from scheming more. One dazzle at a time.

The appointments in Maud's daybook were sparse; Mr. Sullivan was booked for tomorrow night, along with a Mrs. Eunice MacGregor. More empty pages than full ones, the notebook light as a feather as it sat atop a stack of unpaid bills.

She slowed at the corner of Main and Market and squinted at the squat brick tower of First Congregational. Here, too, the parishioners spoke to the dead, their missives sent to heaven and borne on the wings of angels.

The church bell sang out above her. Eight sonorous rings. She was reminded of Sister Matilda, who belted out the hours at the orphanage. "It's 8:00 a.m., girls. BOM, BOM. Time is of the essence and prayer is the essence." The recollection gave her a stomachache. All that petty purity. All that yearning for heaven.

All that seeking and never quite finding.

She had to give Mrs. King and Maud Price and her ilk credit. They reached out and found, dragging heaven right down to earth. They lifted the curtain and let the dead strut and fret their way across the stage. *Here we are,* they said, *and there behind the scrim is the eternally sunlit Summerland.* Technically, the scrim was canvas and Clem lit the Otherworld with a whale-oil lamp.

She closed her eyes and cupped her hands over her ears to block the noise of the street. Maud's parlor materialized, empty and silent. She imagined the round table and those seated in a row of chairs just behind the main event. They would all sing, a call to the spirits, voices loud and off-key, though very intent on their task. A music box would help tame the cacophony. Then a flutter—one corner to another, a disturbance of air behind the most enraptured singer. A winged angel. A whisper to the ear of another. *Ask.*

Maud would clutch the arms of her chair, lean forward aquiver, and answer.

No. Not answer. Write.

A spirit box to hand, a pen scraping and scratching the paper, a note delivered, then read by the poor soul who asked the question to begin with.

Maud had used those once in the past—and how much more effective they were than the doltish planchette. All the sliding around from letter to letter threatened to lull the audience to sleep. No! A letter written from the dead to the living.

Her heart raced and pattered. She hadn't felt such enthusiasm for a project in ever so long, not since the final levitation Mrs. King had performed. Now that was a stunt.

She brushed her fingertips to the rough brick of the church, then swung to the sidewalk, nearly colliding with a pug-nosed dog and its verbena-scented owner. With a quick gesture of apology, she hopped around the pair and continued on. The angel wings required just basic engineering—gears and a few simple mechanics, glass filament wings, and—

"What in the hell? Those are my things. *Those are my things!*" Clementine grabbed up her skirts and dashed down the street. Her boots squelched in the mud, her right foot sucked tight at the corner. She yanked her foot out and stormed toward a policeman who milled around the boardinghouse entrance, waving people away from the mess of clothing and books and a broken-ribbed trunk. A gnarled biddy swiped up a red scarf, twisting it quick around her wrist. Clem grabbed her shoulder as she turned to sneak away. "You give that back, Zebedah."

The old woman craned her neck to peer up at Clem with beady eyes and a sneer that cut right across her liquor-blushed skin. "It's on the street; it's mine."

Clem bit the inside of her cheek, then gave Zebedah a hefty shake.

The woman grunted. She blinked and kicked Clem in the shin. "You deserve worse."

But Clem shoved her to the side. Her heart pounded against her chest. She shouldered around a man in a slouch hat that looked suspiciously like Russell's. A stuffed cotton bustle swung from the gas lamp. A green silk carriage dress sat in a crumple, its neighbor a pair of Russell's suspenders. All the rest was piled against the brick. The ragman already had his long hook in the lot. He stared right through her as he swung a bundle to his handcart.

An object cracked under Clem's boot. She stepped back and stared down at the flattened and ruined dollhouse chair. All around her—no matter where she stepped—the tiny figures of furniture and lamps, small blankets and chandeliers were scattered. Wire and copper coils. A canary's wing cut from tin. She lunged forward to scoop up what she could, cradling the pieces in the folds of her skirt.

"These aren't toys," she said.

A shadow darkened the walkway and was followed by a stolid, square-toed shoe. Mrs. Epp. Clem clenched her jaw and tried to ignore the landlady. But the woman slung her boot in front of Clem's path. "Two months. I told your ne'er-do-well this was the consequence of nonpayment."

A meticulously carved settee with a spot of red velvet sat just beyond Mrs. Epp. It had been designed to recreate Harriet Martin's front room sofa, part of the elaborate kit Clem used to create the tricks. She was proud of that little sofa, with the miniscule magnet glued to the underside and the hidden pockets with so many possibilities for wonders.

But Mrs. Epp made sure to crush it with her boot not once, but twice. Then she pulled her knit shawl tight around her moth-eaten neck and lumbered back to the front doorway of the boardinghouse.

"You can't do this," Clem said.

"I can do what I want, my girl, and this is what I want." She took guard at the door.

"I have things upstairs still."

A squeal of wood came from the alley.

"All away!"

Then came a loud crash and the cracks of wood snapping.

"Your things are downstairs now." Mrs. Epp pulled at the skin under her chin, then slammed the boardinghouse door.

"But—" Clem jogged around the mess, slowing at the alley. The dresser lay in pieces, drawers split and belongings strewn near down to the privies. In the blink of an eye, the sum of it heaved and swayed, overrun with urchins whose clawing hands picked the site clean.

She clambered over the wood, searching for the only thing that mattered in the lot: Almira Parker's velvet bracelet. She dropped her skirts, letting the bits and pieces bounce and scatter, then tossed over a drawer. There lay the bracelet. She breathed a sigh of relief. A pair of grubby hands shot out to grip the velvet band. The boy howled when Clem grabbed and twisted his wrist. He bared blackened teeth at her, and his chest expanded with the threat of a mighty yell. A necklace of green glass beads slithered from his pocket as Clem shook him.

"You yell once more, and I'll slit your throat," she whispered. "Would you like that?"

His lips pressed into a tight line. He dropped the bracelet into Clem's palm. She let go of his wrist, and he grabbed his arm up to his chest.

"Are you going to cry?" she asked.

"No."

His lower lip quivered. He dropped his gaze to the splintered wood, then blinked, long lashes sweeping his cheeks, before darting away to meet his gang. There were three of them, now jostling and shouldering each other, arms full of Clem's and Russell's belongings. A girl ambled by, Clem's bowler bobbling on her head. She swung her shoulders, a half-naked doll dangling from her grubby fist. Its head smacked the brick and its braided hair dragged in the mud. A boy in a torn blue wool jacket barked a laugh and cut a look back at Clem before tearing off along the rail tracks. Their voices came in fits and starts as they shouted in glee for their good luck.

Clem clutched the bracelet in her fist and turned to watch people shuffling along the street with the rest of her things. A policeman walked beside them, his high collar cutting into his neck, leaving a roll of red skin.

"Stoddard," she called, "I want to make a complaint. You can't toss someone out without warning."

He stuffed a thumb to his thick leather belt and tapped the brass buckle. "You can and she did."

"I gave you twenty dollars last night."

"Did you?"

"I . . . I have nothing now, you bastard." There was nothing to do but give the dresser a hard kick. She shoved past him, pushing her way through the thinning crowd to gather what was left of her belongings. The clothing and costumes had all been taken. Not even a single shoe to account for. The trunk had been purloined. The copper springs and pins and dollhouse furniture picked clean off the walk.

Clem clenched her jaw. She marched over to the boardinghouse door and pounded her fist to the wood. "I don't forget things, Mrs. Epp. You can count on that."

෨

Harriet didn't answer the door. Or rather, her cook or man-of-house or maid did not answer. Clem sank to the granite step and pulled her knees up to her chest. She'd wait.

The branches of a weeping willow took up much of the backyard. It swished with the wind, bare limbs sweeping across sodden dirt. A book lay against the leg of a wicker rocker, as if it had been discarded and forgotten in the last rays of summer. It lay open, spine to the ground and pages mottled with mold.

Her chest pinched as she thought of all her models and stage sets trampled to the mulch. So many hours of toil each table and wardrobe and stuffed divan had cost her. And her little automaton bird—just a wing, a few copper bits, and the bellows left. She had been so close to giving it song. Never mind the costumes and frippery and disguises now in the ragman's cart. At least she still retained the plans and notations and designs. Wrapped and labelled and carefully tucked under a false floor of her satchel. It would have been a disaster to lose those too.

Where was Russell? She had so much to tell him of Maud Price's house; it would make his head spin. Never mind the eviction from the ratty, drafty little room—better things lay ahead. Soon enough she'd have plenty of cash. Enough for two wardrobes—three!—of frills and ruffles and promenade jackets. Of fine wool trousers cut to her figure and top hats of the highest sheen. Cuff links. Alpaca skirts. Stripes, not plaids.

There was Harriet's man, Mr. Collins, striding up the side path and mumbling to himself as he glanced at his pocket watch.

"Hello," she said.

He dropped the watch and lifted his eyebrows, the furrows on his forehead deep enough to catch shadows. "Miss Watkins." His gaze shifted up to the door and then across to the windows.

"No one's answering."

He tucked the watch back. "No one is here."

It was an obvious answer to an obvious state, so she just shrugged.

He stepped past her, rattled a ring of keys, and unlocked the door. "I have the item Mrs. Martin requested."

He pulled the latch and did not look back at her, just reached for the muslin-wrapped bracelet.

She handed it over and waited as he pocketed it. He didn't glance at it, not once, but kept his eyes on the brick wall. His jaw shifted one way, then the other. Then he reached in a chest pocket and withdrew an envelope.

The paper crinkled as Clem palmed it. She pressed her thumb to the flap.

"It's the correct amount." Mr. Collins cleared his throat. He stepped into the mudroom.

But the envelope was too thin, too light, and Clem tore into it. She stared at the paltry bills. "You've taken a bigger cut."

"I don't like to wait. The weather and all that mess."

Clem pursed her lips, then forced them into a smile. She couldn't fault him or argue. She'd do the same in his position. "Did Mr. Sprague stop here last night?"

"Mrs. Martin had an early evening."

"Hm. Nothing that needs looked at?"

"It's all in working order."

"No requests, nothing?"

"None."

"Good." Clem scratched her neck. "Tell her I stopped by."

A window squealed open above her. Harriet leaned out. "It's barely sunup—why are you here?"

Clem stepped back to look up at Harriet. "The day's near done, why are you asleep?"

"Why are you wearing that hideous plaid?"

"Why'd Mr. Collins tell a fib and say you were out?"

"Because I pay him to."

"I just had all my things tossed to the street."

"Well, come up and entertain me with the story."

‿⌒

The cuckoo on the clock above Harriet's dresser sprung from its wooden doors to chirp the hour. It spun around and around—ten times, to be precise—then clattered back to its dark little den. Clementine snuffed the cigar Harriet had given her and stretched out on the chaise longue. Harriet had much finery in her room. Cut crystal perfume misters in amber and blue and red littered the top of a dressing table. A sterling silver brush set lay on the cabinet, the brush twisted with strands of her hair. The walls were a pastel green silk, the curtains a heavier and darker fabric. Beside the cuckoo clock hung three oval portraits of Jack Russell dogs, each with a dead rabbit between its teeth. In the corner, Harriet sat on a tufted rocker, bare feet crossed and one foot swinging lazily from under her satin dressing gown.

"Was Russell here last night?" Clem asked.

Harriet dropped her foot to the floor and removed her spectacles.

Clem reached for the cup of coffee on the side table. Steam curled from it. "Put those on again."

"No."

"You look different in them."

"I know what I look like in them."

"Does Russell?"

"That's a ludicrous question."

"You're right." The glasses weren't terrible. They didn't make her look old, per se. Just not like Harriet Martin. More like a faded version of her. Her hair held less luster, her eyes less sparkle, and when she smiled, her teeth seemed just a little bit more yellow. "He is charming, you have to admit."

"I wouldn't know." Harriet's smile dropped just a hair. Enough for Clem to know she was lying.

"You wouldn't know what to do with him if you had him. I, however, do. Normally. When he's not gone underground and left me to my own machinations."

"I thought you liked it like that."

"Hm." The coffee scalded Clem's tongue. She set it down with a clatter and reached for the ewer, splattering water into the glass. She chugged it down, then touched a finger to the tip of her tongue. The damn thing was nearly boiled.

"Problem?"

"Do you try to kill your guests?" Clem stretched, catching her feet in the folds of her crumpled skirts. She pinched a crease between her toes and pulled it up. The hem had come undone. "Do you have thread and needle?"

"We'll give it to Nan. She'll fix it." Harriet put her glasses on and held out her hand. A bracelet of jet stones dangled from her wrist and clicked against another of pearls. "Maybe she can dye it while she's at it."

"You shouldn't look down on other people's clothing." Clem crossed her hands to her chest and lowered her head.

"You can wear something of mine until it's ready."

"Just a needle and thread will suffice. I have things to do."

"If you need money—"

Clem's cheeks burned. "I don't need money. I need a needle and thread." She sat up and swung her legs over the edge of the chaise. "I don't take charity, Harriet."

"A loan."

"Then I'd owe you something, wouldn't I?" Her stomach grumbled. Last night's stale molasses bread had not gone far. Her boots—all clean and shined to a gleam—sat by the door. Mr. Collins had requested them when she entered the house, for God forbid a speck of dirt fall to the floor of Mrs. Martin's. He doted on the woman like a trained monkey.

The oriental rug was thick, deep enough it silenced her footsteps as she crossed the room. Harriet stopped her with a soft hand on her wrist.

"Don't."

"Clem—"

"You're not my mother."

"I'm not old enough to be your mother."

"It's good you're not. You'd be dead. Instead you're here. And beautiful."

"How else should I keep my guests coming back?"

"I would have thought my magic helped with that."

"Will you abandon me? Now that you have the earnest Miss Price to improve?"

"Send a note. I'll get what I can for you, if there's time."

Harriet still cupped her wrist, the touch light. It reminded her of Mrs. King. Affection was never free. It came with a price. Harriet wanted something. She simpered and doted and bribed when she did. Her hair was a flame of auburns and blacks, and the word "Medusa" crossed Clem's mind, as it had before.

"What do you want?"

The light from the window reflected off Harriet's glasses. "It wouldn't be Russell I'd have assisted last night. Charming as he is."

"I see." Clem shook her wrist free. "Pay me more and I might then give you a kiss."

Harriet tsked. "Go on, you miserable creature. I have a sitting in an hour."

"Anything I can help with?"

"You've done enough. For now." She stood, running her fingers on the back of Clem's neck as she walked past. "Use the kitchen door on the way out."

∽

It would rain soon. Or it wouldn't. Sheets of too-bright sun shined, then were snuffed between bruised and purplish clouds. Clem had neither umbrella for the rain nor hat for the sun. Both of which she should have borrowed from Harriet, but didn't.

She kicked a rock. It skittered into the street, disturbing the nap of a lorry horse. The animal shifted weight from one foreleg to the other. The wagon tilted over the sidewalk, weighted down with enough boards Clem's heart pinched for the horse's travail in pulling it. One push and the whole would tumble.

"I feel for you, you poor damn horse."

She rubbed her eyes, then pulled her pocket watch from her belt. Almost eleven o'clock. Russell had best be waiting at Wynant's Tavern. She snapped shut the watch and dropped it to her waist.

"Watch it." A small boy, shoeshine kit tucked under his arm, leered up at her, then shook his head.

"Watch it yourself." Clem sidestepped around the child, then dug her heel to the ground and twisted back around. "Boy. You."

The boy looked over his shoulder and walked on, his steps cocky and wide as if he expected the ground to pitch with a wave.

Clem jogged up and kept pace. "That's not your necktie."

"Nah, it isn't." His fingers, stained black at the tips, feathered up to the tie.

"Then give it back."

"It's not yours, either."

"Actually, it is. So I suggest removing it and handing it back."

The boy didn't; he swaggered and circled Clem. "You need a shine?"

"I need that tie. And the pin. That's mine too." Clem reached out, only to catch at air.

The miserable bootblack smiled and stuck his tongue out like an asp. Then he ducked under Clem's arm and darted into the Main Street traffic, lost as quick as a wink amongst the drays and wagons.

"Damn." Clem grated her teeth. She bit her lip and peered down Main Street toward the railyard. The wind gusted, digging its fingers into her bare neck, slipping under the thin lace collar. She shivered, then slung back her shoulders and trudged along toward the railyard and the warmth of Wynant's. "I swear to God, I'm going to kill Russell one day."

Russell was indeed in the tavern. Not at a back table as was their wont, but right up front, eyes staring at Clem as she passed the window. His elbow sat on a pile of newspapers. He jerked his chin at them, as if he'd done her a favor in collecting them.

"Damn and damn again." She stopped in front of the thick wooden door, pulled in a breath, and pushed the door open. The thick air nearly made her flinch. It was a stale wall of heat and tobacco smoke. It coated her clothing and stuck, scratching its way into the weave of fabric as easily as it did the splits in the wood floors and between the slats of wall. She gave a quick nod to Lucas, the barman, who nodded back, the thick, puckered scar on his shaved head its usual angry red. *Antietam.* It was the only explanation he ever gave for it and enough to shut people up.

"Do you have money?" she asked.

"Twenty-six to one on a cock named Fred."

"I don't know what you see in those. They're cruel."

"But they're buying our breakfast."

"That they are. Well done." She held up two fingers in a request for two ciders, then slid into the chair across from Russell. The legs wobbled, and she gripped the table edge and shifted the chair. "Of course, you could have returned to get our things."

Russell did not move, save tapping his index finger to the stack of newspapers. He closed his eyes and sunk his chin to his chest. "It is all my fault."

"I'm wearing plaid because of you."

He opened one eye a slit. "Yes. You are. It's . . . not bad."

He puckered his lips, then bit down on the lower and waited as Lucas set the ciders down.

They both followed his stooped amble back to the bar, then Russell cleared his throat. "It's all entirely my fault. I thought the rent was due today." He shifted in his seat. "Simple mistake. You'd have made the same—"

"No."

"No. Yes, correct. You wouldn't have." He cleared his throat, then took a swig from his mug.

Clem followed suit. The liquor hit her stomach and sloshed around, for she'd left Harriet's without so much as a strip of bacon. "There's a grimy little bootblack who has my tie."

"The one with the diamonds."

"You saw him?"

"Bugger wouldn't slow down."

She picked up her mug and stopped before taking a draught. Instead, she placed it down as if it were the finest of china, leaned back, and crossed her hands to her lap. "My bird, Russell. I had nearly finished it. My beautiful, cheeping, metallic bird. All I have now is the bellows. And a wing."

"I am sorry about that. I know how much you valued those annoying things."

"Do you?"

"I do."

Her eyes cut from his coat to his collar and down to his cuffs. Her hand shot out and pinched the cuff link. A gleaming gold lion. "I haven't seen these before."

"Of course you have."

"You're a terrible liar." She let go. "Is that where the rent—"

His cheeks flushed, then paled.

"No. You were given them."

"She doesn't mean anything."

"No. They never do." She shouldn't have been surprised, nor let the sting of it matter. He liked his women as much as he liked to fritter away their money at the dogfights. So be it. He still came home to her.

His jaw shifted side to side, the muscles tight. "I await your verdict." His eyes held an edge of something that made her pause. She'd seen it before, when he wasn't aware she watched. Disdain. But then it cleared. The edge of his lips curled, pretty dimples deepening. "You will forgive me."

"I will."

"Thank you."

She leaned across the table, nails scraping into the wood and crimping the edges of the newspapers. "Because I need you."

He sat back, his sigh of relief theatrical. "I am yours."

"Good. Maud Price—"

"Ah. I take it that is where you found the plaid." The dimples grew deeper, two dark holes in his cheeks.

"Miss Price will be holding a séance tomorrow night. A private séance."

"Tomorrow night? We need time to—"

She pushed out of the chair, gathered the papers, and was out the door. She rapped the glass, then gestured for him to pay and to follow her.

He finished the cider, both hers and his, dropped coins to the saucer, and followed. Drizzle coated his shirt and vest; he wiped at the shoulders. "What's the game? Rappings and moans?"

Her eyes narrowed. "Meet me at the kitchen door at dark. Stay along the fence. East fence. Look for the coal chute—it's just past the honeysuckle. One whistle."

"Why are you so keen on this Price woman?"

"I have a thirty percent stake in her succeeding tomorrow night and believing her own delusion. Don't overdo it."

"Do I ever?"

"Here." Clem lifted her eyebrow. She dug into a skirt pocket and took cash from the envelope. "Pick up what you need for the sitting tomorrow. I've got bootblack for your face but you'll need new gloves and quieter shoes. And potash if you can find it. Flash paper. You know the list. And phosphorous. What we had is still under the floorboards at Mrs. Epp's. I'm off for bread and cheese. There's nothing in the house to eat." She stood on tiptoes and kissed his cheek.

"All forgiven, then?"

"My eyes are to the future, Mr. Sprague. And that future is Maud Price." She was off with a wave over her shoulder, skirts held fast and shoulders hunched forward, intent on her path. She listed the tasks ahead. They would be many: Miss Price had sunk far down the medium ladder the past few years. But Clem had an idea and a plan—for an idea was worth nothing without the plan to bring it to fruition.

The drizzle had stopped and the sun came out again, washing the street with light. Clem slung her arms wide to catch the warmth. The future was a grand thing.

Chapter Eight

MAUD

One shouldn't look through another's things. Maud crossed her hands on her chest and stared at the ceiling of her room. One shouldn't.

But the woman had left that portmanteau of hers smack dab in the middle of the bed—which she had made, including an extra punch and fluff of the pillows—before exiting the house.

It was a simple case. Larger than it had seemed as Clementine swung it from her shoulder the previous night. It was nearly the size of a travel trunk. A leather-clad handle, a thick strap, two brass clasps secured with square iron padlocks. She lifted one, tugged, and dropped it with a thunk to the leather. Maud stepped back. She paced in front of the bag, clucking her tongue, eyeing the thing, yanking one lock and then the other, as if one would magically give up its ghost. Her stomach growled. She smacked her hand to it. There wasn't any breakfast; she'd given Clementine the last heel of molasses bread the night before. There wasn't coffee, not even chicory, though she thought there might be a tin of mint tea on the highest shelf. The maid before this last had hoarded it as if it were gold. Maud thought it tasted like boiled grass.

"I really don't have a pot to piss in." She turned on her heel and made for her father's room. Were there really as many bills as Miss

Watkins had said? She'd meant to attack the lot of them this week, or the next. There was a new hat at Mrs. Appelbaum's with a bluebird perched on the crown; there had to be some credit at the hatmaker's. It would be listed at the bottom of the previous receipt.

Her father's desk was neat as a pin. Instead of the overarching ream of papers she expected, Maud counted three neat piles set in a straight row. Each was held in place by a stone. A note had been tucked under each rock:

House
Provisions
Fripperies

She plucked the last stone aside and glared at Mrs. Appelbaum's handwriting. Her heart sunk. *No more credit offered.*

A scratching heat climbed up her spine. The front door was about to be knocked.

"Bother and damn."

She moved to the landing and peered down.

The rap was hesitant. One light tap and then another.

The sort of knock that first-timers gave, their nerves not fully ready to meet the dead, their belief a thin strand.

But what could she do? Here she stood in bedclothes and there they stood on the front stoop. She pressed two fingers to her throat and fiddled with the plain collar.

"Miss Price?" The voice came muffled through the door. A man's voice. Another polite rap. "Miss Price? It's Mr. Sullivan."

Maud scraped her nail on the railing, then turned, leaned against it, and crossed her arms. What could he want so early? Perhaps she could dress. Yes. Dress and open the door. That would leave him, though, out in the drizzle. What if he caught cold? What then?

No. Better to have him think her out and about, better he depart and not catch a chill.

Then he would be in robust health for tomorrow evening's sitting, and by then—if Clementine was as good as she boasted—Maud could bring him word from his wife. She stared at the painting on the opposite wall, a dreadful landscape with men hunched in the snow and trees slapdash in the corners. Not one could be identified as real; they were, rather, like a child's version of pines and palmettos, the cabins in the background missing windows and doors.

"Miss Price?"

She pressed her lips together and stared at the smallest figure, the one near a broken plow. An ox, more blue than gray, with sunken ribs and jutting hips, lurked behind it, looking, as the figure did, at something just outside the frame.

Three loud raps made her flinch.

Even if she dressed and descended, opened the door and let him in, it would be no use. She could not take his hand in hers and thus in Matthias's. *Hello, my dear, it is so good to meet here.*

She pushed away from the rail and trudged to her bedroom, closing the door with a small click, as if anything louder might be heard by the man on the porch in the rain. A sigh rattled in her chest and escaped in a sharp breath. She dropped her forehead to the door.

"I am of no use."

Maud turned to the room, avoided her reflection in the mirror, and crawled under her covers. She pulled the quilt over her head and tucked it under her palm.

◦

The air grew stale and humid. Her skin flushed hot. A bird chirped, let out a wheeze, and chirped again. It didn't stop. It went on and on, chirrup chirrup wheeze chirrup. Loud, as if it had landed on the bed. She tossed the blankets back and sat upright with a shriek.

There was no bird at the end of the bed. There was an intruder. She reached for the bedside table's drawer and grappled for her derringer pistol. She swung it toward the figure, holding it up with both hands.

"That is not a gun. It barely qualifies as a toy." Clementine lounged cross-legged, leaning against the bedpost, a dusty brown bowler tipped back on her head. She held a miniature bellows between her thumb and index finger and squeezed down. Her left eyebrow went up. The bellows produced a chirrup and gasp.

She dangled it in front of Maud's eyes, then clamped it shut, tied a cord around it, and tucked it in the chest pocket of a man's tweed vest.

"That's my father's vest."

Clementine stared down at it. "Yes, it is."

"That's his hat."

"He was a small man."

Maud clenched her jaw. "That's not yours to take."

"You can set that thing down now. Give your arms a rest."

Clementine swung off the bed and sauntered over to the mirror, thumbs stuck to pockets. She tipped back on her boot heels and turned one way and then the other in the glass.

"You're a vain one, aren't you?"

Clementine did not turn, but looked at Maud's reflection. Her mouth slipped into a smirk. She turned the sleeves of her shirt two times, pinching the material into neat folds. "Not very vain." She faced Maud. "Will you dress for the evening meal? It's nearly four."

"Nearly four?"

"Yes. I've roasted a chicken and potatoes. And leeks."

"Leeks."

"Are you going to repeat everything I say?"

"What?"

"Never mind." Clem wandered to the window and peered out. "I think we might have a rain tonight."

"Miss Watkins." Maud swallowed. She curled her fingers into fists and pressed them to her thighs. "I asked for one thing. To find out Maisie Sullivan's fate. Mr. Sullivan himself was at the door earlier."

"Did you let him in?" Clementine leaned her shoulder to the wall and stared at Maud.

"I wasn't dressed. I assume he'll return tomorrow, so I do hope you've found something for me."

"I have nothing for you. Yet. I've had much to do. You are a very heavy sleeper, do you know that?" Clementine kicked off the wall and circled to a rocker. She took a seat, slinging one leg over the other. "But let's not bother with that. Tell me about your Matthias. Is he your only guide? Are there others? Mrs. Martin has a slew, including a Creole maiden and a lamplighter from East London. Sometimes a young Abenaki girl who likes to sing."

"I have witnessed the Maharaj."

"Yes. He has his moments." She leaned back, pushing her heel to the floor and the rocker to sway.

"I do not have such theatricality. I hear voices. On some occasions I may see a spirit. Sometimes I know what is spoken. Other times only that I have been visited."

"Tell me what happens when Matthias visits. Does he bring others? Or does he wish all the limelight? Does he come from the clouds or a doorway or through the wall—"

"You're not being kind."

"I'm only trying to understand. I wish to know you." She crouched in front of Maud, resting her hand on Maud's knee. It was heavy and warm, and Maud did not throw it off. "I wish to help."

"Do you?"

"Of course. I am at your service."

Maud hung her head. She was so tired. Tired to the bone. "I have a paper to deliver next . . ." She threw up her hand. "I have a paper to write. I had started it with him."

"Shall we sing a little? Does he like a song?" Clementine's palm moved in a lazy circle. She tilted her head, her expression one of anticipation. But not for Maud's answer. Clementine's gaze had grown glassy, her lips and cheeks slack. "Mm. Yes, I think a song would do. 'We are waiting and watching for thee—'" Her voice was very low, as if she wished not to startle.

"He likes tunes from the music halls."

"Does he?" Clem frowned and bit her lip.

"'The Old Arm-Chair.' He's very fond of that."

"Then you shall sing it."

"I've tried."

"Try again." Clementine's hand now caressed the top of her wrist. "Close your eyes and sing."

> "I sat and watch'd her many a day,
> When her eye grew dim, and her locks were gray,
> And I almost worshipp'd her when she smil'd—"

Clementine tilted her head and sniffed. "The chicken's burning." She leapt up and bolted for the door. "Do you like white or red?"

Maud shook her head. "I—"

"I only have red, so I hope you'll like it." She smiled and pushed a lock of hair from her forehead. "Get dressed. The chicken will go cold and then what will you do?"

"Eat cold chicken?"

"I hate cold chicken." She hurried to the hall. "Time is of the essence, Miss Price."

Maud dropped her fork to her plate. "I can't eat any more."

Clementine took a drink of wine and stared at her from across the dining table. She had set out two rather large candelabras on either end, each holding a single candle, which seemed to defeat the purpose. Long shadows painted their way across the serving platters and the women themselves were left in a gray half-light.

Still, Maud could not fault the meal. She'd eaten an entire half a chicken, three potatoes, and leeks that dripped butter and salt. Her stomach swelled against her corset; if she were alone, she would unbutton her blouse and untie the stays.

"Delicious," she said, then covered her mouth and swallowed back a burp.

"I'm glad you approve."

"But you've barely eaten."

Clem spun her glass by the rim and contemplated Maud. "I have a light appetite at best." She scraped the bones to the serving platter, then gestured for Maud to hand over her own plate. She slid the whole of it to the side and took her pipe and pouch from her suit pocket and proceeded to tamp tobacco to the bowl. She stuck the pipe between her lips, lit it with a match, and settled back in the chair.

"You make me nervous," Maud said.

"Do I?"

"Yes. You rarely blink."

"I don't? Hm." Clem smirked and relit the pipe. "I've never noticed. But then I don't go around staring at myself in the mirror."

"What happened to your finger?"

Clem held out her hand and studied it. She tapped the nub of her index finger and frowned. "That was an unfortunate situation with an ax. Which was as tall as me at the time, and which I'd not been given lessons in how to handle."

"Who left you alone with an ax?"

"Wood needs to be chopped when wood needs to be chopped. My mother had died, see? And Da . . . There was a cow and there was me and there was the grave I dug for Mother. Luckily old Arthur Asher found me before I bled to death. He couldn't save the finger, but he knew how to use a hot poker to heal it up." She mimicked the action. "Just like that. Distracted me with a card trick, grabbed my hand and stuck the iron to it. I think he didn't know what to do with me after that. He was a trapper. Little girls weren't useful for that. So down the hill we went to the Children's Home." She blinked then, slow, as if she was partway in that world and partway in this one. "No pity, please. The Sisters gave me a marvelous education."

"My mother was sent to the asylum. She died there. She found her gifts more bane than beauty."

"Do you miss her?"

"Yes."

"Yes." Clem picked up the wine bottle and held it to the candlelight. "Would you—"

"I'm stuffed. So, no thank you."

"Then I'll finish." She poured the wine into her glass and tossed it back in one swallow. "Now. I've been trying to sort something out."

"What is that?"

"How famous I can make you."

"I'd be happy with consistent circles and the mortgage paid."

"You don't think well of yourself."

"I think quite well of myself."

"You don't."

Maud's face went hot. "Yes, I do."

"That's not what I see at all." She set her pipe in an ashtray and leaned forward, one hand crossed over the other. "I see the sadness in you. Abandonment." She stood, trailing a hand around the table. Clementine's eyes flicked back and forth as she studied Maud. "You are dejected."

"You would be too."

"Of course." Her voice soothed, like warm cider, like honey. "Loss is the nature of the world, isn't it?" She took a seat, her knees knocking Maud's. "We, at least, soften the blow."

Maud let out her breath and with it came a great sob, as if a stone had been dislodged from her throat.

Don't cry. It makes me cry too.

Maud's eyes popped open. Clem still sat before her, smile beatific. "Who's speaking?"

A breeze brushed the back of Maud's neck. She gasped, snatching at the air behind her, as if she could catch the hat on its arc back to Matthias's head, that tall beaver hat he wore, the one he always swept low and fancy, like a gentleman.

The voice came again from behind her, gauzy and roughened, as if from a long stretch without use. Familiar and strange all at once. *I don't really know where I am. I just wish to talk to my brother Joseph.*

Maud trembled and clutched the edge of the table. "Who calls?"

Seth Stoddard. I'd be much obliged for you to hold up an arm, so I know you hear me clear.

She raised her hand. Clementine did not.

"Seth Stoddard. I'm listening." Not Matthias, and yet someone had come, someone had slipped through, had sought her.

A long sigh turned to a moan, then a mumble. *My wife . . . market . . . hops and horses . . . O! Yes, sir I can't—*

Something banged the window.

Maud winced and twisted to look. The glass had cracked in two.

Clementine rose and crossed to it. She peered out in the dark, then stood on tiptoe and stared down toward the ground before turning back to Maud. "I think a good, solid meal does the trick for you."

"You didn't hear—"

"Not a sound." She tucked her hands to her pockets. "There you are." She paced the length of the room, causing the candles to flame and flare as she passed. "It's a start. He has a chance of returning tomorrow night. In the meantime, we need a signal. Should there be no visitation."

The room wavered as if Maud were watching it through wax. She pinched her temples and waited for her vision to clear.

"Are you well? You do not look well."

"No, I . . ." She took in a deep breath and dropped her hands to her lap. Clumps of soil littered the fabric and seeped into the folds of the skirt. She leapt up, brushing them away. Small pebbles dropped without sound to the floor. "What . . ."

The smell of tobacco smoke burned her nostrils. She turned to Clementine, who stared up at the ceiling, her pipe in her hand. She blinked once and gave a nod, as if she'd just come to some agreement with a thought, then looked again out the window. "It'll be blustery tonight. Look at the clouds."

"Look at all the dirt. Would you look?"

Clementine frowned and squinted. "What dirt?"

Maud blinked in disbelief. "This." But there was no *this*. Her dress was as white as it had been when she lay down for a nap. Not a pebble lay on the floor. She trudged to the mirror and stared at her reflection. Then she darted to the far wall, clambered on a chair, and swept her hand over a picture frame, disturbing only a layer of dust. "Where is it?"

There had to be a device, something with mirrors or glass. "Where is it?"

Clementine smoked and watched.

Maud dove down to search under the table, then dug her nails into the baseboards and pulled the curtains wide. And then she found it. Across the room in the curio cabinet. A small box of mirrors. She grabbed it and held it out to Clementine.

"You have to admit it was clever."

Maud's breath grew shallower. She gritted her teeth and slung the box at Clementine. It clattered to a stop by her foot.

"Where's the other half?"

"I don't give away all my secrets."

She squeezed her eyes to hold back the stinging tears. "And was Seth Stoddard another three-legged monkey?"

"No, Miss Price. He was real. Your spirits need you as much as you need them. You must believe that."

Clementine picked up the box and held it to a candle. The light split into shards of color that danced across the ceiling. She set the box to the windowsill, then pulled a watch from her pocket and flicked it open. "I'll be to your right tomorrow night. Mr. Sullivan to your left. Mrs. Eunice MacGregor will be on my right and Mr. Sullivan's left. Should anyone else come, we will seat them to the opposite side. And find your planchette. Just in case this new spirit has an urge to communicate. Confidence, Miss Price. You must have confidence. Lost things can be found, you see?"

Chapter Nine

CLEMENTINE

Russell had outdone himself. Clem pressed her lips to his, her legs wrapped to his waist, then leaned back against his bent knees. She held up a finger and gazed at the attic door. She had locked it, and stuffed linen in the space between door and floor, but one couldn't be too sure. Then she gave a nod and wrapped her arms around his neck, nose to his skin. "That was a damn fine ghost."

She felt his smile, the stubble on his cheek rough against hers.

"This is a damn fine house," he whispered. Then he rocked forward, his hands to her shoulder blades, keeping her from toppling to the floor. "You are a damn fine woman."

"I am."

His eyebrows arched, and he spread his knees and let her topple, nuzzling her before standing up and stretching his neck one way and then the other. He trod to the pile of chairs, his bare feet quiet as a cat's, and twirled them one at a time from their pile until they were in a row. He pulled the oilcloth from the wooden poster, swinging it around his shoulders into a cape. He paced from one end of the advertisement to the other, picking off a splinter of wood, rubbing and blowing at the dust.

"Seth Stoddard?"

"It has a ring, doesn't it?" He tiptoed to the long table and picked up each of the ink bottles Clem had set out. Then he perused the pens and wiped the nibs. He held up the spirit writing box and pressed a hidden button, releasing a square of blank notepaper. "Dearest Russell," he read. "You are a magnificent, creative creature of cunning skill."

Clem moved to her knees and swiped the paper away. "Dearest Clementine, you are the cleverest of clever girls." She jumped to her feet, curtsied, and followed it with a deep bow.

He glanced to the attic door. "Are you sure she can't—"

"A little laudanum does wonders for sleep."

"Yes, it does." He hopped to the tabletop and gave a jerk of his head for her to join him.

She did, pressing into his side as he wrapped his arm around her. "Look out there."

The moon glowed a watery silver against the inky sky.

"It's like that gong you used with Mrs. King."

"It is."

"Next we'll hear the screech of a loon."

She elbowed him. "Don't call my creations loons. They're songbirds."

"Well, when you put more than two in a room, it sounds more like screech than warble."

"That's the first thing you said to me," she said. "When we met."

"Not true. I called them a wonder."

"Did you?"

～♋～

The first time she'd met Russell, it had been over the top of a cage of tin parakeets that chirped and flapped their sky-blue tails. It had been her fourth—no, fifth—attempt, nights spent after her release from Mrs. King's soirees and séances and sins. The trick was in the bellows. It had been one failure upon another. But her habit entertained Mrs. King, who didn't complain about the cost.

"It will amuse guests," she said. "When conversations run dry."

She showed one to Mrs. King, standing with one scuffed shoe atop another. She tapped her knuckle to her lips, swinging her shoulders, waiting for an answer.

Mrs. King held the tin bird in her palm.

Clementine bit her lip, forcing back a laugh. She crossed her finger behind her back, hoping Mrs. King would not see the similarity in the bird's beak and her own.

"What do I do with it?"

Clementine dug a small key from her skirt pocket. "Here. Wind it up."

Mrs. King was delighted. One bird became a dozen, and an ornate birdcage was commissioned and presented with much fanfare to Clem. "We'll bring it to Sun House. I've invited a troupe to perform for the summer solstice."

Thus the birdcage was packed in straw and crated along with the silverware and four saddlebreds to the grand house Mrs. King's spiritualist fame had bought.

The troupe had presented a tepid and sordid matinee of *A Midsummer Night's Dream*. Clem watched from a ladder at the back of the makeshift stage, being called to change the backdrop and throw dried flowers at various points.

The actors ran back and forth, flinging off costumes and donning others, rushed whispers in the wings before strutting and primping into their scene. Only one man remained backstage. He leaned against the wall, a script in one hand, a bottle of wine in the other. He swigged the liquor and mouthed the lines and his expression grew more sullen as the acts unfurled. He left before the final bows, slipping out the door to the hall.

Later, she found him staring at the birdcage. It sat in the center of the rotunda room, surrounded by ferns and guarded by nymphs and minotaurs that ringed the room. Plaster, not marble, but who could tell? As who could tell the tin birds from the real?

"Do you admire them?" she asked.

He lifted his gaze. "They're a wonder." He raised his wineglass for a drink, only to find it empty. "Oh."

"Do you need another glass?"

"Ah, yes, you're a maid. Yes, please. Another glass."

"I'm not the maid." Her skin flushed.

"My apologies."

"You shouldn't assume things about people."

She gazed out over the room, blinking against the glare of sun on the white marble floor and crystal chandeliers and watered silk settees. The guests had meandered out to the veranda. Most were half in their cups, because actors did like fancy drinks in fancy houses, and Mrs. King's liquor was easy on the tongue. "You're one of the troupe."

"Is that what you assume?"

"It's what I know. All I have to do is look at your costume. There's no lining to the jacket and no cuff to your shirt. You're all made up. Like the birds."

"Yes. Yes, I admit I am."

"But you weren't in the play."

"Understudy." His lip twisted.

"What would have happened? If you had to go on?"

"What?"

"You were drinking then. So what would have happened?"

"I know every word. I could recite the lines in my sleep."

"It was a terrible play."

"Who are you," he asked, "if not the maid?"

Her eyes flicked from one figure on the veranda to the other, then snapped to his. "Do you like the birds?"

"They're very loud."

"Are they too loud?"

"One or two would have done the trick."

She said nothing, just sucked in her cheeks and let them out.

"Five is rather . . . you can hear the clicks of the tails. Do you hear the clicks of the tails?"

A burst of laughter from the veranda. Samuel White, the leading actor, held up his glass, then tossed it back. Gwen Pritchard was forehead to forehead with Mrs. King. Morris Thwaite stumbled and fell into a wicker chair.

"They don't care about you," she said. "It's like you're not here. Here and not here. It's a very odd place to be, isn't it? But it becomes a lovely place, though, once you're used to it."

"What's your name?"

"Clementine Watkins. You are Russell Sprague."

His eyes crinkled at the edges. "Yes, I am."

She would have thought nothing more of him, save he confirmed her belief in the preening quality of actors. But he'd found out Mrs. King's game and thus found out Clementine herself.

Mrs. King had arranged chairs in the ballroom. She herself sat upon a single stool on the raised stage. Clem peeked through the pinhole in the canvas backdrop. The acting troupe had come early and sat in the front row. In between were more evening jackets and silks and bobbing hats. The summer set, whose names glided in and out with society's whims. Russell Sprague, being late, had the unfortunate option of sitting in the back row behind a large hat of peacock and finch feathers. Not that she cared if he came or not, but she was curious what he thought of the mechanical bugs she'd left on his pillow and the pocket of his evening jacket.

"Lower the lights."

Clem lowered the gas, which hissed and fluttered to blue before snuffing out, leaving only a single candle lit on the table next to Mrs.

King. The medium's voice climbed up and careened down. Strange laughter came from the back of her throat and jangled like rusty bells on the marble back wall. She pronounced all sorts of things: King George played sticks and ladders with the grooms and yodeled from the top of the tower before falling in tears over the deaths of Richard's little boys. Boston was due for a large nor'easter, no matter it was the height of summer. Gwen Pritchard's betrothed wished to speak. "He missed you at the graveside, did you . . ."

Clem pulled the mouthpiece of the spirit trumpet to her lips. She did love this device, with the bell high up near the ceiling, the brass piping painted to match the trompe l'oeil walls. She wrapped one hand over the other and hummed. *Gwen, my quite contrary Gwen.*

The flash pot tucked behind Mrs. King's candle went off; Clem could see the bright red of it cast above her. Clem stepped from the trumpet to a pulley handle and waited for the next flash.

There it went—this time with a bang. Enough to blind the group and then, as they regained their vision, just enough light to see Mrs. King suspended an inch from the floor before the mallet struck the gong three times.

"Oh!" a woman cried.

Clem hoped it was Gwen. She reached for the trumpet. *I have no strength in the light, Mrs. King. Can you blow it out and I'll talk to my contrary Gwen?*

She twisted a lever on a wooden box, then tugged a wire. A gasp came from the front, as a smoky image cast itself on the glass above.

It wouldn't look as such from the front. Not in the light and not with the spirit of Gwen's betrothed now floating above Mrs. King's head. Clem stepped back, rubbing her nose, her lips curled in a satisfied smile.

"Catgut. Dyed black."

She startled, one hand curled into a fist, and squinted to see Russell Sprague's face an inch from hers. He pointed a finger. "Look up."

She tilted her head.

"Horsehair catches the light. Catgut does not. Your birds require feathers over their tin plates, the sheet glass out there has a thumbprint on the lower right corner, and the woman could do with an opening act."

He patted her shoulder and took up the trumpet. *That's the right darkness. Now I can speak.*

❧

Now she smacked her hand to his thigh, twisted off the table, and dug her travel journal from the pocket of dead Mr. Price's coat. "Look."

Russell took the journal from her and studied the map she'd drawn earlier. The markings, neat and precise, mapped two floors of a house, with dots and arrows pointing to various corners. Along the margins she had penciled cutaways of interior walls, lath and stuffing and hollows.

"Look at the space between the sitting room and library." Clem tapped the paper. "Look how much room there is for a false wall. And here." She flipped the page and pointed to a back bedroom on the second floor. "If you stand in this corner, what you say is heard here." She slid her hand to a landing, down a set of stairs, and into the parlor. "A whisper so clear it is like breathing in a sitter's ear."

Russell set his elbow to the table and propped his chin in his palm. "Where does the light come from?"

"Candles and sconces."

"Just at dusk, where is the sun?"

"The house faces west."

"The parlor, then entry, and the dining room. I could put a mirror at this corner—what is that, the kitchen? Why are there so many crosses drawn in there? Never mind. And here." He pointed up. "How high is the ceiling?"

"Nine feet." Clem mimicked his position, a hand cupped to her chin, her body curled over the drawing. She hummed and put her thumb in the middle of the hallway. "The spirit will float here."

"She'll need to come down the stairs. Greet the guests. And if we angle this looking glass just enough, the spirit will trail her like a loyal dog."

"But that's all for later. Tomorrow night we'll keep it simple. There's a woman coming, with a note she wishes to communicate with her husband. How is your *Richard the Third*?"

The words came sonorous and majestic: "'My conscience hath a thousand several tongues, and every tongue brings in a several tale—'"

"Mm."

"'And every tale condemns me for a villain.'"

"That's enough. Keep the voice, not the words." She stared at the poster and Maud's ethereal features. "She looks nothing like that. I would be kind in saying she looks like a mouse."

"God, she was famous. Dolls and paper cutouts and miniature planchettes."

Clem grabbed the signboard and turned it to the wall. Then she crossed the room, hefting up her satchel before setting it to the table. She pulled a leather string from around her neck, leaving the key free to unlock the satchel. "I'm going out early in the morning. You'll need to stay quiet."

"As another mouse."

She turned both locks, set them to the side, and then unpacked small wooden boxes, handing each to Russell. Here a box of gears, there one of coils. A roll of cotton and a vial of saltpeter. He placed each where she pointed. Then she removed a black dress—simple widow's weeds she'd dyed herself—flapped it to release some of the wrinkles, and spread it across two trunks. She hung a bustle and corset on the door hook.

"The spirits come out tomorrow night." Russell rubbed his hands. "What will they say?"

"The spirits, Russell, will say what I want."

Death notices came in two forms: a line or two in the newspaper or beribboned in black or white upon a front door. She left Maud's to wander the shaded streets, spying this house or that, looking for the telltale silk bows and tightly drawn curtains. The houses that circled Maud's had not one death to speak of; instead Clem turned her lip at the sway of daffodils and cheery narcissus.

Portsmouth had been so much better for the pickings. One coffin, two coffins, three a day if she was lucky. A cortege to follow of a morning and a body laid in wait on a dining table in the afternoon.

Never mind Portsmouth. It was Maisie Sullivan that Clem searched for now.

Maud really should have kept account of these passings. It made it so much simpler in the long run. Clem herself bought newspapers daily. She kept coded notes about the deceased. No one would be the wiser, should the book fall into another's hands. Most of the pages were given over to drawings of flowers and mechanical movements and various birds. She had learned her lesson early—her first client, Mr. Pope, had been an egregious drunk and had left his own death list on the side table in his séance room. A glass of rum sat on top, soaking the pages. The accusations sent him to Europe under a false name, and Clem from Manchester to Boston on the morning train.

But Mr. Pope had written his own warrant. His clientele was made specifically of relatives of the corpses whose notices graced the first few pages of the newspaper and therefore had the most money and summer homes to visit. They also had the greatest anger when duped. An inkling of suspicion set them in tailspins, and they paid wads of cash to investigators. These were nasty men disguised as mourners whose one intent was to expose the nefarious mesmerists and mystics.

No. Clem read and remembered and tucked away in a coded notebook the least interesting of passings, because those were the people who yearned to believe and, even if they did not, they went away with an entertaining story. They could not afford the sword of vengeance.

Maisie Sullivan's name did not ring a bell, which led Clem to believe she had received no notice at all, save perhaps in the register at her church. But Eunice MacGregor's name did. Or rather that of her husband, Theopholus. Kind husband of 43 yrs, missed by wife, service at . . . etc.

She wandered the streets, passing the empty hulk of a mill, the glass broken and jagged in the windows, the bricks crumbling from a corner. The cottages here were close to the road, the roofs sagging. This had once been the heart of Harrowboro, before the railroad came and wrenched the town north. A small clapboard church with a high steeple beckoned. She could make out a row of tombstones, lit and then shadowed by scudding clouds.

Clem strolled into the churchyard. She tried the dark wooden door. Locked. The stones that lined the side of the church tipped and tottered, some half sunk in the soil.

JEREMIAH HORAN DEAD *1763*

HERE LIES MATILDA PENCE BELOVED MOTHER AND WIFE 1756–1814

The granite on the next was worn smooth, with only a small poppy scroll along one edge. She bent to a small square block and brushed off the wet dirt and bramble.

MARY DAWSON DROWN-ED *1837–1855*

She wandered the obelisks and plain Puritan slabs until she reached the newer plots and their temporary wood markers, fine new grass just peeking from the patted earth.

"May I help you?" She had not heard the minister approach. He held his hands clasped in front of him, as if at any moment he would raise them in a prayer to God. His black coat, caught by a gust, rippled from his figure. He blew at a wisp of gray hair from his forehead. Age spots littered his scalp.

Clementine smiled and shook her head. She raised a palm and gestured around the yard. "My soul is helped by them."

"Ah. The solace of those at rest." He pulled in a lungful of air, the hairs in his nostrils quivering. "It gives me solace, in its way. No more pain."

"Tell me of these three." Clem pointed toward the newest graves. "I will hold them in my prayers."

He tilted his head for her to follow. "Terrence Small." He patted the top of the marker and moved on. "Thomas Thetcher, poor babe."

Clementine gave a gasp and tsk and put her fingers to her lips, mimicking a silent prayer.

"The young are the hardest of losses," he said. "But others cut as deep to their loved ones. Here. Mr. MacGregor."

A fizz of delight ran up Clem's spine.

"He sung bass in the choir."

"A great loss, then."

"Yes."

"How did he die?"

"Nicked his heel and the infection followed."

"My brother died the same." She pressed her hand to her throat and stifled a small sob. "Just a cut. How can it be such? There is not a day I do not think of him."

His hand was warm on her shoulder, there long enough for comfort and short enough for propriety. "I would like to pray for you. Would you pray with me?"

"I will."

The ground, Clementine noted, was not raw here. Mrs. MacGregor's Theo had been buried before the winter froze the ground solid. Sometime in the fall, though November had been strangely warm, so he could have succumbed and been dropped to earth as late as Thanksgiving. A ring of wildflowers—pale-blue Quaker ladies and white bloodroots—circled the simple wood marker.

Mrs. MacGregor must have visited just that morning. For who else would lay out such sentimental nonsense?

The pastor murmured on, punctuating "the Lord" and various other words until he came to "amen."

Clem responded in kind, then swallowed the bitterness that came with the word. "Did you minister him?" She lowered her head. "I'm sorry, that isn't my concern. I just . . . my brother died alone. I have always wished to know his last words. Were they to God? To Mother? Did Mr. MacGregor have the comfort of your ministry? His wife's? Child?"

"Two. Both taken in the war."

"Poor Mrs. MacGregor." She clapped her hand to her heart and staggered back, hoping against hope she wasn't overdoing it. She could see Russell rolling his eyes. She let out a long breath. "Is she all alone?"

The minister reached for her elbows to steady her. "Mrs.—"

"I must go." She stepped away, bothered that he held tight enough to her arm that she had to shrug to loosen his grip. "Give Mrs. MacGregor my condolences."

She lifted her skirt to avoid a particularly large mud puddle and hopped to the next row of graves. Maud's dress was too tight and pinched at the waist and shoulders.

"Mrs.—are you new to the parish? Will you return, friend?" He lifted his hand. "Will you return?"

But she pretended not to hear, swinging the cemetery gate open and taking again to the decrepit street.

She clapped her hands and hurried her pace. The church behind her remained silent, its bell missing from the belltower. The bells in the North and South Churches clanged the hour. The ringing echoed from the hills above Harrowboro. Just enough time to make it to the seamstress and order a new dress. And the haberdasher's for a suit. Mr. Price's clothing smelled like burnt apples. It was a terrible tobacco flavor. She much preferred cherry.

Chapter Ten

MAUD

Dear Miss Price,

The sitters tonight will be placed in a specific order, namely: myself to your right, Mr. Sullivan to your left, and direct across Mrs. MacGregor, who you know is in desperate grief for her husband. Winter infections are vicious and wounds to the heel, dire.

Please acknowledge me, if you acknowledge me at all, as Mrs. Leota Turlock, your cousin come visiting, tho better to ignore me completely, as I am only there to wait for your signal of need, should you give one.

I suggest it be something such as "Do you hear the clapping?"

Your improved planchette is available should the spirits come and you wish to take down chatter, and if need be, the bottom sheet has been marked with some comforting words to Mrs. MacG.

Sullivan's wife is still a mystery, so leave him be for now, unless Maisie waves and shouts.

A small bowl will be placed on the table by the coats;
I will leave a few dollars in it when exiting the house and
do hope the other two are of generous minds tonight.
Remember your recent visitation and be of cheer that
the door is ajar again for those who seek you.
C.—

The table had been moved. It sat near the fireplace, where a jaunty little fire heated the room. The brass candlesticks centered on the table had been lit. The cloth was not the normal lace, but linen that draped to the floor. Her planchette rested atop a stack of blank paper, the pencil sharpened and ready should the spirit urge her to write. To its left sat a small bell with a velvet ribbon.

Four chairs circled the table. Beyond, near the curtained window, four chairs from the dining room sat in a prim line, bookended by two large ferns. The portraits of her grandparents had been removed; their place taken by an oval fisheye mirror. As she passed, her figure shrunk and bulged.

"Sit down." Clementine, dressed again in the borrowed plaid, leaned against the doorframe, arms crossed. She had done her hair in two plaits pinned neatly at the nape of her neck. She wore a simple necklace of gold and amethyst.

Maud sighed. "No trousers?"

"In public?"

"Thank you. For dressing."

Clementine pushed away from the wall and crossed the room. She pulled out Maud's chair. "Sit down."

Maud took her seat. Now she faced the line of chairs. "Are we expecting—"

"You have read my letter?"

"Yes."

"Excellent. You may give it back now. Put your hand to the planchette." Clementine trailed her finger on the linen cloth and then sat directly across from her. "Remember how good you were with it."

The wood, smooth from years of use and nicked on the lower corner, warmed under her touch. Once it had danced across the paper. Now it remained inanimate.

"Put your thumb underneath and slide it toward me."

A loose paper slipped forward as she pressed. The letters on it were wild and stilted. She made out only "often-wise" and "sharp" before Clem pinched it up, then rolled it back under the planchette's trap.

"Only if necessary, Miss Price."

"It *is* chatter."

"I'm sorry?"

"In the note. You wrote chatter."

"Yes?"

"Sometimes it maddened me."

"Let it madden you again."

The bell jingled at the front door.

"I will go out the back. Expect me a few minutes late." Clementine smiled. "Welcome your guests."

∾

If only Mr. Sullivan would stop rocking. And Mrs. MacGregor hadn't doused herself in lemon verbena. The room boiled; Maud had shut the parlor door at the commencement and stoked the fire before taking her place in the circle.

Maud's eyes fluttered open. Mrs. MacGregor's own were cinched up tight, her head flung back, as if it were she entering the trance. Her jowls quivered and swung. "Theo . . ." Her voice trembled.

Mr. Sullivan stilled, then continued rocking.

Only Clementine remained at ease. Eyes closed, a content smile on her face. She gave Maud's hand a quick shake.

Maud squeezed her eyes shut and clamped her jaw. Neither of which were beneficial to calling in Matthias. Not that she expected him. She wished she could float away now. Just float to the ceiling like a wisp of smoke and out through the transom. That would be a wondrous trick. To just disappear and leave the others to marvel.

She took a breath and held it. Counted to six and followed with another. Again. Her shoulders dropped. She released her jaw from its vise. A wash of blue painted her closed lids.

"We are here to meet you, should you wish to meet us," she said. "Our circle is peace."

Mr. Sullivan's knee knocked hers. "I'm sorry."

"It's all right, Mr.—"

All the candles snuffed.

"Oh."

The sitters' faces glowed orange in the coal light. Then the fire hissed and went to black.

Hello. I am here. A deep, gravelly voice sounded from the corner.

Clementine's grip tightened.

Can you hear me? I am ever so far away and close.

The small bell rang, right near her ear, then above the table. Maud's heart banged her chest.

O clap your hands, you nations all, and shout with joyful mirth!
How awesome is the Lord Most High, great King o'er all the earth!

"Theo?" Mrs. MacGregor's voice splintered. "It sounds like Theo. Is it Theo?"

Oh, do sing with me, all! I so miss my Psalms! The bell rang again.

He brought down nations under us, and peoples 'neath our feet.
He chose inheritance for us; His love did Jacob meet.

Mr. Sullivan joined in, stumbling on the words and changing over to a hum. Mrs. MacGregor's soprano came reedy and wild. Clementine sang with gusto, as if it were a shanty song and not one of the Psalms. *Which one?* Maud thought. *Which one?* The bell rang, once above each of their heads.

How your voices carry me! Look at me dance, Eunice my dear, both feet full of health!

The table tipped and smacked down to the floor.

No little nick on the heel will stop this heavenly dance.

Up the table went and down again it slammed.

Mrs. MacGregor's song had turned to blubbering. "Oh, he touched me! Oh, Theo!" She stood, the chair clunking to the floor, the circle broken. "Theo."

I am close and far away, my love. So close, I've left you a present. Remember me. Oh! I must go . . .

The table twisted.

"Hold it down," Clementine said. "We need you, Mrs. MacGregor."

Something thumped hard against the wall.

The table twisted left and right, the four of them shuffling this way and that. A single candle sconce flared. *How?* she wondered. *How?*

Then the table stopped. The chairs lay all around the room. One was on its side atop the sherry cabinet and another looped around the parlor door.

Mrs. MacGregor's skin had gone a pallid gray. She stared above Maud's head, a trembling hand pointing to the mirror, then clawing back at her neck and the string of wildflowers that hung around it.

Clementine covered her mouth. "My God," she muttered.

"That was . . ." Mr. Sullivan blinked and stared at Maud. "I have never in my life—"

Mrs. MacGregor collapsed to the floor in a faint.

"Smelling salts!" Clementine rushed to the woman's side. She twisted a silver capsule and ran it under Mrs. MacGregor's nose.

Mr. Sullivan kneeled to help the woman sit up. He touched the flowers as if they were made of the finest glass.

"May I see him again, Miss Price?"

Three sets of eyes looked at her.

"Yes, Miss Price," Clementine said, "will we see him again?"

A pressure filled Maud's chest, as if a fist twisted against her ribs. She wrapped her arms around her waist and bit back a moan. The room tilted. She felt her head wobble and roll. Then her mouth filled as if with mud, viscous and sour.

Clementine's image swayed before her—hands to her knees, eyes wide and startled. Clementine crossing the room in great wide strides, the silver capsule held out.

Dots of red and yellow floated in air that frayed and hung like tattered webs. She heard a bird, its song cheerful and relentless, its beak pecking her ear. Then a guttural gasping, a high whine like a punctured balloon. *Help me, give me your hand . . .*

She sputtered, spitting water from her mouth and blowing it from her nose. She pulled in a deep breath. The room was again the room: there Mrs. MacGregor, there the table, there the mirror. She clambered to her hands and knees, then struggled to stand, pulling in racking breaths. With each one, her vision cleared. There was the sherry cabinet, the door swung open. There her planchette hanging from a hook on the wall. There the sconces—all now lit. When did that happen? Mr. Sullivan attending to Mrs. MacGregor. Here Clementine, crouched before her, the half-empty ewer in her grip.

Maud shivered.

"Are you all right?" Clementine asked.

"I heard something . . ."

Clementine nodded and straightened. She swung the ewer by the handle and looked around the room. "Have you ever seen such a thing?"

Mr. Sullivan opened his mouth and snapped it shut.

Mrs. MacGregor took his arm and returned to the chair he set upright for her. "Your gift, Miss Price, is a miracle. To hear my Theo, to have this gift from him. From you."

"No." Maud pushed a strand of wet hair from her forehead and tucked it behind her ear. Never had she felt that pain, as if her ribs would crack, as if she were held underwater. She knew of others who had. Not all spirits were kind. Some wanted back in the world. Some wanted revenge.

"Someone has drowned." There had been no peace, not the trails of color and beauty that came when she gave herself to Matthias.

Only anger. Only fear.

"Leave me," she blurted. She pressed the heels of her hands to her eyes and blotted out the group.

"But I must pay you," Mrs. MacGregor spluttered.

She heard the rustle of skirts and Mr. Sullivan's "Let me walk you out," and Clementine's voice, clear and light. "I will leave my payment in the glass bowl, Miss Price. Should the others do the same? Yes, I think this would be a good place to . . . but no, Mr. Sullivan, I'm going the other direction."

The voices echoed in the hall, umbrella handles knocking the bucket, and then came murmurs, for she was certain they held much concern for her and had thus lowered their voices.

"Wonder," she heard, and ". . . my favorite flowers, why I just bought them this morning . . ." and "You remember her, don't you? The Maid of Light . . . I only came today because I wanted a laugh, but—"

Maud dropped a fist and glared at the door and the commotion as the three departed. The front door swung shut. She scooted back to the wall by the fireplace, leaning her head back and pulling in a great breath before taking stock of the room and its contents in such disarray. A fern lay on its side, the soil spilled to the rug. A curtain hung half off the rod.

Her breath caught in her throat. She was not alone in the room.

A man peered out from under the tablecloth. His mouth curled into a smile. "Haha!" He flicked the cloth and crawled out, facing her on his hands and knees. He wore all black, gloves and skullcap included, greasepaint covering his face. "How about that, eh? How about it?"

Then he plopped back, slinging up a knee and resting his elbow on it. "We have not been properly introduced. Russell Sprague." He rotated his wrist and tilted his head in a bow.

"You did . . ." Maud gestured around the room.

"I do apologize for the curtain. Caught my foot on the fern." He stared at her, his hazel eyes pale in the candlelight. "You're delicate as glass."

The front door swung open. Clementine strode in, shutting and locking it, removing the feathered hat and lilac cape she'd taken from Maud's wardrobe and thumping them to hooks. She twisted a curl near her neck, then entered the room. Her cheeks were ruddy from the evening chill. "This deserves wine." Then she clapped her hands and flung herself up on the table, swinging her legs. Her eyes narrowed as she looked from Russell to Maud and back again. "You have met."

"We have met." Russell tipped his head back and then dipped his chin. "My God, the flowers. You must admit, Clem, those were the button on the jacket, weren't they? That was a clever trick, though she near grabbed my hand. I was almost too slow getting back under the table. Did you know Mr. Sullivan has overly large feet?" He held out both hands. "He could snowshoe and walk upon the water with those elephant toes."

"You have made me a liar." Maud pushed her hand to her stomach, forcing it to calm. She swallowed, the liquid bitter and hot.

Clementine rubbed the side of her mouth and gave a short laugh. "I can guarantee that your sitting book will be overfull now. We'll need more chairs. I saw a set in the storage shed. We'll bring them in tomorrow."

"We won't bring anything in." Maud squeezed her hands to fists. "This was too much. This was out-and-out fraud. Mrs. MacGregor didn't deserve such, such—"

"Comfort? Solace?" Clementine winced. "Yes. That's a horrible outcome. And here Mr. Sullivan will fall to his knees in prayer and hope that tomorrow his Maisie may be the one to come calling."

"I do a wonderful woman's voice." Russell got to his knees, clapping his hands to his chest. He gave a breathy sigh and his voice whispered like a young girl's. *There's rosemary, that's for remembrance. Pray you, love, remember.*

"Oh, Lord." Clementine rolled her eyes.

And there is pansies, that's for thoughts.

Maud clenched her jaw and hit the floor with a fist. "I've changed my mind. It's criminal. I won't do it."

"But you already have." Clementine kept her voice low. "That's the tricky part, isn't it? One monkey leads to another, and at the end of the day how will you explain them? Besides, you've money now for another hat."

Maud's stomach clenched. "If you had been patient—"

"The guests would have aged and died."

"We'd have to bury them in the yard," Russell said. Then he stood, pulling off his gloves and pocketing them, humming a bit and smiling at her with such bright eyes. "Are there others out there we should worry about?"

"You're as rude as she is."

Clementine gave a quick lift of her chin and lounged back on an elbow. "Go get the wine, Russell. Let's toast my rude behavior. And the lovely cash sitting in the bowl by the front door. We really should toast that."

Russell gave a theatrical bow and on his way out righted the fern, toeing the dirt into a pile with his shoe.

Maud didn't want wine. She wanted the room put to rights. She wanted to run after Mrs. MacGregor and tell her how sorry she was. She slid her gaze to the hall. "I'll send the money back."

"No, you won't."

"I will."

"You gave her a gift of much value. She returned the favor in kind." Clementine swung her legs, hopped from the table, and began straightening the chairs. "I'd give my life to hear my mother's voice."

Maud scooped soil into her palm and sifted it to the pot of the second fern. Moved it one place and then a few inches to the right. "Was it sickness?"

"No." Clem brushed her hands together, then grabbed up a chair and plonked it in front of the window.

"Is your father—"

"An unfortunate accident."

Maud rasped in a breath. Clem's mother. Was that voice she'd heard, words coiling around Maud's skull like a rope—*Help me*—was it Clementine's mother? The spirit's tendrils had dug into Maud. Shaking her. Clawing under her ribs as if to squeeze her lungs like bellows, pleading for release. Was she the one who clung to Clem, murmurs and mutters pulling at her skirts?

"Move your feet."

Maud shifted aside. Clementine shimmied the table into its original place.

"Is it your mother who follows you—"

"No. I've said before, nothing follows me." Clementine threw her a quick smile. "Your hands are ice-cold. Put them in hot water before the next sitting so no one thinks they're holding hands with a corpse."

There it was again. Maud swiped at her ear, then covered it. There. As if someone called from across a lake, as if the wind picked it up and tossed it, flinging the words to the water to sink. "Did she drown?"

"Curiosity can kill a cat, Miss Price." Again that tight smile and face as blank as glass. "I'll be very late. I wish you a good night." That was it. Clementine strode out.

Chapter Eleven

CLEMENTINE

Mr. Sullivan liked to read. He had been reading for the past thirty minutes, earnestly stooped over the book, a sheaf of paper to the right of it, his pen held aloft and at the ready for notes. Since he sat in a small room in the rear of a cottage that bordered a rambling brook and a patch of fallow pasture, he did not draw his curtains. Thus Clem found the viewing from her perch in the oak tree advantageous.

He swung his head from side to side as he read. His dark hair curled around his ears and at his collar, enough of it that he could still boast youth, as long as his hat remained on. Which it was not now. It hung on a post near his front door, along with his coat, and his overshoes, which he'd tied and hung over their own hook. He turned a page. Ran his hand over it to smooth it down. Dipped the pen in the inkstand again.

Clem hooked her arm to the limb and leaned out, then dropped to the ground. She kept still, hunched and ready to take to the brook and the field should someone spy her. But the other cottages were dark, dogs inside and chickens roosting. She stayed low, taking quick steps across the brown earth and past the coop until she came to the side of the house and the front room window. A dim glow from the lamp limned the room. Sofa, rocking chair with padded seat and back. Both patterned in green ivy. A fireplace empty of coal or wood. A squat book-case near the door. A sewing basket by a small wicker seat. She suspected the basket was a reminder both happy and painful in equal measure.

The front of the house had a single wood step, no portico or cover-ing above the door. One could jump directly to the street and in three great strides be across and knocking at the neighbors'. She scanned the houses—ten on the other side, curving with the ess of the road. Just past the last was a turn to the mills, and even through the wash of maples its brick hulk loomed. She eyed Mr. Sullivan's roof. It could use a few shingles itself.

He didn't have the money for Miss Price's services.

So the cash came from Mrs. MacGregor, who could ill afford it, and yet she had handed over the offering without hesitation.

She suspected Sullivan's days were spent manning a desk and copy-ing orders. Tucked up in the mill office but not part of the bustle and bossing. Perhaps his Maisie worked at Jasper's Woolens and they met at noon bells to share their meal.

There was nothing much else to note. The rooms were dark, no tenants or possible wife present. Clem circled around the back.

Mr. Sullivan bored her. The man read and read, and when he fin-ished, he stretched and yawned. He shut the book and made for the kitchen, turning off the gaslight on his way. The back door creaked as he opened it. It was time for his bedtime piss. The walk to the outhouse was short, no need for a candle and no need for Clementine to do more than slip down behind the bramble and wait.

Task completed, he returned inside, wound the clock in the hall, and retired to the bedroom. Tomorrow he would no doubt rise, take his morning piss, eat one slice of bread and one egg, cock his head for the mill bell, and without another thought join the others as they trod the road to the factories.

Her foot slid on the wet grass, the toe digging into the muck. She sucked in a breath of loamy air. Pulled her foot out with a squelch.

Sullivan's house would be a long wait; she would be a good girl—return to Maud's for a few hours' sleep and return to steal in the window and pinch a beloved object or letter of adoration. She patted her jacket pocket, glad to find her pencil and tracing paper still there and waiting.

Tonight's sitting had been too much shock and bang. Between Russell throwing the chairs and Maud apoplectic and on the verge of a seizure, things had gone nearly out of hand. The sittings needed awe, yes, but the tricks needed to be doled out intentionally—this bit of insight to one person, that cold hand on another's, there a whisper, there a smattering of ghostly light.

True, Mrs. MacGregor had left a lot of money. Eight dollars, four of which were folded in Clem's pocket. Maud would need to write a thank-you. She could invite her to next week's sitting—for there would be no more daily séances, thank you very much. Once a week, two sittings, so the medium did not overtire herself.

The moonlight gleamed bright against the bulk of the mills, turning the bricks a silvery green. Most buildings were dark, the loading docks empty, shadowing the train tracks that ran the length. But an orange glow spilled from one. A dog barked and then yelped, its owner cuffing or kicking it quiet. Just across the tracks she made out the crates half-hidden in the woods, the spark of a match and rumble of voices.

Dogfights. She hated them.

She pulled her hat low, shoved her hands to her pockets, and tilted her shoulders forward. Like she was ready for a fight. She skirted around a burn barrel, heading past the maze of carts and wagons and crates of fighting dogs.

The main fighting circle was empty, the hay blackened with pus and dirt, just a couple of men loitering by the rope corral.

A snap of teeth and a yelp came from the last cart. A ragged red flag was tied to the corner. A man crouched by the crate, smacking the flat of his hand to the wood. "You're damn nothings, you are."

Clem counted three dogs crammed into the box, each tied tight at the neck and heads stuck between the slats. Their nails scraped the wood, digging in as they lunged against strap and slats, teeth bared and bites coming a hair's breadth from his face.

He eyed her, spit a line of tobacco to the dirt, and kept slapping the crate.

The brindle twisted his block head and bit down on the man's cuff.

He stumbled back, leaving the hank of cuff to dangle in the dog's mouth. "Look what you done, Brutus, you damn nothing dog." He turned to Clem. "Look what he done."

Then he rounded back, kneeled and scruffed the brindle's ears. His jaw worked as he twisted them tight and yanked. The dog gave a sharp cry. "Quit your crying."

The black dog in the middle panted, its red tongue, flecked with saliva, lolling and swinging. He let loose the other to cuff this one on the jowl. "Yer a good boy, ah you are."

Clem looked to the final dog. Its scalp sported a mass of fresh welts. The right ear hung by a thread of skin and flapped about as the dog shook its head. "You're a mess," she murmured.

"That's the bitch."

Clem took a step forward, then stopped at the low growl. "There now."

"She's for the bone market. I don't see much else to do with her." He sat on the edge of his cart. He stuck his legs straight out, dirty wool trousers hanging from his knobbed knees. "Too tough for bait, too scared for the ring." A long brown string of tobacco flew from his mouth.

Clem pulled her pipe case from her jacket and watched the dog as she packed the bowl and lit it. She couldn't tell the color of the thing. It looked a dingy gray, maybe brown. Its nose had a deep crevice, as if it had been sliced clean in half and not mended. More scars on the neck, pink and raw under the rope.

"I had a dog once," she said. "When I was small."

∾

That dog hadn't been trapped in a cage like this one. It was a yellow mutt that roamed the brick boundaries of the orphanage. She'd seen it on her very first morning, after Sister Matilda turned the lock on the gate and hurried Clem along in a wash of brick outbuildings and cobblestone. Sister Matilda said, "Never leave the compound. Outside is nothing good." Then she gave Clem's hand a shake and the rosary beads cracked and clattered on her wrist.

The Children's Home occupied one square block, the whole of it surrounded by a high brick fence. This was the borderline. "Inside," Matilda said, "you will find food and education. Outside you will find the Devil. And the dog. Both know no bounds, but in here we do."

Then the dog stuck its snout through a crumbled bit of the wall and snuffled. Its nose quivered as she passed by. Matilda pulled her through the interior door and up a flight of twelve stairs.

The hallways echoed and smelled of bleach and wax and old socks. The high-pitched shrieks and babble of girls floated near the ceiling and slid in streams down the walls. Clem's teeth chattered against the cold, though the potbelly stove at the far end of the hall belched hot air.

They marched by classrooms and boys and girls and the scratch of chalk on boards and the scrape of chairs to wood, then turned left at the stove and up another set of stairs. This floor had very low ceilings and a smaller stove. Matilda pointed to an open doorway. "You are here." She showed Clem to a cot that sat under a window barred with icicles. A set of clothing lay folded at the foot of the bed, along with a brush and wooden comb, a square of soap, and a washcloth.

"God provides," Matilda said, and another voice joined her. "As do we."

A girl she had not noticed stepped away from the next cot. Her skin was as pale as the ice on the window, her eyes as indigo as the sky.

"This is Virginia. She will be your friend." Matilda gave a pat to Clem's back. "You will fit in here."

Then she was gone again, her habit swaying as she made her way down the stairs.

The girl ground the heel of one foot into the top of another. "What happened to you?"

"My mother is dead," Clem said. "And my father too."

Virginia pointed at the swaddling on Clem's hand. "What about that?"

"He cut off my finger so I wouldn't shoot the gun he shot her with."

Virginia smiled, showing off the empty spot that once held her two front teeth. "That's a good story. The others'll like it." She stuck her tongue in the space and sucked it back. "Don't tell it to Mrs. Bletham; she'll put you in the box for telling a lie."

"What about you?"

She shrugged, bony shoulder to ear. "Dropped off with a note. Nothing so good to tell as yours. Was there a lot of blood?"

"From me or them?"

"Either or."

"I don't remember."

"The Sisters say it's best to look forward, anyway." Virginia wiggled her hand into Clem's uninjured one. "We'll be good friends." And she smiled again.

They were good friends. She taught Clem when to keep her mouth shut and when to sneak an extra biscuit, which could be blamed on Mabel, who cried all the time and smelled of mildew. They snuck out early, when the Sisters were at their morning prayers, and fed the dog. Biscuits and eggs. Mutton and sausage. Oatmeal and crackers.

"What should we call it?" Ginny asked.

"Dog," Clem said.

"Mrs. Bletham doesn't like dogs."

"Then we don't tell her."

They sat against the wall and watched their breaths and waved at the sick ones on the second floor and giggled as the Sisters shuttled them back to their beds, their wimples flapping like duck wings.

Ginny grew cold and bored, so she left. Clem didn't care. She loved Dog and its soft velvet muzzle.

At Christmas came a swirl of skirts and women chattering and tsking as they stood in a bunch and handed over toys. Mrs. Bletham stood by their side, her big cheeks red and her breath pungent with brandy. She patted the boys' heads and pinched the girls' cheeks. Sister Matilda kept her nose to the air and sported a dour, grim look, for she did not believe in the Do-Gooders and their once-per-annum generosity. "Charity does not boast," she sniffed.

Clem looked at the table. Jacob's ladders. Tabletop nine pins. Jackstraws. Noah's ark with all the animals two by two. Dolls with porcelain faces that broke when dropped and straw ones that didn't. Embroidery kits and tortoiseshell combs.

None of it mattered. Clem didn't need any of it. She fingered the slice of ham and hunk of molasses bread in her frock pocket and sidled out of line to feed it to Dog.

But the hole had been bricked up.

Clem dropped to her knees and dug at the ground. It was hard as stone. "Dog?"

No whimpering or yelp came from the other side. The snow fell in thick, feathery flakes, sticking to the seams between the bricks. Clem jumped up and ran the length of the wall, calling for Dog and getting no answer.

"It's not coming back."

Clem startled, swinging around to Ginny's voice. "Yes, it is." Her lips were numb from the cold.

Ginny hunched over and hopped from foot to foot. "Sister says to come in."

"I have to find—"

"It's dead. Cook found it this morning." She blew into her cupped hands. "We're about to sing carols. Mrs. Bletham said to find you."

One of the Sisters handed her a doll—Little Maud, with hair as bright as the moon, but missing her slate—the one Clem had wanted so long ago. She curtsied and said thank you to the pack of Do-Gooders. They all sang "O Come All Ye Faithful."

No one talked about the dog. Not that night and not after.

⁓

"Are you only good for your bones, girl?" Clem clamped the pipe in her teeth and sunk down, hands to her knees. The dog kept its gaze on her. Clem felt it then, that buzz that started in her stomach and spread throughout her limbs, just under the skin. "Will you take two dollars for her?"

"For that thing?"

"You expecting more at the meat market?"

He scratched his jaw. "Three and no less."

"That's highway robbery."

"Take it or leave it."

The cur's tongue lolled as it panted, flecks of saliva clinging to its muzzle and chest. Its right ear—what was left of it—shined with fresh blood.

"You've got the breath of Hades, dog." Clem stood. "Two dollars. Take it or leave it."

Chapter Twelve

Maud

"I do believe I'm tipsy." Maud pressed her finger to her lips. "We can't tell Father. I mean, her."

"No. Fathers should never be told anything important. And Clem should be told even less." Russell leaned over the chair to pour her more wine.

She put her hand over the goblet. "I can't."

"Don't be silly. You haven't had more than a drop."

"But I have."

Russell raised an eyebrow and waited, the bottle ready.

"Well, a little."

"Yes?"

"Just a drop." She removed her hand, curling it atop the other in her lap.

"Good girl."

"You have beautiful eyes," she said. Then she squeezed her own eyes tight and shook her head. But that caused a wooziness. She clamped the seat of the chintz chair and waited for the floor to settle down.

"You have a beautiful soul." Russell leaned his elbow on the fireplace and gazed at her. He had changed into a suit with a large cravat finished with a black pearl stud. He had oiled his hair, though the ends still curled around his ears. The firelight curved the lines of his face and flickered in his eyes.

"Oh. I—"

"Shall I mesmerize you?" he asked.

"Do you know how?"

"Alas, I do not have that gift." He took a sip of his wine, then cupped the goblet so the stem swung in front of him. Specks of light shimmered and flitted on the wall and on his clothes.

"Tell me more of the theater. You said it was in your blood."

He smiled, dipping his head and then giving a click of the tongue. "I was born in a tent somewhere outside of Albany. Act 3, scene 4 of *Othello*. I gave a great big cry and nearly caused Iago a heart attack. I grew up in it. My father raised and struck the sets, my mother costumed, and I took any spear-carrying role tossed me."

"Oh, more than that, I'm sure. I can see you as Mark Antony, as Hamlet, as . . ."

"To be honest, my talents have been rather overlooked." He gulped his wine and set the glass to the mantel. "Every actor wants to play Hamlet. It's an actor's dream. Or delusion. No—I've bored you enough. Tell me more of your Mr. Matthias."

"Well, I—"

"Do you see them? The spirits?"

"No." She lifted her glass, but it was nearly empty, nothing but a small swallow left. He'd think her a sot if she asked for another. "I used to, when I was young. But mostly I hear things. Sometimes it's just chatter, other times a laugh or sometimes crying. And then sometimes they're very clear, as if they stood right next to me with a hand to my shoulder. But Matthias, he's who they're talking to—it's as if he steps inside me. He listens and he speaks or keeps—kept—everything organized, I suppose. My only job is to stay quiet enough. I don't really have a skill on my own." Maud opened one eye. "Now I'm boring you."

"Au contraire. I'm endlessly curious." He lowered himself to the floor, crossing one long leg over the other, his attention rapt, eyes only on her.

She pulled in a quick breath. She did not know what to do. Men did not fawn over her. William Marcus had made sure of that. "I have no experience with this."

He frowned. "I'm sorry?"

"This, this, never mind." She gulped her wine and stood. "I should not be here alone with you. It's not proper."

"Blast proper." He jumped up. "I say you do what you want when you want and hang the consequences."

She opened her mouth to retort, but found herself laughing, great laughs that bubbled up and then scraped her throat. "If I did what I want, I'd stay in bed all day."

"Oh, I don't think you would." His mouth curved down and he wagged a finger. "You have too much to offer. You have a gift, Miss Price."

"When I see someone's face light up . . . yes, it's true. It is as if a flame had been lit inside them when they can touch again someone so loved, someone they thought lost forever. It's more than comfort, though that's certainly part of it."

"During the war, it was a nurse that gave that," he said. "More than comfort, you're right. Something to go on living for, something hopeful."

"Yes, that's it. That all is well with the souls above and those here, too."

She felt warmth on her cheek. A brush of fingers. Or perhaps she only wished for it.

"You mend hearts that need it, Maud. How many can say that?"

"Mrs. MacGregor—"

"Think of all the others you can heal." Russell paced to the window, lifted the curtain, and looked out. Then he turned and spread his arms. "Come, look."

She stood and crossed to the window. His hand was soft and warm in the small of her back. He tapped the glass. "Out there are thousands of people who wish nothing more than a word from a loved one. There." He pointed to the clapboard house in the far corner, all the windows dark. "Someone kneels in prayer, asking not for Jesus, but for a son. And just beyond the river a girl sits on a stoop awaiting her father, who calls from Summerland, his words to her silent as the wind. They await you, Miss Price. *Think* of all the people who need you. Why, an opera house isn't out of the question."

"An opera house."

"Think of the Fox Sisters, but far more dramatic. They're nothing but raps and taps and booked for months on a European tour. Stick with Clementine and I—until your guardian angel returns, of course—but even then, there's much we can do."

"I did like the table tipping." She swallowed a hiccup.

"You didn't think it too . . ."

"It was grand. And the flower necklace . . . well . . ."

He turned and sat on the window frame, crossed his arms, and shrugged. "Small details."

"Three-legged monkeys."

"Ha! Indeed."

"Is this how Harriet Martin does it? Night after night?"

He frowned. "Who?"

"Don't tell me you aren't acquainted. She gave me Clementine's card. Is everything Mrs. Martin does a fraud?"

"Every act has something true. We merely give it a stage. And tonight, well, I did notice . . . Something came to you."

"Clem's mother. Her mother did."

"Well." He clapped. The sound reverberated throughout the room. "She is right about the sound here."

"Did her mother drown?"

He blinked and then picked lint from the cuff of his jacket. "I believe it was cholera took the poor woman. Or diphtheria. One or the other. She was orphaned very young."

"I felt it. As something else." Maud pressed her hand to her stomach. The room tipped first one way and then the other. She staggered back.

Russell slid one arm around her waist, the other taking her wrist and guiding her to a seat. Then he grabbed up her glass, tossing the dregs of wine to the fire, and filled it from the water pitcher. "Drink."

The water sloshed as she took it, spilling to her skirt. She swallowed what was left.

"You are right," Russell said. "You've had more than a drop of wine."

"Matthias keeps them to hand."

"Who?"

"I don't know how to open the gate without him. They follow him, not me. They follow him in, they follow him out. He's always careful who he brings, he's said so. Only those who do not harm, he says. Only those. And yet he's not here. Earlier I heard—and tonight. They're here without him."

"Isn't that a good thing? You don't need him. You've got the keys to the house and stable and the whole pasture."

Maud's mouth soured. "I need him."

"You don't."

"You do not listen." Maud's grip tightened on the stem of the glass. "You do not believe."

"But I do." He curled his hand around hers. He stroked her wrist with his thumb. "Your gatekeeper will return."

"I think I need to go to bed."

Russell stood, offering his arm. "I will escort you to the staircase."

"I did very much like the table tipping every which way."

He gave a self-satisfied smile and quick bow.

"Mrs. MacGregor's heart was full, wasn't it? The flowers! I . . ." She took to his side, her shoulder pressed to his arm.

A loud bang came from the hallway, then the parlor door swung open and smacked the wall.

Clementine slapped the frame. A leather rope coiled from her hand to the floor and into the dark. "We have a dog."

⁓

"Esther."

"Naomi."

"Madeline."

"Osiris."

Russell bent to the mongrel and snapped his fingers. "Martin Luther."

"That's a boy's name, you dolt." Clementine gave a sharp whistle. "Jezebel."

The dog glared at them all. She sat in the far corner, a sack of bones and scars, shivering and growling, swinging her wary gaze between them. Maud held a napkin to her mouth and nose, for the mongrel smelled of offal and rot. Blood wept from a gash on her shoulder. Maud followed its path to the puddle on the carpet.

Russell tossed a half loaf of bread to her.

But the dog flinched and sunk further, turning her head to the wall, ribs expanding and collapsing with a great sigh.

"What color is she?" Maud asked.

"Who knows?" Clementine shrugged off her jacket and folded it to a chair. She sank down on her haunches. "You're a good dog, aren't you?"

But the animal pushed her nose even further into the wall, one yellow eye staring at Clementine.

Russell put his hands to his hips and walked from one side of the room to the other. "Martha Washington."

Maud snorted. "Betsy Ross."

"We can knit her a sweater of stars and stripes."

"You knit?" Maud asked him.

"I am a man of many talents."

Clementine inched forward. "I saved your hide. Don't turn away."

The dog whined and scraped her nails to the plaster.

"She doesn't like you much," Russell said.

"Of course she likes me. I kept her from the boiling pot, didn't I?" She made little coos, like one gives a colicky baby. "Ethelred."

The dog panted, her tongue flopping to the side and teeming with saliva bubbles. Then she opened her mouth and snapped it shut, as if she wanted to say how very much she didn't like that name but liked even less Clementine's expression.

Russell raised his wineglass. "To Ethelred." He hesitated before drinking. "That's a boy's name too."

"It fits and so it will be." Clem sat cross-legged and picked at a shoelace, her attention on the dog that surely had fleas on top of the abscesses and bites.

Maud hadn't seen anyone so loopy with adoration. The woman whispered inane nonsense, scooting forward in fits and starts, waiting for Ethelred to slow her trembling before creeping just that bit further. She kept a hand on the rope, ready should the dog bolt. But the poor thing looked more likely to crawl through the wall and take up residence in the horsehair and laths.

"Did you drink all the wine, Miss Price?"

"You're not going to give it to the dog, are you?"

Clementine glanced up at her with a little smile. "My word. Do you give wine to your dogs?"

"I don't have any dogs."

"Did the wine kill them?"

"No, it didn't . . ." She caught her reflection in the fishbowl mirror. Bright red cheeks and nose even redder. Her eyes slitted and puffy, hair all in a disarray. Like a madwoman. A drunk madwoman who had just been accused of poisoning dogs. Even Russell, who looked as small as a tin toy in the curve of glass, peered at her in a supreme sort of judgment. "I haven't done anything of the sort."

Both sets of eyes stared at her.

"You shouldn't accuse people of things like that." She grabbed at her shirt collar, for the room was unbearably hot. She had grown used to the chill and now she couldn't bear the stuffy, oily heat from the fire. "Put the dog outside."

"With all these rooms," Clementine said, "there must be one we can assign her."

"Put her in your room." Maud scratched the skin at her neck. "You brought her; she's yours to deal with. And she wasn't part of the bargain, anyway." Her voice had risen in pitch and sounded much like a spoiled girl's. She gasped in a breath in the hopes of lowering it to a reasonable level. She watched herself in the mirror, her lips flapping open and closed like a fish out of water. She squeezed her hands to fists and smacked her thighs. "You're maddening." She flung out an arm toward Russell. "And so are you."

"Now, Maud—"

"On first names, are we?" Clementine asked.

"Well—"

"I want a contract. I want to know exactly what you are doing and not doing here. I do not want you crawling under a table without warning me, and spinning it the way you did is going to get someone hurt."

"But you just said—"

"It's like you're throwing a dervish around the room and it's going to cut someone's head off."

"I'm very careful—"

"This is my house, and I will be the one who approves or does not of any . . . scheme . . . you come up with."

"You're upsetting the dog." Clem's voice was low.

"I don't care. I do not care." She dug into her waistband for her handkerchief.

Russell proffered his.

She wiped the spittle from her mouth and crumpled the hankie. "Thank you."

"You are more than welcome." He gave a small bow, his expression full of concern.

"Don't look at me like that."

"I'm looking no way at all."

"I do not require pity, sir." Maud pressed her lips together and breathed through her nose. "I am in debt. I acknowledge that fact. I want a contract with an ending date and clear demarcation of roles."

"Petulance does not become you, Miss Price." Clementine wiped her trousers and cupped her hands to her knees.

"I am not petulant."

"You are."

"I'm not."

Clem shrugged and looked again at Ethelred.

"You're impossible."

"And you are in such arrears on this house and at your milliner, it will take ten lifetimes for you to pay it off. You want a demarcation of roles? Here they are. One—Mr. Sprague will have full creative license during the sittings and theatricals. Two—I, Clementine Watkins, am in sole charge of the mechanics, the budget, the ledger, the props, and the guiding idea. Three—you, Miss Price, are to follow what we ask of you—with your approval as to the sequence of events, of course—until such time as you are (a) out of debt or (b) have found your goddamned ghost."

"I'll open the other bottle to celebrate the agreement." Russell strode to the sherry cabinet.

"I do not agree. I don't agree."

"Then I will write a letter to the *Banner of Light* explaining your failures."

"Better that than—"

"I'm growing so weary of your righteousness."

"I am not self-righteous. This is infuriating. I—"

"There." Clementine pointed. "You've done it. Scared the piss right out of Ethelred."

A dark spot grew under the dog's haunches. She whined and swung her head.

"Oh, poor little girl." Russell pulled the cork with a soft pop.

Clementine unfolded her legs and stood up. She shoved her fingers to her vest pockets and rocked back on her heels, scowling at Maud. "You upset the dog. I told you not to upset the dog."

"I have nothing to do with the dog."

"Are you afraid of her?"

"Of course not."

"Why not?" Her eyebrow shot up. Then her lips spread in a smile. "I can guarantee the next sitting will bring a full house. If I know Mrs. MacGregor's type, she will run to the hills to announce her good news, and we, too, may need to cut a hole in the roof to allow the sinners in. Will you have your miracles ready, Miss Price?"

Clementine's eyes gleamed. Maud could not look away.

"I do not like the chairs thrown," she said.

"No throwing of chairs."

"I will ask for your help only if I need it."

"I believe 'I hear clapping' was the agreed signal. Is there something else?"

"This is for people's solace."

"Of course." Clementine's skin was impossibly pale. Her eyes impossibly black.

Maud swallowed and tore her gaze away before she fell into the darkness of them, into her own demise. They would write a contract in the morning, with clear dates. *You must have boundaries and dates and demarcations,* her father had said. *Else the world takes from you all of you.*

Ethelred barked. She had slipped from the corner and the wet spot and sat now at Maud's side. She touched her nose to the back of Maud's hand.

Clem tugged the rope, once and then again, until the dog limped its way to her. "There," Clementine said. "That's my girl. We'll make you and our Miss Price good as gold."

The dog hung her head when Clem reached to pat her, swinging her bleary, one-eyed gaze to Maud. Then she heaved her chest once, tucked her tail, and leaned against Clem's leg.

Chapter Thirteen

CLEMENTINE

The yard was as disastrous as the house. Vines climbed the exterior clapboard, fingering the paint, digging into the wood, and boring through the window frames. Clem followed Ethelred through what was once a garden but was now a chaos of hedge and overgrown willows. She took a pull on her pipe and squinted down the leash at the dog.

"Remember who saved you," she called out.

To which she received half a look before the dog's ear perked and tail stiffened. The bayberry brush and sedge near the back corner of the yard shook. Some vermin or other shifting around. Ethelred lunged at it, tightening the lead in Clem's hand and yanking her forward, until the two had punched through limbs and thistles. Clem's shin banged into stone, and she toppled over a low wall, landing in a thick layer of mud.

Still the dog tugged on the lead, panting and snorting, nose low to the curve of stone.

"Leave it, you damn thing." She set her feet and wrenched the leather, reeling it hand over hand.

A faint high laugh came from beyond the bushes, though Clem couldn't figure its direction. It was too early for anyone to be up. Maud would be snoring away the bottle of wine she drank, and Russell never lifted a lid until well past nine.

Ethelred, muscles taut and quavering, spun around, nose up to the air. She'd heard the laugh too.

Clem let out a breath and loosened the lead, giving the dog room to sniff and explore.

Her shin throbbed. She rubbed it, looking about. The place was more deer's thicket than grotto. It had once been something; she scraped at the mud with her boot heel, exposing the dull gray of granite slabs. Ethelred balanced on a wide board, sending it seesawing and sliding off a circular stone disk.

"Hup, dog." She scrambled up, winding the leash tight to keep the cur away from the cap's opening. The hole of the old well was crude, eighteen or so inches wide. Clem held her palm above it. A chill crawled over her skin and wrapped her wrists. Then came the stench of decay. She wrinkled her nose and stepped away, her boot slipping on the wet wooden board.

The laugh came again, ringing and then cut off.

Ethelred scrambled past her, the leash winding around her knees, threatening to topple her into the well. Clem let go the lead.

"Ethelred," she called. "Dog."

But Ethelred did not return as commanded. Not that Clem expected it.

She heard a sharp whistle from somewhere in the yard, and a woman cooing, "Come on, thing."

Clem pushed her way through the bramble, careful to keep hold of the willow branches so they wouldn't snap back. A length of thorny vine from God knew what bush caught her trousers and shirt cuff. She pulled the bastard vine out thorn by thorn, quite proud when the vine dropped and she'd avoided ripping the fabric. She quite liked her outfit.

A young woman of middling height and girth and frizzled brown hair tied in a bun strode across the yard, stopping in front of Clem.

"Who are you?" Clem asked.

"I'm Rose O'Malley and I work at the Parkers'. Who are you?"

"Well, Rose O'Malley, have you seen my dog?"

"You're a friend of hers?" She jerked her chin toward the house, then cut a look at Clem.

"I'm a . . ." Clem tucked her thumbs to her vest pockets and coughed, because she hadn't meant to be caught out like this. It was careless; she'd assumed no one would be around this early. She thought she'd take the dog and have a smoke and then be back inside before Hall Street stretched its arms and woke to the world.

It wasn't as if she hid, per se; she just wanted control over who saw her as what. The mourner at the séance. The widow come down from the open grave. The ne'er-do-well's wife. The lad dumb enough to bet on a dog. But here she stood in borrowed clothes staring at the next-door neighbor's maid—for even without the apron string hanging from the bundle she held, her rough and tumble hands and yellowed nails gave her away.

"You're one of them, aren't you?" Rose asked.

"One of who?"

"Them. No one wants her here, but here she is, and now here are you." Rose's voice snapped. "My sister Bridget, God rest her, spent a single week there and said it was enough."

Clem crossed her arms. "What was enough about it?"

"The things. The sounds. She said the maid before heard the father."

"Did she?"

"Moaning away, and he'd been dead in his grave three Christmases." She narrowed her eyes, pulled out her apron, and stuffed it under her other arm. "Hale he was and then he was dead."

"That's often how it happens." Clem slid a look over the maid's shoulder to the yard. Empty. "Did you see a dog? I need to find my—"

"I put it in your cellar. I saw you two come out of that house before the dog got loose." She tipped her head and stared down her nose. "You've not said who you are."

"Everyone and no one." Clem took out her pocket watch, twirled it, and flipped it open. "You'll be late, Rose O'Malley. And Mrs. Parker will think you're idling with a lad."

"You're not a lad."

"No, but her dining room window faces our side yard. And she will be sitting there wondering, 'Where is that lazy Irish girl?' Then you'll pop out of this wild garden and I'll shamble along behind, and idling will be the least of what your missus will think."

Her mouth formed an *O*, then she stuck her tongue between her teeth as if she were thinking it through.

"You know I'm right."

"No—"

"Run along and I'll wait a count of twenty. Then you wait a count of twenty, and when it's clear you yell out, 'The bat's in the belfry.'"

"You want me to say, 'The bat's in the belfry.'"

"Yes. And I'll know we're all in the clear."

Rose turned to leave, then threw a look over her shoulder at Clem. "Does she really conjure ghosts?"

"You're idling," Clem said.

The woman pushed through the weeds and her step wasn't as discreet as before. Clem took her tobacco pouch from her pocket. It had avoided the wet and muck. There was still the pipe to find and the dog to bathe. And feed. And train so it didn't bite her hand off.

And Maud to train.

"Bat's in the belfry!"

She sighed.

And maids who needed to learn to Mind Their Own Business.

Ethelred was not in the cellar. Clem peered at the bare dusty shelves and kicked aside a lump of empty potato sacks and then gave a whistle in the corner where the slant of sun didn't reach. No dog at all.

She pinched the bridge of her nose and wished Rose O'Malley a day of hell for leaving the cellar wide open. Now who knew where the damn thing had wandered. Clem wanted to spit, to be done with the beast. It didn't like her. That much was clear.

Clem bent down, hands to her knees, and squinted under each of the lowest shelves—just to be sure Ethelred hadn't burrowed into a corner and found herself stuck.

She shifted a crate. It caught on something on the floor. A hinge. Clem lifted the crate to the side and crouched down. A door had been cut into the floor, the seams tight, a carriage bolt shoved across the faceplate.

It squealed and fought as she jimmied it, then came loose when she gave it one last tug. With a grab at the cast iron ring pull, she swung open the door.

A gust of stale, musty air wafted up a set of narrow steps. Only four, and then a square room of rough wood walls and packed-earth floor. The space was just large enough to accommodate a simple slat-back chair. The sitter would have no opportunity to raise their head, for the ceiling came within inches of the chair's top rail.

But it was the wall that stopped Clem's breath. She stared at the gouges. Long gouges and short, splintered wood and the rust of blood in the fissures.

She keeled back, her hand flat to her chest as she tried to breathe, only to have her lungs fill with the dank, sodden air of the hole.

They had one like it at the Children's Home. Mrs. Bletham called it the Pondering Room. Girls who went in writhing came out quiet.

Clem had been there once for laughing at Mass, and then another for stealing Sister Anne's rosary. Which she hadn't. Ginny, with her knobbly knees and grasping claws, stole it. She liked to dangle it in the moonlight and watch the beads spin. "My brother's sick and I'm going to pray for him."

It was under Clem's pillow when Mrs. Bletham came looking, and Mrs. Bletham consigned Clem to the dark.

"Thou shalt not steal," she said. "You will ponder that."

"I'll watch your doll for you." Ginny twisted her fingers and stared at the doll Clem held. Then her hand snaked out to caress the golden hair.

"No." The doll was Clem's. She'd been handed it directly. The lady from the Society for Orphan Girls had brought it and candy and loads of hymns they were all required to sing. Clem knew all the words, so Clem got the doll. It was pretty, with its white dress and golden-haired cap, and just like the one she had wanted long ago at the fair. Little Maud.

Mrs. Bletham snatched it away. "Ginny will take good care of it while you think on your sins."

She stared now at the small space, her heart smacking her chest, then dropped the door closed with a thud. She'd come back and nail it shut. Nail in the memory of sitting in a box just like it, head cocked to the side and neck burning with ache, anger and vengeance playing behind her lids. So much time to plan one's revenge.

A shadow fell across her. "Any sort of repast down there? A moldy apple? A jar of pickles?"

Russell stood at the entrance, a sheet wound around his body. He gripped it at the neck and, thankfully, at the waist modestly.

"The neighbors can see you."

"Oh. Lucky them."

"What do you want?" Her breath was sour. She stood, brushing off the cobwebs and dirt, then pulled the crates back over the secret room.

"I'm going to faint. You're going to see a grown man swoon and faint right in front of you."

Her legs were heavy and numb as she shuffled up the cellar stairs. As if a hand had gripped her ankle and cut off the circulation as it tried to pull her back to the little square door. She blinked in the sudden bright light. The leaves of the willow sparkled with dew, looking much like a dress cut of diamonds. Russell danced like a faun in his sheet, weaving in and out of the tree's long branches. His hair was flat to his head on one side and a mass of coils on the other. She stopped him and wiped a line of dried spittle that caked the corner of his mouth to his chin.

He leapt like a stag and spun around her.

"You smell like a cask, Russell."

He pursed his lips to kiss her, widening his eyes and batting his black lashes.

"Don't even think . . ."

"Oh. I didn't—" They both turned to the voice. Maud stood on the kitchen step. Her mouth twisted and curled as if she were both shocked and about to be sick. Clem guessed by the color of her skin it was the latter.

"There's toast and tea." Maud swallowed and grimaced. "And the dog."

"Can we eat her?"

Clem smacked Russell in the stomach.

"Ouch. Don't hurt a starving man."

"Don't give the woman a show."

Russell stared down at his exposed body. His lips curled into a grin. "Well, look at that."

Clem clenched her jaw. "You're drunk. Cover yourself up."

He glowered at her, eyebrows pinched in the middle. "She didn't see—she's gone in. Look."

"Don't ruin things, Russell. Get dressed and get sober and act like a gentleman. If that's an act you can actually do."

"Since when have you become a nun?" The sheet rustled as he pulled it closed. He sauntered across the yard, dragging his fingers through his hair in an attempt to tame it. Then he slowed, turning back to her. "I don't always like being told what to do, Clem."

His step was light as he hopped up to the kitchen door. "Toast and tea, Miss Price. Now that will hit the spot."

Clem bit the inside of her lip. She reached for her pipe, digging and clawing at all the pockets, then remembered it was still lost. She circled around, smacking a heel to the ground.

A tapping against glass stopped her. Rose O'Malley peered down at her from a second-floor window.

Clem pushed her fists into her pockets and stared back up.

The maid gave a slow smile, then swung her head round, as if someone spoke to her from another room. Then she returned her attention to the window and lifted the frame enough to peek out. "I can see your pipe." She pointed to the thicket. "It's just there by the hedge."

"How much do you see from there?"

"Oh, I see a lot."

Clem stalked across the space between the houses, pushing through the overgrowth and finding herself between neat garden rows, mounded and ready for the planting of spring flowers. She spun back, the pebbles grinding underfoot.

"Damn."

Parlor. Study. Maud's window. Her father's. The attic.

All on display like a giant dollhouse.

Chapter Fourteen

Maud

Every muscle hurt. Every bit of her skin ached. Every blink was like a rake of sand across her eyeballs. Her tongue was the consistency of a stuffed cotton pillow. She awoke to so much chatter, she wondered if she'd sleepwalked and landed herself smack in the middle of Main Street. But she was in her own bed, with the door firmly locked and the curtains decidedly closed.

She willed herself still, not wanting the shift of a sheet to disturb those who whispered and muttered. Voices surrounded her, soft as the wings of a moth. One batted against her ear. Another coiled and took to the ceiling. Every which way the nattering came. But none of it made sense. Just guttering sound without meaning or words.

Then all at once they stopped.

She listened for them, but only heard Russell's door closing across the hall, and his whistle and hum as he stomped down the stairs.

"Oh God." She had said something about his eyes. Why had she said something about his eyes?

With much care, she sat up, glad for only a small twinge of nausea. She would ignore it. Simply ignore it. Yes. Pretend all is right in the world. She took a few tentative steps and then, when the room stopped swaying and had set itself aright, stood up. Tea. Tea and toast would do the trick.

She squared her shoulders and dressed. Took the stairs and only winced once at so much movement. Tea and toast. A bit of milk. She'd skip the butter. Too rich.

A flash of white flew by the window. Russell pranced around in a sheet with very little underneath. He reminded her of the Minotaur, shaking his head and pawing the ground with a bare foot. He spoke to someone just out of view. Maud cracked the window.

"I'm going to faint," he said. "You're going to see a grown man swoon and faint right in front of you."

Clementine walked into view and stood in front of him to stop his leaps and dance. She wiped her thumb on his chin, then ran a quick hand over his cheek. A lover's caress.

Maud should have known. It pained her—a sharp pain she hadn't expected. For wanting his attentions to be real and true. For knowing they weren't. He'd made her laugh; very few people did. So, of course, she'd acted like a fool. Father had kept this from happening. She couldn't fault William Marcus; he said men were made of ambition and rat dung, and to stay clear of them would be best for all involved. Loneliness, he said, will keep you sharp.

In the kitchen, the teacups rattled in their saucers as she set one in front of Russell and one at her own place. She winced at the sound of his slurps and the crunching acknowledgment that toast did save many a morning, and particularly this one. He shoved a whole piece into his mouth, not at all embarrassed at his manners. He chomped and swallowed, his gaze intent on her as she sipped her tea (tepid and weak).

Ethelred stared at her, too, though with a jowl of drool and mouth of bad breath. She sat with her good shoulder heavy against Maud's leg.

"She likes you." Russell wiped his mouth with a corner of the sheet. "You should keep her."

"I've never had a dog."

Russell raised his eyebrow. "I don't think you've much choice. Besides, Clementine's no good with dogs. To be honest, she's not that good with living things."

He smiled. Yes. Very, very white teeth. Maud's skin flushed hot and then cold. She pushed the chair back and took her cup to the sink. "We should bathe it. Well, after you've dressed." She rubbed her forehead and watched Clem stomp around the yard, bending to pick at things and then kick the dirt. She wore another pair of her father's trousers, ruined now, the rump a muddy, wet mess. "Where are her own clothes?"

She turned to Russell. He was on his hands and knees in front of the dog, tempting it with a slice of bread.

The kitchen door swung open, landing with a loud thwack. "I found my pipe." Clem's gaze narrowed on Russell and the dog and then caught Maud. "Did you open all the curtains?"

"Yes, I—"

"Well, don't." She leaned over the table and lifted the lid to the teapot. "None for me?"

"You're an impossible woman."

"Yes, I've been told as much before. Nevertheless . . ." She drummed the table with her fingers. "Do you have a sewing kit?"

"Why?"

"I'd like to stitch my name in the collar and waistband and—"

"Those are my father's clothes."

"They're of no use to him now, are they?" Clem made a face, as if Maud had said something extraordinarily strange.

"Orphanage habit." Russell tore off a hank of toast and offered it to Ethelred. "You should see how fast she eats."

"Don't feed the dog scraps, Russell."

"Just a bit of toast."

Clem's face darkened. She shifted her jaw from side to side. "It's my dog."

The room stilled, as if the air had been sucked out. Russell grabbed up his sheet and took his time getting to his feet. He tossed the bread to the table. "See what I mean, Miss Price?"

"Whatever rubbish he's told you, it's not true." Clementine tipped her head and gave a tight smile. "You look green and gray."

Maud swallowed. "Too much wine."

"You need a clear head for this business. Two glasses only. Sherry, not red. Agreed?"

"How big a glass?" Russell asked.

Clem's lashes fluttered and then slowed before her eyes snapped to Maud's. "Agreed?"

"Yes."

"Good."

"Good."

Clem sauntered around the table, picked up the dog's leash, and wound it around her palm. "I want you to write a note to Mrs. MacGregor with your sympathies and great appreciation for her trust in you." She reached out to Ethelred, palm up and waiting. "Return her money."

"What?" Russell stared at her.

"Do you need to clean out your ears? Russell's got wax buildup, dog." She scratched under Ethelred's jaw. "Return it and tell her she and any of her acquaintances are welcome at any time. You do not request a fee. You will never request a fee."

"I already do that. You scolded me about that. When we first met."

Clem ran her thumb on the dog's head. "Take it to her in person. Remember why you do what you do. Comfort and solace. Comfort and solace."

Clem's scratching slowed. She ran her thumb along the scabbing edges of Ethelred's ear. Maud bit back bile and covered her eyes, pressing her fingers to each temple.

"You will take it," Clem said, and it wasn't a request or a question. It was a command, much like telling the dog to sit.

Maud peeked through her fingers at Ethelred. The poor thing shook and stilled, cycling between the anxieties of Clem ministering to her shoulder (with a napkin, no less) and then cooing at her.

"I'm not your dog," Maud blurted.

"Did I say you were?"

"You are being rather . . . commanding." Russell crossed his legs, thankfully aware of the sheet. He tucked it along his thigh and gave Maud a pious face. "It will be a lovely gift for the woman, a bright light in her miserable, lonely day."

"You don't know she's lonely," Maud said. She found her mood sinking into a mound of nettles. She wished the two—and the dog—would disappear as quickly as the voices had this morning. She wished she hadn't had so much wine. She wished Matthias would just make an appearance and she could set them packing. Clementine wouldn't really write a letter to the *Banner*. There was nothing she could say that couldn't be refuted. Maud could send a rebuttal, for wasn't her reputation sterling? Hadn't she once been investigated and the newsman himself crumpled as his own mother reached across the divide to him? Why, he'd cried like a baby. Ripped his notes in two right then and there, and Father had tossed them in the fire. Her word counted for something. Her name counted for something.

Or had.

Hence the presence now of a maddening woman and her dog and a half-dressed man.

"I," Clem declared, now standing and staring directly at Maud, "will be in the attic. Out of your way, should you need room to converse with your spirits. I've written you your tasks; the paper is on the dining table. Yours too, Russell."

"Woof," he said.

Clem's eyes narrowed, but she did not respond. "You wanted a contract, Miss Price. It's on the table for your review. We'll sign this evening. You can have it witnessed if you wish."

"Can I?"

"If you know someone you trust, of course."

"Of course."

∾

Meditate. 45 min.

Write down spirit interactions (Seth?) and if none: Repeat meditative state

Compose letter to Mrs. MacG (see example)

1p Deliver above

2p Psychical Society Mtg. Mr. Garrison to speak on mesmeric fluidity. It's nonsense but clap and agree.

3:30p Return for illuminated hands demonstration

Maud smacked her desk and stared out the cracked window. She knew how to use a planchette. For God's sake, what did the woman take her for?

Meal

Free time for bible reading or other such uplifting activity

PS—Russell will be using your father's room as the guest room is cold as a tomb

PPS—I have not forgotten Maisie. Patience is a virtue.

She crumpled the paper and dropped her head to her hands, elbows puckering the contract. This was Father's domain. He wrote them, he read them, he signed them. Now it was her turn. The contract was simple enough: *an agreement between parties in exchange for services rendered. Thirty percent of proceeds to be remanded to Clementine Watkins . . . Expenses tallied and reimbursed. All theatrical effects the property of . . . in all items to receive the approval of . . . until all parties satisfied.*

Maud's stomach cramped. She rubbed it, regretting the third cup of tea. *Well,* she thought, *it was this or the pauper's house.*

She smoothed the commandments and folded the note to her purse, next to the duly transcribed letter to Mrs. MacGregor.

The day, indecisive as April was, required a hat that would not find its ruin in the rain. A good strong wool with a wide brim would do the trick. She opened her wardrobe and ran a finger over the hatboxes. Clementine wasn't the only one with organization skills; each hatbox had been inked with its type and the date purchased, and there sat the blue wool right where she'd expected to find it.

She peeked at the mirror long enough to set and pin the hat, then turned to the door. The list would be tackled. Minus the meditation, which had made her headache ever so much worse.

Russell stood like a sentry just across the hall. He had dressed, thank the Lord, though his chartreuse vest gleamed bright enough to hurt Maud's eyes.

"Mr.—"

He put a finger to his lips, then pointed at the ceiling. His eyebrow lifted, awaiting some response.

She nodded, which made him smile and gesture more grandly. A sweep of a hand to the staircase. Then his index finger and middle finger mimicked a walk. A hand to his chest. A roll of the wrist and a bow to her.

The giggle spilled from her lips before she could stop it.

He swung his gaze to the upper floor, stretching his lips in a grimace of great fear and pain. But the attic door did not open. He shrugged and stuck out his elbow for Maud to take.

～⑨

"I am glad you allowed me to accompany you, Miss Price." Russell held onto the brim of his tall hat and blinked against the gusting wind. "Old Town is no place for a woman of your sort, not at all."

Maud combed aside a tress of her hair, tucking it behind her ear before clamping her hand to the top of her own hat. The brim bent to cover her face, then snapped back and threatened to fly away and never be found again. "April is a pesky month."

"It cannot make up its mind."

She snuck a look at him. He walked with such confidence, chin high, mouth curled in a small smile, as if he was carrying on an amusing conversation with himself. He was quick to tip his hat to passersby; she noted that he tipped it further to the ladies and that his gaze lingered a second more than necessary when they returned a nod.

"You have never been married, Mr. Sprague?"

He gave a quick shrug of the shoulder. "It seems, Miss Price, that the marrying path has not been laid for me."

"Nor for Miss Watkins, it seems."

"We make an excellent pair that way."

"Why her?"

"Why not?"

"Most men don't work for women; they'd find it—"

"I don't work for her. She works for me."

"But the contract—"

"Yes, yes. It makes her happy to have her name there. But I'm in charge of the business and the bank account is under my name. Which you noticed at the bottom of the document, I assume."

"I . . ."

"Sprague & Co., Limited. Sprague. Not Watkins. You should always read your contracts."

"I took a glimpse."

"She works for me." He gazed down at her, then back up to the street. "The wind is miserable."

Maud worked her jaw. He was right; she hadn't noticed. She just assumed. It was a reasonable assumption, given Clementine and her braggadocio. She tucked her hands under her armpits, for the gloves she wore did nothing against the bite of the wind. A carriage sat along the curb, the traces jangling. The two horses' tails whipped one way and then the other, and the beasts stomped in exasperation. The driver sat hunched atop, dozing with his mouth slung open.

How nice it would be to fetch a ride. Maud had half a mind to open the envelope and purloin Mrs. MacGregor's cash. She bit her lip and leaned into the wind, gripping Russell's arm, and the two passed the cab with only one shared look of longing for its warmth behind them.

A rustling noise, deeper than the blustery wind, passed by her and then circled back. She stopped stock-still on the sidewalk.

"Would you not walk so . . ." A man in a checked coat shuffled around her, clipping her shoulder with the corner of the crate he carried. "Watch yourself."

"You should beg her pardon," Russell said, "not the other way around."

"Is that so?" The man spit a long stream of tobacco juice by Russell's feet.

"That was uncalled for."

Zhezhezhezhe. The voice sawed nonsense against Maud's ear. If only it was quiet. "Be quiet."

Russell's eyes went round as he turned to her, leaving the man to stomp away, pausing once to glare at Maud.

Listentoyourlistenzhezhezhe.

She strode to an empty doorway, tucking herself into the corner, resting her forehead against the brick and cupping her ears. Her skin pricked cold along her arms, the chill racing across her shoulders and down her spine.

Listentoyourlistenchild. Listen to yourzhezhe. The voice susurrated then, like a crumbling of leaves in a fist. *Ever watchful child. Ever . . .*

A warm hand touched her. She spun around. "Don't touch me."

Russell stepped back, his hand frozen in midair. He shot a glance each way down the street, then rubbed the top of his head.

"I almost . . . they almost . . ." She punched her thighs with her fists. "Now there's nothing."

"You really do hear them."

"Of course I do." Her head ached. She pushed her thumbs to the soft skin under her brow. "Did I speak?"

"Something spoke." He frowned. "Just like that? A spirit just shows up out of the blue and—"

"Yes, sometimes." Her heart thumped. She took in a deep breath and held it. The doorway echoed with voices, high and low and none making sense, but still a glorious chaos of sound. She let her breath out with a laugh. "They're all around. I heard them this morning, too, before—and Seth Stoddard. Perhaps he's . . . perhaps Matthias . . . oh!" She squeezed her hands and pressed them to her stomach. "Mr. Sprague, do you think . . . Why do you look at me so?"

"You are cured."

"Is it possible?"

"Of course it is." He reached for her, then hesitated. "Although—"

"Although what?"

"They aren't yet on the bit, so to speak. You do need them to mind."

"Yes." Her bubble of elation burst, leaving just the throb of her head. The spirits no longer nattered about. They had slipped away, leaving only echoes of the busy street in their wake.

And yet, it meant hope. She needed to sit and listen for them. She bit the inside of her lip again, for wasn't that Clementine's first commandment? *Meditate. And if you fail, do it again.*

"I think I've upset you."

"No." The clock tower intoned the hour. One o'clock. "Mrs. MacGregor—"

"Nearly there."

She took the elbow he proffered.

A few spits of rain mottled the sidewalk and packed-earth street. How quickly one stepped from the new town to the old. Just at the corner the building had been a fine red brick and the window of the mercantile gleamed with pots and stoves and a rack of porcelain dishware. There was dishware here, too, broken and crushed in piles near the hollowed shells of the old mills. Spindly tufts of grass fingered through cracked mortar, yellowed and dead from the long winter.

Russell hopped a stream of muddy water that sliced the street, then picked her up by the waist and lifted her over.

"You are light as a feather," he said and kept his hands circled to her waist.

"You can let go." Maud stiffened and lifted her chin.

"Ah. Yes. My apologies." He cleared his throat and set his hands to the back of his hips. "Here you are."

"Are you coming in?"

"Oh, no. I have my own list to follow."

"But—"

"I find it easiest to let Clementine think she's in charge. The world is much nicer that way. I'll meet you right here in, say, an hour?" His mouth pursed tight. "Sixty minutes, Miss Price. Then we shall partake of the spiritual realm and all matters without matter." The mud squelched around his boot as he turned away. "Well, that is . . . these are my best boots." He gave a small wave and sauntered up a side street.

⁓

"Oh no, Miss Price, I can't take back a penny of that." Mrs. MacGregor waved the letter, the banknotes clipped between the paper and her thumb. She smiled, a great wide smile that loosened the wrinkles around her lips and deepened them around her eyes.

Maud's stomach roiled. She couldn't look at Mrs. MacGregor, at how her gaze glistened with the zeal of a believer. How many times had she seen it before? The woman buzzed and glowed with fervor. She touched Maud's shoulder, as if touching a sacred idol.

"But I leave you out on the porch. Come in, come in."

Maud stared at the rutted street and the cottages that clustered together, roofs overlapped, some sunken. A fat gray cat sat in a clump of weeds and licked itself. Then it pinned its ears and dropped flat.

"I don't want to keep you," she said. "I should have written first. Or at the very least left a calling card."

"No no no no." Mrs. MacGregor ushered her into the parlor, bony hand around Maud's wrist and leaving her no choice but to sit on the worn sofa. The woman's grip did not leave Maud. She sat beside her and shook her head as if Maud were the Second Coming.

Which caused a horrible dark guilt to crawl its way under Maud's skin.

"Do you see him now?"

"I don't see . . ."

But the woman's lip trembled.

"Can you try?"

The room held very little. The sofa in faded paisley. A round table and oil lamp. A quilt hung over the mantel, patterned in diamonds of rags. A framed photograph. A man dressed in his Sunday best, gaunt cheeks and long white mustache, hands crossed to his chest, shoes shined and so black against the linen-lined coffin.

She dipped her head. The rag rug was a mix of blues and reds, pocked with burn marks from a pipe. Mr. MacGregor had, in life, paced as he smoked. The rug had not been turned to hide it. No, Mrs. MacGregor left it as it was. Waiting his return from the long forever night.

A rasp and thump came from the next room.

Mrs. MacGregor patted her arm. "I think I've left the window open." She stood, a wince as she straightened. "Age is a curse, it is, it is." She hobbled from the room, leaving Maud and the memento mori of Mr. MacGregor to fend for themselves.

Maud picked up the photo, turning it to the gray light that came from the single window. She pressed the image between her palms and closed her eyes.

But all she felt was the smooth glass and the leather frame, and all she heard was the old woman's shuffle from one room to another.

"I married him first spring I turned sixteen. He was a stone mason even then; followed his father in the trade. And we live in a house of wood."

Maud opened her eyes.

"Lost two babes—one at four days and the other in the war. Thomas, and Webb, who was at Andersonville Prison and died like the others of starvation and cruelty. Sometimes I think I hear him cry for me at night, for we was closer than close." She twisted her hands until her knuckles went white. "Theo rode to Macon and brought him home. Cut his tombstone. Only time we'd not supped together all those years. Only time."

"Theo is right behind you. His voice is very raspy."

"I told him. It's what comes with a pipe. I said, 'Theo, it's ruined the carpet and now you can't sing a note without a cough.'"

"He still sups with you," Maud said. "Leave him a plate and fork."

~ා

"Thank you for the tea. It was very kind." She slipped the money under the lace on the mantel and rubbed her gloved finger over the photograph. "You are always welcome, Mrs. MacGregor," she whispered. "When you miss your Theo."

The woman crossed her arms over her chest and pinned her eyes shut. She bowed forward as if her grief would bend her in two. "God is with you, child."

Maud opened her mouth to speak, then thought better of it. She instead donned her cloak, gave Mrs. MacGregor a kiss on her plum cheek, and took her leave.

The wind was like a sudden slap. Russell waved his hat from across the way. She hurried toward him, careful to hop the ruts.

He reached in his hat, as a magician did when scrounging for the poor rabbit crammed under a false bottom, and pulled out a rose. It was still in bud, white petals tipped with red, as if he'd picked it and swirled it in paint. He ran the flower under his nose, pulling in the scent, then handed it to Maud.

She mimicked him. Put the bud to her nose. But there wasn't a scent at all. Nor were there thorns. Just a stem of green leaves, some mottled, some curled brown at the edges.

All silk. As was the rose. An exquisite replica.

If she hadn't brought it close, it would have fooled her. "It will never wilt," he said.

She wanted to both showcase it in a vase and hide it in the slop bin. "It is a wonder."

"Yes, it truly is." He plucked it from her hand and slipped the stem in the buttonhole of her cloak. "A wonder."

Harrowboro Gazette
April 27th

Curiosity took me to 328 Hall Street on Tuesday last, to participate in a séance held by Miss M. Price, once known as the Maid of Light and in whose gentle hands I have much to laud.

The decline of Miss Price's powers is as much rumor as it is errantly false. Indeed, without the huckstering personality of her now deceased father, William Marcus Price, who—had you the opportunity to see Miss Price in her heyday—sorely inhibited the clarity of her visions, now the true soul of the woman sings out. Now we have Miss Price in a simple parlor room, with one table for six and an overflow seating of eight, all of which seats were taken by brethren and the curious alike.

We all began with a song to unite us and call the guides and energies to us. Miss Price led the ersatz choir. She is of earnest features, small and soft-spoken, her gaze often turned to the spheres that inhabit her inner world, and thus by the time the music ended, we all felt she was prepared for any communication of spirit during the sitting.

And indeed we were visited. A young Dutch tulip farmer by the name of Jan Hoerner came to call, a fine fellow of good humor who showed himself briefly and took time to pat Mrs. V—'s shoulder and leave a rose for Miss Price, as he said he loved her and would wait at the gates of Summerland for her final visit and take her hand in matrimony before a bevy of angels.

Mrs. V— was visited by her uncle, who chose to write a short note of his contentment and joy to be with his Clare again. Though we were not privy to his relationship with Clare, it did seem strong and pure. This put much faith in myself that Heaven is as wondrous as our religions and Miss Price show to us.

For those who doubt, I urge you to make an appointment with Miss Price forthwith and quick. Due to her health and the immense strain on her by those calling from the spirit world, she

has curtailed sittings to Tuesday and
Friday evenings only. I have heard
through various friends and colleagues
that multiple spirits came to the second Friday sitting to play tambor and
flute.

Martin Knox

Harrowboro Gazette
May 8th

To refute Mr. M. Knox: Maud Price, the
so named "Maid of Light," and her ilk
(of which there are lamentably too many
in our H'boro town) are but deceiv-
ers of the vulnerable, offenders of
the Word, and bilkers of cash. They
take the mantle of Prophesier from the
shoulders of Ezekiel and Zechariah and
scores of others well-known to the true
devout and twist the Throne of Heaven
to their own dictates and direction.

Heaven, to remind Mr. Knox of his
Good Book and the Book of Revelation
specifically, is not an Otherworld of
flying ghosts and disembodied voices
(that sound so similar from parlor to
parlor one wonders if a traveling thes-
pian has been hired at a reduced rate
by a cabal of so named mediums and
clairvoyants), but Heaven, sir, will
come to earth as a New Jerusalem.

The notoriety these charlatans hold proudly besmirches the good folk in attendance who do honestly seek comfort and connection and wish to assuage their inquisitiveness as to Heaven's shape and form—and be assured their beloved departed no longer suffer.

We are given reports from "The Beyond" that all is wonder and good life and "more will be told if you come again—my energies only hold a few minutes, so come next Wed-Fri-Mon and see!" And thus more lucre greases the palms of these fakes and more poor citizens lose their Christian beliefs.

Be aware that Miss Price and her evenings are as duplicitous as Mrs. H. Martin and Mr. Hopkins, even if she does not attempt such feats as levitation and mesmerism.

If I had my say in the ways of the world, all such swindlers would find themselves in the New Hampshire State Prison.

Argus Jackson

Harrowboro Gazette
May 11th

I am a simple woman, but I can attest that my Theo did come speak to me and still does and that is due to Miss Price.

Mrs. Eunice MacGregor

Chapter Fifteen

Maud

"No. Again."

Maud stuffed the coin back to her skirt pocket—the third one along her right hip. Clem had sewn three such secret pockets, the precision of stitches so fine, Maud had difficulty finding them even when she held the skirt two inches from her nose.

The opening was very small; Maud could just wriggle her pinky in to retrieve the penny.

Clem called today's lesson "The Gift." The goal, as with Mrs. MacGregor, was to give the sitter an object of much value to them, but not to anyone else at the table. The awe and flabbergast, Clem stated, leads to a bubbling of memories and associations—in other words, the guest conjures their ghost themselves.

When Maud asked where the objects came from, Clem waved her off. "You pay me for that. Your job is merely to deliver the goods."

The scheme gave Maud the feeling she was part of a nefarious gang. Which, in addition to a fizz of guilt, gave her a buzz of excitement.

Clem's schedule for the household spared no time to breathe. Activities were communicated via missives tacked to the door. Clem herself remained in the attic most of the day, leaving only to walk the dog before dawn and in the dark of night. It was only in the early evenings she deigned to make an appearance in the house, as if she were a pasha and all had to stop whatever else they were doing to listen to her wisdom.

Russell had been assigned his activities too. He spread them across the dining table one morning.

Inquire at the Orpheum Theater about rates.

Replace the wallpaper in the library, the false wall shows.

More meat scraps for the dog. Roast chicken for her, breast only.

Close the curtains.

Bring the post first thing.

"Yours?" he asked.

Practice.

False boxes to open. High voices and low. Tipping the table with a knee. Writing tablets with secret drawers and how to switch one paper for another. "I designed it myself," Russell told her, and only checked once to see if Clem had suddenly taken root in the room.

Evenings were spent in front of the fire, sipping wine and playing hands of cards with Russell, who was fiercely competitive at cribbage. Who knew where Clementine went?

Days, though, were spent passing each other in the hall, each holding their commandments from on high.

Once she'd stopped, a sheaf of papers pressed to her chest, and stared at Russell. "She rewrote my speech to the Psychical Society."

"I will help you rehearse it," he said.

"I don't wish to bother—"

"She provided me the possible questions you'll receive."

"Oh."

"Indeed. Oh."

And instead of cribbage, Maud memorized and recited, and she found she liked Russell. Odd as it was and he was, she liked him very much.

She turned her attention back to Clem. "Where's Mr. Sprague tonight?"

"At a card game. Or the theater. Or a tavern. You're not concentrating."

Clem moved beside her at the séance table, hands crossed in front of her, one eyebrow cocked, her unlit pipe stuck between her lips. She wore an old dinner jacket of William Marcus's and had welcomed Maud to the table in a moth-ridden silk top hat that must have come from the attic. It sat jauntily on her head, her hair tied back in a loose bun. She looked much like the leader of a pirate gang.

"All you need is an eyepatch," Maud said.

The eyebrow went up another notch. "Hand over your treasures, wench, or I'll—"

"All right, all right." Maud sighed and dug again in the pocket. The coin refused to budge.

"No."

"I'm barely moving."

"You have to be exact. Like a ballet dancer. It's all choreography. Not digging around in your pocket and huffing in frustration."

"I was not huffing."

"You were."

"I can barely get my finger—"

"You're going to have to try harder."

"Maybe something else?"

"No."

"No? Just no?"

Clem spread her hands and slid them across the table. She turned her palms up. "Here. I bring you nothing." Then in a swift motion she turned her palms to the table, tapped her thumb twice, and lifted her hands.

An earring lay before Maud. A simple gold teardrop with a ruby encased in diamond chips.

"Where did you get that?"

"It means something to you?"

"It was my mother's. She searched for it everywhere. I looked for it, I . . ." She turned her gaze to the dark hall, the memory of her mother crystal clear, the earrings dangling. How she touched them throughout the day. An unconscious habit, but it set them to swing and the rubies to catch the light. Mother would stop at the hall mirror, give a pleased smile, and continue with her duties.

"She wore those when she was happy," Maud said. "Then she lost the one."

"And that made her unhappy?"

Maud's gaze snapped to the earring. "Where did you find it?"

"You have the match, don't you?"

"In my jewelry box."

"Well, now you have a set." She leaned forward, a penny held between her index and middle fingers. "And here's the coin from your pocket."

Maud clutched at her skirt, turning the empty pocket inside out. "How did you—"

"Little gifts, Miss Price, bring great rewards."

Maud cradled the earring in her hand, felt the stone warm on her skin. Then she clipped it to her ear.

"Now *you* look like the pirate."

"Quiet." She plucked the penny from Clem's fingers and began again.

The following night, Maud lay on the kitchen table, her hair pulled tight into a bun, nothing but a sheet over her chest. She stared at Clem. She stared at the tin bucket she held.

"It doesn't hurt. I promise on my life it will feel slightly warm and then slightly comforting."

She was certain that, had she not acquiesced to this, Clem would have daubed the wet cotton strips on her face as she slept and not minded if she breathed or not. She held two straws of rye grass between her palms.

"Put them in your nose, now."

Maud did as she was told.

"Good. Now we begin." Clem dipped a strip in the gypsum, held it before Maud, and bent close. "You should close your eyes."

"Yes, I—oh!" The strip landed heavy on her forehead. She felt the prods and pokes as Clementine spread it over the bridge of her nose. "You sure it won't pull my eyebrows?"

"I've done this a hundred times. Trust me."

There wasn't much else Maud could do. The strips were comforting at first, warm and supple. Clem hummed as she worked, stopping to inform Maud where the next strip would land, lulling her into a gray-tinged drowsiness.

"Do not smile."

She felt Clem's fingers against her lips as she molded the gypsum-soaked cloth. It tickled. She wanted to smile.

"Just think," Clem murmured, "of all the famous and infamous whose faces have been cast for eternity. Mary, Queen of Scots. Marie Antoinette. Martin Luther. Robespierre."

Death masks.

Clem pressed strips to her ears, muffling her voice and the hums. The gypsum hardened and shrunk. Her head was jostled as Clem added layers.

The reeds were her only access to air. She pulled in as much as she could, but it didn't reach her lungs. She grabbed out to stop Clem, to have her crack the mask off. She grew light-headed, then jerked as if her body were falling into infinite space. She spread her hand to her stomach; she was hyperventilating, that was all. If only she could slow her breaths. Then a soft hand lay atop hers, and she stopped spinning in darkness, her breaths slowing, the inhalations and exhalations intentional.

The murmurs continued in wave upon wave, blue inflections and red when the cadence changed. Clem's voice or the stream of spirits that slipped between this world and Summerland, Maud did not know. She could not answer, her mouth molded shut and her inner voice mute. She could only watch the sounds slide and bleed, split and waver. Form and unform in shapes that resembled humans. Cloaks and umbrellas and wild feathered hats and yellowed lace. Then a voice near her ear, sweet with clover, impossible to forget. *Isn't it beautiful?*

Her mother's cheek against hers. *Listen.*

"Beautiful." Which came out a moan and jolted her from the rush of color and back to the dull gray of her encased lids.

A knock echoed and drummed on the casting. Then came the removal of the mold, Clem shifting and tugging until it popped free, the reeds dragging against Maud's nostrils and leaving her to breathe freely.

She sat up, blinking against the white light glaring through the windows. Clem held the cast up, turning it to Maud. "You will forever be young." She cradled it, walking across to lower it to a box of straw.

"What's next?" Maud asked.

"More gypsum, some sandpaper, and glow paint." Her smile was as wide as a cat's after a tumbler of milk. "Now your hands."

～೨

The river of color did not return, no matter how long Maud sat in silence. Nor did her mother's voice. Sometimes she heard a muttering, or words that hung like gossamer thread, thin and watery. Other times, the sound was the snore of the dog.

She smacked the armchair. "Bother. Bother and damn."

Ethelred awoke from her sleep at the side of Maud's chair, stretched and scratched under her ear. She gave Maud's hand a lick, then circled around and lay down again with a large huff.

A shoe nearly hit Maud's head. She heard it fly by her ear, watched it land in the potted fern.

"Sorry." Russell's voice came muffled from behind the new false wall. Then a hidden door, just to the left of the séance table, flapped open. He stuck his head out the small square. "Apologies."

"Why do you have to throw a shoe?"

He made a long face. Stared at her, then at the shoe. "It's thrilling."

"I don't think it's thrilling to have a man's shoe stuck in the fern."

"It will glimmer."

"What's the point?"

"I aimed for the door. Clem can pick it up."

"If she is here."

"Right."

Clementine had not, in fact, been here. Not in the last four sittings, not at breakfast save to grab up sausage and a bowl of water for the dog, not at all the rehearsals with the false wall and mirrors, and not ever at night.

Her notes had been there. Her notes were always there. Tacked to the door. *Listen for ghosts. Practice handkerchief routine.* Folded under her teacup. *Watch the mirror at the top of the steps. Double-check your reflection shines in hall mirror. Clumsy last night, practice planchette 50x.* Stuffed in the brim of her favorite hat. That one still riled Maud.

I borrowed the green hat with the finch. It was definitely worth the money. Which you earned, so no guilt.

As Clementine predicted, the evening sittings filled with guests. Not just the table itself, but also the seats that lined the wall. Letters of introduction came, to be answered by her hand, though Russell dictated.

New cards were made. New advertisements to the *Gazette*: *The Maid of Light Has Returned. Tues & Fri sittings. Curiosity and an appointment the only requirements.*

At first, Clementine sat to her right, acting as just another believer. She came in the guise of a cousin, Mrs. Turlock. She arrived earlier than the other guests, making certain to take the spot. Gave Maud's hand a quick shake to carry on, or a quick touch with the stub of her index finger when Maud's voice quivered.

And when Maud's throat dried, as it did often, because she still had a small pang of conscience, the grieving Mrs. Turlock moaned and pointed this way and that. "Sister Matilda, do not forsake me!" And "I see Mrs. Bletham clear as if she sat next to Mr. D——." Which gave Maud time to shift her pages aside and make the contraption spit out a letter or two. Then Russell took over with floating hands and orbs of light. And after it all Maud took a wine bottle to her room and stamped out the whole of it in drink.

Last night the man beside her—a Mr. Markle—spent the evening accidentally rubbing his shin against hers and even went so far as to grab her thigh, causing the table to rise and fall with a thump.

Clementine should have been there. It wasn't fair of her not to be. Maud had barely mastered the coin trick, had only conjured one or two small items—posies and ribbons.

She had to admit the effect worked. That one object brought tears and gasps. The postbox overflowed but, more importantly, so did the bowl subtly situated by the front door.

Tonight she had been given no objects. The box she had come to rely on, the one Clem set just inside her bedroom door, was empty, save for a single note:

Let us have some failures, Clementine wrote. *No medium is without them.*

A sharp click of dog nails came as Ethelred left the parlor and took to the hall. The beast looked in at Maud, and then howled.

Maud jumped in her seat. She'd rarely heard the dog bark; now here she was, baying at some moon in her head. Then Ethelred stopped, sat on her haunches, and stared again at Maud.

"You speak."

Ethelred answered with another yip.

"I think she wants out," Russell said from behind the wall.

"Are we allowed to take her out during the day?"

"I have no note from on high that we can't." Russell closed the little door, which returned the painting of winter geese to its proper place.

"Do you need going out?" Maud leaned from her chair and patted her skirt.

The dog padded over.

"You're a drooly thing." She took her handkerchief from her cuff and rubbed the dog's jowls.

Russell pushed open a thin length of wall and sidled out. He stretched his arms wide, twisting his torso one way and then the other, dislodging the tail of his shirt. "By summer I won't be able to breathe in that space."

The dog rested her head on Maud's lap. She peered up with her strange yellow eyes and sighed.

"Don't let Clem see that," Russell said. "She doesn't like to share things."

"Where does your mistress go for hours and hours?" She ran her finger under the dog's half ear. It was velvet soft, the scar where it had ripped smooth as silk.

Russell sank to one of the chairs in the "peanut gallery," as he called it, draping his arm across the backs.

Maud could feel him watch her. Her skin pricked along her neck and down her spine. She gave a small shiver.

"What is it like, when the spirits really come?"

"Loud." She brushed her hand over Ethelred's shoulders. "Like putting your ear to a French horn and having all the notes blown out at once."

"And Matthias?"

"He was like a conductor, I suppose. He gave the notes their right order of play."

The sun dimmed outside the window as a cloud scudded by.

"We're not all fakes, Mr. Sprague."

Ethelred's eyelids drooped as Maud stroked her back.

The light returned, sharp on the planes of Russell's face. He frowned but did not look away. It was as if he were puzzling something out. Puzzling her out. "Why did he leave you?"

She curled her hand and sat back. "Why would he stay when the Otherworld beckons?"

"Like heaven."

"It *is* heaven, Mr. Sprague."

He ran his hand through his hair. "Why, then, do they not all go? I'd pound at the door to be let in."

"We hold them here. We the living. Love. Guilt. Even fear. We're often the prison. Or the other way around, too, should they have something to say to us." Her mind slipped to the figure that hovered and whispered behind Clem the first day they'd met, here in this room. A soul clung tight to her. "Sometimes they cannot let go."

"Unfinished business."

"Yes."

"Never met someone who didn't have that." He stood. Ethelred flinched at the movement and kept an eye on him. "All right, then. Let's work through some bits. Get some of the poor dead souls' business dusted and done."

"Don't make fun of me."

His smile dropped and he gazed at her with somber eyes. "Oh, Maud. I would never do that. Your ghosts need as much solace as the mourners."

"Sometimes more."

"Yes. But it's the living I can help."

"It's not all for the money?"

"I am not ashamed of saying the money is an excellent byproduct of our service. However, one of the most lovely things about working with Clem is the end result. Watching someone go home gladdened, or at least amused." He picked up the shoe and tossed it from one hand to the other. Then he held it up to her. "Take this shoe. It is not merely a shoe. It has a mate. A mate that longs for it. This piece of leather contains special powers."

She shook her head. How mercurial Russell was. One minute a clown and the next as serious as a priest. She could not look away. It was like watching the acts of a play performed in high gear. Like watching two or three mixed and matched for the fun of it.

"Pay attention to the footwear," he intoned.

She stifled a laugh. "It looks like a simple shoe."

"No no no, my dear. The mate to it is still sitting in Mr. Dreyer's hall closet." He threw himself into the chair opposite her and set the shoe on the center of the table. "This is his seat tonight, by the way."

"Mr. Dreyer lost his son."

"Indeed. Carl."

"Whose shoe . . ."

". . . this is." He lifted his eyebrows. "Mr. Dreyer, in the depths of despair, drops his head to his hands and wails 'Where oh where did I lose that shoe? My last link to my boy.'"

He leapt to his feet, and in one long stride reached the hidden door, then slipped himself inside.

A square opened in the wall. Out floated the papier-mâché face of a young child. It wavered as if lost or searching for something.

"Father?" Russell mimicked a sniveling young child's voice.

Then the face turned its eyeless gaze on her. Which would have startled, save Russell's thumb and forefinger wiggled in the empty sockets.

"That is my shoe. Who took my shoe, and why is it here?"

The mask flew back. The square shut tight. Russell crept to the table and sat. Then he smacked the back of his hand to his forehead and peered into the room as if it were as dark as midnight. "Here here. Ho ho! My son!"

Maud laughed out loud. "Stop."

"Sh. This is a serious séance. Do not break the spell."

She covered her mouth, but the laugh bubbled out. "Sorry."

One hand covering his eyes, the other arm slung back in a melodramatic pose, he jumped from the chair. "What? What be that object on the table? Why, my heavens and hells! It smells of my Carl's feet!"

He lifted the shoe, cupping it between his hands as if it were the most fragile of objects. "Be not lonely, shoe. Now I have two of you to remind me of my dear departed boy."

"And what happens when he returns home and finds it's not a match at all? That it's only a prop?"

Russell blinked. "It's his shoe."

All Maud's mirth drained away. "Where did you get it?"

"Well, Clem—"

"Stole it."

Russell opened his mouth to answer, but then frowned and tossed the shoe to the floor. "Never mind." He gestured to the table. "Let's go over the letters."

She stared at the planchette sitting in wait, the letters ready for her review. The device had been so cleverly made, the concealment of the prewritten notes near impossible to distinguish. And should someone reach for it, a skeptic or one overcome with grief, the press of a small button rolled the evidence right away.

"Nothing yet for Mr. Sullivan," she said.

Russell shrugged. Then he reached for the stack, lifting the corners with his thumb. "There's a dried posy here. Don't let it slip. Mrs. Gardiner expects them."

"I don't want to use the planchette tonight."

"Then don't."

"No."

"All right." He tucked his fingers in his pockets and walked each side of the room, perusing the walls, stopping to check cabinet doors, running the nail of his pinky along a nearly invisible seam. "In fact, I agree with you. Lose the contraption. It takes too long, and if there's one thing I know, it's not to leave gaps in the show. I don't know why Clem insists on it."

"Have you always done her bidding?"

Russell, who had been bent to peer in the fireplace, straightened and stared at her. "I don't do her bidding."

"You follow her orders as much as I."

"Well, between you and me," he said, with a glance to the open hall door, "I let her believe so. But I, too, have artistic control. In fact, I don't like to boast, but I have a better bead on dramatics." He pulled out a chair across from her, gave a wary look at the dog, then sat and crossed his legs. "But while we have the planchette, you should read the letters, just to make sure you know the—"

"I do read them." Maud remained still, her muscles taut with a sudden anger. "How does Clementine get this information? How does she know all this? Franny Gardiner hanged herself in her cellar. She was seventeen. Seventeen. Why? Because her father kept her from the man she loved. Because she was ruined. He came here for what? Forgiveness? That's the letter she wants me to read. *You were right and good to stop me, Father. I could not see it.* I can't read that. *He* was at fault. Not Franny. I won't give him solace he does not deserve."

"What would you say instead? His wife will be here too."

"I wouldn't say anything. I'd wish for Franny to speak."

"Something truthful."

"Yes," she said. "Something true."

Then he kissed her. Warm lips on hers. And then they were gone. He rocked back. "Well. You are a very fine kisser."

Her heart clanged, smashing like a mallet to a cymbal. She drew in a breath and slapped him. "Don't do that again."

He rubbed his cheek, which bloomed red in the shape of her palm. "My apologies."

166

She stood, pressing her lips tight, and sidled around the table. Ethelred scrambled up to follow her. "Why did you do that?"

"You're the last bit of good I know."

"Then let me be good."

She stepped into the hall. Closed the door and took a deep breath. Then she squeezed the bridge of her nose, turned to the stairs, and gasped.

Clementine sat at the top of the landing, a hand to each trousered knee. She beat one heel into the wood stair.

"How long have you—"

"We really should get you on a stage, shouldn't we? So you can show us all the latest talents you've acquired. Your dramatization of Franny's downfall was captivating."

"What did you hear?"

"Just a small revolt. And other nonsense."

The grandfather clock tolled. Clem snapped open her watch. "Hm. Two minutes fast." She sat back and made a show of crossing her arms and pursing her lips in thought. "So which is off? The hideous clock or my watch? I think the clock. Is it overwound? Is a pinion worn smooth? Is the pendulum rod bent?"

"Why does it matter?"

"Everything, Mouse, has a job. Which makes the clock go, and makes it toll the hour at the right time. Which, right now, it doesn't. And that, left to itself, will lead to chaos."

"Of course it will."

"Sarcasm doesn't become you."

"It's a few minutes off. What possible difference does it make?"

"If I as a child was two minutes late to supper, I lost the privilege of eating it and was consigned for an hour to the Pondering Room. It only took one time in the dark to stop being late."

"The Pondering Room."

"Much like the box in your cellar. How often did he put you there? Your loving William Marcus? How many times did it take to stop being two minutes off, like your clock?"

Maud's vision tunneled. Her skin puckered with damp, with the scratch of beetles on her arms and neck.

"I found it a satisfying place to sit and think. But by your expression, I see that's not the case with you."

"He made me go there when I couldn't conjure, when I—"

"When you didn't do your job."

No air. Maud dragged what she could through her mouth, but her throat clamped down. Ethelred nudged her fingers with her warm, wet nose.

Clem's gaze flitted down the stair rail. She beamed and clapped her hands. "There's my girl."

But the dog hunkered behind Maud.

Clem's mouth tightened. She bounded down the stairs and gave a long look toward the closed parlor door, a hand raised to the knob. But then she shook her head as if escaping a daze and hooked her fingers to Ethelred's collar. "Do you need out? Has no one let you out?" She dragged the dog down the hall to the kitchen. The door swung shut with a thud.

A hiss of sound flew past Maud. *Her . . .*

She spun to it, as if she could catch more words. But there was nothing more. A crackle of sound. Nothing else. Nothing more.

The door swung open again. Clementine peered around. "By the way, Franny hung herself with the rope from a potato sack and used an upturned apple bucket. She did have second thoughts—there were scrapes where she tried to loosen the . . ." She drummed her fingers to the door-frame. "Never mind. Star-crossed lovers. Wasn't ever going to end well."

Chapter Sixteen

CLEMENTINE

Russell held his hands to his chest, waiting just inside the attic door for Clem to look up from the table. It annoyed her; it was a telltale sign he'd left some responsibility by the wayside and now wanted to give penance for mucking things up.

"What have you done?"

"Why would you think I've done something?"

"You're in your servile mode. So you've done something."

"I am offended at the implication."

"Hm."

"I've merely brought the post."

She flipped down the jeweler's loupe to return to her task. She was in need of a cog. She scanned the materials arrayed on the table before her. A neat row of inks, a tidily stacked ream of paper. Coils in one box, pins and gears in two others. Another filled with the tin bodies of canaries and finches and a blue jay—all awaiting feathers. She'd glue them on at some point. Wings stored by size in a small cabinet. A mannequin's arm. A hand missing two plaster fingers. Four sets of glass eyes in blue, brown, green, and topaz. The shell of a woman's face leaned against a pile of books that had been removed from a crate. The jaw sat to the left of the mannequin's cheek.

Russell cocked his eyebrow and glared at the table. "You're working on that again?"

"I am."

The automaton. Russell never called it by its name. He referred to it as "The Thing" and as her "ghastly pastime." He prayed to all gods and devils it would never reach completion. Sometimes she feared the same, for no matter the drawings and plans she pored over late at night, there was always another coil or spring or tack or ratchet wheel needed.

My crowning glory, she said. *One day,* she also said. The one day was nearly here.

"Why can't you work on the mechanical birds?"

"They're simple." She pinched a cog that had found its way to the box of spindles and held it out. Too large. "They're amusements."

"I'm fond of them." He took a seat on a trunk across from her.

"Amandine is better."

"You've named the thing."

"I have."

"You'll scare the sitters into the grave with that."

"Not the grave, Russell. We do need a live audience. To pay the bills."

He sat on a trunk and held up a bundle of letters. "And I think we're well on the way. The sittings have gone well, don't you think?"

"They're getting stale."

"That's only because that Sullivan fellow continues to sob his way through them."

"I haven't found his dead wife. She's not in my book. She's not in a graveyard, at least not here. I think we should put him off."

"He's coming tonight, I'm afraid."

"I'm tired of posing as Mouse's cousin. And you set off that flash pot too near the ferns last night. I saw your arm. Simplicity, Russell. If we could just have simplicity."

"You keep calling out for some Sister Matilda—in fact, you cry out so often you step right on Maud's meditation. You don't even give her a chance, and I've barely wound in the catgut before you're on to another effect. So don't talk to me about simplicity. You're like the three witches in *Macbeth* all rolled into one."

"Really."

"And Lady Macbeth. When you're in a mood."

"We've had full houses for three weeks." She snipped a wire coming from the mannequin's wrist and bent it to a loop. "You didn't like the collar button I bought you."

Russell's hand went to the collar of his shirt. He twisted the silver stud, then smoothed his hand down his shirtfront and vest. "It's quite lovely. Just not for daytime."

"It's a ruby. Not diamonds and emeralds." She swallowed and bent close to her work so he couldn't see the flush on her cheek. She had been so sure of the gift. The jeweler assured her it was understated and yet bold. "Just read me the post."

He cleared his throat. "Three letters of introduction. An Alexander Elliot has asked to bring a party of five. He's included a check. The Otts request an evening at their home, party of ten."

"Write the Otts for a complete list of attendees and that Miss Price will be honored. Mark the Elliots down for this coming Wednesday."

Russell stuffed the notes in his pocket and sat back, hand to his knee. "Thank you for the gift."

Clem held up a wooden hand. She pulled a wire dangling from the wrist. The index finger curled into the palm, then the middle finger followed. The ring finger quivered, then jammed partway to the palm. "You are very welcome, Mr. Sprague."

"That is . . . horrific."

Clem sighed and set it down. "I should feed it to the dog and start again."

171

Ethelred groaned from under the table and stretched. A wide leather strap wound from her neck to Clem's waist.

Clem leaned back in the chair, hands gripping the table edges. "I'm going to make it look like Maud."

"Well . . ."

"Can't you see it? She'll be at the top of the stairs and in the sitting room at the same time. But I think the effect would be better with a spirit cabinet. For the shock of it. Better on a stage. Hm." She stretched her arms out, then wrapped them around herself and patted her shoulders. "Where's the Mouse?"

"I left her to practice her lecture." He took a seat at the table's head, shifting aside the box of eyes.

"She fancies you."

"Don't be an idiot."

"I'm not. Let her fancy you. She can yearn for a first kiss on that mealy mouth of hers." Maud fancied him; Clem heard it in the trill of her laugh, part nervous and part desirous. And Clem wasn't sure how she felt about that. It was useful, certainly. To some extent. The woman listened to Russell. He didn't have to explain things and justify them. He smiled and told her there would be a false wall built, and wouldn't it be wonderful fun? Or that a hand touching the shoulder of a mourner did all manner of good for the world.

Clem let out a snort. When she asked Maud to even consider moving her chair half an inch, she received scorn and a twenty-minute diatribe on authenticity and honesty. She rubbed her forehead and narrowed her eyes.

"Don't break her," Russell said.

"I'm helping her."

"You're helping you." He sniffed. "And me, of course. You can be a steamroller at times, though."

"What a compliment."

"She's fragile."

"Don't tell me you fancy her."

"Of course I don't. Though I am good at playacting it."

"Because it's useful."

"Of course." Russell picked lint from his trousers and nonchalantly flicked it away. Then he settled back, crossing a leg and smiling at her. A movement outside the window caught his eye.

Ethelred sat up with a growl. Clem gave a yank to the leash. "Get down."

The movement came again. Dark light dark light, just past the limbs of the tree. Russell pushed out of the chair and strode to the window.

"It's just the maid watching from the house next door." Clem held up the automaton's hand. She pulled a wooden peg at the wrist, lifting the index finger. "Tuesday laundry." The next peg stuck, then the middle finger joined the first. "Thursday is pots, pans, and the weekend meals." Another peg tugged, until the ring finger snapped up. "Friday is to air the bed and spy."

The girl stopped midway to closing the curtain, her brows touching in a frown.

Clem set the hand to the table, laying her own on top and caressing it with her thumb. "I think we should hire her. If she can cook."

Russell tilted his head and watched Rose. "She's a young thing."

"Trainable."

"Lovely to look at."

"She has a mouth on her."

"Can she keep secrets?"

"With enough of a threat, yes."

"Can she make blancmange?"

"If she can't," Clem said, "she's no good."

"No good to us at all." He lifted his lip in a half smile and ran his thumb along Clem's chin. "What do you think?"

"I think you should close the shutter."

"Excellent thought."

❣

Rose O'Malley liked money as much as she liked to spy. She pocketed the bill Clem gave her, escorting her up the servants' steps to the very tiptop floor and then out the door to the roof. Luckily, the pitch wasn't very steep, and the slate shingles were rough enough Clem's shoes did not slip. She wanted to watch the procession of people coming for the evening séance, and the neighbor's roof gave the best view of the approaching carriages. She tucked herself in an alcove and crossed her legs. The Plunketts' carriage, a bloated number in high black gloss and shiny brass lamps, came first. It wasn't a surprise; they had made a point of showing up early when Harriet Martin's was their preferred circle of solace, eager for the nearest seats to the medium, as if she were a stand-in for the right hand of God. Clem wondered what Harriet had done to lose their loyalty.

Then came the Arnetts, whose great-aunt had passed three years before, but it seemed a sum of money had gone missing, and Auntie Arnett held the key to its location. The men in derbies sauntered along the sidewalk, having come up on foot from town. They had been assigned the peanut seats.

The Gardiners walked arm in arm, still with black band on his sleeve, full widow's weeds on the wife.

Clementine took out her watch and turned it to the moonlight. Mr. Sullivan was late. She bit her lip and squinted out at the street.

Rose crawled out to join her, tucking her skirts under her legs and bracing her heels to the lip of slate roof. "I told you it was a good view."

Clem didn't answer. She checked her watch. Looked down the street. Sullivan jogged around the corner and picked up pace near the house. He kept a hand to his hat brim, the other clutching a holdall and a folded umbrella.

"Him again." Rose gave a small huff.

"How often do you come up here?"

The girl lifted her shoulder to her ear and let it fall. "Time and again." Then she grabbed Clem's elbow and shook. "Look. He's up to tricks. Always poking himself around."

Mr. Sullivan did not go directly to the door but skirted the streetlamp and circled into the side yard. He tiptoed to look in the dining room window, but the curtain was shut tight. He took off his hat, tapping it against his chest as he continued his examination of the exterior. Soon he'd get around to the cellar and then Ethelred tied to the maple.

"Rose, I need you." Clem dug in her pocket and pulled out two more bills. "It's two dollars if you go down and say you're Miss Price's new maid and get him into the house. Take his case and umbrella and seat him at the table. Can you read?"

"Just the necessaries."

"Can you keep secrets?"

"For three dollars, I'll take whatever you want to the grave."

"I'll pay you three dollars a week for maiding and cooking."

She sat back against the slate, crossing her arms under her head. "I can make eighty-nine cents a day as a doffer down at Whitley's mill. Why would I take less?"

"Then why aren't you working there?"

She blew out a sharp breath. "My whole family's at Whitley's."

"Four dollars a week. Mondays off." Clem threw out a hand for a shake. "Offer's invalid if you don't go down now."

"I have this job."

"I can tell your employer what you stole from them."

"I haven't stolen a thing." Her chest deflated. "That's not Christian of you."

"You're right. But it is more fun."

Rose snatched the money, stuffed it under her shirt cuff, and scrambled through the attic window. Clementine waited until she saw Rose in the yard.

The girl startled Sullivan, then gave a simpering curtsy. She pointed to the front of the house and jabbed his elbow, circling around to herd him in the correct direction.

Clem crawled back through the window and took the steps as light as she could. She kept to the brush and overgrowth, putting a finger to her lips as she passed Ethelred. In the kitchen, she lowered the wick in the oil lamp until all light ceased, giving her easy access to the hall. The parlor door was shut. Two sconces flared on either side of the entry table and mirror, another near the landing. Sullivan was looking for something. She was sure of it.

Rose had been good as her word: Sullivan's case had been tucked near the front bench, the umbrella duly placed in the stand.

She waited for singing to commence, then jogged to the bench and case. It was locked, but a twist of a hairpin did the trick. She held her thumb to the latch until the song swelled to high, unreachable notes, then left it to snap open. A sheaf of papers lay under a crumpled wool scarf. She pulled the papers out and scanned the notations and drawings.

The singing stopped. Maud rang the bell again to call the room to dark and silence.

Clem shoved the papers back and clicked the lock. Then she made for the library.

The room was empty, Russell having taken his place within the wall fifteen minutes earlier. The murmurs of the guests came through the shelves. She pulled out the third volume of *Plutarch's Lives*. "Russell."

Maud's voice rose and hovered as she began her invocations.

"Russell."

He waved his hand through the book-sized opening for her to leave him be.

She gave the hidden door a push, releasing the hinges to squeeze herself inside. It was pitch dark; she felt around until she caught Russell's elbow. A glowing hand appeared as he swung it into place.

"What?" he whispered through clenched teeth.

She stood on tiptoes, so her mouth was right to his ear. "No effects."

He turned his head, the stubble on his cheek scraping her lips as he nodded. She backed out, closing the library door with care before sidling into the hall.

"Who is here?" Maud's voice from the parlor. Tremulous and low. "It is your Franny, Mr. Gardiner. She asks to speak. Will you let—"

"Franny?"

Clem put her ear to the door. She clenched her jaw to keep from yelling. "Read the damn letter." The words slid through her teeth as she hissed them.

"Yes, sir, she tells me you . . . here. She writes."

Good. The woman would do what was told her. Clem glared at Sullivan's case; that would need more thought. She turned to the kitchen; Rose might be there. Or she may have gone off again with the three dollars stashed to her bosom.

A strange long keen stopped her in her tracks. The sound was unearthly. Loud. Then it dropped low, words murmured and spit.

"What the hell are you doing?" Clem whispered. "What in the hell?"

The door flew open, banging to the wall. Gardiner barreled out, his face white with rage. His wife followed on his heels, then the others, all a melee of coats and umbrellas and yammering. "I wanted her safe."

Clem stepped into the dark at the end of the hall.

"I loved my Franny." He pointed a finger toward the room. "This is not her—she forgives me. She must. I'll sue you for fraud. That wasn't her." The muscles in his cheek twitched and trembled. "I loved her."

The hook ripped from the wall as he yanked at his coat. Mr. Plunkett flapped his hands as if that would calm the group.

Maud stepped from the room, her face a pale gray. "I do not control what is spoken, Mr. Gardiner."

"How dare you? She was my heart."

"Get out."

Rose, who had not been in the kitchen after all, but lurking across in the dining room, now gave out umbrellas and swung open the front door. "She wishes you out."

"Who are you?" Maud asked.

Rose gave her a wide-eyed look and flash of a curtsy, then turned back to her task of shoving the guests out to the stoop. "Mind the rain. Ooh, sorry to stab you, Mrs. Plunkett."

Then they were out and only Maud stood in the hall. She covered her face with her hands and took in a long breath. Her hands slid down. Her lips moved. She gave a shake of her head. Then turned on her heel and stared back in the parlor.

Clem was going to kill her. Maud had left the man free rein of the room.

"Mr. Sullivan? I am overextended, Mr. Sullivan. May we try again tomorrow?"

"Of course, Miss Price." He ducked his head and bobbed it as he passed her to the hall, hesitating at the gaping hole where the hook had been and then at the crumble of plaster on the floor. He retrieved his coat and tucked his case under his arm, knocking the umbrella stand. He reached for it and caught Clem's eye.

"Mrs. Turlock?"

"No, that's Miss Watkins," Maud said.

Clem squeezed her hands into fists. "I've returned to my maiden name."

His gaze flicked down her suit then back up. He gave her a puzzled smile.

"Where are you from, Mr. Sullivan?"

"Pardon?"

"Straightforward question. I'm from Laconia originally. Where are you from?"

"Does this matter?" Maud's head swung to stare at Clem. Her eyes were glazed, her blink slow. Her lower lip quavered. "I have a terrible headache, Clementine."

Clem hurried forward to take her elbow. "You can see she's given all her energy to the spirits, Mr. Sullivan. Her health is delicate, as most . . . well, someone was an unbeliever tonight. It's sapped all her magnetic energy. It would be most kind of you to leave her."

The door swung open. Rose bustled in. Rain splotched her apron. She pushed back a lock of hair. "One more, eh?" She gave a troubled sigh. "Should I wave for a cab?"

"No, it's quite fine." He put on his derby and tapped the crown. "I'll call again, Miss Price. When you're more clear-minded. Mrs.— Miss Watkins. From Laconia."

"Thank you for the visit." Rose held out his umbrella. He took it, his look bemused as she shuffled him outside.

Clem clenched her hands in fists and forced herself to take a breath. "Do you know how many hours—how much planning? All you had to do was read that letter. Instead you accused the man of causing his own daughter's suicide."

"I didn't accuse him." Maud clutched her skirts.

"You did."

"She told me. Franny told me."

Clem's eyes widened. "*She* told you."

"Yes. Don't you see? I *heard* her. Not chatter and jumbles, but her words. As clear as a bell."

"You should have shut her up." But, of course, Maud wouldn't; Clem wanted to rip her earnest little heart out. "How convenient. Your powers return right now in this show with this man. Who has the money we need for the next show."

"You're the one who spends it all. You're just like William Marcus."

"Thank Franny the next time you talk. Her timing was impeccable."

"He led her to her death."

179

"I don't care if he cut her head off and fed it to the pigs. Do not insult the guests. Ever. And never leave someone alone in the room. Do you understand me?"

Maud stuck out her chin and glared back. "She came through. I heard her." But there—a flinch. Infinitesimal, but there nonetheless.

"You didn't hear her."

"I called her. And she came."

"Don't lie. I don't like to be lied to."

The woman's chin trembled. "I didn't—"

"You give solace. That's what people come for. They do not wish the truth. We've been over this. Many times."

Clem stepped back before she gave in to the urge to shove the woman through a window. She wiped her hands and turned away.

Rose stood in the shadows of the dining room, eyes wide as saucers.

"Rose, this is Miss Price. Miss Price, this is our new maid. Since you can afford one, we now have one."

Russell stepped out from the library. "What in the hell is going on?"

"Nothing. All is forgiven and forgotten."

"What did I tell you, Clem?"

"I don't know, what did you tell me?"

But Russell ignored her. His eyes were on Maud. "Are you all right?" He gave a glimmer of a smile, one Clem had seen before. When it had been bestowed on her.

Chapter Seventeen

MAUD

A hat sat atop Maud's dresser. She peered at the thing, resting on its wooden block. The striated wings of a pheasant curved out from the crown, the quills dipping and swaying as she passed. Black feathers—a raven's or crow's—fanned the front of the crown, and red hackle feathers of who knew what poor bird circled the band. She poked at it, afraid the whole would squawk and fly at her. But it did not. It sat in pride of place with a thick card leaning against the wooden base.

> *You deserve both a new hat and my apologies for my behavior.*
> C.—

But it was not at all a hat Maud would choose for herself. It had a funereal quality, somber and tinged with a cloying sadness. The red feathers gave no vibrancy but looked as if the bird who owned them had come to a violent end.

She couldn't wear this. It was beautiful, certainly; Maud knew her hats and this was of the highest quality. Clementine must have had it specially made. But it was extravagant in its scope, and inelegant, and she would have to duck to get through a door.

And it did not feel earned.

Much as the apology did not feel genuine. Clem had been furious after the Gardiner fiasco. She had forced Maud to write a note to Mr. Gardiner, to explain that her energies had been co-opted by another spirit, that the magnetism of the room had been reversed, that she had spent the next three hours in conversation with Franny herself and forwarded the transcribed notes from their conversation. She debased herself.

At least she had not been sent to face the man in person.

The hat was not an apology. It was a treat thrown at her for obeying, much like the dog.

Maud lifted it from the stand and lowered it to its silk-trimmed box on the floor. The lid let out a huff of air as she pushed it tight. She stared at the box, then pushed her toes to it and shoved it under her bed. She sat on the new down quilt and slapped her hands to her thighs. A lot of money had gone out the door of late. The leak in the dining room had been repaired just yesterday, the room repapered so the walls matched exactly. All the bedding had been upgraded. Her father's room had been rearranged to add new flooring, with false boards and wires and magnets. The desk gained a new lamp and a crystal inkstand. The carpet up the stairs had been removed, the back felted and then replaced so footsteps were muted.

And Rose. How much was the maid costing?

It gave her heartburn. She needed a dose or two of Sanford's Jamaica Ginger, but she'd finished that with last Thursday's gravy-laden lamb and buttered leeks.

It was out of hand: she was a liar now. An illusionist. A fraud. Perhaps there had never been a Matthias at all, and the guide she loved and who strengthened her was no more than her father's will. All of it woven from her imagination to please William Marcus and avoid the box.

She fell back and sighed. How she wished she'd brought the rest of the port with her.

A small rustling sound made her sit up and look toward the door. A slip of paper lay halfway under the door's sweep. Her heartburn grew worse. Clementine no doubt lingered right outside, wanting an immediate response.

"You could just come in and tell me what you want," she said, loud enough she winced. "Are you waiting for thanks for the hat? Then thank you for the hat. It's very . . . you."

There was no answer. Just the ivory note glowing in the lamplight. Waiting.

"All right." She padded across the floor to retrieve it.

Come to the kitchen.

Not Clementine's handwriting at all. Russell's.

❧

The landing was dark; Rose had extinguished the lamps earlier, having taken the night off to visit her family. The moonlight had no chance of breaking through the clouds. The front windows gaped hollow and black, as if nothing existed outside but an infinite void.

She trailed her fingers along the wall, feet bare and quiet on the rug as she took the stairs. The hall was dark, only a thin sliver of light coming from under the kitchen door. She swung it open. A stump of candle illuminated Russell's face. He looked up from the table and held a finger to his lips. Then he gestured Maud closer, lifting a chair and gingerly setting it down for her.

He gave a deep bow, picked up a towel, and fluttered it like a flag before turning to the hob. A pot was lifted. Two cups filled with liquid. He held them up.

"Warm milk." His breath caressed her cheek when he neared and set the mugs down. "With cinnamon and honey."

Like her mother made once. Perhaps all mothers made such drinks of comfort.

They drank in silence. He wiggled his eyebrows for no reason, then frowned, then made silly faces. He held up a finger and pointed it directly at her forehead. "I shall now read your mind."

She stifled a laugh behind her hand. "Why are you whispering?"

"Your thoughts are very quiet. And—" He pointed up. The sound here carried to the servant's rooms. Clem's rooms.

He touched the tip of his finger between her brows. "Ah," he said. "The warm milk agrees with you." Then murmured under his breath, "And you are taken aback at a man forward enough to place his bare finger upon your naked brow."

"It tickles."

He widened his eyes. "That is the ethereal fluid flowing. It is quite powerful in you."

"Is it?"

"Oh, yes."

Every part of her tingled. She thought she might disintegrate. He really did not have any sense of propriety; she really should move away. Instead she closed her eyes. Wondered when she had grown so fond of him. Of his asides of inscrutable Shakespearean quotes. Of his need to double-check his cravat and collar buttons and sideburns when passing any bit of glass. His laugh, which came direct and honest from his belly. How he made a point of asking her how she slept each night. How he escorted her on errands, his hand lingering near her elbow should she need assistance. She leaned forward. "Tell me about your mother."

"My mother?"

"Yes."

"But I am reading *your* mind."

"It is very curious."

"My mother has a very quick temper," he said. "My brothers and I got away with nothing; nor did we want to, because the tongue-lashing was brutal. We called her Lady Macbeth. Which she did not appreciate. She was very good in the role; my father never liked to play opposite. She got the best applause."

"Both actors?"

"They've given up theater for a dairy farm and now live in Saco. My original hometown."

"Cows."

"Goats. But let me return to you. You have the most exquisite thoughts." His finger caressed the top of her brow then ran down her cheek, soft as a feather.

Her eyes popped open. He had moved so close, his chair tipped forward on its front legs.

"What are you doing?"

"Reading your mind." Now his lips were a breath from hers. "You wish a kiss."

The chair's legs gave way with a screech. Russell grabbed at the table but ended up on the floor, his arm hooked over Maud's thigh.

The mood had snapped like a twig.

"So that's that." He crossed his eyes, then jumped up and righted the chair.

"Best this way," she said. "Friends."

"Friends. Of course." He sighed. "More milk?"

"Please."

She watched him as he took the bottle from the ice box and poured it to the pan. He dipped his finger to the milk as it warmed, focused entirely on his task. "Can't let it scorch."

"Do you seduce all your clients?"

"No, I—ah." He shook his finger and then lifted the milk from the hob. "Now I've scalded it."

A heaviness came over Maud. Of course this is what he did; she wasn't stupid. Clementine used him for this. All the attention meant to dazzle her, to make her docile.

"You're a very good actor."

"I'm not, actually. I come from a line of very good actors. I am just not one of them. Black sheep. Ham hock talent. And listen to me. I'm not a seducer. Well, I am. I have been. In the past. But you . . ." He put his hands to his hips and gave her a bemused look. "You. Are just . . . good. You make me want to be good. Except for the kiss, though I think I read your mind correctly. You are—"

"I would have let you." She picked at her robe and stared at the candle. "Did she tell you to do this?"

"Of course not."

"You wouldn't tell the truth anyway."

"Maud—"

"Don't." The candle flame flared and shivered. Maud stared at the wick and dragged in a breath. "She's coming."

The dog came first, barreling through the door and skidding under the table. Russell's chair teetered and dropped against the wall. Clementine, in a nightdress, followed behind. She blinked and stared at Maud. She wiped the side of her mouth with the back of her hand and smacked her lips, like a child just awakened from sleep. But her skin was not flushed from slumber; it was sallow, dark around the sockets. She pushed a hand through her tangled hair, then swung her gaze from Maud to Russell.

"I'm making milk," he said. He held the pan before her.

Clem focused on the pan. She gathered the sides of her gown and held the fabric tight. "For me?"

Russell smiled, the corners of his eyes crinkling. "Yes."

"With honey?"

"With double honey." He gazed over Clem's head at Maud, shooting a glance for her to grab another mug from the shelf.

Maud twisted from her seat and took down a mug. She held it out to Clementine. But the woman did not move.

"I've done something terrible, Russell." Clementine pulled her nightdress higher, balling it to her stomach. She slung her head back and grimaced. Sobs shook her body. But there were no tears. No sound.

Russell stirred the milk in the mugs and circled around her, setting only two mugs to the table. "Sometimes this happens," he said.

"What has she done?"

"Nothing at all. It's just a nightmare. We all have them." He turned back to guide Clementine to a chair.

A chill slipped across Maud's skin, then was gone. Ethelred whimpered; her tail thumped twice.

Russell held a cup to Clem's lips.

Her lashes fluttered. She wrapped her hands over his and took a sip, her eyes never leaving his.

"You should go," he said to Maud.

"You should go," Clem echoed.

Maud stood, pulling her robe tight to her neck. She nodded. "Good night."

Neither gave notice. Only the dog paid mind, watching her from under the table before jumping up and following her to the hall. An icy hand coiled her wrist, then let go with a long sigh. The hall was pitch black; she glanced over her shoulder to the kitchen. No light. Just murmurs that wove around each other, too low to make sense.

Chapter Eighteen

CLEMENTINE

Her head ached. She squeezed her eyes against the morning light and ran her tongue along the roof of her mouth, tasting curdled milk and bile. Russell's arm was heavy, wrapped around her waist, hand against her chest. She curled her own around it. Tried to breathe in rhythm with him but couldn't. The nightmare would not dislodge its claws. It never did. The harder she struggled, the deeper it dug. Because it wasn't all a dream. It was her secret, packed away, hidden from the waking world so she could pass the days. So she could get by.

I was only a child, she thought.

It started the same as it always did: Ginny running through the snow, blue coat wide like a kite, black hair wild like a wave. Breath frosted in tendrils behind her. Always out of reach.

"Give it back."

Her voice sharp. "No."

She'd taken Clem's doll. Pushed her over as they climbed the stairs and scooped it right up.

Clem limped and hopped; her knee had smacked the stair edge, and now Ginny was far, far ahead, near the well. The snow squeaked under her boots.

"You have your own." Clem lunged forward, just missing as Ginny spun away.

"I want this one." Ginny stuck out her lower lip. "You keep that one to remember me, and I'll keep this to remember you."

At the end of the week Ginny, but not her brother, who was sick, would be whisked from the orphanage and the room they shared and taken to Portsmouth. Which was the other side of Timbuktu as far as Clem was concerned. "You're moving to a big, big house with lots of dolls. You don't need to take mine."

Clem didn't want Ginny's doll. She mistreated it, dragging it around by a foot through grit and lint, leaving the white skirts to grow grayer and grayer from her dirty little hands. "I don't want yours. I want mine. It's the only thing I have that's mine alone." She reached for it and tugged, but Ginny's grip was tight as a vise.

They both pulled, heels dug into the ground. But Clem wasn't as strong as Ginny; she'd given much of her meals to Dog and didn't mind pinning the waist of her skirt or the grumble of her stomach.

Ginny's upper lip curled. She yanked hard, her whole weight into it and shoulders twisting.

There was a ripping sound. Then Clem stumbled back, the doll's arm squeezed in her grip, but nothing else. Ginny held the rest of it.

"You ruined it. It was mine and you—" Clem clenched her fists and shoved her. Ginny's head hit the stone and bounced. Then she collapsed like a marionette, making Clem laugh. She picked up the doll, brushing flakes off the dress. Then she reached for Ginny's hand to pull her up. "Come on. Vespers soon."

Ginny stared straight up, not minding the snow falling on her open eyes.

Clem crouched down. Shook her shoulder. "Ginny."

But Ginny did not answer.

Clem had cleaned the doll, wiping dirt and other things from the porcelain cheeks, and jiggered the eyes to open and close. She sewed the arm on, double stitches to make it strong. Late at night she held her under the covers. *Little, little Maud Doll,* she singsonged, *you'll be fine with me.*

Russell shifted onto his back, mouth slack, face smooth, guiltless. Her chest contracted with envy. If he knew—she clamped the inside of her lip. He wouldn't be here. He would not stay up at night holding her. Yammer on about new mechanicals she should think of making—*an elephant, can you imagine, Clem, my dear? Now tell me the gears and bibs and bobs for that.*

She lifted his hand and kissed his palm. Never mind the women and faro and the stink of his shoes after he'd watched hours at the dogfights and come home empty-handed.

"I love you, Russell Sprague. As sure as the night becomes day."

Bells clanged in the distance. Clem peered at the window. The sky glowed red-orange. Ash left black streaks on the glass. Not morning at all. She bolted up. "Russell."

"Mm-hmm . . ."

"Get up." She threw the covers off and peered across the rooftops toward Main Street. Reds and yellows roared in the night sky; even here she heard the satisfying pops and cracks of wood. Fire bells clanged from all directions. She stood on her tiptoes to peek down at the street. Maud and Rose stood with other neighbors, some pointing, others with hands to their chests in prayer that not a soul had lost their life.

Russell stepped behind her. He rubbed a hand through his hair. "Downtown?"

"Near the tracks."

"You don't think—"

She pushed the paned window wide open and breathed in the bite of smoke. Ash floated and stuck to the casing. She scanned the church spires, just to be certain. "I think it's the Archer's Dry Goods."

Right by the old boardinghouse. It wouldn't be long until confirmed. Russell had forgotten to take the bottles of phosphorous from the hiding place when they'd been thrown out of their room. Such a safe place to store it and such an unfortunate place for it now. She wouldn't tell him. He'd drag himself round with guilt at the mistake.

A bright white flash split the sky. So bright Clem covered her eyes. Then came the roar of the explosion and a ball of fire.

Even from the top floor she heard the gasps. Maud had both hands to her mouth. A mother held her child to her chest and cried out, "Look at that, look! Have you seen such a thing?"

The fire show died very quickly, as did the gawpers' attentions. They went this way and that to their homes, no doubt to write Aunt Bessie in Nashua or Uncle Harker in Bangor of the great conflagration they'd witnessed. Then they'd snuggle into their beds with their dogs at their feet and wake the next day to the smell of cinder in the air. It would give them a slight pause, mostly of annoyance, before the laundry chores and bank clerk duties began.

People, Clem thought, *have the empathy of goats.*

She sighed and turned to Russell. His jaw was tight, lips drawn flat and thin.

"You look angry," she said. "Why are you angry?"

"Did you set that—"

"An accusation of arson. Oh me oh my."

He grabbed her by the arm.

"That hurts."

"My God, Clem. Is that the terrible thing—" His whole body shook. He didn't let her go. Kept hold and waited for an answer.

She plucked up her pipe from the bedside table. She couldn't face him and see the doubt. "You don't really think I—"

"I don't know what to think of you sometimes." He lifted his vest from the chair and shrugged it over his shirt. The space between them seemed a chasm, dark with doubt.

"Will we have a spirit cabinet?" She wrapped her arms to her chest and wandered toward him. "At the Otts'. I think a cabinet."

191

His gaze went to the window, then he bent to pull on a boot. "Maud dislikes cabinets."

"Does she?"

"She does."

"Well, I want a cabinet."

"No cabinet." He stood up straight. "I'm going to ask you one more time. Did you have anything to do with that fire?"

"No. And I didn't burn Mrs. King's townhouse down, either. If you're going to dredge that up." She clenched her jaw and threw the unlit pipe to the bed. "You have to admit, it was a spectacular explosion."

He stuffed his wallet in his coat pocket and looked at her. How tired he seemed. "Do you love anything?"

She reached for his cheek, only to find him out of reach, already at the door. She gave a start. "Are you walking away from me?"

"What's it about?"

"What?"

"Your nightmare."

What would happen if she told him the truth? *I dragged her up and heaved her over the edge of the well. Bump bump splash.*

"What would you think if I did set that fire? I didn't, but if I did?"

"I'd hate you."

"Well." She wrapped her arms tight and turned to the window. "I should hate you for even thinking that I could. I help conjure the dead. I don't create them."

Chapter Nineteen

MAUD

Maud's hand shook as she set her notebook to the podium. She dabbed her upper lip and forehead with a handkerchief and stuffed it back to her belt. The meeting room was thick with pipe and tobacco fumes. How she wished the resolution to forbid smoking in the Psychical Society offices had passed. It had been such a close vote; if it hadn't been for Harriet Martin going to the other side, Maud would be able to take a breath of clean air.

But there was Mr. Garrison, cross-legged and knobby-kneed, puffing away, one eye blinking to stave off the sting of smoke. And the others, all crowded in the little third-story room, thigh to thigh and shoulder to shoulder, squinting through the smoke as they carried on their conversations. Harriet sat near the door, her fan flicking wildly and causing the peacock feathers on her hat to bend to the point Maud thought they might snap. Her skin was a shade of green that didn't bode well. Maud hoped now the woman regretted her vote.

Mr. Garrison stood, turning to the encircled crowd and ringing a small bell. "Fellow travelers, be met."

The room quieted and gave Garrison their attention.

"Mrs. Boothby will lead us in an opening song."

Mrs. Boothby, who Maud was certain did not converse with Emperor Alexander of Russia or Lord Dunraven, and who she was even more certain did not speak the language of Pythagoras and thus could not have held a long teatime with him, rose from her chair. She was a woman of short stature with little chin and a sharp nose. She dipped and bowed and gave tight smiles that seemed meant for whoever she conversed with in her head, rather than the person to whom she passed the ballad's lyric sheet.

"'The Ballad of the Slate-Seizer,'" she said. "Sung to the tune of 'Jock O'Hazeldean.'" With a gloved finger held high, she hummed a note, then the group started in on singing.

Maud had no lyrics sheet. She stood at the podium and picked at the paper in front of her. Here were the words she would say, not written by her, but by Clementine, and she was about to speak them as her own to her spiritualist colleagues. It was a marvelous speech, on rational spiritualism and the morals and theology it shared with the Christian mind and prophecy, on Revelation and worship and rhapsody.

Clementine's orphanage had spared no expense on education, it seemed. That much was clear in the endnotes and asides she'd starred for Maud to pay particular attention to. And yet she'd mentioned a room as dark and confined as the one built for her mother. And then for her.

Maud took out her handkerchief and wiped her face once more. She stared at the paper. These were not her words.

The voices rang around the room, off-key though full of vigor. The floor shook from the stomp of feet.

How many liars surrounded her? Not just Enid Boothby; she was ridiculed by the others, if only under their breaths. But Mr. Garrison, who commanded large audiences in Boston and Manchester and down the coast to Savannah, who spoke of the need to accept spiritualism as a true religion, had he walked the Otherworld? Had Mr. Mumler in his yellow check suits and Miss Orland in her single room?

Or were they honest and it was she who had sinned?

The warbling ended. Mr. Garrison rang his little bell once more. "The floor goes to Miss Maud Price, to be followed by questions and discussion of her lecture's themes."

He took his seat and gave a nod for her to begin.

She folded her handkerchief away. Her throat felt tight as a vise. She swallowed and swallowed, sure no sound would come through. The rear door opened. Harriet slowed her fan and looked to the latecomer.

It was Mr. Sullivan, who shuffled sideways between the last row of chairs and the wall, his hat held above his head so as not to be crushed. But there was no seat and nowhere to hang the hat, so he set it back to his head. He looked neither left nor right but directly at Maud. Someone tugged the arm of his jacket and received only a dismissive glare.

He believed in her. He needed her. She felt it in her bones, how much need he had for the truth.

"Miss Price?" Garrison gestured for her to commence. Then he sat back and pulled at his sideburn, a sure sign she'd displeased him.

"Yes, yes."

Mr. Sullivan raised his gaze from the pocket notebook he held, awaiting her words.

She cleared her throat. "Obadiah, Nahum, Joel. How came their prophecies save but delivery by celestial beings—their words sent from God to the spirit-home all souls inhabit . . ."

❧

"You provoke the church, you know. Not that it doesn't need the shaking up. Still." Harriet Martin pinched a rose-topped tea cake between a pair of tongs and transferred it to Maud's plate. "I did very much like the song at the end. I didn't know you had such a sweet voice."

Maud had a terrible voice and knew it. *Grating as a field mouse with croup,* her father said. It hadn't been in the notes the evening before; she'd read the lecture aloud to Russell and she knew where it ended. But there in a dash of black pen was the direction: *LEAD THEM IN A ROUSING SONG.* And the verses of "Far Away Where Angels Dwell" had been torn from a book and glued to the paper.

Harriet bit into a poppy seed cake. Her hair flamed in the afternoon light; her frock was a deep evanescent teal. Maud suspected she'd taken the seat by the window just to attain this glow. Certainly others in the room noticed. A few women scowled and shoved their spice cakes and crumbles to their mouths before slurping down their tea. Then there were the men. They did not slurp or scowl, and it was to them Harriet gave infinitesimal nods.

"Would you prefer the lemon?" she asked and pointed to Maud's plate.

"The rose is fine. Thank you." Maud took a bite, pressed the cake between her tongue and palate, then swallowed it down before the cloying taste registered. She followed with tea, which was a very good solid black tea. "You're kind to bring me here."

"You looked as if you needed some sustenance. After such a laborious lecture." The corners of her mouth curled and dropped. "Not written by you."

"Pardon?"

"George Malcolm Pruitt. You wouldn't know the name; he's not well known in circles. He wrote theses and arguments and all manner of tracts on the superiority of spiritualism as a religious sect. 'A Step beyond Christianity' had a wonderful quote of—"

"I didn't write it."

"No. Of course you didn't. George did. My first husband. He was mad about heaven. Spent his days writing and his nights in states of trance." She stirred milk into her tea. "I don't blame you. In fact, I should apologize to you. I referred the woman to you, after all."

Maud pulled in a sharp breath. Then another. No words came to her. Just a sinking feeling of dread and disbelief that pooled in her stomach like glue.

"You were desperate. And our community is so small, it was the right thing to assist. The others were starting to talk and—"

"You sent me a plagiarist."

"I did not expect—"

"She said she was a believer."

"In herself, yes." Harriet pinched a lemon cake from the top plate. "We can split the lemon. I saw your face with the rose."

"I don't want the lemon."

"As you say. You don't mind if I do?"

"What have people been saying?"

"Nothing important. You know how rumors go."

"What were they saying?"

"Honestly?"

"I ask no less."

Harriet sighed. "All right. It's been said that since your father passed, you'd . . . lost your way. Certainly you've struggled to connect with your guides; you've told me so yourself. It's what spurred me to help you. We all help each other. We're a house of cards—you know that as well as I do."

"Are we all frauds?"

"My God, don't use that word. No, of course we're not."

"Then why do you use her?"

Harriet clapped her hand to her chest. "Me?"

"Yes, you. You're the one who sent her. I assume she's taken the opportunity to turn your entire life upside down too."

"I should have mentioned the need to keep her in hand."

"What does that mean? She and her partner have—"

"Shh."

Maud gripped the edge of the table and forced herself to a whisper. "They've taken over my house. There's even a dog."

"No."

"Yes. She said she would help, just until I could—I am not a—I'm real. I hear the souls." She shoved herself back in her seat. "I'll make them leave. They have to leave. I could go to prison. What do you know of her? Of him?" Her cheeks exploded with heat. She cupped her face and rocked in the chair. "And she buys whatever she wants. You should see the clothes. All of them far too grand—even the men's suits. And she labels them with her name. As if I'm going to steal them. C. Watkins. In red thread."

"Oh, Maud."

Maud took a sip of tea and wished she hadn't. "Can we get water?"

"Russell's very charming, isn't he?"

"He's all right."

"Did you sign a contract?"

"Yes."

"Hopefully not in blood." Harriet pressed the tines of her fork to the cake and took a bite. She raised an eyebrow. "It's very good. You sure you don't . . . ?"

Maud shook her head. She wanted to pound the table with her fist. Instead, she watched Harriet finish the small cake and chase it with tea. This was not the place for a scene.

"The lemon was the best. We'll order two next time."

"When I'm around her, I'm discombobulated. I'd rather be poor. I'd rather lose the house."

"Would you?"

"I don't care."

"You would very much care should you wake in the poorhouse. It's not a kind place." Harriet set her napkin by her plate. She lifted a finger to the waiter.

"Why doesn't she do it herself? Why involve me?"

"It's her ace. If something goes wrong, you're the one who falls." Her gaze flicked over Maud's head. "Speak of the devil."

Maud turned.

Clementine clapped her on the shoulder. The stub of her index finger dug under her collar bone. "You didn't finish your cake."

Then she gave Maud a small pat on the back. "Russell was waiting for you. Waiting and waiting."

"I'm here with Harriet."

"Yes, you are." Her eyes glittered like orbs filled with light. They flitted everywhere, stopping for only a moment on one object or another before snapping back to Harriet. "I've sent three notes your way and haven't heard a word. I'd feared you died. Or forgotten me."

"One being equal to the other." Harriet smirked.

"Of course." Clementine pulled over an empty chair and sat, her skirts billowing and settling. She picked a sugared lemon rind from the serving plate and chewed it. "Let's order more."

Sheissheissheis. The voice again. Just past Clementine's shoulder. Weaving and hissing. If only the voices made sense, if only—

"You look like a fish, Miss Price."

"Do I?"

Clementine twisted around. "What is so interesting at the tables behind us?"

"Nothing."

"Well, then, let's eat."

"We've finished."

"But no, Miss Price, we have not." She wove her fingers together and tapped her knuckles to her chin. "How do you feel about a ride to the country? Two nights. Ten guests with a chance for more and a lake to boat on?"

"What have you got going?" Harriet asked.

"The Ott boy. You remember him. Fell out of a tree."

"The Otts." Maud's stomach soured.

"That's right, you've been there." Clementine gave a tsk. "Terrible tragedy. Not you going, of course. But the little boy." She made a tumbling motion. "Split splat."

Maud stood, her hands fisted and pressed against her thighs. "How dare you."

Harriet covered her nose and mouth, but the laugh still escaped.

Clem hooked her elbow over the back of the chair. "You have no sense of humor, do you?"

"That's someone's child." Maud's voice shook. "Get up."

"Why?"

"I believe you're being escorted out," Harriet said, "and scolded. Though, really, Clem, going through George's papers. That wasn't called for."

"I was going to tell you. It's just . . ." She took a breath and shrugged both shoulders. "His work is so valuable. And I'm sure it went over well—did it go over well, Miss Price?" She clapped her hands, took up the rose cake, and popped it in her mouth. Then she leaned over the table and gave Harriet a peck on the cheek. She whispered something.

Harriet's skin paled. She gave a slight nod.

Clementine straightened. She caressed Harriet's cheek. "You do understand."

"Of course." Harriet lifted her cup. The tea sloshed to the saucer and across the cloth.

"Now then, Miss Price, I am all ears for you and your scolding." Clementine pushed her chair in. Tapped Maud's shoulder as she strode past to the door. "Come, come."

"Harriet?"

"Go along."

Maud wanted to say more, but the waiter had taken a towel from his pocket to wipe the stain. Harriet pasted on an appreciative smile, all attention on the concern of the waiter. She murmured as he took up the cups and dabbed the fabric.

Harriet opened her silk purse and removed two coins. "I'm a clumsy oaf," she said to the man. "Here."

The bell on the door gave a sharp clang as it hit the glass.

Maud turned. Clementine was already on the street, the dog leash wrapped around her wrist. Ethelred's nose steamed the glass. The dog swung her head to look up at her owner, then she tucked her tail and circled around her skirt to sit on the curb. A flash came then. Clementine's watch, swinging from its bright gold chain.

"She's impossible," Maud murmured.

"But not someone to keep waiting." Harriet's hand trembled. She stared at it, then jerked it back, made herself busy with snapping the purse shut and rearranging the new cup and pot.

♋

Clem sighed, opened her umbrella, and swung it over her head. Ethelred walked ahead, not minding the drizzle. People gave them wide berth, eyes averted, stepping quickly from the sidewalk to let the three by.

". . . you won't do it again."

Maud had no idea what she wouldn't do again. She loped to catch up, to hear the rest of what the woman was saying. She grabbed Clem's elbow. "Stop walking. I need to speak."

Clem did. She lifted her eyebrow and waited with an expectant gaze. "Speak."

"That was someone else's work."

"Yes. Of course."

"Of course?"

"You had half an idea written and I had a whole one that would do the trick. You pay me for that."

"It wasn't your idea to take."

The dog lumbered over, tongue lolling, and sat directly between them. Clem scratched her behind the ears and smiled at Maud. "She's a good dog, isn't she?"

"Don't change the subject."

"Did I pick the wrong dog?"

"What?"

"To put my money on? I don't mean Ethelred . . . but you, Miss Price. Have I put my faith and reputation in the wrong person? I wonder if I have." She stopped scratching the dog and instead took up the leash.

"I'm the one with the reputation—wait." But Clem didn't. Maud gripped her own umbrella and jogged forward. "I'm the one with the reputation—"

"That is in tatters. That I am fixing."

"What did you say to Harriet?"

"Nothing of any consequence to you." She stopped and looked in the window of a butcher shop, eyeing the sides of lamb. "Do you like lamb?"

"No. I don't."

"Then we'll settle for steak. Come along."

Clem tied Ethelred to a tethering ring on the curb. A small bay, whose reins were tied to the next ring, gave her a long look and stamped a foot.

"Stay, dog."

The line in the butcher shop was long, women calling in Portuguese and English, hands raised and waving crumpled bills. All cuts of meat filled the glass case, the separate types delineated by a chopped head: cow, pig, lamb. The whole of it stank of blood. Maud covered her nose and mouth and didn't care that Clem smirked at her.

"I'll wait outside," Maud said.

"You're going to pick the meal." Clem frowned. "Are they speaking to you?"

"I'm sorry?"

"The sows and bulls."

Maud wanted to hit her. Right in the mouth. "You are the rudest woman I've ever met."

"Chops. We'll have chops." Clem unsnapped a small purse on her belt and unfolded bills.

"This isn't right."

"Comfort is comfort." Clem turned to the butcher and ordered four chops and a bag of offal and bones.

Which she handed to Maud to carry.

"I've got the dog," she said.

Maud held the knit sack to the side. The paper soaked red on the bottom. "It's going to leak."

But Clem wasn't listening. She stared out the window, though what she could see past the carcasses Maud couldn't guess. A woman entered, carrying heavy bags. Limp carrot greens hung over one bag, the other was stuffed with loaves of bread. Her dress and shawl were of the same gray as her hair. Her mouth was pinched tight.

Maud thought that if her collar were as tight, she would look the same.

"Mrs. Epp." Clem gave the woman a nod.

"Mm-hmm." Mrs. Epp pushed past Clem.

"The beef loins are excellent today. Fresh from the farm."

The woman categorically ignored Clem. Clem leaned her elbow to the glass cabinet and didn't move until Mrs. Epp turned her head.

"There you are. Hello, Mrs. Epp. It's so very nice to see you this fine day. I am so glad you all survived that terrible fire. I hear from the paper the boardinghouse is being rebuilt with generous donations from the community." She put a hand to her chest. "Why thank you, Mrs. Sprague, it is a joy to see you, too—"

"Sprague?" Maud shook her head. "Sprague?"

Clem looked at Maud and blinked, as if she were just seeing her. "Oh. That. It's nothing."

She swiveled on a heel and marched out the door.

"You're married." Maud followed her to the sidewalk.

"We needed lodging. She only accepted married couples. You'd do the same in the situation." She untied the dog, then snapped her umbrella open again. "I don't believe in marriage. It ends very badly. What matters is getting the chops to Russell, who is not my husband but is a very good cook." She spun toward Maud. "Has he offered you warm milk?"

Maud picked at the wood handle of the umbrella. "Why would he do that?"

"I vaguely recall that he did."

"I hate warm milk. I wouldn't accept it."

Clementine narrowed her eyes. She dragged her teeth on her lower lip. "Hm." Then she hurried on, long strides as if the world was hers. *It did help,* Maud thought, *to have a monstrous dog clear the way.*

Chapter Twenty

CLEMENTINE

Dogs spinning plates. Four black spaniels clicking and clacking on their toes. There went one plate and then another, crashing to the floor. A towheaded boy sprinted out with broom and dustpan to clean up the shards.

"Sisyphus." Clem slunk down in her seat and yawned, never minding the sharp nudge of Harriet's elbow to her shoulder. Russell flapped his playbill in front of his face and gave her a sidelong glance.

She was bored with the look. Bored with the dogs.

But soon they were off, wagging their tails as if breaking twenty or so plates was the greatest of fun, and a stagehand pushed on a white upright piano. The pianist approached from the other direction, long strides accentuated by his black-and-white striped pants and red tailcoat. He bowed three directions—house left, house right, house center—and ignored the balcony. He sat with his back to the audience and began a rollicking tune; the crowd below joined in.

Clem leaned forward, wrapping her elbows over the brass rail, and peered around. The Orpheum showed its age. The tapestries hung lackluster and faded along the auditorium walls. The gilt on the wainscoting and piping on the proscenium arch had a dullish sheen. The aisle flooring could use, if not a full replacement, at least a good sweep. Still the place had footlights belting the lip of the stage and gaslight chandeliers, and good acoustics.

Russell leaned forward, his shoulder to hers. "Well?"

"It's not Boston," she murmured. "It's not the Globe."

"Trapdoors, though."

"Mm."

"No dress circles to worry over."

"Will her voice carry?"

Russell rested his chin on the back of his hand. "Mm."

A sting on her back jerked Clem upright. Harriet shoved the tip of her fan into Clem's waist and scowled.

Clem waved Harriet off, let out her breath, and sunk down yet again. The money they could make with a theatrical far outstripped the sittings. Two ballerinas in tutus swirled around each other onstage, both warbling impossibly high notes.

Clem drummed her fingers to the armrest. Russell, still with his head lolling on his arm, stared at her and not the stage. She gave him a smile that he didn't return. Instead he resumed watching the dancers.

She thought how much more interesting they'd be as ghouls. Not easy to pull off, but the seats raked just enough she could add glass and smoke and they would look as if they floated straight up from hell or fell in disgrace from heaven. God, to see Maud's face at that sort of illusion might be worth it. A ragged laugh sawed up Clementine's throat. Harriet gave her a sharp look. She had on a pair of glasses; the dancers' reflections spun in each lens. At intermission, she would slide them off and tuck them away, sidle and sway through the middling audience as they made their way through the lobby for a breath of air and smoke on the sidewalk.

Clem's insides tensed with doubt. She'd left Harriet, who lived for the approbation of a crowd, and chased Maud, thinking she'd want the same.

The applause filtered up to their seats.

"Shall we stay for the second act?" Harriet asked.

Russell stood and stretched his arms. "I'm off."

"Where are you going?"

He looked just over Clem's shoulder. "I have a tip on a card game."

Harriet tsked. "Poor man."

The three shuffled with the crowd down the curved stairs. Those behind Clem forced her forward. A warm breath slid across the back of her neck. "You've outdone yourself."

She pulled her elbows in tight and twisted to find the voice. But there was no room. The crowd swayed and descended. Who stood behind her? Clem slowed enough Russell pressed into her. But then he squeezed past her and made it to Harriet's side, as if the touch repelled him.

A thumb caressed her earlobe and jaw, then dropped to her arm and gripped hard, fingers digging into the fabric. "Don't look back. Just know that I know."

Then her arm was free and throbbed from the sudden release. Her heart clanged and punched her chest. She bit down on her lip and swallowed. People like to scare people. She knew that better than anyone. She wrenched herself around.

An old woman stared at her with rheumy eyes, each hand gnarled over a cane. Her companion, a portly man, wiped the top of his head with a handkerchief. "What are you looking at?"

She pushed past, stopping to sweep her eyes over the audience. But it would be impossible to know who had spoken.

She raked her hand to Russell's sleeve. "Someone's following me."

"I doubt that."

"Stay with me. I want your opinion on the acoustics."

He didn't answer but collected his hat and the women's cloaks and umbrellas from the hatcheck room. "Will it ever stop raining?" he asked no one in particular and held the door for them.

The sidewalk was slick with soggy flyers, the air thick with cigar smoke. She grabbed his arm as he raised it to call a hack. "Stay with me."

"Not tonight, Clem." Russell stepped over a puddle, opening the door of an empty hack before the driver slowed to a stop. The oil light on the carriage flicked and sputtered. A black horse swung its head and crunched into its bit. Russell was a blasted man, really. Pompous. Arrogant. Minimally talented. His ire at her showing in his impeccable manners.

He held out his hand to Harriet and assisted her up. She looked at Clem over her shoulder. "Coming?"

"You're going to the card game, too?"

"Don't be ludicrous. I'm going home. There's brandy there."

Russell handed coins up to the driver.

"I guess I'll stay for the second act, then. It's your loss. There's going to be soliloquies."

"Suit yourself." Harriet cranked the window closed and knocked the ceiling with the handle of her cane. The cab lurched forward.

Russell strode off, head ducked against the spitting rain.

Damn them both.

◌

The second act proved worse than the first; the audience had thinned after the spinning-plate fiasco and only a few remained to splutter applause. Clem stayed in the shadows under the loge, scanning the audience. A man two rows down turned around, his spindly arm hanging over the chair back. He lifted a finger in greeting.

The man next to her gave a quick wave back, mumbling sorries as he shuffled past her, trying to avoid her toes and failing. The two men shook hands and spoke as if they were gladly met in the town square, not interrupting a droning rendition of Mark Antony's penultimate speech.

Once the show ended, she waited for the auditorium and lobby to clear, watching through the glass door as the carriages took the last of the stragglers, and then she made her way to the street. The night sky lumped low with clouds; the underbellies were yellow from the glow of the gaslights. She buttoned her coat and ambled to the corner. At least the rain had stopped. She dug her pipe from her coat, then stepped into the theater alley, alee of the wind. She tamped the tobacco and clamped the stem between her teeth.

She leaned her shoulder to the brick and smoked and stared out to the street and the single carriage that squeaked as it passed. The spokes spun shadows across the opposite wall, a blur of light and dark, split only by a darker silhouette that hovered at the mouth of the alleyway, then shot forward.

"Who—"

A gloved hand covered her face, shoving her against the rough brick. The pipe twisted in her lips and fell with a clatter. She bit at the glove leather, struggling for purchase on skin underneath, but the hand squeezed down, pressing her skull to the wall until she feared it would break in half.

"You will be quiet, won't you?"

She slumped her shoulders and nodded.

He relaxed his fingers enough for her to breathe and then wrench her shoulders away. But she wasn't quick enough, and a sharp punch to her ribs bent her in two. She clutched her waist and staggered, stumbling against a barrel. Her vision funneled to a single dot of light.

Then she was jerked upright, held by the neck, a thumb and forefinger threatening to squeeze tighter.

The man's stubble scraped against her jaw. "I know who you are. I know what you did."

He lifted her so her toes just touched the ground and shook her, as if she were nothing. Then he set her to her feet. She gulped in air, wincing at the burn of it in her lungs. She tried to stand, to see who he was. But her vision swirled, as if she were on a skiff spinning toward oily black rapids.

"What do you want?" Her voice was ragged, each word cutting her throat. Her mind ran through past clients, those she'd set up, collected a fee, and left to their own devices. "Did Mrs. King send you?"

But he didn't answer. Just shoved a wad of paper in her mouth. She swung her arm out, clawing at his face.

"I know." His fist came hard to her brow, sending a pulse of pain and then panic and then nothing at all.

∾

A pair of blue eyes stared at her. The lashes fluttered up and down.

A lamp swung to the side and then close enough she winced and turned her head. She couldn't breathe; something blocked her throat. Then a pair of fingers stretched her lips and scratched at her tongue. She bit down, jaw tensed and teeth bared.

"Jesus and Joseph, I'm trying to help." The boy dropped down and pushed his feet into her ribs, the pain searing like a knife.

She let go. He dug out the wad of paper and dropped it to his side. His knees glowed from the holes in his trousers. "You got a shiner coming."

"Son of a bitch," she rasped.

"Son of a bitch is about right."

The lamp swayed above her, lighting the face of the erstwhile Mark Antony, still in greasepaint and red-lined lips. "This is a respectable alley," he said. "Your likes belong in the Bottoms."

"She's not one of those." The boy wiped his nose and blinked those long lashes. "I seen her in the balcony."

The man's face froze. He looked to the street and then back to the stage door. "We'll need to move her, Archie."

Clem dabbed at her forehead, holding her fingers out to see if there was blood, but everything swam.

"My dear lady, you have been accosted." Mark Antony's voice tromped over her like ants. "Which is unacceptable on any part of the Orpheum's premises." He gave the lamp to the boy and gently prodded and pulled her to a sitting position.

She flailed her legs and kicked out. "Get your hands off me." Then she got to her knees, gritting her teeth as she grabbed the lip of a barrel and dragged herself up. The stage door flew open, releasing a spray of laughs that petered out and returned as gasps. The actors swarmed around her, shiny faces and stinking sweat. Even one of the dogs sniffed at her boot.

"Who's the management here?"

Mark Antony bowed. "I am thus. Theodore Rumson."

"Mm." Her stomach roiled, and bile burned in her throat as she tried to move. She tottered forward, grabbing Archie's shoulders for balance. "You're a good boy."

"Archie, get the police."

"No police," Clem said. She stepped back and turned to the street. There was nothing to say. "Call me a cab." She shambled forward, tugging at her coat. The ball of paper caught on her skirt hem. She swiped it up, waiting out a bout of nausea, then continued.

The boy sprinted into the street, looking left and right and then waving both hands.

It took all her strength to get to the cab.

Rumson followed close behind and dug in his pocket to pay the driver. "We should call the police. We really should."

"How many traps in the stage?" Her voice sounded as if the words ran across sandpaper.

"Traps?"

"Yes, that's what I said."

"Three."

"Good. I'll call on you next week."

Clem lay on Harriet's bed. The cuckoo clock spit out the bird, and the bird chirped once before returning to its dark hole. The rag covering her eyes had grown heavy against hot skin swelling fast enough to pop.

"What does it mean?" Harriet's voice floated from the far side of the room. A spoon clinked against a glass. Then Harriet pulled the rag away and set it on the table. She held out the glass. "Water and brandy."

Clem took a sip, the warmth slipping down to her belly. "Mostly brandy."

"As it should be." She shifted her hands, crossing them in front of her and waiting for Clem to finish. Her forehead wrinkled with concern and wariness. She took the glass and busied herself with neatening the side table. Folding the rag. Shifting the lamp. Wiping the base of the glass with a kerchief. Wiping her eyeglasses with the same, not minding the swirling streaks. "Why were you in the alley to begin with?"

"I was smoking."

"I've warned you where that habit leads."

"Haha. Give me those. You're going to scratch them." The cotton was damp and smelled sharp from the liquor. Clem rubbed each lens, holding them to the lamp and rubbing again. "There."

"Thank you." She slid them on. "The world is clear. Now tell me what it means."

Clem closed her eyes. The paper hadn't been meant to choke her. It was meant to be read. It was meant to be remembered. It was meant as a threat.

The writing, spider-thin and long-tailed, had seared itself behind Clem's lids.

> *I can print the truth in the* Gazette *or be silent. That choice is yours to make, Miss Watkins.*

Sullivan. She'd seen his handwriting on the notes in his satchel. She didn't think he had that sort of threat in him. And damn Maud for leaving the parlor. Rule number one: do not leave a room unattended.

"Has a man come by your sittings looking to communicate with his dead wife? Tall, stooped shoulders, mild to the point of milksop?"

"Mr. Sullivan."

"Yes."

"He came two nights ago. And he's scheduled for tomorrow—" She checked the clock. "Tonight. The letter's from him?"

"I have to get to the house." She pushed herself up, holding tight to her ribs and thankful for the wrapping. "He's a skeptic. He's found something and I need to fix it. And I'll need to look over yours this week."

"I have sittings—"

"No, you don't. I need to decommission everything. We're going to have to start over."

"I can't afford you again."

"You can't not afford me." She pressed her hands to her thighs. "I'm this close to making Maud . . . Will he be at the early or late sitting?"

"Early."

"He's not going to ruin her. Me. I won't be ruined. I'll find out what he has."

"And then what?"

"Be rid of it. I won't be blackmailed. I've worked too hard."

Harriet spread her palms then contracted her fists to her lap. "If it comes out—"

"You'll say you never met me. I know the drill." The clock ticked. Clem heard a scrape of the gears and clutch in the rhythm of the brass pendulum. "Your clock needs repair. I'll do it when I—"

Harriet grabbed the letter and ripped it in thirds. Then she pushed the pieces into the lamp globe, shaking her fingers when the flame came near. Her chest rose and fell with shallow breaths. "Make sure it doesn't come out."

Chapter Twenty-One

MAUD

"Can I have my dog?"

Maud set the book she had been reading—or skimming, as it were—to the seat of the rocker. She had not been able to sleep; the house was too quiet, too empty without Russell and Clem. She hated to admit that the knock had brought relief. Ethelred uncurled from her feet and stretched, then shook herself. She set her head on Maud's knee and wagged her tail once.

Then Clem knocked again.

"You are being requested." Maud patted the dog.

The landing was dim. Clem had already started up the stairs. Midstep, she bent in half and cried out, one hand to her rib cage. Her foot slipped off the tread to the one below and her entire body shuddered. "Ah, damn. Come on, dog." She slapped her leg and looked down at Maud, one hand feathering her swollen and bruised brow.

"My God. What happened to you?"

"I fell off a horse."

"Are you drunk?"

Clem let out a bark and then doubled over. "Jesus."

"Let me help you."

"No." She grimaced. "You'll need to go on your own. Rose has everything."

"I don't need Rose."

"Yes, you do. They'll all have maids."

Maud's stomach twisted. She would be left to herself. Not a sideshow, not a puppet of Clem's.

"You do exactly as I've written. Remember how much the Otts have paid for this. Now come, dog."

Ethelred slunk up the stairs and sat at the top, waiting as Clem pulled herself by the railing.

She did not come down in the morning to see them off. Just left another note on Maud's door:

> *We cannot rely on the vagaries and fancies of your spirit friends. That's not how you will rebuild your career. Until you are again the Maid of Light—when you can guarantee consistent manifestations—until then, follow the script.*

Russell had not come home at all.

⤸

"Oh, look." Rose poked Maud's shoulder and pointed past Maud's nose to some tree or hillock or large slab of granite, her voice piercing in its enthusiasm and close vicinity. Her voluminous bosom flattened against Maud's side as she clambered for a better view through the mud-splattered window, forcing Maud into a corner of the carriage, pinning her to the door. She wrinkled her nose at the girl's sweet smell and the lingering must in the sleeve of her shirt. The kitchen never fully lost its dampness; the maids always trailed the odor.

"That's a hawk, Miss Price. I think that's a hawk. Do you think so?" Rose turned her bright brown eyes on Maud, expecting an answer to her query.

There certainly was a view: a sweeping field littered with stones large as houses and the bulk of Mount Monadnock rising from the earth and mist.

Rose's mouth hung open. Her gaze darted all around, and her body grew taut and vigilant, hoping for another sighting of the bird that might be a hawk.

"I think it's flown away," Maud said, pulling her numb hand from under her leg and nudging Rose with a shoulder.

"It might have."

"It might have gone to your side."

With a twist of her head and body, Rose soon had her nose to the glass on her assigned side.

Maud took a long breath.

"At least we didn't go the Post Road. That Brawders House turns my skin to gibbering shivers." Rose peered from window to window. And she hummed. Hummed and pointed and poked. Maud was sure she'd never been anywhere except kitchen basements and washhouses. The note from Mrs. Parker next door contained not a whit of frustration or ire that her maid had been stolen away.

She is good at laundry and light of finger. We wish her the best in her new employment and wish the same for you.

Sent via post, rather than walked across the yard. But Maud was inured to the neighbors and their upturned noses. It wasn't as though she could up and leave. The house, though a burden that sucked much of the money into repairs and lately "reconstructions," was still her home. She couldn't drag it somewhere else.

A wheel hit another cleft, lifting Maud from her seat and banging her right down. Rose squinted at her, head tilted and mane of hair ready to tip her over.

"What are you looking at?"

"You don't look like a psychic."

"I'm not a psychic. I have no idea what the future holds."

"Mrs. Parker says it's all the Devil's work, but you're nice as candy. My sister once saved three weeks' wages to talk to a gypsy at the fair because she thought her Tommy had gone out on her and she was afraid to ask him directly."

"Rose," she said.

"Yes?"

"Would it be too arduous a task for you to be quiet?"

Rose chewed on a loose bit of skin at her thumbnail and considered Maud. "You want me to shut my mouth?"

"I do."

"Well then." The seat wheezed as she sat back with a huff. "All you had to do was say." She tore the skin off and spit it to the floor. Then she lifted the basket at her feet with a low, incomprehensible grumble and rifled through the contents. Her eyes brightened when they found her treasure.

"Cheese." She unwrapped the cloth and held it under Maud's nose.

Maud pushed it away. "Eat on your side."

"I'm only offering." The grumbling returned, though the cheese was thankfully removed from Maud's face. She dug through the basket again, producing a small pocketknife. She shaved a layer of mold from the end before cutting a thick slice. "Miss Watkins said you'd be like this."

"I don't want to talk about her."

"She said you'd say that too." She bit off a hunk and chewed. "It seems to me you don't like her at all, but you do everything she says."

217

"I don't do everything she says." And now she could spread her wings and not have them clipped. God knows what had happened to Clem the previous night. Maud wished she could sympathize. Instead, she felt she'd been given a gift.

Rose swallowed. "I know you don't always see them. The spirits. I've seen the rigging Mr. Sprague's put up everywhere. I wouldn't ever open my mouth about those troubles, you can count on me for that. She says if I make so much as a peep, well . . ." Rose drew her finger across her throat.

"There won't be rigging here. Nor tricks."

"Well, she did also say—"

"Rose."

"I think it best if we do as she says. That's all." She turned to look out the window. "There. There's the hawk. I think it's got a snake."

"Rabbit," Maud said. "It's got a rabbit."

∾

Mr. Ott yanked open the brougham's door and beamed up at Maud with a gap-toothed smile. The remaining threads of hair he possessed were flattened across his pate and forehead by the rain, which ran in rivulets along his shoulders and down his bright blue coat. "Miss Price, you are most welcome."

A houseboy hurried across the yard with an umbrella, holding it tight against the wind that blustered and pulled him off course. He arrived in a huff, ruddy cheeks and half-buttoned jacket.

"Sorry, Mr. Ott."

Ott waved a hand. "Never mind, never mind." He grabbed the umbrella's handle and hefted it from the boy's hand, tipping it to cover the step Maud was now expected to take from the vehicle to the glop of mud and pebble in the drive.

The house had not changed much from her previous visit, though some things showed life returning. Straw had been pulled from the front beds, the paths groomed, the roses were bare of their muslin covers. Potted geraniums lined the steps. A lilac over the doorway dared a few blooms. The windows gleamed silver, newly washed, curtains opened to the early day.

Rose squeezed against her to peer out at the house. "Grand as a pasha, ain't it?"

Maud shrunk to the side and twisted herself free. Clem may have insisted on Rose attending her, but she did not have to like it.

"Stay with the luggage." She took the hat Rose proffered and pinned it on, then held out her gloved hand to Ott, who enveloped it immediately in his mitt.

Her foot slipped on the wet step. She grabbed the side of the carriage and Ott's shoulder to right herself, avoiding the umbrella as it swung around toward her head.

Mr. Ott shoved it at the houseboy, who raised himself to his tiptoes to hold the parasol above their heads. But the rain spit at such an angle to sodden the feathers along the brim of her hat. Ott righted her on the ground. Then he spread his arms and crushed them around her, clapping a heavy hand to her back. "This is an honor."

He stepped away. The boy didn't know whose head now required the umbrella, so he tipped it one way and then another, teeth chattering as he did so.

"Perhaps we should get out of the rain," Maud said.

"It is a ferocious one, isn't it?" Mr. Ott opened his mouth and then snapped his teeth shut. "Like a lion."

"Or at least like rain."

"Yes. Can't have you with a head cold. Let's get in." He waved the groom to lead away the horse and carriage and Rose, who Maud hoped would be assigned a stall in the stables and leave her well enough alone.

"Nancy will be most happy to see you. And Celia is beside herself. She says she has a particular thing she wishes to discuss with her brother and hopes you will give her a private reading."

"Of course." A stone settled in her stomach. Here was the family she'd first deceived; the guilt did not sit well.

Mr. Ott led her across the drive, stones slipping and scrunching underfoot. She held her cloak closed against the whipping cold, glad for the soft, thick wool. Really, Clementine did know her fabrics.

My present for your trip. She'd even sewn Maud's initials in the collar.

Ott took her elbow, guiding her up the granite steps. Lilac blossoms lay crushed and brown on the stoop; he shifted them with the side of his boot and shot a sharp look at the boy.

Faces pressed against the front window, at least six sets of eyes following their path. Then the door swung open, and she was pulled into the foyer, Mrs. Ott lifting her cloak from her shoulders and handing it to the butler. The door shut the boy out in the cold, no doubt to clean up the rotten blossoms.

"You are here." Mrs. Ott squinted at her. She crossed her arms over her mourning dress. The jet beads of her bracelets clacked against each other. She shook her wrist to settle them. Her hair was whiter than Maud remembered, her skin paper thin, though she could not have been more than forty. The death of a child took a cruel toll. "But you are wasting away, Miss Price."

"Am I?"

She turned at the loud clearing of a throat, surprised to find Mr. Garrison standing before her. He pursed his lips and pushed at his glasses, then gave Maud a sharp little bow.

Garrison had not been on the guest list.

"Mr. Garrison, a surprise."

"I thought you might be pleased."

"Will we be holding a competition?" Maud plastered on a smile.

Mr. Ott barked a laugh that echoed in the round dome. "What a grand idea. I think we should take sides and see who lassos the most spirits."

"I defer to Mr. Garrison's experience."

"But you're the one who brings my boy, so my money's on you." He smacked his belly and touched her shoulder to face the guests. "I am remiss in my duties. Let me introduce you around. You, of course, need no introduction at all, but this ragtag group does."

He began with a short man with a crown of red hair, whose name was Judd, or Jedd. He took Maud's hand and shook it. She dipped her head and remembered he had an uncle dead at a very old age, though she could not remember the deceased's name offhand. Her head buzzed. It was as if one pink shawl (Miss Brennan) bled into a cravat (Mr. Timpkins) then a bustled woman whose words whistled as she spoke and a man who wore a broomstick for a mustache. All the while her headache grew.

Still she allowed the men to peck the top of her hand and the women to dutifully shake two of her fingers, and all kept up their manners. She twisted an embroidered flower at her waist and murmured greetings in return.

"They are quite keen." Garrison bent to speak in a low tone to her.

"It seems more than ten."

"I count twenty."

They passed the birdcage and the canary. It ruffled its feathers and tucked its beak into what was left of them. One stuck against the bars of the cage.

"I wish a word with you, Miss Price." Garrison pinched the corners of his mouth into what passed as a smile for him. She'd seen it enough at the psychical meetings; Harriet commented he bathed in and drank lemon juice and eschewed the sugar out of spite.

"Of course."

"Morning breakfast, then?"

Mr. Ott's face loomed before her. "You will need a rest. Nancy says it's the right thing to do."

221

"I would be . . ." Somehow, they had circled back to the foyer and stood at the foot of the grand stairs. Celia stood at the first landing, the gray of her mourning dress drab against the peach of the silk paper that curved the walls around her. "Miss Ott."

"Celia, my girl, just who I need. Would you show Miss Price her room?" He lifted a hand to the assembly that had followed. "Miss Price requires her rest."

"She's not Queen Victoria," Celia muttered.

Ott sucked in his lips and shot his daughter a look.

She ignored him and instead turned to take the next flight up. "Come with me, Miss Price."

Maud followed, slowing at the landing to look down at the group. They wanted so much from her; the anticipation and curiosity crackled and jumped.

"Aren't you coming?" Celia leaned over the railing. Her ringlets bounced, but they were the only soft thing about the girl. All the rest had drained at the death of her brother. Now she was angles and metal and rust.

The group below had wandered back to the front room, the spectacle of the medium overtaken now by other entertainments. Mrs. Ott swept past the room's doorway, a maid, balancing a tray of coffees, dragged in her wake.

"She's with child."

Maud looked up at Celia.

"They're changing out Tom's entire room. She says I'm fourteen now and it'll teach me what it's like. To be a mother." Then she continued up the stairs, stopping once more to gesture to Maud to follow. *Much like Queen Victoria,* Maud thought. She pushed a wilted ribbon from her shoulder and gathered her skirts. She sighed. Much like Queen Victoria.

Chapter Twenty-Two

CLEMENTINE

Clem's ribs hurt. She couldn't stop the throbbing headache that made her wince with any small turn of her head. She flicked the pulled curtain to peer out at the street, then flopped it back and stumbled over the dog. "We're about to be blackmailed, Ethelred, and damn Russell is nowhere to be found when you need him."

She pulled the dog's good ear and blew out a breath. What the hell did Sullivan see? She ran her fingers again along each seam in the wall, but even an inch away the paper edges blended. She checked the wires that pulled at the chairs, rolling the rug and peering at the boards. The table held no secret drawers, the ceiling no extra chandeliers; she had designed the room for simplicity. It was too intimate for technicals—though she hoped to approach Rose about singing in her little bedroom, as that sound went right up the chimney and would land with great effect here. It would land with best effect in Sullivan's lap. Maybe she should have the girl shriek like a banshee and give the man a final heart attack.

She dropped to his seat. "Oh, my dear Maisie," she imitated in a drippily teary tone, "to speak once more would give me faith in God. Miss Price, oh blubber blubber—"

The mirror. Her face bulged and distorted in the glass. As did the table and its legs and even the wall behind Maud's seat.

"Damn. You look like a beast." She rushed the mirror and growled. Then she grabbed a spirit tablet from the cabinet, setting it precisely where Maud would work her own writing board. She sat herself in Sullivan's chair and snuffed the lamp.

The room was swathed in black. Ethelred made a small whimper.

"Shh. Let me think."

Maud gave an introduction, how the souls wished to share their joy with the living and other such rot. The circle sang a ditty of invocation, maybe another if they felt the spirits. Hands were clasped. "We will now," Maud said, "give a knock to Summerland's doors, and invite who opens them to leave their realm and join ours."

Clem slammed her fist to the table. The thinnest strip of light slid under the hall door. All Sullivan needed was to open his eyes and look straight in the mirror. Maud's replacing a blank paper for a rigged one might not be obvious, but it would be suspicious. All he needed was a minute by himself to turn it over and move the lever to see how it all worked.

Out in the hall, the brass mail slot squealed. Two thumps of mail. At least the postman twined them in packets rather than letting them spit all over the place. The flap smacked back in place.

Clem gritted her teeth and stood. She shambled over to the window and yanked the curtains open. Rain spattered the glass and slid in streaks. Like Mr. Sullivan's over-emotive tears.

She wouldn't pay him a cent. She'd invite him to examine every inch of the room and the house and up her skirt if he wished. If Russell ever deigned to show his face, the house could be put back to rights. She'd stop the sittings altogether. Who needed them, anyway? For the weekend, the Otts had given them three times what they would make in a month. Enough for a down payment on the Orpheum for a night. Two if she milked her injuries.

Mr. Sullivan held the evidence to block it all.

"Dog?" she said. "Damn and hell to the parlor tricks. And to Sullivan too."

∽

The Scientific Unmaking of Mediums, Clairvoyants, Mesmerists, and other such HUMBUGS of the Spiritualist Movement. Vol. 2.
    —Alfred Sullivan, Esq.

The man, Clem thought, did not lack arrogance. Esquire, indeed. This is what the bastard was working on. There was no dear departed Maisie—as she suspected all along. Just journal after bound journal of obsessively detailed ramblings and newspaper articles pasted to the margins—séances from Providence to Albany, from Kennebunk to Saco, then a turn to Concord and west to Maud's homely sitting room.

She sat at Mr. Sullivan's desk, the one she'd seen him bent to, and flipped the pages of one tome after another.

Taps revealed, apples used. 1873, Lawrence. Mrs. Leland Frost.

The debunking of voice boxes. 1868, Walpole. Josephus Blinken.

The unmasking of Onawa, Apache girl, and Jim Blanchett, convict transport to West Indies. 1875, Morristown. Miss Faraday.

How to escape a spirit cabinet in five sketches.

The trick of the guillotined head.

Spirit writing and the falsified note. 1877, Harrowboro.
Miss Price & co.

Damn the man.

She slammed the last journal shut and sat back in the chair, sliding around on its wheels as she stewed. She swung the seat around to glare at the bookshelves before her. Gilded titles: *Biography of Mrs. J. H. Conant, the World's Medium. Plain Guide to Spiritualism. People from the Other World.* One after the other. All the leather spines cracked from use, the gilt flaking.

He'd need a dray horse and cart to drag all these around.

She twisted the chair back to its rightful spot, set her elbows to the desk, her chin to her palms, and stared at the window shutters. All this unmasking. All this degrading. She had been right about the bastard all along. So simpering and soppy, so prim and proper, droopy eyes always on the verge of feigned tears. Looking for his Maisie. Just an easy lie to gain entrance and, like Cleopatra's asp, bite his host and leave the venom.

She flipped open her watch. Fifteen minutes until Harriet's show ended. No hacks came to this part of town. He'd have a twenty-minute walk back if he didn't stop for a drink.

The books required burning. At least the one with Maud. She would burn the pages, these and any on Harriet.

With a jerk, she pushed the chair back and stood. She kicked the leg of the desk, which hurt her more than the damn wood, then hopped about, waiting for the throb in her toe to stop.

She'd burn it all down. The sticks and thin boards of the cottage would go up in a flash. Add a bit of copper sulfate for a good, green-flamed spectacle. She gave the house five minutes of life at the most. But there was the neighborhood to consider. The cottages here sat cheek by jowl with each other and moldered in the shadow of the shoe peg factory. She had no desire to harm the innocent.

The book it was, then. Burn it in the stove as a warning she was on to him. And write a note to remind him his stay in Harrowboro was at its end and that all houses of clairvoyance were effectively shut to him.

She stared at the cold fire grate. The poker and tongs hung from long hooks in the wall. A box of matches sat on the mantel, a basket of kindling on the floor. She tore pages from the book, crumpling and stuffing them to the small firebox. She added slivers of kindling in a ring below. Poked more through the wrinkled papers. Struck a match on the sole of her shoe and dropped it in. Like burning a witch, she thought. Blue flame to red to gold.

A stack of wood sat behind the kindling basket. She tossed a log to the burgeoning flames. Took the tip of the poker to it, turning it with the hook so the driest of bark faced the flames.

"This is a surprise."

Clem jolted back.

Sullivan stood in the hallway. She'd not heard a sound.

"You should be at Mrs. Martin's."

His lips curved into a frown.

God, he looked the part of the sad widower. Stooped shoulders, lowered head, weary eyes. He raised his hand to rub his jaw, then watched the flames consume the paper. His neck bore scabs and long scratches.

From when she had fought him off in the alley. She tightened her grip on the poker and took a step back. Her hip caught the corner of the desk. Her heart jumped to her throat.

He studied her, his doe eyes flitting across her, mouth playing at a smile. He picked at a scab, squeezed it between his thumb and forefinger, and flicked it to the floor.

"I contemplated burning the whole place down," she said. "But then I thought, where would you go on this horrid wet night?"

"Kind of you."

"I have my moments."

"You can burn all you want; I'll write it again." He gestured to the books. "I've wanted to believe. It's led me far and astray. Taken my eyes from heaven to the rotted soil of man. Or woman."

"Yet you don't mind digging in the dirt for a blackmail coin or two. Hasn't done you well if this place is the extent of the earnings."

"You're a clever girl, Clementine. Or Mrs. Turlock." He tucked his hand under his jacket and pulled out a small notebook, the cardboard cover soft and ripped at the corners. "The mechanism on the planchette was quite inventive. The little gifts? Miss Price needs more practice with that." He raised his eyes to the ceiling. "And you yourself pace."

"What?"

"Upstairs. When you are not the royal consort, so to speak. There's no need to prevaricate; I've seen your lot pull tricks for years and years."

"So what do you want?"

"Not money."

"What, then? Another feather in your self-righteous cap?"

"People should know the truth—"

"There isn't such a thing. You know that as well as I. There's only spectacle and illusion. Give people their solace, Mr. Sullivan. It doesn't harm anyone. I'd even call it a type of charity."

"It's lying. You've done it so long, it's like a well-worn coat." His eyes narrowed, the gaze hard as chips of ice. "All the way back to the Children's Home."

"What in the hell are you talking about?"

"Before your engagement with Miss Price, you did odd jobs for Harriet Martin, referred to you by your old employer, Mrs. King, whose employ you left under vague conditions. Mrs. King was very fond of you. Or rather, of her own generosity and charity. You must have read her biography. She writes about the waif she saved from a snowy Boston street. A waif named Clementine Watkins, onetime tenant of the Laconia Children's Home, in fact. A home run by a Mrs. Bletham and a bevy of nuns, including one Sister Matilda. Excellent education at the Laconia Children's Home. I was so keen on Latin. Until the smallpox came. Kiboshed an entire semester."

"You were at that place?"

"Do you know they gave out surnames based on the year of arrival? I'm an *S.* Sullivan. There was Sloan and Sloat and Savage and Stanton. You came with the *W*'s."

"So what?"

"You wouldn't remember me; I spent most of my time in the sick ward. Do you remember that ward? It looked over the shops and ice-house and well. You'd point up and wave to us." He raised his hand, curled down his index finger, and waved. "You and my sister. Thick as thieves, the two of you."

Clem's ears rang. Her throat grew tight. She remembered it: the girls and boys standing on their cots to gaze out at the others, hands to the glass, knuckles tapping until someone turned to look up.

⌒

Little Ginny chucked her chin to Clem's shoulder and burrowed against her back, soaking in any warmth from the snow. She reached around to stroke the hair on Clem's doll and blew long breaths of mist. "Think we'll get it?"

"The pox?"

Clem felt the girl's shoulders lift and fall.

"Mrs. Bletham's already ordered their graves dug."

"She hasn't," Clem said. "You're lying."

"It's what I heard."

The little patients above scratched at the windows and waved down. Clem waved up, her skin bright red from the cold, clear of pustules and scabs, the scar on her severed finger smooth and white.

⌒

Now she rubbed the ridge of it with her thumb. She tipped her head. "I'm not going to give you any money. You have nothing on me. So I thank you for your hospitality and—"

"You killed my sister. And disappeared."

Clem bit her teeth into her upper lip. Then she laughed. "I have to give you credit. Your research skills are as keen as any journalist's. Or mole's. Dig enough tunnels, they'll connect."

"I never thought they would." He pulled an envelope from his jacket pocket and held it out between them. "But now I have this."

He shook the envelope. "Don't you want to read it?"

"No. I'm not interested."

"But it's from Sister Matilda. All the way from Nova Scotia. Don't you want to—"

"Sister Matilda is dead."

His shoulders shook, and his smile grew wider as he laughed. "No, no. She did suffer a terrible fall, that is true, right down those back stone steps. After dragging poor Ginny from the well."

Clem's teeth chattered. Then she shuddered, as if she'd been dropped into the cold well water herself. Sister Matilda had seen what happened. *What have you done, sweet girl? What have you done?*

"I don't remember you. And I don't remember a Ginny. You have the wrong person, Mr. Sullivan."

"Why did you hurt her?" His voice came from high above, echoing against stone. He leered over her, all else blocked out but his watery doe eyes.

Then he was prone, staring up at her, heels scraping into the planks, hand grappling for the poker hooked into his temple.

Clem crouched down, hands to knees, and watched his blinks slow. His eyes dull. His hands dropped, one smacking the stone of the hearth. Feet sliding and then still.

She plucked the envelope from where it had landed on his chest when he fell. It was empty. Of course it was.

"She took my doll. That's why."

⌒৩

Clem bent her head to the rain and wrapped her cloak tighter. Her hand trembled. Her whole body shook, as if she'd been hit with lightning, the electricity bolting through her muscles and along her skin. She felt it surge and wane as she strode away from Sullivan's. Throat to belly to groin. Power and emptiness. Wobbling feet that slipped on fallen leaves and a hand gripped so tight to the poker, she thought it welded forever to her hand.

She should do something with it. Throw it in the millpond or toss it in the river near the Bottoms.

Her head fizzed and whistled. She hadn't thought. Just swung the iron and listened to the soft thump at his temple. He'd been so surprised, eyes widening and staying that way as he crumpled to the floor. Now she had the poker and he lay with a smashed glass and spill of rum to complete the scene. Spectacle and illusion. Unfortunate bang to the head. Hearths are very hard.

She didn't remember him. He was just one of the little sick ones, and Mrs. Bletham did have graves dug. More than half were filled, white-cotton strips tied to each stake, names and cause of decease embroidered in black.

Lafayette Underhill—Smallpox.
Jocelyn Wright—Smallpox.
Benjamin Sloat—Smallpox.
Isaiah Sloan—Smallpox.
Virginia Sullivan—Smallpox.

Mrs. Bletham kept accidents and other inconveniences out of her reports. Donors did not like facilities that left children to fall down wells and drown.

She pushed a wet hank of hair from her forehead and stared at the hulk of the peg shop. The windows wavered and blurred in the downpour, black sunken eyes amidst the rust red of brick. The cottages lay just down the hill. No one the wiser. Smoke curled from chimneys. Candles and lamps glowed yellow behind closed curtains.

She had to move on. The street before her was empty, but for puddles clogged with leaves and water sluicing from the downspouts of the manufactories that lined the road. Just two blocks up the hill, she'd join the nightlife—patrons leaving a late dinner at the Eagle Hotel, passengers alighting from the 10:30 Nashua stage, and hacks and carriages lining up to receive a fare, for it was a damn cold and wet night. The first of the audience would be exiting the Orpheum, the men already with cigars poked to their lips, the women sending trailing goodbyes to their friends, murmurs of "Did you ever see the like . . ." and "Don't forget to call on Thursday—we're having music . . ."

No. She could not go past there. Not with the gas lamps and marquees flooding the street with light. Home would be best; she could peel off her clothes and settle in as if she'd just decided an early night would suit her best.

A lantern's light painted the brick. A night watchman hurried around the corner of the far mill. He hunkered under an umbrella.

Clem clenched the poker tight and wondered how she'd explain it, or how a woman alone in the middle of the night got to be in Old Town. She grated her teeth, scouring the loading bays and trash bins for anything she could toss to catch his attention and throw him off his sentry path. It would give her a few minutes to dash to an alley then out the other side. She'd find her way through the yards and liveries all right. She knew the routes.

There wasn't a stone or board to throw. *Don't be furtive,* she thought, *just hold up your head and stride right past him.*

She could have kicked herself. *Stupid,* she thought, *stupid to let herself go like that.* Lose control and have no plan at all. Stupid emotions led to stupid problems—like having to pass a watchman on a street when you've just killed a man.

Nothing to do but do it. Don't be furtive. Hood pulled up, poker hidden in the folds of the cloak, head high. Maybe a hum of a tune—what was the one Maud hummed without knowing?

> *"I sat and watch'd her many a day,*
> *When her eye grew dim, and her locks were gray . . ."*

"You there." He held the lantern high.

Clem picked up her pace. Straight toward him, never mind her shoes dragging in the water that gushed toward grates. She didn't stop, just nodded her head as she passed by. "God be with you this mad night."

He circled around but did not follow.

"Thank you for the light, sir."

She tossed the poker at the millpond, the splash covered by the heavy plonks of rain to the water's skin.

Up ahead, the sidewalk surged with men stumbling from a tavern, shrugging on coats and soft caps. She stepped into the alley and back behind the saloon, ducked under a fence into a livery yard, and walked along the stable wall until she came out on Third Street. A white steeple pierced the night sky, which meant a graveyard she could cross, and then it was a hop and skip to the house and fire and warm clothes.

She'd ask Rose to make up a bath. She'd sit in it and drink a bottle of wine and give Ethelred a pat.

But Rose was gone. She'd sent her with Maud. To keep an eye out. Had her practice walking in the pitch dark and waving her luminous hands about, should the Otts' guests prove restless.

The rain stopped. The air grew viscous, each of her breaths drawn with an effort and exhaled like coughs. She was so very close to the house, why wouldn't her feet move? The road, quiet here by the gate to the church, the moon bathing it in watery silver, billowed out and tilted. She gripped a post to keep from falling, leaning her back against the fence to wait out the ache in her side. Wait out his eyes, so surprised as he fell, so unbelieving as the life sapped out of him.

She pushed the gate to the cemetery. Stepped into the loam and along the mourner's walk.

He deserved it. His sister had too.

⟡

She tore off the cloak, letting it fall by the cellar, and ignored Ethelred's barks from the kitchen. The rain had soaked the yard, leaving a churn of mud. Her hands slipped in the moss and wet as she tried to keep purchase on the old well's cover, get underneath to shove it upright and away. The pain in her side came like a knife stuck deep. She called out, curling around the red heat of it. Gritted her teeth and waited out the flares before her.

Blood is black in the moonlight. Splatters and strings of it patterned her shirt and skirt, clumped her hair like sap.

Her hands shook and could not twist a button. She tore at the collar of her shirt, fingers tacky, sticking to the fabric. Dragged the sleeves off her arms. Twisted the skirt around and wrenched it down until the button ripped from the wool.

Ethelred barked and barked.

"Shut up." Her teeth chattered.

A lamp shined in the neighbor's upstairs window, the yellow flicking through the leaves and brambles. Then it moved on, leaving her the dark.

She tugged the drawstring of her petticoat and stepped out, then bunched the garments and shoved them in the well.

They didn't fall. The well was full of rotten leaves and dirt. She stuck her fist to the middle and pushed down until the muck swallowed it all with one suck of sound.

Chapter Twenty-Three

MAUD

Celia's jaw jutted forward. She set the toy soldier to the dressing table. "You brought me this."

Maud stared at it, then at the reflection of the toy and Rose across the room, unpacking her trunk. "I did."

There was very little she could say. *I deceived you. I have no idea where Clementine found the toy, and I don't wish to guess.*

She'd been given a chance now at redemption—with the Otts, with Matthias, with her own honor. And this gave her a lightness of spirit, as if with each passing minute, she moved closer to making it right.

Rose crossed between them, setting Maud's brush and comb and mirror on the dresser. She did not take any notice of the toy, saying instead, "You'll be changing from your travel clothes, miss?"

"Yes, thank you."

Rose gave a nod and turned back to the trunk, unfolding the tissue from one of the dresses and making a show of holding it out before sticking it in the wardrobe.

Celia glowered at Rose. "You can leave."

"Pardon?"

"I'm talking, and you can leave." Celia tightened her lips and stared at Rose's feet rather than her face; a habit picked up from her mother, no doubt, and Maud knew it would one day bring resentment and insubordination in her staff.

Rose noticed, too, and gave a half curtsy, accompanied by a sneer.

"The other maids are downstairs. You can go with them, and Miss Price will pull the bell if she needs you."

"Yes, miss."

"What's your name?"

"You can go, Rose." Maud gave her a quick smile.

Rose laid another gown over the trunk's top and turned for the door.

"Not that way," Celia said. "Over there."

Rose gritted her teeth and gave a fawning nod of her head. "I'm so appreciative you showed me the way." She twisted the knob on the servants' door. "So appreciative of your kindness."

Maud covered her mouth and coughed to hide her laugh. The woman drove her mad, but she had to admire her gall.

"What are you laughing at?" Celia turned her head with a snap.

"Nothing. I've got a tickle."

"Oh." She frowned, her pale brows touching. She dragged her lower lip along her teeth and pressed her palms together in front of her.

"You are well?" Maud's bum was numb from the carriage ride. She shifted on the dressing room chair and straightened a leg. Her foot tingled and she wished she could take off her shoe and stretch her toes. But the girl's back was straight with determination and she wanted to say something particularly to her.

Maud thought back to the previous meeting, to passing the toy and remarking on the silent canary, to Celia's sobs and cornucopia of thanks.

"How are you, Celia?"

"I want to talk to Tom." She pointed at the soldier. "That's everything left. They've taken all his clothes away as if he never had been."

Maud's heart tapped her chest. "What would you like to say?"

"Bring him here and let me talk to him."

"They don't appear like that."

"Please try." Her cheeks flushed. "I need to tell him I'll always remember. I need to tell him I'm sorry and Mother's having another baby to forget him, but I won't."

"Oh, Celia." Maud reached out to her, but the girl flinched away.

"No. You call him to me."

Maud nodded. "Close your eyes, then. I will ask."

"I want to watch."

"Then at least take my hand."

The girl's skin was cold, as if she'd just come in from the yard. A hiss came, like wind across sand. Maud squeezed Celia's hand tight. "Hello. May I ask who's there?"

Maud fought to hear over the thump of her heart, struggling against the din of the wind to hear just the smallest of whispers. But it circled away, pulling the sound with it, and leaving Maud just the thud of her pulse.

"I'm sorry." She opened her eyes. The room shimmered and then slipped back into place. Celia would throw the toy at the door.

And she did. Her skin purpled with rage. She picked the soldier up from the floor and threatened to throw it again. "You're like the rest of them. You weren't the first Father dragged us to. I know you were nothing then, I saw you. I saw how you made up sounds and pretended you heard him, but you didn't hear him, did you?"

"Celia—"

"You didn't."

Shouldn't do that, Celie, you'll get a big smack.

She froze. Maud froze.

The little boy's voice came from the head of the bed. But there was no boy. Just dried pansies pressed behind an oval of glass.

"How did you do that?" Celia glared at her.

"I didn't."

Oh Celie, come join me here. It's ever so nice. She approached the bed, arm extended as if she thought she could catch a mirage.

Not there. Come play. The voice swung around, now on the opposite side from Celia. *Do you want to hear a secret?*

Now it traveled across the floor, like a clumsy snake. "The spirit is weak now. Aren't you, spirit?"

Can I come—

"It's too weak, Celia," Maud barked, loud enough the girl jumped. "It's gone."

Celia's eyes glittered. "There isn't anything." She dropped to the floor, drew up the dust ruffle, and peered under the bed. Then she sat back and stared at Maud. "I'll figure you out. You mark my words. My parents may think you've brought him back, but I know it's as fake as your sympathy."

"That is where you are wrong. My heart breaks with yours."

The girl grimaced, the yearning to believe the voice had been her brother's warring with her very warranted disbelief. "You wait." She stumbled up and tromped from the room.

Maud squeezed her hands to fists and clenched her jaw in anger. "You can get out of the trunk."

The dress flipped off and slid to the floor. Russell sat up, one arm over the trunk's edge. "That was very good, wasn't it?"

She folded over, shoving her face to her skirts, and let out a muffled scream. Then she sat up. "Did she send you?"

"No. I came for you. I really am here to—"

"I don't care. I don't want you here."

He made a long face and crawled from the trunk, tucking in the edge of his shirt and swiping back a hank of hair that fell right back to his forehead. He bowed, then lifted the dress Rose had abandoned and placed it on its hanger in the wardrobe. Then he turned to the upright trunk, pulled out a drawer, and shut it right back. "I'll leave this to Rose."

She leapt up, slamming the first trunk shut and pushing at the lid to the other. "None of you listen."

"Careful of the spirit trumpet." He pointed to her feet and the elbow of black-painted brass that disappeared under the bed. "That's a new design. I picked it up from the brass works only two days ago."

"Why are you here?"

He spread his palms and shook his head, as if the reason had fled just a moment prior.

"What other tricks have you set up?"

"None. I swear. Well, Clem tutored Rose with the gloves in case you . . ."

"In case I fail."

"She doesn't want you to fail. No. No no no. That would be a terrible misrepresentation."

"So you brought that contraption. Now you can report back to her—"

"No. That's not—"

"What is it, then? Why else would you be here?"

He sank to the edge of the bed, legs wide and fingers playing on his knees. He contemplated the peach silk walls and gilt dresser. Picked at the comforter and pushed at the trumpet with his toe. "I like you. No. That's—listen. You have a séance tonight and I promise to do nothing. Unless you give the code, of course."

"I'm not going to give you a code. I am here in good faith. I haven't been in good faith since you and Clementine barged into my house. God, don't you see?"

"All I wish to mention is the Otts are a meaningful family. And if it goes right—"

"I don't want you here. I don't want your help. Go home and take care of . . . whatever she is to you."

"She doesn't need taking care of."

"You are heartless, aren't you?"

"Me?"

"She could barely make the stairs when I left. I think she broke ribs, but never mind trying to help."

"What are you talking about?"

"She fell from a horse. That's what she said."

"Where would she get a horse?"

"I don't know. Where do you get glowing faces?"

"That's just phosphorous on wood." He looked up at Maud. "Is she all right?"

"She left written instructions at my door this morning. My guess is it's only sore ribs and a bruising to her vanity."

"Are you sure?"

"The note suggested she was already on the mend."

"Well. No Clementine to bother us, then. I expected her to show up." With a slap to his knee, he rose. "I haven't felt so free in ages. This . . ." He pulled on his lower lip and gave a nod. "Well."

The servants' door opened. "I'm to dress you for dinner." Rose pulled a pin from her lips and stuffed it to her hair. "That's what I've been—"

"Rose."

"Mr. Sprague."

"Which way to the kitchen?"

"Left."

"Door out?"

"Right through the butler's pantry."

"Good." He bowed to Maud, then Rose, then left.

The door swung open again. "I want you to win." He loped to the bed and pulled the trumpet from underneath, twisting it into two pieces. "Au revoir."

Rose stared after him, then back at Maud. "I see how it goes."

"You don't see anything. Get me dressed." She sat with a thump at the dressing table and gripped the brush. She held it up. "Are you getting me ready?"

"He is a good-looking gentleman."

"He's not a gentleman."

"They never are. Not really. I had a lad once named Nero—Nero, can you believe that? Who would name a child such a—"

"Rose."

"Yes. I know. Be quiet." She put her finger to her lips. "Shh. Shhh shhh shhh." She stood behind Maud and laid her hands to each shoulder. "It's cold."

"What?"

"If you say, 'It's cold,' I go like this." She flopped her hands all around. "With the gloves."

Maud squeezed her eyes shut. She smacked the brush to the table. "That will not be required, Rose." She bit down hard enough she thought she'd crack her back teeth. "I am not a puppet."

"I'm the one who's got to flip-flap my hands."

"That's a marionette."

"I know that."

"Just dress me for dinner."

"And be quiet."

"And that."

Rose unpinned Maud's hair, separated it into four sections, and took up one long tress. She pulled the brush underneath in one rough yank, catching a tangle and giving a sharp tug. She regarded Maud in the looking glass. Then her eyelashes fluttered and lowered, and she muttered "Sorry" and picked up the comb. "She said I should remind you of the book."

"What book?"

"In your reticule." Now her finger slipped through the tangle, working the knots. "The cue book." The knot snapped and Rose grabbed the brush again. "In case you get lost."

A book of life and death. Names and dates and connecting arrows from one guest to another and to a corpse somewhere rotting away. Maud's chest tightened like a fist. She looked toward the reticule, the call of the book like a siren's song. She could take a brief look. Just to make sure; just to have a name to request. Just in case. Just a small necessity. Rose would lie for her, if she gave her enough money, she was sure of it.

Maud pressed her hand to her mouth and stared at herself in the mirror. "No."

Rose's eyes snapped up and caught hers. "Miss?"

"Burn the book."

 

There was no way to get warm. All the windows were open to the night sky, letting in the damp chill. Three candelabra sat across the dining table, the fat, squat candles fizzing out at each gust of air, relit each time by a server in white gloves and a black tailcoat.

"He's warm enough." Mrs. Peckham, just to Maud's right, shot an eye full of envy at the server. The dinner guests hunched over their soup bowls, slurping in the tepid warmth.

"It's a lovely soup," Maud said.

Mrs. Ott dabbed her lips and waved for the server to take her bowl. "New asparagus with tarragon and . . . something."

Mrs. Peckham, whom Maud met only when seated next to her, scraped the bottom of her bowl and slurped the dregs from the tip of the spoon. She considered Maud over the handle. "I don't go in for demonism, but Nancy insisted."

Garrison, just to Maud's left, leaned forward. "You will find no demonism, but the transcendent beauty of the spheres."

"Or ghosts." Judd of the wild red hair lifted his glass and drained the wine. "That's what I'm looking forward to. Things that bump around and—"

Mr. Ott glared at him. "It's not play."

Judd's face lost its ruddiness. He held out the goblet for another pour and quaffed half of the wine before setting it to the table. His eyes bulged from his head as he stared across at Maud, the whites pink and lids puffy from the liquor he'd no doubt swilled all afternoon. "Still ghosts," he whispered.

Garrison gave a tight smile and turned a shoulder to cut him from the conversation. "The speech you gave. At the Psychical Society."

Maud's spine stiffened. "Yes, I appreciate any opportunity to speak."

Her bowl was cleared, replaced by a plate of roast and charred leeks. The blood and juice of the meat had congealed atop it like a scab.

With a nod as his own plate was served, Garrison took up his fork and knife and made a clear cut to the beef. He chewed the bit and swallowed, then cut another into a smaller piece, his knife squeaking across the porcelain. "We are a small band, Miss Price. It would do to keep the wagons rounded, as they say out West."

"I don't understand."

"Your sittings come with comment. Much comment. And, I must be honest, a sliver of resentment."

"I cannot help someone's envy."

He lifted a leek. It drooped over the tines. "Of course not. That is each our own sin to confront." He sucked the leek in his mouth, not in any way disguising his distaste of it.

Maud knew resentment would follow her; it had in the past. Her father pooh-poohed the letters of judgment that she was *too* successful, playing *too much* to the crowd. "Do not," he said, "ever listen to the grumblers. If they had half your gift they'd use it, but as they don't, we'll use their fine notes to clean our bottoms."

"As head of our Society, I do hear all issues, as you know. And spiritualism itself is suspect, as new movements are. It is also fragile. Between the Woodhull scandals and the Davenports playing contortionist games, we are vulnerable to attacks on our faith." He flicked his nose with his thumb, moved closer, and lowered his voice. "I have received a letter of exposure, with diagrams and intricate detailing as to certain . . . tricks."

"And how does that relate to me?"

"It is about you, Miss Price."

"I haven't—"

Garrison looked down the table to Ott, who held his wife's hand, patting it unconsciously as he ignored her and spoke to Miss Brennan. Her curls bounced as she listened. Maud heard the word "gosling" and nothing else.

"Whatever was said is not true." The words cut her tongue as they left her mouth.

"We will need to circle, Miss Price. Should this make the newspaper, all the rest of our group would be susceptible to ridicule and the loss of our cause. We don't want that, do we?"

"I have done nothing wrong."

"Still, we will need to circle. You understand." He leaned away, turning his attention to the conversation on his left and leaving her with her overcooked leeks and graying meat.

Mrs. Peckham chewed a leek like a cud and stared across at the grand painting of cherubs cascading from heaven.

Let me go to the fair and show. A ring-a-lee. A ring-a-lo.

"Pardon?"

The woman turned her head toward Maud. "What did you say?"

"You said—"

Judd jumped from his chair and grabbed at his hair, standing it on end. "Ha!" Then he plopped back down and continued to eat.

"New money," Mrs. Peckham said.

The back parlor had been turned into a sort of playhouse, with gilded chairs, a raised platform, and green velvet curtains hung like wings to each side. Candles flamed from surrounding sconces, but even with the mass of them, the high ceiling remained bathed in darkness.

Maud found Celia there, standing center stage by a tufted armchair and round table. "I've checked everything." She lifted her chin and gave Maud a stubborn, hard look.

Maud sighed. She had wanted a moment's peace before the attendees swarmed in. She wanted to catch again the voice that sang *a ring-a-lee*.

"I am aware of all things counterfeit. I will tell my father—"

A tapping came from behind the curtained glass, then continued across to the next. "Someone wants in."

Celia frowned and gave a small shake of her head. "Just like that."

"Someone knocked on the window."

"But there's no window there." She marched off the dais and slung back a curtain. "It's for effect. Mother says it makes people think of sunshine, though I don't know how, as they're closed all the time. You're just trying to rile me."

"How old are you?"

"I'm fourteen."

"I would have thought you sixty-eight with your suspiciousness."

"That's rude."

"It is. I'm sorry. Do you think I might have one moment . . ."

But in came Judd with a sway and hiccup. He took the front seat and slapped his knees. "I do like a good strong fright."

Then the others came, Mr. Ott waving them to various seats. Garrison escorted Mrs. Ott to the front row. She held a long black handkerchief tight to her fist.

"Your mother mourns."

"We all mourn."

Ott came around to face the crowd, hand raised to quiet them. "There we are now, there we are."

The room took on an odor of sherry and the third-course haddock. Fans snapped open: against the smell or due to the stifling heat in this room as opposed to the ice box they'd left, Maud could only guess.

"We are all, of course, here for our honored guest, Miss Maud Price."

A round of polite clapping came and went.

My love . . .

Maud tipped her head to listen. The voice was like honey. So familiar and so wanted.

Ott cupped her elbow and dragged her forward. "This little woman brought back my boy."

Celia, who now stood against the back wall, gave a snort.

"Let her do the act," Judd said.

"Yes, yes." The servers slipped in the door to take positions by the sconces, followed by the maids. And Rose. She held up her hands to show they were bare of gloves, luminous or other.

Mr. Ott dragged Maud back to the small stage and fumbled in his pocket for a match. He lit the squat candle on the table and turned to the servers. "Put them out."

All at once the room went dark, only the halo of light by her side. "My foot."

"Ah, sorry." The chair scraped the floor as Ott sat. "Carry on."

Maud took a long breath. She clenched her hands, then shook them to relieve the creeping prick of numbness. *Listen,* she thought. *Just listen.*

Catch the cat—John Douglas asks to speak—how long I've been—

Her mouth moved, voices crawling over her lips, taking shape in blues and yellows, a cheek, a gray braid, wizened skin, falling boy.

It was a roil of water and sand. She listened to it all as if she were held underwater, stones in her pockets, silt on tongue and under her lids. Her ears thrummed with sound, loud flapping, birds hefting themselves above the sea. Bird wings, silk fans, a blur of hands. Applause and foot stomps.

"Walk forward, daughter."

"Mother." The word was more breath than sound.

Her mother stood before her, hands held out in wait. She had dressed in her best poplin, light blue and trimmed in black silk tassels. Not the soiled garment Maud had last seen her in, when the men came for her. Her hair was braided neatly, with a blue silk ribbon that matched her eyes. Those eyes alive again, turned to Maud, not inward to the voices and worlds she traveled and ultimately lost herself to. Eyes sparkling, not flat with derision as they were with William Marcus.

"One foot in front of the other, there's my love." She pulled the chair back, gesturing for Maud to sit, and as she did, sat within her. Maud slumped forward. As if her bones and sinews had been stripped out and set aside to make room for the spirit. "So many come to see you—let us give them a show."

Then Maud sat up straight. Her legs her mother's. Her arms. Her voice hers.

"Hello, my dears. My name is Carolina Price. It is so good to meet you all."

A voice of rust and wood and air. One Maud had so desperately missed.

"So many wish to speak." Carolina picked up her pencil and pad. "Who," she intoned, "wishes to ask?"

Maud blew out the light.

Here. This was hers. No more hating herself each morning. Bright eyes glinting from the crowd, the single candle a beacon for the dead. Whispers came, words streaking past her ears, circling her chair. A boy's laugh. The tap on the nonexistent glass. A medieval ditty.

"Do you feel them?" Her eyes raked the ceiling and arced over the room. "They are all around you."

She pulled in a sharp breath. Oh, how she'd missed this.

"Mr. Timpkins, there's a Harriet calling you quite loudly. She was a loud thing, wasn't she?"

"Oh yes!"

"Yes indeed."

"Ah, Tom says he's beside himself to have a little brother. It will be so, won't it? And Celia will be the grandest sister, as she was to me." An old man's voice bubbled in her throat. "I've got a cane chair up on the porch with me, Timothy. You shouldn't fuss so and the sunsets are grand. And you know to give a coin or two to Mrs. Potts; she's bare of cupboard now."

A single bell jingled.

"Mr. Judd, now I'm looking right at you. We don't start with songs and lectures. We get right to the truth. Your gran wants you back in church and there to sing. Here's a note to remind you."

Papers fluttered to life, floating midair. Hands reached to catch the message, to flatten it to a heart; the crush of notes a susurration, a breath from the beautiful world. "No more now, dears." The colors became waves and whispers. Goodbyes.

A pulse of pain hammered her temple. A sound of crushed shells. Spatter of stinging liquid.

Now you've killed me.

"Careful, my love."

Maud lurched from the chair, falling to her knees as she reached for her, fingers touching nothing. She let out a long sob.

"Give us the lights, damn you all, give us light." Garrison rushed to her, the flicker of candles reflected in his glasses. He touched her cheek and forehead, then twisted around. "The spirits have sapped her energy."

The room wobbled and accordioned, all the faces pressed up tight in a distorted ball, then swooping away as if pulled by strings.

"Is that it?"

"I saw something. In the corner."

"Nothing happened."

"That was my gran all right."

"What does it mean?"

Garrison helped her to her feet. She gripped his arm. The floor shifted and tipped. "That was," he said, "unexpected." He helped her from the platform and addressed the others. "Miss Price is too weak from the journey. The spirits will come another time. I am happy until then to provide a short lecture on the difficulties in reining in magnetic forces."

Mr. Ott stared at Maud from his seat, jaw slack. Then his mouth grew into a wide smile as he stood, taking her hand within his and pumping it up and down. He turned to his wife. "What about that, Nancy, what about that?"

"It was Tom, wasn't it?" she asked.

"We will ask for him especially. Tomorrow."

"You see?" Mrs. Ott buried Celia in a hug, rubbing her back with a ferocious verve. Then she kissed the top of her head.

Maud raised her eyes to the room. Rose stood flat against the back wall, her face white as the apron she wore. Russell, costumed as the other servers, beamed.

∞

She could not bear the light. She pressed the cloth over her eyes, listening to the low hum of guests on the floor below. All had wanted something more, had pawed her arm and tapped her back as Mr. Garrison escorted her from the room. *Please and please and please* they cried in silence. But the words and pleading might as well have fallen into a dark canyon. She could not catch them. And her mother was nowhere near.

It had been so long. Once Maud had sought her—desperately. Hours upon hours seeking the Otherworld, spirits and souls all around, and none her.

You see it. Don't let him take it. The last words Carolina had said to Maud before she passed.

The cloth cooled. Maud slung it off and pushed the heels of her hands to each lid until the dark sparkled.

He had taken it. With all his pretty words and seductive compliments, he'd taken the gift she shared with her mother and turned it into something cheap and paltry. Forced her to speak when no voices were there, until her throat burned. Forced her in front of crowds and skeptics alike and smacked the side of her head in private when she failed to give them what they asked.

Her mother had warned her as best she could then. Perhaps she'd returned for the same reason: *Don't let her take it.*

Chapter Twenty-Four

CLEMENTINE

That bleed of light into the parlor was unacceptable. She had nailed that footing in herself. Had checked it once and again, been satisfied, and taken it off the list. But when she got on all fours to determine the problem, shined an oil lamp to one side and laid her head to the other, the issue was clear. A long crack split the slat in two. As if it had been kicked.

"My damn fault." She bit into a chicken leg Rose had cooked and left in the ice box, tearing off a chunk and washing it down with a swallow of whiskey. A bottle she'd kept to herself, though when she held it to the kitchen window it looked like Rose had managed a few nips for herself.

Or Clem had drunk more than she realized. The light out the window had dropped to a purply-blue. She set the bottle down and burped, then splayed her legs under the table and stared up at the ceiling.

"There are two hundred and seventy-eight crosses in here, dog."

But Ethelred didn't answer.

She squinted her one good eye at the stacks of letters spread on the table before her. So much pleading. She scraped one up. The words doubled and tripled and skittered on the page, so she tossed it atop the unopened pile for Russell to attend to.

"But is it enough to give me grace?" She gave a tsk, then lurched up. The crosses wheeled around her. She spread her arms to steady herself and waited out the unholy spin of the room.

"I think I'm drunk, Ethred. Ethelred. Apologies."

The dog eyed the chicken leg still in Clem's hand and sat.

"Chicken bones'll kill you." She ambled to the slops bucket, lifted the lid, and tossed in the leg. "Stick with me, dog; you won't die of a splintered bone on my watch."

The hall seemed longer, though it maintained the same dour gray as always. She made a chirp and listened for the echo of it all the way at the third-floor ceiling. At the dining room, she grabbed the doorframe, leaned in, and hooted like an owl. The sound rushed past her and shot into the parlor. Ethelred's nails clicked as if she walked on the wall.

"Who needs spirit trumpets with a house like this?" She grappled for the railing and clung tight. Her foot missed the step once and then again. On the third try, her boot stayed where it should, which was an excellent sign she'd make the next step. Up the stairs she went, her shoulder dragging against the wall. The top step came too soon; she tripped and dropped to her knees. "That is not becoming of a lady." She glared at the rug and the pattern of sinuous vines and morning glories. The dog nuzzled her arm, her nose cold and wet. She swung her arm away. "I'm getting up." Then she glared down and bared her teeth.

Ethelred's lip lifted.

"Good dog." She twisted around, grabbing her ribs though there wasn't a reason to. Nothing hurt. Which had been the plan. Add laudanum to the whiskey, just a few drops more than to Maud's nightly milk, just enough to take the edge of pain away and let her think.

She grabbed Ethelred's shoulder for balance and stood. Russell's door remained shut, the note she had pinned earlier in the day still hanging from its nail. She'd have to manage this by herself. All of it. But what was new in that? She ripped it down and crumpled it.

Then she stumbled up to the attic, shoved her key in the lock, and shouldered the door open. The air was damp and chilled. The window had been left open. She passed the worktable and touched Amandine's shoulder through the drop cloth that covered her.

The window frame had swelled and wouldn't shut. It thunked against the house with each gust. She yanked the curtain closed, sat on the bench in the dark, and pressed the palms of her hands to her eyes. "I've taken too much of the tincture, Amandine." Then she scrabbled for the oil lamp, dug a match from her pocket, and lit it.

Ethelred glared at her from the doorway.

"Come here, sweet girl."

But she lay down, first on her front elbows and then dropping her haunches.

Clem sighed and roughed her scalp. "You're my good dog."

She wanted her pipe. A smoke would clear her head. But it was in the Orpheum alley. She squinted and rubbed her eyes and stared at the double image of Amandine, clothed in white like a ghost. With a quick jerk, she reached for the cloth and pulled it to the floor. Maud's visage looked down at her. Clem picked a blue glass eye from the box at the end of the table. She pushed it into an empty socket, then followed it with its mate. They were a deeper blue than Maud's. She'd need to order another pair. She ran her hand around the mechanical doll's chest, fingers glazing the linen and stuffing that created the curves. Then she lifted a small clasp on the back of the skull and swung a door open. She hooked wires to each prosthetic eye and leaned around to examine the movement as she tugged each strand.

Blue eyes and plain face. Mouth too small and chin too sharp.

"How is it at the Otts', little Mouse?" She crossed her leg and balanced her elbow to her knee. "Have you called up the ghosts?"

Her skin prickled and the cold came like a vise. She shrugged and stood in front of Amandine. She fluffed the automaton's hair and coiled one strand around her finger, pulling it out so it bounced and danced by the ear. "Would you like the limelight?"

She reached back, pressing her cheek to the mask, and took hold of a key near the base of the neck, twisting it round and round. Then she slid her hand down to the middle of its wooden spine, took hold of the next key, and wound that. The switch was last. She hooked her finger to it.

"I could make you famous, you know. You just need to do what I say." Her lips swiped the rough edge between the mask's ear and the metal box concealed behind the wig. "Do what I say."

She flipped the switch and stepped away.

A soft whirring filled the cabinet Amandine sat on. Her head lifted and turned toward Clem. The eyes opened; glass orbs slid to the left, then snapped forward.

Ethelred dropped her head against the floor and growled.

The automaton stopped.

Clem clenched her jaw. "Come on."

A small tick joined the whirring.

"Come on."

Then the left hand turned its palm up. The arm lifted. The fingers curled in, save the index, which touched the plaster lips in a request for silence. Then the head tilted back, the lids dropped, the stare became one with the stars and Otherworld. The other hand raised itself from the lap and pointed at Clem.

In the theater, she'd speak. The spirit trumpet projecting her voice, the audience looking all around the auditorium for the source. "The spirits are restless," Clem murmured.

A metallic snap sounded from the cabinet. The hand dropped from the wrist. Clem watched it fall. She took the limp wooden hand in hers and held it against her heart. Then she flipped the switch and pulled each eyelid shut.

〜

"We are agreed." Clem stuck her hand out for Rumson to shake. He peered down at the contract, stroking his fingers along the part in his hair as he pretended to peruse it once more. As he pretended to be keen and sharp. But she'd caught the shove of the bottle to the drawer, and no amount of perfumed hair oil and cigar smoke tamped the smell of liquor.

Her upper lip broke out in clammy sweat. She took a large gulping swallow. Whoever suggested two cups of vinegar for a night of excess needed to be shot. Every joint and muscle ached. Never mind her ribs, which required binding and hurt like hell. Her head was a scrambled mess, though in her favor, Rumson did not look on much better footing. She needed a druggist and a sensible balm. A tincture of coca would do the trick.

She stared over Rumson's head at the posters taped willy-nilly to the office walls—*Aida* and *Othello*. The Scarlatta Twins, direct from Milan. Posters with bright girls on swings and brooding men with skulls. Each with torn and yellowed corners. The theater had seen better days. Now the house sat empty, the plate-spinning dogs on a train to the next town. And the marquee had not been changed. Which meant Theodore Rumson had no choice but to sign.

"It's a simple set of terms," she said.

His fingers stopped. "Yes."

"And fair."

He settled back in his banker's chair, the springs muttering at the sudden weight. His breath rattled as he stared first at her outstretched hand and then at her. God, what a pompous, devil-breathed man. If his Mark Antony was bad, his playacting at "cunning theatrical producer" went even further. He wanted her to twist, to think he was doing her a favor, when indeed it was she doing him one.

"I do not normally sign legal documents with a woman."

"I could bring my lawyer. He's very interested in the alley incident, so two stones, you know."

Rumson smacked his lips. He raised his hand to dig at his scalp again and thought better of it. The chair squealed as he leaned forward and reached for a pen. He uncapped the ink and dipped it in. His tongue stuck out as he dropped the nib to the signature line, and he sucked it back in as he turned the paper toward her and handed over the pen.

"Just think," she said, "you can boast that you had the vision to sign Maud Price first. Once the tour is done, we'll come right back where we started. To you." She pulled a breath and turned the contract back his way. "We're missing an initial."

"Are we?"

"Yes, here: 'The workings of the act are not to be disseminated by production staff or management—'"

"We've had magic before—"

"'—by production staff or management. Consequences of this are—'"

"I am aware. I've done this my whole life, woman. Theater remains in the theater."

Clem handed him the pen. "Just so you understand the ramifications."

He stabbed the pen to the clause and dropped it to the desk with a wheeze of relief.

Clementine removed an envelope of money from her reticule and pushed it across the desk.

He clawed it up, feathered the bills, and then stuck out his free hand. "To opening night." His stomach grumbled and burbled. He eyed the desk drawer.

"Yes, thank you," she said. "I would adore a glass."
"You would?"
"To toast the partnership."

❦

Clem folded the theater specs and measurements into her purse and lowered the veil from the brim of her hat. She sent a quick thanks to Sullivan for the goose egg on her brow. It led to Rumson quaking at the thought of a lawsuit, which he could not afford. He needed her money and she needed a stage. Sometimes, she thought, things fall into place just as they should. No more Sullivan to poke around in Maud's business and her own past. It had to be done; anyone with goals and ambition would understand.

Rumson watched her through the upstairs window; she dipped the umbrella and gave him a nod of the head. She raised the tip to the marquee. "Your biggest letters, Mr. Rumson."

Then she unfurled her umbrella and stepped out to the street. Grace could be damned.

Chapter Twenty-Five

MAUD

The morning light glistened with fog and ice crystals. Maud squinted and turned her head. Her headache had raged most of the night and only dissipated in the early morning. Then Rose came with a tray of coffee and a molasses biscuit and a note to meet the Otts in their private parlor. She dared not turn her head; when she did, on rising and allowing Rose to dress her, the room fractured into shards. A familiar discombobulation, one she dreaded both in its presence and in its absence.

And yet, she'd take the whole world shattering to pieces if it meant her mother had returned.

"Oh, Miss Price, Miss Price." Mr. Ott scooted forward on the settee and took her hands in his. "You give so much."

The freezing rain chittered against the windows, melting upon contact and running in rivulets down the glass. A log popped in the fire. Maud's chair was so close to it she had started to sweat. The blanket across her lap did not help. But Mrs. Ott had been so obsequious, so careful with her comfort, and now she did not have the heart to remove it.

Maud returned her attention to Mr. Ott. "Yes."

"We would like to provide our patronage to you." He gave a determined nod of his head, as if the idea had already been discussed and agreed to.

Maud slid a glance to Mrs. Ott, who also bobbed her head, her emerald and diamond earrings swinging.

She chewed her lip. She had won the bet. She was free of Clementine. She would no longer live with the not-so-silent threats of exposure, the not-so-polite reminders of how far she'd fallen from grace. She was free to decide on her own now.

Under the Otts' auspices she could return her home to some order. Get rid of the dog that snuck in and hogged her bed. Leave behind the anxiety of some trick going wrong (Russell did have exaggerated ideas about the order of phenomena, the flying shoe having been replaced with floating eyeglasses and a wax hand that touched the guests' shoulders when things became, in his opinion, too damn slow). Decide herself how many sittings, or if she wanted to just sleep in for a day. Or not answer the mail.

The Otts were powerful. He had been a state assemblyman and a rumored stop on the Underground Railroad. He owned half of Main Street and held the debts of others, as well as stakes in most of the mills. She stared out at the curve of maples and the brilliant green of spring leaves. Beyond that, the fog shrouded the mountains in white. A groom led two horses across the yard. Everything here held such order.

"Miss Price?" Ott leaned forward, his hands still entwined with hers. "I see you are wavering. Let me convince you further. We would provide all funds for you to allow your gifts the freedom and time to grow."

"Five hundred dollars per year," Mrs. Ott added. "With a housekeeper. Of your choosing, so of course you can keep—" She wrinkled her nose. "Well, the choice is yours, but a good solid Methodist—"

Mr. Ott set a hand to Nancy's knee. "The details of her help can be discussed later, love. The main points are as such: five hundred per year, as mentioned, a dwelling all your own."

"I have a home."

"There's a lovely carriage house just beyond the turn of the creek," Nancy said. "It would be yours."

"And my responsibilities?"

"Well, doing what you do," he said. "And lending you out. I have colleagues in Jaffrey, Nashua, Keene, Concord . . . And if you haven't seen Portsmouth—"

"I've seen all of those places."

"As a child, yes, but now, Miss Price, you can return with even greater fame. We'll build you a spirit cabinet. I hear those are all the rage."

Her shoulders sagged. "My current manager would call that a three-legged monkey."

"A what?"

"Sometimes the spirit does not come. What happens then?"

"We bring in the wine. Ha!" Ott smacked the chair arm. "When they're in their cups we can tell 'em Queen Elizabeth arrived with her armada."

"Henry . . ."

"Or not. No. We give you all good faith, Miss Price."

She could shake his hand right now. If, indeed, she would be left to her true calling. It felt, almost, like a gift of return to service.

"Will you charge?"

"Don't need the money. Just your presence at events and balls."

Maud pictured Clem just behind them, pipe in her mouth and that horrid smile. She scratched under her arms, pursed her lips, and hopped up and down.

Maud straightened, resting her hands to her lap. "I see. I will think on it."

Was one set of handcuffs better than another?

❦

The rain thumped the roof of the carriage. It was useless to speak; the words would be lost in the hammering. Maud and Rose sat in silence, each holding a strap and staring out windows that showed them their own reflections or the wash of the lamplight on the bark of a tree. She had wanted to leave earlier, but Mr. Ott had insisted that the storm was too strong and the roads too rough.

She smiled. It had been what she wanted, overall. A chance to prove herself. A chance to atone. Even Celia relented from her sullen judgments in the end. And her mother had come at last. She gave a small laugh.

Rose's head bounced and swayed. Her lips moved, face transparent in the glass, eyes hollow and mouth an oval of black. Russell had shown her a trick effect much like it, and then proved it worked by appearing in the dining room window when he was meant to be at the table. Maud jumped and Clem stared and Rose dropped the meat tray.

The carriage slowed and came to a stop.

"Why are we stopping?" Rose asked.

"I don't know."

A hurried rap came to Maud's window, then the handle twisted. Rose tensed and pressed herself to the corner.

The door snapped open. Russell barreled inside, taking the seat across from them and yanking the door shut. Rain dripped from the brim of his hat to his lap. He didn't smile. "Are you the Maid of Light?"

Maud nodded. "Why, yes, sir, I am."

He stood as best he could in the space, head bent at a funny angle, and dug around in his coat. "I have pilfered champagne."

Maud clapped her hands. "It is something to celebrate, isn't it?"

"I'd say." He twisted the wires off the cork, tossing them to the floor. The cork flew out with a pop, bouncing off Rose's window.

"Could've taken off my nose."

"Dear Rose, I would never wish harm on your lovely nose. You may have the first drink."

"From the bottle?"

He handed it to her, his eyebrow pulled up and a bright flush to his face.

She grumbled under her breath and took it.

"Now wait, we need a toast."

"Drink first, toast after, that's what my Da says. Then you've got the good part done up before things go awry."

Russell winked at Maud. "Should we follow Mr. O'Malley's eminently good instructions?"

Maud put her hand to her heart. It beat so, like a bird too long caged. She thought that, should he look at her one second longer, she would faint. Like those silly women in silly romances.

"Are you all right?"

"Oh. Yes."

Rose held the bottle out. "A toast to, I don't know what—"

"Parting the veil, girl, and our Maud holding the curtain wide."

"Oh, well, bottoms up, then."

The bottle was handed round. Russell looked at Rose and then at Maud before knocking the glass behind him for the carriage to move on.

⁓

The gas lamps along the street had been lit, though it was not later than four. Water, and the detritus caught in it, flooded the streets. Dung floated on the skin of it. Branches caught in the spokes of the carriage wheels, knocking and scraping the underside. At the turn to the house, Maud spied a dog standing chest-deep in water, head swinging back as if it waited to be told whether to move on or retreat.

Russell closed one eye and then the other. "Poor fella."

Rose's skin had gone a sick-colored gray. "We shouldn't have had two bottles."

"Just think of it as mother's milk, Rose my Rose. You will sleep like a baby with pleasant dreams of . . . I have no idea what your dreams consist of, but you will have them."

"Washing the sheets and cleaning up the dog's poo in the yard, mostly."

"Hm." He leaned against the side and slung an arm around his knee. "I think you need a few more experiences, Rose. I do think you do."

"I was supposed to only drink milk." Maud cupped her left eye and watched the pellets of rain. "Damn the milk."

Russell laughed.

"Damn her," she whispered.

"She's not that bad."

Rose whimpered.

"Why do you sound like a wet cat?" Maud asked.

"I don't."

Russell pointed out the window. The house loomed in front of them, rain pouring over the lip of the roof, gushing through the square of yard and down the walkway to the street. All the windows were bare of curtains, each room ablaze with lamplight. Ethelred stood with her paws on the sitting room window frame, the glass steaming with each breath. The dog barked, jaw snapping silently behind the glass.

Clementine stepped into view, her silhouette leaning forward to peer out. She waved.

Maud shook, as if all her bones had come loose from muscle and skin. Her vision blacked, and she felt herself trapped and clawing, nails scraping clods of dirt from a wall. Then, just as quick, it faded, and she turned to Russell. Felt his hand warm and secure in hers.

"Time to boast and shine," he said, then opened the carriage door. He turned back, eyes bleary, and pointed from one to the other. "Don't wobble."

❧

"What do you think?" Clem held her ribs, took a swig from a vial, then set the bottle on the dining table. She held up one of the papers—a sketch of a stage, a figure down center, and another sitting in a cabinet just behind.

She bent down, giving a small shake of the head before resting one hand on the table and drawing a large moon and clouds. But it didn't seem to satisfy her. She rubbed the eraser to it, blowing away the crumbles and leaving long red streaks where it had been. "It goes over here." She licked the tip of the pencil and drew it all again on the other side of the stage.

Ethelred paced behind her with a whine.

"Quiet, dog."

"Can we at least change?" Maud asked. "I haven't even taken off my gloves."

Clem snapped her head up. "Why?"

"Because we waded through water," Russell said, "and smell like a sewer."

"You don't smell any worse than the dog. Sit down."

"No." Maud's voice quavered.

"No?"

"You're impossible. I'm going to my room."

"You're drunk. And you don't smell like a sewer, you smell like the bottom of a brewer's tank."

Clem was taut as a rubber band, flipping the pencil over and over, eyes darting to another paper that showed a cross section of a theater with pit and fly tower, rigging marked above and traps circled below. "Three hundred seats. It's a small space, but that's a positive. First night we'll do invites only—Russell, there are stacks of requests for sittings; we can start with those. Rumson is agreeable to sharing all the names the next nights, so we can run down the deceased." She stared at the ceiling and blew out four soft breaths. "We might get a few new ones if the river breaches by the mills."

"Jesus, Clem." Russell dropped to one of the trunks the driver had left in the hall and loosened his collar. "What are you doing?"

"I'm creating our new show." She waved at Maud. "While you've been off country-housing—"

"That's what you call it now?"

"I hope you made use of the book."

"I burned it."

Clem hesitated, the pencil an inch above the seating chart, then continued jotting a note on the margin. "Oh? Well, next time warn me, and I won't go to the trouble."

"She didn't need it," Russell said. "Clem, if you'd seen it. We can't do a damn thing like it. It was wonderful."

"That's where you were." Clem pursed her lips. She slid the candelabra closer to the paper and continued to write. "So you went off like a gallant prince to save her. Did he rescue you? Alas, I was being robbed in an alley and spent most of the time in bed with a steak on my face. Thank you for noticing, Russell."

"You can take care of yourself. You always have."

"Did your Matthias magically reappear, Miss Price?"

"No."

"Ah. Well, that's . . ."

"My mother did."

"Oh." Something ugly crossed Clem's face, contorting her smile. "Excellent." She tapped the pencil to her chin, then tossed it and scooped up another sheet, holding it out and shaking it. The paper contained a crude sketch of a man in long robes with a beard to match. "You will recreate the Maharaj, Russell." She twisted around and tipped her head at Maud. "He has a remarkable mind-reading stunt."

Russell stepped forward. "She doesn't need an opening act, Clem."

"Of course she does. It's the theater. There's always an opening act."

Maud ground her fists to her stomach. "No. Mr. Garrison—"

"What of that prig?"

"You're meant to help me save my reputation. Not turn me into a sideshow."

Clem frowned and shook her head. "I have returned your reputation to you. Not made you a sideshow. I have made you better than you were; certainly you can agree on that. Look at the waiting list for your sittings, look at how much . . . every other medium charges twenty-five cents a head, you garner ten dollars. The Otts were an entrée into an entire slew of their ilk. And now—"

"I want to wake up without hating myself."

"Alas, I can't help with that." Clem took a pushpin from a small wooden box and stabbed the costume sketch through the wallpaper and into the wall. "So your guide has returned. Your *mother* now. Matthias gave up? Had to call Mummy?" She gave the tack a twist. "We will provide backup and small effects. Nothing changes. Except we're done with sittings here at the house. They don't make enough money, anyway."

Maud stumbled forward and took hold of the back of a chair. She still felt the movement of the carriage. The champagne sloshed about in her gut. "We had a signed agreement. You can't renege on it."

"Are you calling me a liar? I wouldn't do that." Her gaze was stone and ice. "A parlor is too small for you anyway, Miss Price."

"The Otts offered me patronage."

"It's not in your contract. Absolutely not."

"My contract ended when the spirits came back and they have. I am free to—"

"No, no, no. Number one: you signed a contract that states categorically that all parties must be satisfied. And I am not satisfied. No. Not at all. And number two: you just signed a contract for a run at the Orpheum. Congratulations."

"That's forgery."

"You weren't there. As your manager, my job is to look out for your interests. I did it as a favor."

"I don't want your favors anymore."

"Oh, but I think you might."

Maud's throat closed, as if Clem were not across the room but pressing her thumb to her neck. A garbled voice rushed past her ear and disappeared through the wall. She sank to a chair.

Clem grabbed another paper and tack and stuck it to the wall. "You will wear white. As you always do. With weaves of luminous paint. Won't that—"

"You've no right to sign for her." Russell touched Maud's shoulder.

"And when have you grown morals?"

"Give me the contract."

"Be careful of flatterers and princes, Miss Price. They promise so much and deliver so little."

"Shut up, Clem." Russell's face grew dark.

"Except the clap. But that's been taken care of."

He grabbed Clem's arm and shook her. "Shut up."

"Why her, Russell?"

"Stop it." Maud pulled Russell's arm, but it was like stone.

"This isn't your fight." Clem stared up at Russell, her chin jutted out.

"She doesn't need you anymore." Russell's voice was low and taut enough to snap. He pushed her against the table.

"All the curtains are open, Russell. I don't think you want this on your theatrical resume."

He blinked, mouth agape as he stared up at the window, then shoved her away. He turned to Maud, his eyes glazed and empty, hands raised in a plea. "It's not who I am."

Maud couldn't see anymore. She stumbled back, calf hitting the side of a trunk, then grappled past it to the stairs and up to her room, shutting out Russell's voice as he called to her, Clem's mewling whine as she mocked him.

"I can't do this." She gripped the edge of the dresser and pulled in a gulp of air. The woman would be the ruin of her. She looked up at the mirror. At her reflection and a double behind her. A life-size doll sat on the rocker, dressed in pure white with a modest collar, a pink bow at each cuff. It stared at her with thin lips and blue eyes. Just like her. Or rather, a too-sharp version of herself. Every element precisely honed. As if it were her death mask.

A slip of paper peeked from the doll's hand.

Maud plucked it up, making the thing's thumb click.

My name is Amandine.
I am so happy to meet you. We will be the best of friends.

Chapter Twenty-Six

CLEMENTINE

"She doesn't bite." Clem lounged in the library chair, her feet up on a wood stool she'd found under the stairs. She took a bite of toast. Rose made perfect toast. "You should eat your toast, Maud, before it goes stale."

"I've lost my appetite." Maud didn't turn from the window. "That thing has my face."

Clem bit her lip and stared at the ceiling, urging herself to patience. "She is called Amandine and she is called a theatrical effect."

"You didn't have to leave it in my room last night."

"I don't understand why you fight me."

"I don't want that thing. It's bad enough—I should have the police come and drag you out."

"Then you'd be in breach of contract. And all your money is now tied up in your return to the stage."

"Someone has sent Mr. Garrison comments. About me. I don't need a theatrical effect on the stage to give anyone reason to doubt me."

"What sort of comments?"

"Diagrams. Accusations. About things you've done."

"You're culpable too." Clem set her toast down and crossed one leg over the other. "Did Garrison give you a name?" It would be Sullivan. Of course it would.

"Mr. Garrison threatened to shun me, were the insinuations proven true. That he'd circle the horses, or something like that."

"There's nothing to worry about. I'll take care of it."

"Whoever it was sat next to me. It could have been you."

"Why would I do that?"

"To make me afraid. To make me need you." Maud's eyes slipped away. To the door, to the window. She gave a start, as if someone had pushed her from behind. "Oh." Her lids fluttered. She pressed the heel of her hand to her temple. Her skin drained of color.

"Are you going to faint?"

"Someone's coming to the door."

"It's too early for the post." Clem stood, swiping crumbs from her trousers and joining Maud at the window. "There's nothing to see out here. The vines are practically growing through the glass." She ran her finger along the path of a stem.

Then the knock came.

The hall remained quiet.

"It's Harriet," Maud said.

"Harriet doesn't get up before ten."

Another knock, then Russell's feet pounding down the stairs. "Jesus, where the hell is Rose? I'm not the butler."

"Did your fair prince spend the night in your room?"

Russell bent and stared through the rails. "Hello? Anyone dressed enough to answer the door?"

Maud rammed Clem's shoulder and pushed past her to the hall. "I hate you."

"But you need me. And that's what counts."

Ethelred's nails clicked on the hall floor. She lumbered past the library, tail wagging as she ignored Clem and followed Maud. Clem dropped to the leather chair. "Even the dog."

Then Rose passed by.

"Rose. Rose. I know you heard me."

But she did not answer.

Harriet swept in, her coat still buttoned. She shut the door and tossed a folded newspaper on Clem's lap.

Clem bit the inside of her cheek and scratched at the paper. She didn't need to open it; Sullivan had been found. She hadn't thought it would be so soon. "Why have you gifted me this? Did you lose your glasses? Do you need me to read to you?"

"Why don't you look on page three?" She paced to the window, then back to Clem.

"Don't hover."

Harriet tugged the paper up and folded it back. "Look."

Clem took a breath and flicked the paper in front of her. "Higgins is putting cigars down to rock-bottom prices. I wonder if they've cut prices on pipes."

ACCIDENT AT MILL COTTAGES

Mr. A. L. Sullivan found Friday by Miss B. Dreyer, laundress, on the floor of his cottage, 32 Mill, with a wound to his head from an apparent fall. Dr. Page was called to attend him and determined the injury fatal. No family is known. Any reader with information please contact Aberthwaite Mortuary.

"Poor Mr. Sullivan." She refolded the paper and set it on top of a pile of old *Banner of Light*s. "We could send flowers, but who would enjoy them?" She ran her thumbs under the lapels of her vest, then stretched her legs and crossed her feet on the nearby settee.

"You went to his house—"

Clem put her finger to her lips. "Shh." She gestured for Harriet to come close and grabbed the back of her neck when she did. "What you say in here can be heard in the kitchen." She brushed a strand of Harriet's hair from her nose. "And I don't want Rose to forget the coffee."

Harriet struggled to get away. Clem dug her nails into her muscles and rubbed the ridge of bones with her index finger. "Do you want coffee, Harriet?"

"Mm-hmm."

"With cream?"

A drop of spittle landed on Clem's trousers.

"Now look at that." Clem let go at a tap on the door. Harriet lurched up, rubbing the back of her neck as she fell against a footstool and onto the settee.

"Is it the coffee?"

"It's Maud."

"Come in."

Maud's gaze swung from Harriet to Clem. A vein at her temple stood out. "The police are here. They want to ask about Mr. Sullivan. They say he's dead."

Clem tsked. "I just found that out myself. Terrible thing."

❧

"Jonah Hewes." The officer stood near the china hutch in the dining room, hat tucked under the arm of his pressed blue suit. Mustache of a fine ginger, clipped tight. He touched the corner of it, as if there were hairs there to smooth. A habit his wife no doubt had grown intensely weary of. He'd likely follow it up with a secretive flick of the tongue to make certain it was neat.

Which he did. And included a quick side-glance to the mirror for extra measure. He watched Clem from there, his eyes hooded and his expression shifting from himself to her. He tipped his head and frowned as he took in her trousers and vest. "You are?"

"Clementine Watkins."

He blinked, lashes nearly transparent. "We won't be needing you."

Clem didn't know this officer, but she did know the other one. Officer Stoddard, who had taken her twenty dollars and promised to guard her things. He set his hat to the table and crossed his doughy arms. "Watkins? Divorced already, Mrs. Sprague?"

"I wasn't ever Mrs. Sprague."

"Just a convenient fib?"

"Mrs. Epp had her rules."

Stoddard touched his nose and then pointed it at Clem. "Indeed, my girl, indeed."

"Well." Clem rubbed her hands. "What can we do for you? About poor Mr. Sullivan."

Hewes stuck his chin out and sucked it back in like a turtle. "We'd like a word with Miss Price."

"Just trying to get a grasp of things," Stoddard said. "You know how it is. Nothing of concern, filling in the blanks, etcetera."

"Are you accusing her of something?"

"Mr. Sullivan is a client." Maud's voice quavered. "I don't understand why you're here; I haven't seen him since—I don't keep the appointment book, that's . . ." Her gaze drifted to the ceiling.

"He's not accusing you of anything, Maud. You weren't even in town when—"

"Friday. He died on Friday. I—" Maud put a hand to her temple. "He hit his head."

"As we read in the paper. Just this morning."

"Mrs.—Miss Watkins." Stoddard gestured for Clem to leave. "You understand."

Clem bit down hard enough she thought she'd break a tooth. "Of course."

"Thank you so very much." He blinked and smiled. His eyes, nearly lost in the rounds of his cheeks, were not those of the merry man he portrayed. They were vigilant. And greedy. Calculating what he could squeeze from someone's wallet. "Though we might need a word after."

Damn man.

He pushed the door shut behind her. "Now, Miss Price . . ."

Clem's chest tensed, anxiety squeezing it like a vise. She shouldn't have shown her face. Maud shouldn't have called her. Clem dropped her head to the door and stared up at the high ceiling. A dust web swung from the chandelier, spinning one direction, then another.

Russell's whisper slipped from the library. She strode down the hall. No sense in creeping around when there was nothing to creep for. That only happened in melodramas and penny dreadfuls. She pushed the door open.

They all turned at once. Harriet, Russell, and Rose. Whatever was about to be said wasn't.

"What are you all nattering about? You sounded like chickens with head colds. Should I lop off your heads so you feel better? Open up the windows?"

Rose sat on the edge of the leather chair, the paper curled in her grip, her attention held by her shoes and laces.

"Why are you in my seat?"

Russell glared at her. "Don't talk to her like that."

"You're up," she said. "And somebody's not saying something, and the coffee isn't poured. But never mind, dear Rose, you rest yourself and I'll take over the duties." She lifted the pot and held it over a cup. "Harriet?"

"No, thank you."

"Russell?"

"No." He turned back to the window, arms crossed.

"Rose?"

"Yes, please."

She poured and handed over the cup and saucer. Rose slurped. "Could I have sugar?"

"Drink the coffee."

"Yes. I will."

"It's not like Maud's being accused of murder. You all look as if you've already seen the woman hang. She wasn't even in town. They're probably going to your house next, Harriet, and Boothby's. That woman can tell them about her dinner date with Pocahontas. And everyone else on the list. We have so much more to worry about, what with the show. This is a simple visit from the police to settle the bits and bobs and hours of someone's life."

"What list?" Russell looked at her over her shoulder.

"I—" Her throat clamped. She shrugged and swallowed. "They always have lists."

"How would they know to come here? Or question any of the other psychics?"

"I don't know. Why don't you ask them?"

Harriet studied her, her face masked with the calm she used so well in her séances. Then the edge of her mouth twitched, the movement infinitesimal. But Clem saw. She'd observed her enough. It was her confirmation she'd found the tell, that she'd guessed something right.

"This is ludicrous. Some man got drunk and fell. Damn tragedy. I'll miss his fee." She set the coffeepot to the side table. "I'm going to find the dog. It'll be a saner conversation than anything else in this house."

⌒

She found Ethelred outside, hunkered against the kitchen door. Her snout and feet were covered in mud and twigs.

"Does Rose always leave you free to roam around?"

The dog's tongue lolled out. She licked the back of Clem's hand.

"That's a first." She gave her a rub, then picked dried mud from her fur. It started to rain. "I should have brought a hat." She crouched close, sharing the dry area of the stoop. "I saw dogs twirling plates on sticks. If I was one of your ilk, I'd be embarrassed to have to do that. I won't make you do that. You just be your natural self."

Ethelred gave her another lick, this time on the soft part of her wrist.

"Can I tell you a secret? Mm?"

Rain glopped and bounced on the step and rattled its way through a downspout.

"I'm going to make you a friend."

She wriggled loose a sticky glop from under the dog's missing ear, rolled it in her fingers, and flicked it to the granite. "What the hell have you been rolling in?"

Chapter Twenty-Seven

MAUD

"I'm sorry. I have nothing for you. Mr. Sullivan came to speak to his wife, Maisie. That's the only contact we've had."

Stoddard sat and listened, his breath like an ox's, his huge hands twisting and twisting the hat. An old habit, if one took in the state of the ribbon on the brim.

The other officer did not approve of mediums; he kept to the farthest seat, flipping the pages of the appointment book she had retrieved from her father's desk.

"Mr. Sullivan visited quite often."

Hewes raised his head, touched his mustache, and gave her a curt smile. "Why is that?"

"Spirits do not appear at will. Maisie—"

"Oh, come, Miss Price." Hewes's smile turned to a sneer. He flipped the appointment ledger shut and pushed it to the middle of the table. "Don't think you're the first clairvoyant pulls a stunt like this. Promising *the next time* with your hand held out for coin. I'd rather a cheap fortune-teller at the fair. She's an honest liar and a bit of entertainment."

"Then you haven't sat with an authentic medium."

"No, miss."

He's got a sister.

"You have a sister."

"What of it?"

Allendale.

"I don't—something about Allendale, I can't decipher." She could not catch the next words. They were as random as the rain plonking the window.

Hewes shoved back the chair and stood. "I am an officer of the law. And a Christian. I do not truck with your type."

"Jonah . . ."

"Yet, you are here in my house accusing me—"

"We're not accusing you; we are just making rounds to see who this man was. His body's in the morgue and no one's come to claim him. Your name was in his calendar."

"He was hunting frauds." Hewes cocked his head. "He had a whole room of documents laying out all the ways—"

"Jonah."

Maud's breath caught. Sullivan had sent the letter. She'd been so sure of his grief, but it was not solace he had wanted. It was proof. Something to ruin her. "I don't know what that has to do with me, Mr. Hewes."

"People do things they shouldn't when their backs are to the wall."

She gave a nod. Blood thumped in her ears. Pain tore again through her temple, flaring and sparking against her skull. She stared up at a ceiling. Not her ceiling. Not her body. Arm reaching, man's hand outstretched, gold ring, onyx stone. Someone else's hand now caressing his. A woman's. Caressing and caressing.

Now you'll be quiet.

A rough pull and ring clutched.

Shh-shh.

Then the woman crouched above, yellow-specked eyes curious. Waiting.

That's what it looks like.

Clementine.

Maud stared at her reflection in the looking glass. At the wisp of blue, Sullivan's face appearing like smoke, a lost look to his eyes. Then, like smoke, he and the blue were gone.

She dug her hand to her skirt and forced a puzzled look. "He was a client, and I am sorry for his death. Perhaps he will communicate with me, and perhaps he will not. I can send you a note if he does."

Stoddard picked up his hat and stood. "One last question."

"Of course." Her heart hammered hard, drumming her ribs.

"Where were you Friday and Saturday?"

"In the country. At Theodore Ott's, on Pack Monadnock."

"Who was with you?"

They won't believe you if you tell, my dear.

"All of us. Mr. Sprague, our maid. Clementine."

"That's all." Stoddard turned to leave and knocked his fist lightly on the wall, then peered at the sketches of costumes. "The Maharaj. Well. Does he do magic? He looks like a fella who'd do magic. I like good magic myself, unlike Jonah."

The men shuffled out.

Maud dropped her head to her hands. "My God. My God."

"What's this? Haha!" Stoddard's voice boomed through the door. "Shook all the mud on you, Jonah."

"Keep it away," Hewes said.

"She won't hurt," Clementine said.

"She's as ugly as they come. Ha! Look at this thing. Come get kisses from Papa." Stoddard descended into a series of coos and clucks.

Then the front door shut with a thud. A small, framed watercolor of lilies slipped on its nail.

Maud rasped in one breath, then another.

The knob on the door turned. Clementine stood in the hall, hair drenched with rain, shirt stuck to her arms. She shivered once. "What did you tell them?"

"What did you do?"

"My job."

Something down the hallway caught Clem's eye. She wiped the back of her arm to her forehead, combed her fingers through her hair. "Good. Rehearsal this afternoon. We've been given a two-hour slot." She pulled at her earlobe and looked back toward Maud. "Flash pots. Yes." She stuffed her hands to her pockets. "I knew I forgot something. Russell—" Then she strode away.

◦

"Harriet!" Maud lifted her skirts and jogged down the sidewalk. She blinked against the sting of rain, then lowered her head and hurried her pace.

But Harriet did not slow down. She glanced back once, then tipped her umbrella and crossed the street to Third, arm already up to hail a cab.

"Harriet, please." Maud bolted forward, splashing ankle-deep in the rush of water along the curb edge. She grabbed Harriet's arm, pulling it down, spinning her around. "She killed him. I know it. I saw it."

Harriet raised her arm again, waving for any hack to stop. But all passed her, horses' manes plastered to their necks and water dripping from their bellies.

"She hit him with something. She took his ring. My God, she killed somebody." She wiped her face. "I just lied to the police. I told them she was with me."

"Would they have believed you if you'd told something else? What court of law would believe you?" Harriet studied her. Then she shook her head and continued walking.

"Don't walk away. Please."

"I can't help you."

"I don't want this anymore." Maud grabbed at her throat, then bent over trying to catch her breath. "No, Harriet, don't go."

She reached for her skirt, but Harriet was just out of reach, hurrying forward. Bent against the gusts. "I can't help."

"Why? Why would she do something like that?"

"Sullivan was going to blackmail you." The tips of her eyelashes were beaded like glass. "It would ruin you. It would ruin me."

"You knew she'd do it."

"No."

A man stepped out of the Eagle Hotel to roll back the awning. He gave a nod as they passed, then unwound the rope.

"What does it matter if she ruins me? It's not worth anything. It's like the blood is on me."

"If you want to keep your life, it matters a great deal."

"She wouldn't—"

"Yes, she would. If you had a way to link her to him and she found out? What would you do then? Wait in your bed for her to hold a pillow to your face? I can't help you. I value my life."

Her laugh was acid. Then faded away. She pointed across the street at a theater marquee. The letters bold, each one like a thrust to Maud's gut.

MAUD PRICE MAID OF LIGHT

THREE TUESDAYS

LET THE DEAD SPEAK!

"Play along with her, Maud."

"I can't."

"Until you have real proof, play along."

⁓

"She's not staying in the crate. Mr. Leeds is building a cabinet for her down in the shop." The automaton sat upstage, half-crated and resting in straw. Clem ambled around it, thumbs to her vest pockets, a smug smile on her face. She looked rested and bright, her expression smooth of trouble or guilt.

Archie followed her, his mouth an *O* and eyes wide. "She's like a doll."

"That's it, Archie. She's just three keys and a switch." She clapped her hand to the boy's shoulder and winked. "Don't tell anyone. Tell them it's a wonder of the world. People have a need for wonder."

The boy lifted Amandine's hand, straightening and bending each knuckle. Then he set it to her lap as gently as if it were the finest china and pulled one of her eyelids down. "This beats the dancing bears."

Maud pushed her shoe to a long gash on the stage, wondering if it came from a bear who wanted off his chain.

Russell paced off the width and depth of the stage, every so often turning as if he were involved in a conversation with someone else, thrusting his arm forward as if it carried a weapon. He cleared his throat and let out a rattling sigh. Then words came sonorous and majestic:

"O, let me not be mad, not mad, sweet heaven!
Keep me in temper; I would not be mad!"

He spun on a heel and walked to the lip of the stage.

"How now! Are the horses ready?"

"Does it suit you?" Clem asked him.

"It's adequate. There's a dead spot up right stage and just left of center, but if you move the table—" He pulled it a few inches. "It's a better sightline anyway."

Clem hopped down the stairs and marched up the aisle, taking a seat midway up the orchestra section. "Yes. Better."

A stagehand stepped around Maud, a ladder slung to his shoulder. "Pardon, miss."

"My apologies. I'm the one in the way."

"Miss Price," Clem called. "Sit."

"Petty tyrant," Russell whispered as he passed by and took hold of the ladder. "You are wonderful."

"Time is of the essence, Miss Price."

Maud slid into the chair, which, like the table, was screwed down to a moveable platform.

"You will appear from the fog," Clem said, "as if the spirits surround you."

Maud nodded and stared all around at the ropes and curtain wings, then up at the catwalks in the fly tower. A man sprawled on his belly above, lowering a silver moon by a thin line of black silk thread.

"Up," Clem said. "You'll hit her in the head."

Clem spread her arms across the backs of the chairs. "Now speak."

"I'm sorry?" Maud asked.

"I can't hear you."

"What do you want me—"

Clem cupped her ear and leaned forward. "Still can't hear you."

"Push from the diaphragm." Russell, halfway up the ladder, pressed his hand to his stomach. "Breathe," he mouthed, then held the moon steady while the stagehand tied off the string.

"I am Maud Price . . ."

Clem dropped her head back and gave a dramatic groan. Then she snapped out of the seat and jumped to the lip of the stage. "Like this, Miss Price. Push your hand to your belly and lift your arm and speak. 'Have you prayed tonight, Desdemona?'"

"That's actually whispered," Russell said. "In the scene."

"I know that. I'm just proving a point." She cleared her throat and set her feet wide, hands on her hips. "'I come to bury Caesar, not to praise him.' Like that, you see?"

"Maybe I'm not ready for the stage."

"Oh yes, yes you are. Three hundred sold-out seats say you are." She jumped off the stage, dark purple skirts billowing and then flicking around her as she strode under the balcony to the very back of the theater. "Again."

Maud pulled in a huge breath and clenched her fists to her stomach. "You're just like my father."

"Excellent. Clear as a bell. Archie, join me downstairs so we can test the traps." Clem strode down the aisle, scooping up a notebook and papers, then stopped again at the edge of the stage. "Review the seating chart tonight. I've left it—"

"On my door, I know."

"On your vanity, actually." Her eyebrow lifted. "Russell will rehearse the sequence of notes with you."

"And what about that thing? Are you going to dress her?"

"Of course. Just like you." She moved to the steps. "When I return, we run the show, then strike it. The Melton Company is playing *The Weak Woman* tonight. We have complimentary seats, should you wish to stay. I do not. Come, Archie." She snapped her fingers and opened her palm. A flame danced on the skin.

"Do that again."

She narrowed her eyes at Archie and considered him. "Can you sing?"

"Dunno."

"I'll teach you. I have an idea I want to try out, dear Archie. Come along."

The boy followed Clem. To him, she was a wizard who lit fire from thin air and created life from metal bits and linen strips.

"Can I wind up the birds?" He trailed Clem through the exit wings to the spiral stairs that disappeared to the pit and warren of rooms below.

Maud glanced at Russell.

His face was gray with dismay. He had watched Archie too. "The Pied Piper."

THE NEW ORPHEUM THEATER
ACHER STREET OPPOSITE THE EAGLE HOTEL
THE BEST BILL OF THE SEASON!

MAUD PRICE

MAID OF LIGHT

STILL GREATER NOVELTIES!

THE MAHARAJ

AMAZONIAN BIRDS

A SONG FROM THE OTHERWORLD

THREE NIGHTS ONLY (TUESDAYS)

MODERATE AND POPULAR PRICES

75 CTS. 50 CTS. 25 CTS.

Chapter Twenty-Eight

CLEMENTINE

Clementine leaned a shoulder to the ticket booth, taking one last moment before the crowd shifted through the doors to the Orpheum lobby. Gaslights ran the circumference of the room, climbing the stairs that led to the balcony seating. The floor gleamed with polish. Blue and gold cushions lined the benches along the side walls. Two ushers in red coats stood on each side of the theater doors, playbills at the ready.

Clem curled her hands to fists and then relaxed them. Took a breath and let it out. Then she gave a rap to the ticket booth door. "Let them in."

A rush of voices filled the room, echoing from the ceiling and wood floor. Coats and bustled dresses, canes and top hats. Harriet Martin gave her a slight nod, her fan never stopping its movement, her attention seeming to be entirely centered on the group she came in with. Mr. Garrison was two steps behind, a great frown on his face and arms crossed behind his back.

Stuck-up prig.

A schoolgirl shouldered past Clem, her tickets held above her head.

"We're in the back rows but not together," she said, and when she turned, Clem recognized her as Celia. That horrid Ott girl. "There's just standing room otherwise."

A woman in purple crinoline jostled the girl and glared before wedging herself forward.

"Celia!" Her mother. Dressed to cover a pregnancy, but the pink flush of her cheeks gave her away. Mr. Ott took his wife's arm and gave her a distracted peck on the cheek.

A slight girl in glasses sidled up, tugged Celia's elbow, then stared at the ceiling. The lights paled and flattened her face. "Are you afraid already?" the girl whispered.

Celia clutched the tickets to her chest. "Of course not."

"You should be afraid," Clem murmured.

The girls looked everywhere for the voice, but not at Clem, though she stood right behind them.

The auditorium doors swung open, then slammed shut, leaving the wood to quiver from the force. Leaving the voices to dribble away to nothing.

The spectacled girl let out a giggle. "Theatrical enough?"

"That's all it is."

Then the lights went out.

Murmurs became whispers. Lips to ears. Just the rustle of fabric. The grind of a boot. A cough silenced with a hand.

The crowd became one silent body, compressed and squeezed tight. "What's this?" a man asked. Then the lights came on again. His eyes snapped open and his jowls went lax as he pointed to the balcony staircase.

Russell was unrecognizable. He wore a turban and gold-beaded cape. He tipped his head, setting the crystals braided into his pasted beard to flash in the gaslight. They swayed and clinked. His eyes popped open. They were a milky white.

Damn man always added more than was necessary.

He lifted a velvet gloved hand, turning it palm up. "The spirits are restless," he said. "They are waiting."

The lights cut to black.

"Join us."

The theater doors opened. Green mist billowed and beckoned.

"This way," an usher called, waving the playbills above his head.

"Here we go," Clem whispered.

The crowd loosened, moving around her to their seats. Then the lobby was empty, the ushers pulling the doors closed.

Clem bounded up the balcony stairs and pushed through a side door to a narrow backstage passage. Maud hurried in front of her, skirts brushing the rigging, the hem snagging. Maud grappled with the fabric, her hand trembling.

"Calm down." Clem unhooked the skirt and smoothed the material. Then she folded back the veil. "Why are you up here?"

Maud's skin was sallow, her eyes unfocused.

"Take a breath."

Maud gasped in air and held it before blowing out. "It's too much."

"Everything you've worked for is here. It is your triumph, Miss Price. Show everyone your beautiful Otherworld."

༄

Clem muttered apologies as she sidled past the patrons standing against the back wall and gave great thanks to a man who lifted his brown derby to her and didn't mind giving up a little room. She found herself directly behind Celia and her friend. They sat with hands held tight, cheeks close as they whispered and pointed.

The man next to Clem scratched his beard. "It's all set up real, innit?"

It was all marvelous. All of it. A rush of pride came to her at the sight of the seats filled and everyone at the ready for wonders.

Maud should be just off stage right, Archie under the trap, one hand to the pulley and waiting for the cue.

One chair, center stage. The table with planchette and pencil. Upstage center the spirit cabinet decked with vines. A painted backdrop of celestial stars. A swath of diaphanous curtains hung like mist above it all. The can lights along the floor glowed blue.

Then came the ringing. Like a finger run round the rim of a crystal glass. Pure like an angel's song.

A gasp came from down front. Fingers pointed up. Heads tilted.

"Oh, look." The schoolgirls clutched hands.

Long wisps of vaporous white fog rippled along the ceiling and slipped like gossamer to the stage. It was a grand effect. Clem resisted the urge to jump with joy at the achievement.

Russell entered from the wings, floating just above the boards, arms spread, palms up. He stopped, center stage, and faced the audience.

Celia let go of her friend's hand and leaned forward, clawing her knees. Her friend twisted her gloves so tight Clem wondered if she'd tear them in two.

He flipped his long cape so it pooled on the boards and concealed much of the trapdoor. "I am the Maharaj Gupta." His voice swirled around, dark and guttural. "Schooled by way of Liverpool and Londonderry. I am of neither India nor England, of neither here nor there." He shook his head, so the beads in his beard trembled and flashed. "The spirits are everywhere. Can you feel them? Will you sing to them and invite them in? The words are on the back of the playbill. We will sing to 'Mine Eyes Have Seen the Glory.'"

He spread his fingers and laid his hand to his chest. "Such heavenly voices you have." A flash sparked next to his head, then two more, so bright that even in the back of the house, Clem had to squint. Then they sputtered and ended in ash as white as snow.

"He'll burn himself," the man next to her muttered. He brushed at his mustache with a tobacco-brown thumb, then elbowed Clem. "Phosphorous."

Celia turned in her seat and stared. "Be quiet."

The theater grew hot. Silk fans snapped and fluttered. Playbills ruffled. Clem's palms were slick with sweat. She wiped them on her skirt and scanned the seats. Three rows down, on the aisle, Mr. Sullivan turned his head toward her. He gave a slow nod before attending again to the stage.

Clem pulled in a sharp breath.

But then she looked again, and it was a stranger turning to talk to the woman seated behind him.

"Oh, so many wish to sing with you," Russell singsonged, a child's voice now. He stomped his boot and scraped the heel.

Clem squinted. Light seeped through the trapdoor's seam.

"For God's . . ." She stepped over some toes and squashed others as she made for the aisle, slipping through the lobby door and then bounding up the balcony stairs.

The walkway was empty save for the stagehand, with his elbows hung over the railing as he watched Russell call another song to life. She grabbed a rung of the ladder, descending past the main stage to the trap room below. A single caged oil lamp gave a modicum of illumination. Enough to see a second oil lamp hanging near the trap.

Clem turned the lamp off, just catching the flash of Maud's pale arm as she turned the corner into the dark opposite. She took off after Maud, squeezing past a barrel and coiled ropes, then jogging the warren of dressing rooms and prop tables. Here another gaslight was on, the light dim and hiss constant. Archie stepped about the prop table, arranging and rearranging the bottles and flash pots.

"Who left the lantern on by the trap? Archie?"

His face crumpled. "Ah, hell and bother."

"Never mind. Miss Price has the letters?" Clem asked.

"Ayuh."

"You oiled Amandine's arm twice?"

He squeezed his face like a prune, then relaxed it. "Ayuh."

"If I hear one squeak—"

"No."

"All right, then." She pointed to the table. "Mr. Sprague can have half those flash pots next show. He'll set the damn place on fire, otherwise."

Archie stared at her.

"What do you think of those eyes he's got?" she asked.

"I think they're mad frightful."

"Don't tell him." She cuffed his ear, then tugged his hair. "Get in place to drop the trap, then upstairs with you. Quick as you can."

Muffled applause seeped through the boards. She strode past the table to the stage right stairs, taking them two at a time. Maud stood waiting for her cue, eyes closed and lips moving with silent words.

"Start with the simplest," Clem whispered. "Mrs. MacGregor is in J16."

Maud did not look up. She gave a quick shake of her head and continued to mouth words, fingertips touching her chin.

"You know the order. You know who to ask—there's no need for such prayers."

Maud's skin was white as death, her mouth a black slit and eyes just as dark. "No one would listen to them, anyway."

Across the way, Mr. Leeds nodded, his hand readied on a rope. Russell moved from the lip of the proscenium. "The spirits are all around. They are waiting to speak," he said. "Join us, departed ones. We are your opening, your window, your voice."

The auditorium doors to Clem's right slammed open, then slammed shut. Once, then again. Red smoke enveloped Russell. He was gone.

Leeds gave a swing of his arm and wrenched the rope. The can lights dropped to a low glow. A muslin backdrop unfurled and landed with a brushing sweep. Maud's skirts rustled as she took the stage.

She sat at her plain wood table, prim-backed, empty of expression. Her head swiveled one way, then the other, as if hinged like a doll's.

"Spirits have surrounded me since childhood. I thought everyone saw the spirits attached to them. But when I learned that was not true, I knew my responsibility to you. I am your medium. Be comforted, for your spirits can guide you."

Maud flicked her hand. A flash of golden light appeared from nothing and hovered in front of her. With a snap of her fingers—here Clem mirrored the movements—the light was gone.

"I am here to guide the departed to you and then escort them to the Otherworld, to everlasting Summerland, where there is only peace." Her voice was tremulous and reedy, as if it came from another world. "I am Maud Price. The Maid of Light. And I return to you."

One clap was joined by another, then the room reverberated with applause. It did not matter the years gone by, nor the forgetting, perhaps once in a while saying, "Do you remember . . . ?" Maud had returned to them, to be adored and ogled in turns.

Clem blew out a breath in relief.

Then Maud slumped forward, as if she were a marionette and all her strings had been cut at once.

Clem gestured across to Archie. He pulled the wire holding the spirit cabinet doors. The green vines slithered to the floor. There perched Maud's double. Amandine's eyes glittered as she surveyed the audience. A turn of the head. A blink. Hand lifted and finger pointed in slow sweep over the crowd, stopping on seat J16. A slip of paper dropped from seemingly nowhere, and how Clem wished she could see Mrs. MacGregor's expression as she read the note from her decaying husband.

Clem peered around the back scrim. Archie gave her a bow, then took a deep breath and put his mouth to the spirit trumpet she'd attached to the wall and then across the ceiling. She crept again along the wings and closed her eyes.

An angelic voice wafted from the back of the room.

In the sweet by and by
We shall meet on that beautiful shore . . .

The audience gasped. Clem held back her laugh and gestured to Leeds. He pulled another rope, releasing petals that fluttered behind Maud and scattered across the stage. Archie's voice wavered on the last words, fading to nothing and leaving the room silent.

Maud—the real Maud—tossed back her head and returned upright. Her mouth hung open, gaping and empty.

Russell crept up beside Clem and set a hand on her shoulder.

"Oh, Lord . . ." Clem's thoughts scattered. The woman wasn't going to talk. She was just going to stare out at the crowd like an imbecile, and then what?

But then Maud reached out, curling her fingers around an invisible hand. She pulled it to her chest and let out a sob.

Someone coughed in the audience. Russell bounced on his toes. "Come on, come on."

Then she laughed. "Hello, my dears. I come from very far. It is so good to meet you all."

It was not Maud's voice, though it came from her. Not male, not female. A voice of rust and wood and air.

"You better damn well stick with the script," Clem whispered.

Maud picked up the planchette and pen. She scribbled something to its surface and held it up. "William Johanson, I see you. Your . . . I cannot hear with all those waiting, Sadie . . . Sarah. Yes, there she is. She thanks you for the view. Does that mean something to you?"

Johanson. Row 12, seats D and E. Sarah Johanson, sister, died at eighty-one. Interred April 1873 at Horse Hill with a fine view across to Mount Monadnock and maples to shade in the summer.

"So many wish to speak."

"Robert Darwin." Clem mouthed the name as Maud spoke it. "Where are you, sir?"

Amandine tilted her head and pointed to the audience, stopping on Robert Darwin's seat.

"I am here."

Maud's pen scratched the paper. "Your Olive says you give more broccoli to the pigs than to yourself."

"My God. My Olive, my God."

A single canary trilled from the rafters. Then another joined in, and a gilded cage floated from the heavens.

There was no God. Just brass and smoke and mirrors and mechanics.

∽

Clem sauntered across the empty lobby to the ticket booth. She checked her watch. Twenty minutes of quiet until the audience drifted through the doors and made their way down the streets and back to their lives. Some would wander as somnambulists, half in this world and half still floating in the Otherworld with their dear departed relatives. Some would clutch their letter from the dead and return to press it like a flower into their Bible.

Her chest filled with—dare she say it—the warmth of pride. Yes. Yes, indeed. Russell may have taken liberties, but he knew how to spook a crowd. And Maud came through with flying colors. They'd have to run through the drop trap again, but that was nothing, nothing at all. She spread her arms and tipped her head back and gave a silent thank-you to her own damn ingenuity.

At her rap, Rumson opened the ticket booth door, ushering her inside. A single oil lamp lit the space. The glass had been boarded up for the night and locked. He slid the cashbox toward her and tapped the top. "We've got a hit."

She lifted the lid and stared at the neat bundles of bills. Then she swiped them out and counted. "Reconciled with the reservations?"

Rumson stared at her, then pulled at each cuff of his red coat. His mouth stretched down. "We can recount. Should you not trust—"

"I don't trust anybody, so how's about one more thumb through?"

He nodded and cleared his throat. "Mister Arkins, two. Sarah Merlson, four . . ."

When they'd finished, Clem counted out the percentage that went to the house and staff, then slipped the rest of the money into the box and signed the cash sheet. She tucked the box under her arm. "You're not a believer, are you, Mr. Rumson?"

He eyed her but said nothing.

"Everything in there is real. Save a few pyrotechnicals, all in all Maud Price is the real deal."

"I've seen an elephant at the end of *Hamlet* and had three ponies balance cats on their noses before the first chorus of *Aida*." He scraped his nail along his jawline. "I book shows and take tickets. I don't judge the acts."

The lobby was not empty when she stepped from the booth; a lanky man in a brown checkered suit lingered just inside the doors. He rolled a silver dollar across his knuckles and whistled. "If you blindfolded her and put her in the cabinet, then moved the audience around, I might believe it."

"What would I do with the automaton?"

"Does she talk?"

"I'm working that out."

He made an intricate loop of the coin from one hand to the other and then into his coat pocket. In its place he flicked out a calling card. "Jeremiah Fitzwilliam."

Clem took the card. The man smelled of lemons and cooked onions. His photograph flattered him, smoothing out the pocked skin and disguising his receding chin. It couldn't hide the vulture set of his eyes, or the utter confidence of the pose.

"Mr. Fitzwilliam."

"From Keene."

"From Keene."

A reel of laughter came from the house. They both looked. Fitzwilliam gave a clucking noise then tapped the card. "I have a theater that's in need of an act. You have an act in need of more theaters. They like her. They'll like her more if we up the temperature, so to speak."

"I already envision the possibilities."

"I have a few thoughts myself."

"Are you in Keene on Friday?"

"I'm on a talent tour until next Monday. All the way to Bangor, if you can imagine that."

She held out her hand. "My business partner and I will see you Monday."

Chapter Twenty-Nine

MAUD

"He looks like a lizard." Maud turned the card over and handed it back to Clementine. She rested her head to the carriage glass and closed her eyes. It took everything for Maud not to fall apart. Her mother had not come. No one had come. Maud was left under the hard lights, alone. She had played the script Clem made her memorize earlier, her mouth souring and temper soaring as the show progressed. And now Clem had presented this *opportunity*, and the man, this Fitzwilliam, looked, even in white cravat and silk top hat, like a human salamander.

"Who cares what he looks like? He's got a theater. Don't be so ungrateful."

Maud stared at her profile. "I'm not ungrateful. And you look green."

Clem stretched her feet to the seat opposite and slung her arms around her midriff. "I should have walked."

"Show us the money again." Russell smelled of greasepaint and sweat. He picked a bead of glue off his jaw and wiped it into his hand-kerchief. "We are very grateful for that."

"I'll buy you a new suit." Clem's smile gleamed in the passing streetlamp.

"I was eyeing a houndstooth, even if it's summer coming soon." Russell dipped his head close to Maud's. "I am a wonder in houndstooth."

"You look like a walrus in houndstooth. But maybe you like that, Mouse." Clem kept her hands crossed atop the money box. Her gaze was sharp as a razor. "Was it lonely onstage tonight, Maud?"

Clem's mood change felt like a slap. Maud held her breath, waited for the cutting words, the "I said you needed me." A diatribe on how little faith she had in Maud. It was sure to come; it didn't matter what Maud said now.

"Her ghosts are afraid of you, Clem." Russell's voice was light. He stared at his reflection in the glass, stretching his neck and wiping at a streak of white greasepaint with his handkerchief. "Maud did a spectacular job. Two standing ovations aren't something to sneeze at."

Clem tapped the money box but said nothing.

Russell smiled across at Clem. "A compliment can go a long way, you know."

"Yes, you're right." She pushed out her lip and then sat up straight, giving a nod and a smile. "You did an excellent job tonight. I couldn't have memorized and spouted pre-planted information any better than you. So hurrah for you. Now how about one for me?"

Russell shook his head and slunk down. "Jesus, Clem."

"You know I could do it all myself."

"But it's my name they come for." Maud ground her teeth. "Me."

Clem stopped tapping the box. "I know that."

"Good."

Clem turned back to the window. The tapping started again. Russell went back to picking off glue and wiping away makeup.

"I'm famished," he said.

"Rose is cooking a big meal." Clem tilted her head and gave a secretive smile. "It was meant to be a surprise."

"Well, thanks for ruining it." He folded his handkerchief away. "As long as there's cake."

Maud sighed. At least the ride was short; a luxury most times but a necessity this night. The rain had not ceased. Maud took in Clem's suit. The gold ring on her middle finger. The pearl in her cravat. The shoes she'd shined but not brushed of mud. The dresses that now filled one of the servants' rooms.

"Where did you get that ring?" Maud asked.

"What?"

"That ring." A buzzing filled her ears.

Russell lifted Clem's hand and turned it to the kerosene lantern. "It's very plain." He twisted it around. "Why would you want a man's ring?"

She pulled away. "Because I wanted it."

A small hand, nearly transparent and flecked with water, clasped at Clem's fist. Clem gave a great shiver. "It's so cold."

⁐

The house was dark. No porch light, no hall light, the fires out, the house chill and damp. Maud shivered and pulled her cloak tighter around her.

"Where the hell is Rose?" Clem removed her hat and tossed it to the console. "Rose." She shouted the word as if calling the dog.

Russell lit a lamp in the parlor and returned to the hall.

A candelabra lay on its side at the doorway to the dining room. A tureen had overturned on the table. Soup in a viscous gray had streamed over the edge, pooling on a broken plate. A loud crack came from under Russell's boot. He hopped back and shined the lamp on the shattered remnants of a wineglass. A thin sheen of grease ran along the rug and in a line down the hall.

"What is all this?" Maud's foot slid. Spears of asparagus littered the foyer.

Clem raised her hands to her head. "It's all ruined." She lifted a limp spear and threw it at the table. "Damn you, Rose, I swear to God—" She tromped through the hall and swung open the kitchen door. "Rose, you damn—"

"Rose!" Maud called up the dark stairs.

"What about the dog?" Russell asked. "Ethelred?"

"That was Sullivan's ring," she said.

"What are you talking about?"

"She killed him."

Russell pulled away as she reached for him. "No. She's not like that."

"I saw it. Oh, Russell, please."

"No more."

The bang and clonk of pots came from the kitchen, followed by Clem's sharp voice. "She's ruined everything."

"Please believe me, Russell."

He strode toward the kitchen, then stopped, the lamp held before him, his eyes on it and not her. "I believe you." He reached out his hand for her to take.

The counter and floor near the washbasin was a morass of pots and pans. Smoke curled from the corners of the cast-iron stove. Clem took her skirt in her hand and yanked the handle, coughing as the black smoke billowed out. She fanned the haze and peered in, then slammed the door shut. "The cake."

Rose's small room was empty, the bed made up and pillows stacked in a neat pile, just as she did the upstairs rooms.

"Where's the dog?" Clem asked. She shoved the heel of her hand to the back door and bolted outside.

Maud leaned over the washbasin and peered through the window. Russell's lamp swung, catching Clem yanking her feet from the heavy mud, lurching as she searched the yard. Then the light caught on crossed apron ties, and Rose's body immobile, one side of her face buried in the mud.

Russell set down the lamp and rushed out, dropping in front of Rose and tugging her arm to try to turn her over, struggling to get her upright.

Maud slipped through the muck and landed on her knees. She wiped at Rose's face, digging filth from her mouth. She looked up at Clem, who remained motionless. "Did you kill her, too?"

Clem blinked. Her face purpled and she lunged forward, knocking Maud over and grabbing Rose's shoulders. She gave her a vicious shake, and then another. "Where's my dog?"

"Stop it." Russell clamped a hand to her wrist.

She wrestled it away and lunged forward, grabbing Rose's collar and twisting it. "I do everything for you."

"God, stop it." Maud clawed at her, twisting and pulling at her arm, her grip useless in the rain and muck.

Rose wheezed and fell into Clementine's lap. "Get off me." She scraped at Rose, struggling to push her off.

Rose dug her hands into the ground and gasped. Then she staggered to her hands and knees but couldn't stand. She sunk to one hip and stared up at Maud. "I lost the dog."

Russell lifted her to his arms. She slung her arm around his shoulder and sobbed.

"That's right," Clem said. "You should cry."

"Shut up. Just shut up." Russell cradled Rose's head and carried her to the house.

Rose curled herself in the mounds of pillows and quilts Maud and Russell piled on her. She stared at the square window of her room, shivering and stilling.

Russell stooped forward on a stool, hands to his knees, watching Rose.

"You should drink this tea," Maud said.

But Rose shook her head. Her cheeks were a bright red: a good sign she was warming up. She could have been out there for hours. They'd left for the theater at four. It was now close to midnight.

Outside, Clem called for Ethelred. Whistles and pleas. "Come, girl. The wet'll kill you." Around and around the yard she went, then the calls faded as she made her way to the street.

"With all this money, couldn't you have cleaned up the yard?" Rose wiped saliva from the edge of her lips. "All those branches and how am I supposed to catch a dog with a roast in her mouth?"

Maud laid her hand on Rose's arm. "You're feeling better."

"She'll kill me for the dog," she whispered.

"No, Rose. She wouldn't." It sounded as false as it felt.

Russell gazed at Maud, his mouth taut, eyes searching hers.

"The ring—that's proof. Harriet said I needed proof." Maud's voice quavered. "Then we can go to the police."

"It's not proof. It's just a ring," Russell said.

"She killed him." Maud swallowed back dread. "If we let her . . . I saw her hit him. She's wearing his ring. He cried out. She said, 'That's what it looks like' and watched him die." The panic burned up her throat. "And the girl, always around her. Her too. I think her too." She boxed her ears. "I don't want this anymore." Her back hit the wall, legs giving out, ice tearing through the marrow of her bones.

You've let in the dark. Her mother knelt before her. *You've let it in.*

Her chest heated and heart hammered sharp enough she pushed her palm to it to still it. "Help me." She rocked forward.

"Maud." Russell's image wavered before her, as if made of spun glass. "Darling."

Jumbled words and nonsense, then: *Listen.* A voice like hail on a roof.

"Help me."

Look. The voice narrowed to a pinprick, replaced by flashes of light and dark. Iron poker swung in a wide arc. Sullivan's arm held above his head to protect. Gold ring. Too late. Blood spraying, like moths with garnet wings. The sound a hush and gurgle. *That's what it looks like.*

The room rushed back. "So much blood." Maud pulled in a breath. "Where are the clothes she wore?"

The screen door banged open. Clem staggered through, her cloak and hair soaked, lips blue from the cold. The clang of a loud pot reverberated in the room. "Why are you all in here? Ethelred's out there. Alone." Her face crumpled, mouth twisting as she let out a sob. "You're all useless." She wiped her nose on her sleeve. "Are you better?" she asked Rose.

"Yes, miss."

"Good. I'm leaving the back door open. You can sweep out the water in the morning." She took the stairs up to the attic, her steps slow and heavy.

Maud closed the door to the room. She kept her voice low. "Rose and I will search the house when you go to Keene."

"If you find something—"

"We'll—" Russell knew everything. One whisper in Clem's ear would be fatal. Or the two would continue past Keene, disappearing like mist. "How can I trust you?"

"You can. I swear on my life. No. I swear on yours. On Rose's."

"If I find nothing . . ."

"You will."

He's not the dark. "I'll send a telegram."

"And I'll," Rose said, "look for the dog."

Chapter Thirty

CLEMENTINE

"You signed this?" Clem crumpled Fitzwilliam's contract to a ball and threw it at Russell's head.

He flinched, then watched it roll across the sheet of the hotel bed. He chewed on an unlit cigar and glared at her. The cigar stunk of musty tobacco and men's egos. "That is my signature."

"And you didn't think to bring it to me?"

Fitzwilliam had shunted her aside, leaving her to while away her time in the hotel restaurant. Negotiations were men's purview, after all, he had said. And bought her coffee and a cherry tart. She wished she'd just said no. Pounded on the door and seated herself at the table. Not that the men would have let her in.

She paced the cramped room. Russell's room. Hers was down the hall, as he'd insisted. His things were scattered everywhere: the toiletry kit on the dresser, the suitcoat hung in the wardrobe, the luggage—brand new and given by her—open on the chest at the foot of the bed. Shoes packed, shirts folded, collars to their box. Once it hadn't mattered; everything in a mess together, every decision discussed.

"You need to renegotiate this." She scooped up the contract and pushed it toward him.

"No."

"I'm not listed." She dragged in air, then blew it out again. "I'm not even listed, Russell. Just you and—"

"You're not with the show, Clem."

She gave a start, then turned to him. "Of course I am. It's my show."

"Stop yelling."

"I'm not."

He raised an eyebrow.

"I'm trying to have a discussion."

He unsnapped his travel case and removed a small tortoiseshell comb. "We're revamping." He leaned to the mirror, combing his sideburns and then taking the brush up to swipe over his hair. "I will give a speech on spiritualism in general and then Maud—"

"You've become a believer?"

"I believe in her." He wiped the comb with a linen towel and repacked his toiletries. "Is your trunk ready?"

"Amandine . . ."

"That thing is never going onstage again."

"It's why people will come. I'm going to make her write. And speak. It may mean stuffing Rose in the cabinet and giving her a few lines, but—"

"People come for Maud." He tossed the case to the bed and opened the wardrobe.

"Fitzwilliam approached me." She poked her chest. "Me."

"He's old-fashioned at heart, what can I say?"

"You can say, Russell, that all contract stipulations need to be discussed with your partner. Who is me."

"You are not with the new show." With a sigh, he sat on the bed and crossed his legs. The bed coils squealed. Clem hated the bed, and the cheap iron headboard and faded wallpaper and mostly his smug face. She lurched forward and smacked his cheek. His head snapped to the side, the cigar falling to the pillow. He reached his hand to the red print on his cheek.

"No, I—I'm sorry, I didn't . . ." She kneeled before him, touched his knee and elbow, and then pressed her hand to his chest. "You need to go back to him. If we're coming all the way to Keene—if he wants a cut into the tour—then we need three nights minimum."

"*Aida* is coming from Manchester. He has two free nights."

"All right, then two nights. But a different percent. What he wants is highway robbery. It would take three full houses to pay us all."

He wasn't listening. He'd turned his head to look out the window. She pulled his coat lapel. "Russell, look at me. Please look at me. You love to look at me. You've always loved to look at me."

His mouth rolled into a little smile. It was enough for her to catch onto. Enough to see he hadn't spurned her completely.

"We're a team, Russell. We create magic."

"We create lies. And you kill to keep them."

"No . . ." She pulled at his lapel. "You think that's—"

A knock came at the door. Russell pulled her hand away, slowly, stopping to grasp it once. "I can't follow you anymore."

Then he dropped her hand and stood, careful to step over her skirts, deliberate in his gait as he moved to the door and opened it.

"Russell Sprague?" The courier, thin and too old for the job, leaned into the room; Russell blocked his view, but still Clem felt his eyes follow her as she stood.

"What are you looking at?"

"Nothing, ma'am."

Russell reached back to the dresser for his wallet and took out a bill, exchanging it for the missive. "Thank you."

A coil of jealousy spun up her spine. Only two people knew they were here, and she doubted Rose had any reason to send a note. "What does our Mouse have to say?"

Russell slit open the telegram with his thumbnail, read it, and folded it away. "Your dog has returned."

"My dog."

"Oh, Clem." He stared at the floor, the muscles in his jaw tight, fingers clawing into his hips. "Go pack your things."

❧

The hired hack left nothing for comfort. Russell gripped the reins and cooed to the horse, a small, skittish black mare who was lathered white with sweat even in the chill. "There, girl. There, there."

"Was this the only available nag?"

"The only one." Russell's elbow dug into her arm. He muttered an apology and kept his gaze forward. He hadn't looked at her once since they'd left the hotel. Since he'd read that telegram. He'd folded it to the chest pocket of his coat for safekeeping. Had it been about the dog, he'd have tossed it.

Maud had written something else. Clem bit her lip. She pulled the travel blanket closer around her thighs and waist. It stunk of old wool and the leathers of the livery's tack room.

The road turned, sharp enough the vehicle tilted as it took a steep path. Branches scraped the soft roof and slapped along the buggy's sides.

Her stomach heaved up. "We should have taken the Post Road. Going over Monadnock—"

"It's the best way." He ran the back of his hand over his jaw but said nothing more.

"Is this how it's going to be from now on? Silence?" She stuck out her chin. "What's in that telegram?"

"I told you."

She sneered. "No. You told me what you wanted me to hear. What was it really? Congratulations for doing the dirty work? How long have you two planned this? Why even take me along?" She wiped spittle from the side of her mouth. "She can't get through a single show without me; I work to the bone—"

"It's not a show. It's who she is." His voice was low and hoarse. "You use her as a prop. You use everyone like that damn doll. Wind us up to make us work and pull out the key to stop."

"No. That's not true. That's her talking. She's poisoned you." Clem let out a breath. "We're a team, Russell. We've always been. We've—"

"What you've done—"

Clem's ears rang.

"I've done nothing."

"You killed a man. For what?"

The coach jolted forward. Clem threw out a hand to stop from ramming into the front of the box. She grappled for the reins, yanked, and pulled. "Tell me what's in the telegram."

"Stop it." Russell twisted the leathers away from her, then fell against her as the horse shimmied and backed against the buggy. He flung himself off her, half-standing and gripping the brace of the roof. The horse's nostrils flared wide. Its ears flicked and then lay flat. A hoof stomped hard. Then it stepped back again, the carriage rolling and slipping against the slick road.

Clem shoved Russell and grabbed at the whip, pulling it loose with both hands, swinging to crack it on the horse's haunches.

"Don't." He held her arm, squeezing down on her wrist, not letting go, the pain coursing until her vision grayed and her hand went numb.

The whip fell to the floor. She pulled her arm back, holding it against her chest. A sob bubbled in her throat. She swallowed it down.

Russell's hand shook as he reached for the whip. He shoved it to its socket, then sat, chest heaving, reins slack. The horse, instead of bolting, dropped its head.

"I've never used you as a prop," Clem said. "If anything, you've used me."

"That's not fair."

"Isn't it? All the ideas are mine. The money should be mine. Your affection should be mine. But you bleed the money and give yourself to everyone but me. All those whores. All those times you lost a hand of cards. And crawled back to me. 'What's the next game, my Clem, my dear?' Isn't it true? Well, I don't care anymore. Take the show and take Maud. You'll see soon enough. It's me—*me* you should love."

He shook his head, ran his hand through his hair, then turned to her. His eyes were as hard as glass. "You are no longer part of Sprague and Company. New contracts between myself and Maud Price have been signed and witnessed. You, my dear, are going to prison."

Her heart cracked against her chest. "For what?"

"Don't pretend."

"What is in that telegram?"

"Proof."

Words twisted in her throat and came out a strangled cry. "You've taken me away so she could find something and ruin me. There's nothing to find. I'm not stupid, Russell." She saw the arc of the fire poker as she threw it in the pond. All the clothes down the old well. Her heart thudded. She wiped her upper lip and neck of sweat. "What proof?"

He reached in his pocket, retrieved the telegram, and held it out to her.

She snatched it. Unfolded it. The words were a hangman's noose.

WELL FLOODED. SHIRT FOUND. PROOF.

"I feel sick. I want out." Clem clawed at the handle, then kicked the door and scrambled down. Her stomach seized as she turned in a circle, stumbling in the sedge, so close to a sheer drop her vision tilted.

"Clem—"

"No. I won't go any farther."

Russell set the brake and alit, lunging forward to grab her. She twisted out of his reach and circled around him.

"You betrayed me, Russell. You shouldn't have done that. We had the world at our feet."

"Get in the buggy, Clem." He stood on a shelf of granite, just the white of sky behind him.

"No." Then she ran at him and pushed.

Chapter Thirty-One

MAUD

Maud gripped the edge of Officer Hewes's desk, her nails digging into well-worn grooves. Clementine's shirt lay spread-eagle between them, as if it were awaiting the iron. He tilted his head, his flat gaze moving from the rust-red cuff, the blood soaked and stained into the threads, up the arm, tracing the splatters and splotches like a map. He puckered his mouth and breathed out through his nose. Then he pinched the shoulders and held it up to the weak light that filtered through the interior window. On the other side, people clamored and pressed against a tall desk, working to gain the attention of the intake officer. Two souls slipped through the crowd, their shouts silent to the living but a loud, insistent buzz to Maud. She covered her ears, gave a quick shake of her head, then peered up at Hewes.

"Is something awry?" he asked.

"Awry?" What an odd word. What a stupid question. He held a shirt stained in a man's blood—that was what was awry. But she said, "Nothing is awry."

He turned his attention back to the shirt. "You found it . . . ?"

"In the yard. I told you. In the yard. There's an old well and the rains—"

"You stated your dog found it." He laid the shirt again to the table. "You said, I quote, 'My dog dragged it through the kitchen door while the maid cooked oats.'"

"Yes."

She wanted to reach across the desk and grab Hewes by the collar. He'd asked her this three times, and there wasn't any other way she could state it. She had not been to bed. Every room, every false wall and hidden mirror, every drawer and cranny had been turned inside out and inspected. What she and Rose looked for she did not know—but something urged her to seek. Only the attic remained unassailable. Clem had changed the locks and added a thick padlock for good measure. Maud took a hammer to it and then the door, but it was useless. The other servants' rooms remained empty, the mattresses rolled to the iron cots.

Rose dug through the laundry and then the incinerator box, coming up covered in pasty ash but hands empty. "We have nothing." She bit her lip, but it didn't stop the keen of panic. "Are there no dead to help?" she asked.

The rain had not stopped. By morning, the mud had turned to a viscous, moving thing: limbs and branches and broken cups floated in the yard, banked against tree trunks, and tangled in the overgrowth. Then the old well flooded.

The water breached the lip of the kitchen door, swirling on the floor. Maud and Rose picked up their feet and watched it circle the chair legs.

Ethelred ambled in. She dragged along a piece of stained cloth, dropped it to the kitchen floor, and shook off mud.

"Oh, dog," Maud said.

The linen expanded like a sail, sleeves splayed wide, collar open. Bloodstains ran like vines and crushed berries along the weave. And stitched to the inside collar: *C Watkins.*

Maud grabbed Ethelred up and kissed the top of her head. "Thank you, oh, thank you, dog."

Hewes's mouth curled in a grimace. "I remember the dog." Then he raised his eyebrows and gave her the ever-patient look men gave women they found silly. He lowered the shirt, folding one arm on top the other, then the whole of it in two. "I do not understand, Miss Price, how you connect this bloody shirt—which could have been a castoff used by the help when butchering chickens; my mother had one that hung in the barn—how you connect this to Mr. Sullivan's death."

"We don't have chickens."

The clock above his head struck. Three tinny clangs. She glanced at it, then out to the waiting area. Rose stood near the entrance, by the spittoon, in the midst of unwinding her scarf. She caught Maud's eye. Her glum expression said it all: no return response to the telegram sent hours earlier.

The scarred chair next to Maud was empty; how she wished Russell were here now. To put this ridiculous officer in his place. To take her hand.

Hewes returned to his seat. He threaded his hands behind his head and leaned back. "It's you I should be suspicious of, you know. Sullivan was on to your type. Perhaps you wore this shirt and somehow tossed him against his fireplace mantel. With your remarkable strength."

"It is her shirt. And she wore it and she hit him with a poker. I witnessed it plain as day."

"And I should have faith in that?"

She bolted up and smacked her hand to the wood. "What is faith, Mr. Hewes?"

He opened his mouth to speak, but she didn't want to hear whatever condescending words he chose to hurl. She wanted him to listen to her.

"Faith, Mr. Hewes, is the conviction of things unseen. You are a Christian. You told me so. I have faith in God just as you do. I have faith in the afterlife. I feel and hear and see evidence of things unseen and I saw the man die. I saw Clementine Watkins's face. I saw her wait and watch as he fought to stay in this world. It wasn't his time."

His lips thinned and his skin flushed a dark red. He straightened in his seat, wrapping his hands to the arms of the chair. "Do not ever confuse my faith with yours."

"Mr. Sprague is returning with her this afternoon. He'll vouch for me, for all of it."

"That is enough, Miss Price."

"No, you listen to me—"

"I said enough. This shirt is not proof. Your mental instability is not proof."

"I'll make her confess. Come to the house. I promise she'll . . ." Maud's chest burned. Freezing air rushed from behind her. The room shrunk to a pinpoint and then expanded like a balloon before wobbling back into place. "Russell . . ."

Hewes stood, banging the chair against the wall. The desk officer slid a glance toward them, then turned back to his duties. "Go home."

$\sim$

Rose jogged alongside Maud, the hatbox that carried the shirt swinging and bumping against her skirts. "What do we do now?"

Maud twisted the sodden ties of her bonnet and shook her head. "I don't know."

"Maybe they're home. It's nearly four o'clock."

"If that is so, then we act as if nothing is different. Do you understand, Rose?" Her breath stuttered. Russell would not be there. She was certain of it. Something had happened, a terrible something that turned her bones to ice.

Scorched bricks from the boardinghouse fire blocked the sidewalk. Maud slowed for a dray to pass, then continued along the curb.

Everything smelled of smoke and ash. There was nothing left of the building but posts and a black hole of oily water and scorched wood. Clem held all the cards. Just as Harriet had said she would. If Maud accused her of murder, Clem would expose Maud as a fraud. As a liar. As someone with a grudge who hung on to her reputation by a thread. All Clem had to do was pull back the curtain on the game and Maud's word would shatter and be ground to dust.

The shirt stained with chicken blood. Mr. Sullivan too drunk to avoid a fall. The wraith that clung to Clem nothing but a figment of Maud's imagination or a hoax made up to raise the hairs. And Russell—

No. She pressed her hand to her stomach and closed her eyes. No.

A block down, a horse reared in its traces. The buggy rocked and slipped sideways. The driver's seat was empty, harness reins dragging in the mud. The horse's head twisted around, muzzle pulled to its neck. A rein had knotted around its pastern. Then the leather snapped loose and the wagon leapt forward, careening in front of the dray and barreling up the middle of the street. Water flung out from the wheels.

It was soon upon them. Maud yanked Rose away from the flecks of horse sweat and slobber and clattering hoofs. The buggy hurtled past, spraying grit and brown water. Rose's boot caught in the mud. She pulled it out with a loud squelch and looked at Maud with wide, wild eyes. "Now what?"

She wanted to shake Rose and scream that she didn't know. That Russell might be dead. That Clementine would get away with murder. That she could not protect Rose and the girl should save her own skin. That she could not protect her own.

A piercing whinny came from down the street. Two men had caught the traces. Their heels dragged in the mud as the horse reared. Then an officer lumbered over from a side street, smacking his truncheon against his thigh. He stayed shy of the horse's hooves, instead pointing the club this way and that and nodding approval when the horse settled and the men were able to lead it to the livery.

Maud lifted her skirts and rushed toward him. "Officer Stoddard."

He didn't hear her; his attention was still on the buggy and horse.

She raised her voice—*it needs to reach the back of the theater*—and yelled. "Mr. Stoddard."

He squinted down at her. "Officer, now, be respectful."

"I'm Maud Price, do you remember me? You came to my house, about Alfred Sullivan."

"And I took in your show just this while ago." He pushed his hat back on his head. The strap dug at his chin. "You look white as a ghost."

"I need you to . . ." But he'd laugh at her, or treat her as Hewes had and wave her away as a nuisance. "How much?"

"Pardon?"

"How much do I have to give you to . . ." She turned back to Rose, who had not moved from where Maud had left her. Her thoughts jangled around. *Think.*

"For what?"

"I'll give you one hundred dollars to sit and have cake with my maid."

"And how about an autograph?" he asked. "For my niece?"

"Yes, yes, if that's what you—I need you to hear a confession."

"What's this?"

"One hundred dollars."

☙

Hour after hour Maud sat hunched on the bench in the hall, jerking forward to peer at the door each time there was even a small sound— the rattle of the mail flap when the wind came just right, the clop of a horse, a crack as the house settled. The lamplighter had come and gone. Stoddard, too, after the cake had gone. He declared the whole of it a waste of valuable police time. Though he took the money just the same. Now the rain swallowed the noise of the street, and the tick of the

317

clock became Maud's only companion. With each passing minute, her confidence faded. She dropped her head to her arms and sobbed. For Russell. For her own terrible choice. *Find Maisie Sullivan.* One small request had led to this.

Rose came from the kitchen. "Nothing?"

"No."

"It's late." She bit down on her lip. "I'll let out the dog and close up the house." Rose's voice took on a tinge of panic. "Is that what I should do?"

There was nothing else to do. "I'll turn off the lights up here." Maud stood. She pushed her hands to her pockets, her right brushing the derringer and flinching away from the steel. "I think we should both stay upstairs tonight."

"They'll be here tomorrow. Sure as the rain."

⁓

But the house was silent in the morning. When Maud woke, the bed was empty, as if Rose had not lain there during the night, clinging to Maud and shivering with fear. Only a dent in the pillow witnessed her having been there at all. Maud extricated herself from the sheets and crossed to the door.

"Rose?"

No answer.

"Ethelred?"

The dog would be with Rose, in the kitchen. Or outside in the yard. Maud shot a glance up toward the attic; the door remained bolted tight. She darted down the hall to Russell's room and gave a tap to the door.

"Russell?"

She turned the knob and peered in. The bedding had not been slept in. A half-empty ewer sat on the dresser, but nothing else. The room was cold, as if the window had been left open. But the latch was as tight as it had been the night before. She peered down to the yard. Rose had already dressed. The wind lifted the hem of her bright red shawl. She wrapped it tighter and picked her way through the muck in the side yard. Ethelred trailed behind, snuffling the ground and then the air.

Maud rubbed her bare arms and walked back to the hall. The damp clung to her thin chemise and drawers, seeping through her skin to the bone. Why hadn't Rose started the fires? A scraping sound stopped her midstep. It came from the top of the attic stairs. She held her breath, listening. Her ears rang from the quiet.

Then it came again, clearer. A pan sliding across the stove. The sound traveled to the attic and then whipped back to where it began. How well Clem had used it during the sittings. Now it was Rose, back in the kitchen.

Maud let out a long breath. Just Rose in the kitchen. The dog waiting for the sausage Rose fried up especially for her, even after swearing up and down she'd never do any such thing for a mere dog.

She slipped back to her room, shut the door, and turned the key in the lock.

Another scrape. Wood on wood.

In her room.

She's here.

Chapter Thirty-Two

CLEMENTINE

"Hello, Mouse."

The key dropped to the floor with a ting. Maud tensed, shoulder blades touching. "The police are downstairs."

"No, they're not."

"In the kitchen."

"No." Clem had seen Stoddard through the kitchen window the night before, shoving cake in his fat face and eyeing Rose's bum when she turned to the stove.

Maud lifted her chin. "Where's Russell?"

"Not coming back, I'm afraid."

"What did you do?"

Clem tsked. "Why do you always blame me?"

"I don't—"

"He fell off a cliff. Right over the edge." She swallowed. He'd been so surprised. His eyes wide, arms spinning like a windmill. She laughed at him. Then she waited for him to climb back up and give a great low bow. But he didn't. And this stupid woman was to blame. "I would like an apology."

"For what?"

"Everything." Clem spread her arms. "You took everything from me, and I expect an apology."

She wiped her mouth with the back of her hand, then turned it to look at the blisters and ripped skin. "This is your fault too. Damn horse."

Maud shuddered, as if she were a windup mechanical with a gear out of place. "The buggy."

"Russell never taught me how to drive. I really should have pushed for that, before—"

"He's not dead."

"How would you know that?"

"I just know."

Clem grasped her hands behind her back and picked at a blister. The edges of her vision sparked silver and black. "Don't make things up."

"Why would I do that?"

"You've gotten used to it, haven't you? But it doesn't change things, whether it's true—"

A knock stopped her.

"Miss Price?"

Maud glanced at the door. "Rose—"

"I'd be careful what you say," Clem murmured.

Rose shook the knob. "Why's the door locked?"

Clem made a motion of dressing.

"I'll be out in a minute. I'm just . . . changing now."

Ethelred's muffled bark came from the other side of the door.

"Well, that's all right, miss. I was worried when you didn't come down and—"

Clem stepped next to Maud and pinched the back of her neck. She put her lips against Maud's ear. "Have her go to the shop and get eggs."

Maud gave a small mewl. "Rose . . ." Her voice gave out.

Clem jerked her neck.

"I'd like eggs for breakfast, Rose."

"We don't have any eggs."

"That's why I need you to go to the store." Maud pulled in a lungful of air and released it. "Maybe there's a chicken they've just butchered; you could ask after that."

"A chicken?"

"Have her leave Ethelred in the kitchen," Clem whispered.

"I'll be out soon. Ethelred should stay here."

"Yes, miss. If you're sure."

"In the kitchen."

"Miss?"

"The dog."

"Yes, miss. Come, dog. I'm on a mission for eggs . . ."

Clem kissed Maud's cheek and released her. "There. Not so hard, is it?"

Maud sidestepped.

"What are you doing?"

Maud pointed to the end of the bed. "I'm cold. I want my robe."

"No. You really don't need it."

"What are you going to do?"

"It's not what I'm going to do." Clem smiled. "It's what you're going to do." Clem flipped back her coat and checked her watch, swinging it for Maud to see before stuffing it back into her pocket. "While you and Rose have snored the night away, I have had a lot of time to think. The cellar stays remarkably warm, by the way. But that's neither here nor there. I have come up with a plan."

"Are you going to kill me?"

"Don't get ahead of the script." Clem smacked the top of the dresser. "You make me so angry sometimes."

"How—I—" Maud did look like a failing mechanical. Eyes popping from her head, shivering and shaking, losing balance on one leg and catching herself with the other.

"Why are you so scared? You can meet all your beautiful friends in that beautiful beyond you're so fond of."

"There's no reason to do this. They don't care about the shirt, if that's what you—"

"Stop talking." She held up her finger and crooked it. "Come here."

"No."

"Little Mouse, I just have something I want you to sign."

"No."

Clem grabbed her arm and dragged her to the dresser. Maud twisted and jerked, kicking out and tripping over her own feet. Then Clem wrapped her arm around Maud's neck, forcing her against the dresser, shoving her hard enough it wobbled. The mirror swung on its pins. "I won't go to prison. It's like the box, isn't it? Like a living grave, that's what it is."

Clem looked at herself. Her skin was pink and mottled with gray, her eyes puffy, the skin below a deep lavender. Her hair was spackled in mud, as was her coat. One glove off, one on. The skin on her palms burned and throbbed, the blisters from grappling with the reins of the horse peeled back and oozing pus. She rubbed her cheek against Maud's, forcing her to look at their reflection. "We could have been so famous nothing could hurt us." Then she ran her hand along Maud's bare arm, took her hand, and pressed it to the corner of the paper on the dresser's top. "Read."

Maud swallowed and stared.

"I can no longer live with my deceptions. I am a fraud and a murderer. I killed Alfred Sullivan for his threat to my reputation."

Spittle dropped from the corner of her mouth, leaving a dark mark on the words. *"This is my last confession. God forgive me."*

Clem slipped a pencil from her pocket and held it out. "Take it."

Maud's fingers were ice against hers. She fumbled the pencil, not stopping its fall. She lunged to the side, but Clem tightened her hold on her neck and wrestled her back to the dresser. Then she grabbed Maud's derringer from her coat and put it to Maud's temple. "You left this on your bedside table. Details, Maud. Now pay attention. It would look best if you signed it. But I'll do it for you, if you don't." Clem shrugged. "Either way."

"What does this get you? You could have run the minute Russell knew. The police don't care about the shirt; they don't care what I say. They don't believe me. What do you get from doing this now?"

"I get even."

Maud stared at her. Then she screamed and jammed her elbow to Clem's side, into the same rib that had been kicked. Clem doubled over against the pain. The gun skidded across the floor. Maud scrambled for it, but Clem jerked her ankle as she passed, sending her splaying forward. The bedside table toppled over. The oil lamp shattered. Kerosene splattered the curtains and pooled on the floor and rag rug.

Clem struggled to her knees, then stood, each breath like a stab.

And froze.

Maud sat against the bed, elbows to bent knees, the gun pointed at Clem's chest.

"Oh, you're not going to do that."

"You killed Alfred Sullivan."

"He put his nose—"

"Say it." The gun didn't waver. "Say you killed him. Say what you did." Her eyes were black with fury. "Then you sign the letter."

"No."

Maud pulled the trigger.

The impact knocked Clem backward against the wardrobe. She stared at her arm and the small tear in the cloth of her coat.

"My God, you shot me." She held her hand to her shoulder. Blood leaked between her fingers. She stumbled forward, smacking into the wall, then staggered to the dresser.

"I'm the one leaving this room," Maud hissed. "Not you."

"Not a mouse, then."

Maud's lids drooped. She snapped them open and stared up at Clem. "Ginny Sullivan."

Clem's ears rang. The room wobbled.

"Your wraith. She's right here."

Say you're sorry.

The voice came clear as a bell, the words vibrating like the highest strings on the piano.

"Ginny?"

Clem looked at Maud and saw Ginny's eyes, dark as stones. Water dripped from her hair and stained the threads of her jumper. The doll swung from her hand, cotton-stuffed arms hanging down, blond locks twisted with brown sludge.

Say you're sorry for hurting me.

"I didn't mean it. I didn't." Clem dropped to her knees. "Oh, Ginny, I didn't."

The indigo eyes faded to pale blue. Just Maud. "She was a little girl."

"She took what was mine. Just like you. You took everything. Even my dog."

It was so damn cold. Even her coat, the finest wool there was, did nothing. She had to leave soon. Before Stoddard returned, before they found Russell. Shut Maud up for good. Maud and her righteousness. She hooked her finger to her vest pocket, dug out a match, and scraped it across the wood floor. It sizzled and flared. "Drop the gun."

"Put the match out."

"You have no choice but to do what I say. You're sitting in lamp oil."

Maud's breath grew shallow.

The flame ate its way down the matchstick. "You drop the gun. I blow out the match."

"You're going to throw it, anyway."

"You have my word."

"Do you know what Ginny's saying now? She says to shoot you." Maud pulled the trigger again. Just a click. And again she tried. And again it clicked.

Clem snatched Maud's wrist and twisted the gun loose. Her foot slipped in the kerosene, and she slammed to the floor.

Someone pounded the door. "Miss Price!"

"Help me." Maud sprang forward, tripping on the hem of Clem's skirt, then shoved her away with her heels. Clem struggled to get up, her good arm as useless as the other. Then she saw the snake of flame along the cuff.

"Miss Price!"

"Rose. Get the police."

"They're here; they have the luggage. Mr. Sprague's and hers. Oh, open the door."

The kerosene shimmered blue, the flame spreading across the rug and running up the wall in greedy licks.

"Fire!" More pounding. Voices eaten by the rush and roar of flames.

The walls bowed in and out. Then the plaster bulged and hollowed, the lath boards cracking and releasing, splitting in two, then three, the flames lapping the paint until it bubbled black like cankers. A chunk of plaster and horsehair fell. Then the window blew out.

Clem pulled in deep breaths, letting the air hiss through her teeth as she released it.

Help me anyone I can't reach—

But there was no one to help her.

A single high note rang, then voice upon voice, louder and louder. She could not move, could not cover her ears, could not pull in a full breath. As if she were smothered in gypsum and wax.

"Move."

The words came from her own mouth. They pounded and pummeled her ears, once, and then again. "Move." Flames crawled along the hem of her dress, tracing up the sides of her coat like the bars of a cage. Each breath seared her throat.

More yelling. More smoke. Maud grappling for the paper. The confession. It floated out of her reach, the corners crumpling to ash.

No more air. Smoke. Nothing more to breathe.

New Hampshire State Prison
September 1877

Rough floor. Rough wall. Clem rubbed her finger to it, felt the notches and serrations. Nail marks. Hers. The other girls'.

You will sit and think, Clementine.

No. Not girls. Other prisoners from other cells. Guards pounding truncheons to iron doors. Sound bending and straightening. All their voices gathered in the corners of her cell and scrabbling in the grout. Never stopping.

Damn Russell for not dying.

At least there was no proof she pushed him. He said and she said, and Clem had learned more theatrical skill than he thought. All it took was one beautiful swoon and a torrent of tears. His admitting he'd spurned her for another. The acquittal tasted sweet as honey.

As did the dismissal for Mr. Sullivan's untimely death; Harriet would need to be properly thanked for the alibi. If she ever chose to write.

But the fraud—or, as the courts put it, "obtaining money by false pretenses"—Russell really didn't need to accuse her of that. As if his own hands weren't as dirty as hers.

And little Mouse had become a snake. Saying on record that she had been duped, had been punished with days locked in the cellar box until she feared never to see light. Truly, it turned Clem's stomach. After all she'd done.

She ran her tongue along her cracked lips, then flicked her thumbnail against her index finger. Twisted her wrist. Pretended the trick. Fire from nothing. Easiest trick in the world. A bit of light to brighten the dark.

Her ankle itched. Then the top of her foot. The back of her hand. The burns had healed enough to torment.

Sallow lantern light bled through the keyhole. Never day, never night. Only never-ending time. She leaned against the wall. Studied the shape of the lock. Envisioned its interior workings. And laughed.

Harrowboro Gazette
September 10th

MEDIUM CALLS IT QUITS

Mrs. Maud Sprague née Price announc-
es her retirement from spiritual circles. Readers will remember her from
her notoriety as the Maid of Light,
and from the Watkins trials of the
summer. She and Mr. Russell Sprague
sail for Europe for a world tour ti-
tled Mechanical Wonders, Tricks, and
Treacheries. "We wish," she states,
"to show mourners the various forms of
humbuggery and guide them to the right
paths of solace."

Chapter Thirty-Three

Maud

October 1877

Four months. Maud hadn't seen the house, hadn't wanted to know. Most of the time had been spent by Russell's hospital bed. Giving statements again and again to Stoddard and Hewes and the court. Hiding from the press. The Otts had been generous in providing both sanctuary and sympathy. Clementine Watkins rotted in a cell. Five years' imprisonment for fraud. Nothing for the attempt on Russell's life and her own. Sullivan and his sister would receive no justice, not in this world, but Maud hoped they had found peace in the other.

One last walkthrough and collection of the mail that had piled on the floor before turning over the key.

It was all over now.

The October day sparkled, as did the cab Russell ordered, and the brass buckles on the steamer trunks strapped to the roof. Even Ethelred shined, her coat a glossy gray. She'd grown fat. Rose was generous with the treats, as was Russell, though he vehemently denied it.

Dublin seemed so far away. And the Gaiety Theatre had over two thousand seats. Russell had convinced her that exposing fraud was as popular with audiences as creating it in the first place. "We will take Amandine apart and put her back together right onstage. The exposing is far more interesting than the illusion. Phosphorous, for instance, can ignite, explode, and glow. Sometimes all at once. And mesmerism. Then we can show them a mind reading or two. How it works and all. Yes. We should add that too."

Honest work.

There it was: the Maid of Light replaced with Amandine. Russell was most excited to unravel other ruses: he'd sketched them out and figured the mirror work. But she'd seen him sneak a look at Clementine's notes. The woman was clever. Maud did give her that.

He had surprised her with the luggage on their wedding day. "You had no one to give you a trousseau. So I thought, why not me?"

She put her hand to the glass and sighed, then turned to the room. Empty, save the rugs rolled to the far side, its weave stained with years of water and must. How tired the wallpaper looked, nearly as faded as the rectangles where the mirrors had hung. She stamped her foot. Waited for the sound of it in the parlor across. The floorboard creaked as she turned from the room to the hall.

She stopped at the doorway to the sitting room. Here, the stacked chairs. A fern brown and dead in its pot. The table lay on its back, legs straight to the sky. Sunlight poured through the bare glass, illuminating dust motes that spun like strands of silk thread. The fireplace had been swept clean, the mantel dusted, the wall repapered, and the false one behind torn down and burned in the yard. There was no need to look upstairs. She and Rose had closed it off, though the smell of char still lingered.

Enough. She took her coat from the vestibule stand, shrugged it on, and then followed quickly with her hat, sliding the hatpins through her hair and smoothing a feather on the wide brim. She double-checked it in the mirror. It was a very nice hat. She unclasped her purse and removed her gloves. A noise startled her. Then it came again, from somewhere on the second floor, first in her father's room and then up near the ceiling. Her chest tightened. She knew it silly; no one was in the house.

But there. Another sound: a weak chirp. This time from the landing. She set the gloves on the table, then gripped its edge with her fingers until her nail beds turned pink.

"She's not at the top of the stairs." Her words tumbled from her lips. She stared at herself in the mirror. "She's not at the top of the stairs. She's in handcuffs and chains. You're imagining things."

A bird flew above her, wings wild and flapping, feet scraping the wall. It jerked its head, black beaded eyes studying her.

Maud let out a laugh. Just a common wren. "Did you come down the chimney?"

It flapped its wings to the wall. Opened its beak wide. Then it swooped toward her, so close she flinched and reeled away from it. It hung in the air, one wing lifted, the other hanging loose, then dropped to the floor with a metallic crack.

The tin bird's feet clawed the air. The beak snapped open and shut. A little gift. Trinkets and posies. Three-legged monkeys.

Maud ground her teeth and stared. Then she stomped it with her boot and twisted it flat.

∽

"Manchester first?" Maud settled herself in the carriage, squeezing her feet between a hatbox and Ethelred, and leaned into the crook of Russell's arm.

He tapped the silver handle of his cane. "Everything settled?"

"Just the mail to attend."

"We should throw it all out the window," he said. "New shores now, my dear. New dreams."

The carriage rumbled through the streets, passing the prim white clapboard houses and gaudy brick of Main Street and the hulking granite of the Orpheum. Both leaned to watch the stagehands lift wooden crates from a lorry and haul them down the alley. She thumbed through the post, not wanting to read any of it. Bills, mostly. She handed two over to Russell. "The Orpheum again."

"We're not paying," he said, stuffing the envelopes into his coat. "That contract was made null in the courtroom."

Then he sat back, pulling her closer to him. He gave her a peck on the temple. "Manchester tonight, then Boston. Then across the bounding main. Are you ready?"

Her stomach soured. "My God, will it work?"

"Of course it will work. It's honest." Russell raised an eyebrow. "I have an idea for a new—"

"Let's start with what we have." Maud cupped his face and kissed him. "I love you. But I want to get through the mail."

She cracked the wax on an envelope, slipping the paper out and unfolding it. She held it to her forehead. "My mind states it is one of two types. *Miss Price, you are seated next to the prophets* or *Miss Price, you are the Devil.* Which do you bet?"

The paper was thin as onion skin.

> *My Dear Maud,*
> *It is with great delight that I hear of your nuptials. Mrs. R. H. Sprague! Fancy that.*
>
> *I do hope the event itself was a happy one and am sorry to have missed it—or rather—missed giving you my most ebullient wishes for happiness and health. But the church was too cold and the pews so empty of guests. Not a friendly spiritualist in sight. Well, it's to be expected—you did choose to turn their tricks inside out.*

Anyway. It was much warmer to wait in your carriage. I gave Ethelred a nice scratch under the ear. She's getting soft; you might want to watch the treats.

A world tour! I take credit for your new fame, of course. Since I created everything and you're so blithely giving away the secrets. A few notes:

Don't let Russell get out of hand, you know how he is.

Keep the wallet away from him.

Make sure to oil Amandine's parts. She rusts at the eyelids; you don't need that to go wrong at the wrong time.

Don't overfeed the dog.

You are soon at sea—to Dublin first, is that correct? You're on the Abbotsford, *which is a smallish liner, but cozy is a good thing for newlyweds. You can stay locked in your room with no one to bother you. Who would disturb your first bloom of bliss?*

Who would do such a thing?

Who indeed?

Until We Meet Again,

C.—

ACKNOWLEDGMENTS

I am so very grateful to the following people for their part in the creation of this novel:

Alicia Clancy, you are a writer's dream editor. I feel so lucky to work with you. When you give input and share your ideas, I always wonder "Why didn't I think of that?" I am in awe of you.

Mark Gottlieb, I love talking history and story ideas with you. I appreciate your wise words and guidance. Thank you for your support and friendship; I couldn't ask for a better agent.

Lake Union editorial team: Jen Bentham, Amanda Gibson, and Laura Whittemore, I am ever grateful for your enthusiasm and keen editorial eyes. You make this novel sing.

Faceout Studio & Jeff Miller: I am so in love with your cover art.

Danielle Marshall, you are a force. Thank you for your vision and your fierce commitment to authors.

Historical research is not all musty newspapers and historical archives and old books. Sometimes it requires a contemporary angle. In this case, I was blessed to find two incredible sources whose generosity of time, talent, and knowledge take my breath away. Professor D. R. Schreiber, the Historical Conjurer (www.historicalconjurer.com), is an expert in eighteenth- and nineteenth-century magic and magicians, and the tricks used by mediums to dazzle the sitters at their séances and shows. He is also a marvelous showman in his own right, traveling the country and performing historical magic shows. Clementine gives a tip of the hat to him, and I give my utmost gratitude. Medium Renee Richards (www.psychicmediumreneerichards.com) provided me insight into her own experiences and history as a psychic and medium. She gave me an up-close look at the truly thin veil and the interconnection between this earthly world and the celestial, as well as her experiences working with souls in the other world and the effect it has on a medium. Without Renee, I could not have written Maud.

Musty newspapers and old books were of course perused. The International Association for the Preservation of Spiritualist and Occult Periodicals was a treasure trove of information on the spiritualist movement, with a digital archive of hundreds of spiritualist newspapers. The main source for this novel was *The Banner of Light*, a weekly American spiritualist newspaper published from 1857 to 1907. Other works from the period (and some slightly after) include *The Secrets of Stage Conjuring* by Robert Houdin (1881); *Spirit Slate Writing and Kindred Phenomena* by William E. Robinson (1898); *Seership! The Magnetic Mirror* by Paschal Beverly Randolph (1870); *Plain Guide to Spiritualism* by Uriah Clark (1863); *Biography of Mrs. J. H. Conant, the World's Medium of the Nineteenth Century* by Theodore Parker (spirit) and John Day (1873); and *People from the Other World* by Henry S. Olcott (1875). While the novel takes place in the early years of spiritualism, there is no escaping the works of Harry Houdini, who was determined to out every medium as a fraud. And thus, I include *A Magician Among the Spirits* by Harry Houdini (1924). Modern research works include *Supernatural Entertainments* by Simone Natale; *Radical Spirits* by Ann Braude; *Talking to the Dead: Kate and Maggie Fox and the Rise of Spiritualism* by Barbara Weisberg; *Chemical Magic* by Leonard A. Ford; and *The Spectacle of Illusion* by Matthew L. Tompkins.

Thanks also go to the following people:

#bookstagrammers, you make the Instagram book world so damn fun! Thank you for your passion for books and authors and stories.

Dana Kaye and the Your Breakout Book gang, I value all your wisdom and experience and support as we navigate our way through the maze of marketing.

The Novelitics community: You all inspire me. Thank you for showing up each week and early every morning for our write-ins. I am so glad for our community.

Cathy Yardley, you're my first port of call to discuss story. Thank you for your wise words and terrific advice.

Alan Hlad, thank you for being a most amazing accountability partner. We both got our books done. What's your word count this week?

Katie Nelson of River City Historical, you came to my emergency research aid and went beyond the call of duty. I love working with you and am looking forward to more projects.

The Litwits: Yes, you have been officially listed in the dedication. You three make my days bright. You've pulled me through the swamp of Act Two, held me up while I worked through edits, made me laugh daily with ridiculous texts and even more ridiculous GIFs. You are all adored by me, I tell you. Adored.

Dana Blakemore, you are my everything. Thank you for always being there to listen to convoluted plotlines and the tenth iteration of a chapter. Thank you for being my calm harbor and my rock and my happiness.

And readers. Thank you for your letters and emails and support of my writing and books. If you have a book club, I'd love to Zoom visit and thank you in virtual person (and in real person!). You are why I write.

BOOK CLUB QUESTIONS

1. *The Deception* is a story that is not so much about the existence or otherwise of spirits, but about ethics. Do you agree or disagree?

2. Spiritualism was hugely popular during the time frame of this book. Why do you think this was? Do people still have the same desire to know that their loved ones live on, or has this waned in the present day? Why or why not?

3. Mediumship was a job women could do in a time when there weren't many opportunities for a woman to support herself. How much do you think this would have influenced the sincerity of the profession?

4. How much do you think Clementine is a product of her childhood circumstances? As these circumstances become clearer throughout the book, does this influence how you think of her?

5. Clementine is driven by ambition—to gain recognition and fame through tricks and illusion. How does this resonate, if at all, with social media and celebrity in our current society?

6. Do you trust Russell's love for Maud, or is it merely one more deception? What in his character leads you to think this way?

7. Maud was under her father's thumb as a child, and her mother was institutionalized because of the same gifts that Maud displayed. Why do you think it went one way for her mother and another way for Maud? Did Maud learn to control her gifts more appropriately, or do you think something else was at play?

8. Why do you think Maud lost touch with her spirit-guide in the first place, leading to the circumstances that brought Clem and Russell into her life?

9. Maud was desperate to regain her mediumship gifts, to the point that she was willing to enter into deception. Why? How complicated were her motivations?

10. The author calls herself a skeptical believer. She has seen ghosts—on the Gettysburg battlefield, along the street, and in her own house, among others. But she also sees how easily our desires to communicate with loved ones can be manipulated, making us willing participants in our own deceit. What are your own beliefs?

ABOUT THE AUTHOR

Photo © 2020 Upswept Creative

Kim Taylor Blakemore is the bestselling author of *After Alice Fell* and *The Companion*, as well as young adult novels *Bowery Girl* and *Cissy Funk*, winner of the WILLA Literary Award. She is also the recipient of a Tucson Festival of Books Literary Award and three Regional Arts & Culture Council grants. In addition to writing historical novels about fierce and dangerous women, Kim is the founder of Novelitics, which provides coaching, developmental editing, workshops, and community to writers from around the US and Canada. A history nerd and gothic novel lover, Kim lives with her family in a small town in the Pacific Northwest and loves the rain. Truly. For more information, visit www.kimtaylorblakemore.com.